DEATH'S TASTE

A CHILLING ESSEX MURDER MYSTERY

DS TOMEK BOWEN CRIME THRILLER SERIES
BOOK 5

JACK PROBYN

ABOUT THE BOOK

On a windy and blistering cold morning, Morgana Usyk, owner of one of DS Tomek Bowen's favourite haunts, Morgana's Café, visits Mulberry Harbour a little over a mile out to sea.

A short while later, her body is found in the shallows, floating beside the harbour.

Early reports and eyewitness accounts they saw the killer fleeing the scene. But when storm Alisha rolls in, washing away all evidence, Bowen and the team are left stranded.

Now the water's rising.

And Morgana's is not the only body they're going to find in it.

JOIN THE VIP CLUB

Your FREE book is waiting for you

Available when you join the VIP Club below

Get your FREE copy of the prequel to the DS Tomek Bowen series now at jackprobynbooks.com when you join my VIP email club.

CHAPTER
ONE

Over a mile away from the Southend shoreline sat an enormous concrete structure called Mulberry Harbour. The Phoenix caisson, which was eight metres wide and sixty metres long, and weighed over 2,500 tonnes, had been commissioned for use in the D-Day landings of June 6 1944. It, along with hundreds of others like it, was designed to help tanks and other heavy military vehicles reach the beaches of Normandy, but this particular link in a very long chain had sprung a leak on its maiden voyage and never seen action.

Ever since, it had lain stuck in the same fateful position, wedged in the sandbanks of the Thames Estuary, a staunch defender against the tide.

While generally off limits, over the years, the harbour had become a hotspot for tourists. Those brave enough to venture out towards the blotch in the skyline were subject to a gruelling 1.2-mile wade through mud, sand, and the bullish incoming tide. Photographers and dog walkers were known to have made a visit, largely to see what all the fuss was about, while swimmers and adventure lovers ventured out for its historical and physical benefits. There was even a fun run in the summer in aid of the RNLI.

The best time of year to visit, as with almost everything, was during the summer months, when the climate was much nicer and the tides much more forgiving. The only thing to be cautious of was the wind. During the winter months, the gale-force winds, particularly along the Thames Estuary, can change the direction and speed of the tides with ease, and before you know it, a thirty-minute stay at the harbour can quickly turn into twenty, fifteen, sometimes less.

That, however, wasn't enough to deter the hundreds of people who visited during these months.

Andrei included.

He hugged himself against the bitter, brutal February winds as he traversed the sand and mud. By now, the waterline was up to the soles of his shoes, and small splashes of water bounced into the air, dirtying the laces of his trainers. They weren't the most appropriate footwear, but they were all he had. That, and the thin parka jacket and jeans.

The harbour was a little over fifty yards away, fast approaching. The rectangular structure jutted out of the skyline, lost against the black and ominous clouds in the background. He craned his neck skyward at the bleakness, at the rain that was threatening to come hurtling towards him.

Little did he know that wasn't the only body of water rapidly making its way to him. Ninety degrees to his left, the tide was pulling in. Fast. Meanwhile, on his right, a little over three hundred yards away, was a small group of people, tiny figures on the horizon, converging on the tourist spot.

By the time he reached the edge of the large body of water that surrounded the sunken harbour, the waterline had swelled and was already up to his laces, his feet sodden. Within moments, his toes had numbed, and his wet socks felt like they were gripping his skin, wrapping themselves around his feet and toes in a vicelike grip. Each movement was rough and coarse on his flesh.

As he came to the edge of the pond, he paused, frozen. Not by the wind. Not by the numbing sensation rapidly making its way up to his ankles. But by the sight in front of him. A figure, lying flat in the freezing water, a bleak, vacant face staring into the sky. A woman, neatly dressed, with a dash of make-up applied. Though it didn't look like it now, her hair had been nicely set, the waves that she'd put in with hair straighteners that morning still visible as they floated in the water.

Hovering over her, up to his knees in the water, cradling her head, was another figure. A man. Dressed in a thick black coat with a black scarf around his neck, he looked as though he should have been pitch side at a football match, not a mile away from civilisation in the middle of the Thames. Shock plastered across his face the moment he saw Andrei. He immediately let go of the woman's head, the momentum of the fall submerging her face under the water before her natural buoyancy pushed her back up again.

'What...?' the man said, but before he could continue, the sound of voices assaulted them, carried by the wind that seemed to buffet them from all angles.

Andrei licked his lips, tasted salt, and then turned to face the group. Six of them in total, a little over a hundred yards away, all dressed like they were making their way up the Alps in below-zero conditions rather than the mudflats of Southend.

When Andrei turned back to face the figure, the man was gone. All that was left of him was a silhouette disappearing in the other direction, and his deep footprints in the sand chasing after him.

CHAPTER
TWO

The mobile radiator that was rapidly radiating heat burnt his leg through his trousers. He could feel the fabric starting to melt onto his skin, but there was no room to pull it away; his therapist's office was in the middle of a refurbishment, so they had been forced to continue their professional relationship in a less than large enough space, in what Tomek could only describe as a small broom cupboard. He'd wandered into jail cells that were bigger than this, but he wasn't in the mood to complain or kick up a fuss. It wasn't her fault that the ceiling had leaked. It wasn't her fault that the last two weeks' worth of rain had come cascading down on everything inside her office. It wasn't her fault that it had taken her two weeks to reschedule and find time to fit him in.

'I like it,' he lied. 'It's more... intense.'

'That's the opposite of the vibe I want,' Isabel Fox replied sincerely. 'Coming here shouldn't be intense. The reason you, and the same reason everyone else, come to visit me is because some aspect of their life is already intense. You're supposed to come here and feel the opposite.'

Tomek shrugged. He guessed he was used to it. His entire life was on the edge of intensity, living on the balance, only a small gust of wind or a gentle nudge in the wrong direction away from descending into madness. But it was what he'd known for the past thirty years, and he wasn't about to change it anytime soon.

'Isn't that what makes us all human? That primordial fear of being hunted and killed? Our very existence and survival are predicated on the fact it *should* be intense,' he said.

Isabel pursed her lips. 'You've gone deep pretty early on for a morning session. I had hoped for a quieter start to my day, but I guess you're right. The only thing to bear in mind, however, is that you're not the prey anymore. As a species we've evolved to become the predator. So you can begin to unwind and relax that instinct of yours.'

Tomek didn't agree with that. At least, not while there were murderers and rapists out there who were very much still living out the instinct within them.

Isabel was in her late twenties and had a PhD in understanding how the human brain worked and a pair of welcoming eyes that were enough to put even the hardest individuals at ease. She'd been recommended to him by his boss, DCI Nick Cleaves, and at first, Tomek had been put off by her age, assuming she hadn't enough experience – both professional and in life – to diagnose or help him with his issues. But after their second consultation, he'd warmed to her – perhaps it had been the eyes – and his opinions on the entire process had changed.

Isabel jumped straight in.

'So... how was *it*?'

'That's a pretty broad question,' Tomek said. 'Depends which angle you're coming from. If you were to ask *him* that question, it would have been the most satisfying meeting of his entire life.'

'And for you?'

'The opposite.'

Today they were discussing the meeting that had taken place with Tomek's brother's killer. When he was nine, his brother had been murdered in a park around the corner from his school. He'd been stabbed repeatedly, beaten with a brick, genitally mutilated, eyes gouged with battery acid. And Tomek had been the one to discover his brother's body. Two minutes too late. He had come face to face with his brother's killer, Nathan Burrows, and it had been thirty years since Tomek had last seen the man's face.

Until a few weeks ago.

'How so?'

'He told me nothing. Actually, no. That's a lie. He told me *something*. He told me it was all in my head. That there was nobody else there on the night Michał died. That I'd imagined it, and that for the past thirty years, I've carried with me the potential image and hope of another killer standing by his side for no reason. That I've been thinking of someone who doesn't exist, who has never existed, and will never exist.'

A brief pause entered the room as Isabel made a mental note. Hesitation played out on her face.

'How did you feel about that?'

Tomek shrugged, nonchalant, tightening up the same defences that he'd worn for the past thirty years.

'How do you think? I don't know what to believe anymore.'

'Do you believe *him*?'

Another shrug. This time, he dropped his gaze onto his knee. He began rubbing circles with his nails into the fabric. 'A part of me did. While the other part of me says I know what I saw. I have those nightmares for a reason, and I saw Charlie in one of them for a reason. I heard his name.'

Charlie was the name of his brother's second killer. The one Tomek was convinced existed but hadn't been able to prove. He'd unlocked the name in a nightmare once; heard it as the two killers had fled the scene.

'Did you mention Charlie to Nathan?'

Tomek replied that he had.

'And how did he react?'

Tomek thought about that for a moment. Cast his mind back to the prison meeting room. Surrounded by dozens of other inmates and their friends and family. Talking, discussing, some arguing while the majority enjoyed each other's company. And then he'd mentioned Charlie's name.

Eyes closed, Tomek pictured the man's reaction.

'Nathan's eyes widened slightly,' he explained. 'And he smiled. More of a smirk than a smile. A grin, actually. But it was subtle, discreet. A little flicker of the lips. One of those smug ones you pull to yourself when you've just fixed the window or undone a tough jar lid when no one else could and you don't want to come across like a wanker. Nathan looked as though he recognised the name... but not quite. Then he shook his head and told me there was nobody by that name, that I'd imagined it all.'

'What do you mean, "but not quite"?'

Tomek opened his eyes and was blinded by the brightness. The room was fitted with some of the brightest light bulbs he'd ever seen. He was willing to bet the person who fitted them was as smug as Nathan fucking Burrows.

'I dunno,' he replied. 'It was weird. He looked as though he recognised the name but *didn't* at the same time. Do you know what I mean?'

The look on her face suggested she didn't. 'Do you think you might be wrong?'

Tomek offered her a blank expression in return. 'I told you, I don't even know what to believe anymore. One minute I can see the silhouette there, standing over my brother beside Nathan. The next I can't. One minute I can hear his name being called as right as rain, then it's gone. My mind keeps fucking with itself. Going over and over. And I'm getting no closer to answering anything.'

Isabel let a short, powerful puff of air out of her nostrils. 'Have you had any more nightmares since your visit?'

Shaking his head, Tomek replied that he hadn't. That the nightmares, which until that point had been fairly regular, had now abated.

'That's good, isn't it? That sounds like progress to me. How do you feel after you've been to see Nathan? Do you feel as though you've received some form of closure, even though it may not have been the answer you were hoping for?'

'Closure? What're you talking about, closure? Are you suggesting that I should believe him? That I *should* take his words at face value and believe everything he says? The man's a killer. It's in his DNA to fucking lie. He's protected Charlie for all these years, he's not about to give him up now.'

'So, you *do* still believe that Charlie exists?'

Tomek considered a moment. His head was beginning to hurt; spin like a carousel. Just as it had done for the past few weeks. Since the meeting, he'd struggled to sleep at night. He'd struggled to focus at work. He'd felt distracted almost every waking moment of the day, his thoughts drifting towards Nathan, the room, the meeting, the smug look on his face as he'd lied to Tomek.

Charlie.

Deep down Tomek knew he was right, that his brother had been brutally murdered by two individuals, and that Nathan was lying to him, trying to convince him otherwise. The belief was so firmly rooted within him – thirty years of pressing deep into his psyche – that nothing was going to unearth it. But on that day, Nathan's words had planted a deadly disease in his mind, one that was currently rotting and eating away at the roots surrounding his belief. Could he have imagined the figure beside Nathan? Could he have imagined the name he'd heard in his nightmares? When it had happened, he'd been investigating a string of vigilante murders targeting recently released prisoners, and a suspect named Charlie Hampton, the boyfriend of a probation worker, had come up in the investigation. It couldn't have been that, could it? His subconscious throwing in a random name he'd heard as part of another completely unrelated investigation?

He didn't want to think so.

'I know it was my suggestion to visit him,' Isabel continued, after realising there was no forthcoming answer to her question. 'And I realise that it may have had an adverse effect on you and your voyage into your brother's death, but I want you to take a step away from that world for a while. As much as you possibly can, I want you to forget about it. I want you to immerse yourself in other aspects of your life – your relationships, your friendships, Kasia, work. I want you to focus on the things that you can control. Because right now you can't do anything about your brother's death and what Nathan said to you. And the more you try to focus on it and worry about it, the further and further you'll spiral. You will find your answers one day, I promise you that, but the only way to do that is if you give your mind some rest from it. Then, when you return, your brain will have had time to absorb new information, process it, and enable you to look at this whole situation with a clear mind. From there, you can make the progress you need.'

Easier said than done, Tomek thought as he thanked her for her time and left the broom cupboard.

CHAPTER
THREE

Tomek was sitting in the café, in his usual spot, in the corner of the room, the diamanté mirror sparkling above his head, coffee in hand, warming up his fingers, one eye on the door, waiting for DCI Nick Cleaves to enter. His chief inspector had caught him on the way out of Isabel's broom cupboard and right before he'd gone in for a meeting himself, and had suggested they have a catch-up and a coffee. 'Like a couple of mums,' Nick had said right before he'd shut the door.

Fortunately, Tomek had just the place in mind. A nice little place he knew very well. It was busy, more than large and loud enough for the two of them to have a discreet conversation, and the food was divine. The perfect hump day pick-me-up.

The café was called Morgana's and had quickly become one of Tomek's favourite haunts. He considered himself a regular after being introduced to the place by his girlfriend, Abigail. They had met there one time professionally, and Tomek had even convinced her it had been home to their second date. He'd been there almost once a week since. The café had raised his expectations of everything he'd hope to find in a similar establishment. The food – greasy, flavoursome, just the right amount of salt (even thinking about it made his mouth salivate) – was matched with an almost impeccable service. Morgana, the owner, and the company's namesake, was a one-woman band, catering to all the clientele under her care on the restaurant floor, which changed as often as a set of traffic lights. She did a fantastic job of managing the whole restaurant, leading from the front, and Tomek admired her greatly.

As he sat there, he counted ten other tables with at least one body occupying them. A veritable Essex milieu: tradespeople wearing thick, clunky desert boots in their dirtied tracksuits with an expensive designer watch adorning their wrists, coming in for a late breakfast; an elderly couple, still wearing their thick winter coats inside as they devoured red meat and beans; a middle-aged man with a stomach the size of a space hopper sitting with his legs akimbo to compensate for the extra space required for his gut; a young mum with her even younger son (who should have been in school) playing on a tablet while she tried to force food into her newborn's mouth as it was wedged into its pram, unable to move. There was no judgement in there. Nobody was better than anyone else. They were equal. Just there for good food, good vibes, and a good price – a motto which, until recently, had been printed in sparkly diamanté pink lettering and affixed to the walls with glue.

Before Tomek could look around the rest of the café, the bell sounded at the entrance, and in stepped DCI Cleaves, wearing the face of someone looking for a fight.

The intimidating expression relaxed a little as he made eye contact with Tomek. They shook hands and seated themselves at the table, then ordered coffee and some food. Scrambled eggs for Tomek. Double bacon, double sausage, and double egg roll for Nick – the double heart attack special, Tomek called it.

'Scrambled eggs...' Nick began in his defence. 'That's pretty dry. You feeling all right?'

Tomek patted his hand on his stomach, feeling the insides ripple in the aftermath.

'Watching the old waistline.'

'At your age? You've still got a few more years before you get to my size.'

Tomek turned and gestured discreetly to the man with the space hopper stomach. 'And how many years do you reckon you've got until you get to *that*?'

Before Nick could reply, the waitress interrupted, carrying their coffees on a tray. As she set the drinks down on the table, Tomek asked, 'No Morgana today?'

'No, she has not come in this morning,' the woman replied with a heavy Eastern European accent. Tomek recognised her, but was unable to place her accent. 'And the deputy manager isn't here either, so I'm in charge.'

'Well, I don't think anybody's noticed, so you must be doing something right.'

The waitress turned up her nose at his comments, then hurried away in a huff.

'What'd I say?' he asked as he turned back to Nick.

'Basically, that she's doing a shit job but everyone's too busy or enjoying the food to care. Congratulations,' Nick continued, 'you've upset someone who probably doesn't get paid enough to survive while insulting them for doing their job. Nice one. Bet you feel *real* good about yourself now.'

'You're one to talk,' Tomek scoffed. 'I've seen the way you talk to some of the team.'

'Fuck off.'

'Case in point.'

'That's different. It's a work thing.'

'Whatever helps you sleep at night.'

Tomek had often considered Nick to be a father figure. A stern, strict, and slightly overweight one. And Tomek reciprocated that familial bond. After Nick and his wife's son had ventured into the armed forces unexpectedly, Tomek almost stepped into the role, filling the void that their son's disappearance had made in their lives. They argued, they shouted at one another, but at the end of it all there was adoration there, mutual respect for one another. The same, however, could not be said for many of Tomek's colleagues.

'How was Isabel?' Nick asked.

'Fine. You?'

'Yeah, fine as well.'

'Good. Good chat. Glad you brought me out here for that. You paying for this on the expenses or have I got to pick up the tab?'

Nick's brow furrowed. 'I was going to pay for it out of the kindness of my heart, but now you're being a cheeky cunt I don't want to.'

Tomek didn't argue. There was something on the man's face, something that he wanted to say, something that had been weighing him down considerably. And Tomek knew the man well enough to know that he just needed to give him the time and space in which to do it.

It was a few more moments before Nick spoke again.

'It's about Lucy...'

Tomek paused, listened, and began fearing the worst.

'She's getting worse. She's not improving. She still struggles to stand and walk properly. She still doesn't look as though she's a hundred per cent with it. It takes a while for her to respond at times, and even then they're not coherent answers. She's just... *existing*. I thought by now she would have made *some* improvement...'

A few months ago, just before Christmas, Tomek's daughter Kasia and Nick's daughter Lucy had met up with a group of friends for some underage drinking on Bell Wharf beach in Leigh-on-Sea. While putting one of her dad's stolen bottles of vodka in the bin, Lucy had been attacked and her body thrown to the ground, leaving her in a pool of blood and a massive lump gouged out of the side of her head. Since her release, after a two-week stay in hospital, the doctors had said that there might be permanent brain damage. That they couldn't say for certain.

That only time would tell.

It looked as though time was giving them all the wrong indicators. Though there was still hope, and Tomek wanted to remind him of that.

'Not improving is not the same as getting worse,' he reminded Nick. 'Actually, it's better. You just have to remember that these things take time.'

'We don't have time.'

A lump formed in Tomek's throat. He was about to ask what the rush was but then held his breath as he waited for the words to fall out of Nick's mouth.

'Maggie wants a divorce.'

For a moment he'd feared that Nick was about to tell him he was dying, that he had some incurable illness that was only weeks away from killing him. But this was much worse. Losing Maggie would be just the same as death for Nick. Tomek knew she would take the girls with her. That he wouldn't be able to fight it in court. He was never home as it was. How did he think he could look after his teenage daughters while managing a full-time job as the head of Southend's division? He would have nothing to go home to, nothing to work towards and nobody to work for. The brain and heart of his very existence would be ripped out. And then where would he go?

Tomek was already beginning to envisage it. The downward spiral. The utter collapse of his boss's life. And he was certain Nick had spent many a night thinking about it too.

'Why?' Tomek asked, trying to keep the fear out of his voice.

'Because of what's happened to Lucy. She's struggling. I'm struggling. It's getting to us. And we don't know what to do about it.'

'Breaking up isn't going to help.'

'Try telling that to her. She's got it in her head that that's the solution.' Nick prodded his temple with vehemence.

'What did Isabel say?'

At the mention of the young therapist's name, Nick's eyes widened. 'Don't even get me started on *that*. We're not allowed to mention her name in our house. I'm not even allowed to talk about my sessions with her – when I've got them, how they went, and when I'm seeing her next.'

'Why not?' Tomek asked, even though he suspected he already knew the answer.

'Because she thinks I'm having an affair with her.' More prodding, this time with an aggression that briefly concerned Tomek for Maggie's safety. 'It's the most ridiculous fucking thing I've ever heard in my life. She's young enough to be my daughter!'

Tomek had run out of things to say. It sounded like Nick desperately needed help, and Tomek was the least best placed to offer it. He had no clue what it was like when it came to marriage; he'd only just found himself in a boyfriend-girlfriend situation for the past week. He was still a newbie at all this. And if that wasn't enough, then his string of former ex-girlfriends, of which there were only two, and both of whom were in prison, spoke for itself. He couldn't even pick a decent partner to settle down with. There was always something wrong with them: first, the drug dealing and subsequent addiction; and second, the vigilante serial killing. Neither of which, he liked to think, he had a direct hand in. With Abigail, however, it was different. She seemed, in direct comparison to the previous two, as normal as normal could be. Vanilla, almost. Which was exactly what he needed right now. Less of the drama that might be found on the first page of *OK!* magazine and more of the stuff that never made it into print.

Mercifully, he was saved from the silence by the food. The heavenly aroma wafted from his plate up to his nose, immediately relieving the stress he'd felt from the hour before. The food had the same impact on Nick. As he took a bite of his breakfast, without saying another word to Tomek, it seemed all his worries and fears – about the divorce, about his disabled daughter – disappeared as quickly as the wisps of steam that climbed into the air from his mug.

'Fuck me, that's good,' he said.

'I'd rather not do that, if it's all the same to you. But, yes. Yes, it bloody well is. Bloody lovely, if you ask me.'

'How do they make it taste *so* good?'

'I imagine that sizzling sound you can hear in the background isn't the noise of the chefs testing the hi-hats on their drum kits. I think it's the sound of fat cooking. And a lot of it.'

'Or maybe the secret ingredient is crime,' Nick replied.

'Sorry?'

'It's a *Peep Show* reference. Super Hans...'

The reference was lost on Tomek, who'd been put off the show by its first-person point-of-view camera angles. It had unnerved him for whatever reason, and he'd never been able to get into it.

'I guess you were probably too young to watch that when it came out,' Nick continued.

'Or maybe I just had better taste in TV. Or, come to think of it, I was out doing things, living my life rather than sitting indoors watching sitcoms.'

They continued eating the rest of their food in a silent stupor, neither willing to sacrifice stopping in order to continue the conversation that had already come to a natural close. After they'd finished, they sat back in their padded chairs, with their hands on their stomachs, and for the next ten minutes watched as the steady stream of customers continued to come in and out of the entrance.

Hoping that no further talk of wives, daughters, divorce and depression jumped between them, Tomek asked spinelessly, 'Shall we head to the office?'

CHAPTER
FOUR

It was nearly midday by the time they arrived at Southend CID headquarters in the heart of the city. The promenade leading to the station's entrance was unusually busy, as hordes of ravenous journalists were hovering outside, huddled together like smokers in the winter – except these smokers didn't have the helping hand of a stick of nicotine and tar to keep them warm, only each other and the blood of their victims.

Tomek didn't recognise any of them. Then he looked down at his phone and saw he had two missed calls from Abigail. As one of the senior reporters for the *Southend Echo*, which had in recent weeks struggled to survive as their owner had been arrested for sex-trafficking offences, it was her responsibility to keep her finger on the pulse and wear any leads down to the bone. She was tenacious, bold and relentless, all attributes that made her exceptional at her job. It also helped that she was going out with Tomek, and so knew how to wheedle pertinent information out of him for her own gain. Like now: she was waiting there for him round the back entrance to the station where reporters and press were typically prohibited.

'What're you doing here?' he asked.

'Come to find out what's going on.'

'So have we.'

Nick was a few inches behind him, and as he stood there, Tomek could feel the man's piercing gaze burn holes into the back of his neck, urging him to hurry.

'You remember my boss, don't you?'

Nick said nothing. Instead, he sighed deeply, grunted, then shoved past Tomek and headed in. Tomek followed shortly behind, apologising silently to Abigail as he went. She knew she wasn't supposed to be there, and now she'd been caught – they'd *both* been caught.

He looked forward to that bollocking later.

Upstairs, on the second floor, Southend CID headquarters had become a flurry of activity. A hive of bodies frantically hurrying in and out of the major incident room, an orchestra of voices talking over one another.

The first person to stop and address them was DC Nadia Chakrabarti. Now eight months pregnant, she looked as though she was ready to burst. She walked with one hand on her stomach while the other supported her lower back. The bags under her eyes suggested she hadn't slept in weeks, and yet the make-up on her face did a half-decent job of trying to cover it up. Tomek wouldn't have blamed her if she wanted to come into the office every day in sweatpants and a thick Primark hoodie, looking like she was late for her first day at university. In fact, he would have encouraged it.

'Morning, Sarge, Chief Inspector,' she said slowly, in stark contrast to the speed at which everything else was happening around them.

'Nadia,' Nick replied, jumping in before Tomek could even register his name. 'What the fuck is going on in here? There appears to be something I wasn't made aware of.'

As soon as he said it, the atmosphere in the room quickly quieted down, as though the team had finally noticed his presence.

'A body's been found, guv,' Nadia replied. 'A few hours ago, in the Thames Estuary. Out by Mulberry Harbour.'

'Mulberry Harbour? The old World War Two memorial thing?'

'I don't think you'd quite call it a memorial, sir. But yes...'

'And you say this happened a few hours ago?'

Nadia nodded.

'Why the fuck wasn't I called? I should have been notified the moment this came in.'

'I... I think Rachel looked at your calendar and saw you were on some personal leave this morning, sir.'

That quickly shut Nick up. So much so that he made his way past Nadia and stormed into the incident room, immediately searching for someone else to shout at.

'Where is she?'

'Who?'

The unsuspecting individual who had the misfortune of answering Nick's question was DC Chey Carter, or Cheyenne Pepper as Tomek liked to call him. The young constable's face fell as soon as he realised he was speaking to Nick.

'Victoria. Where is she?'

'*She* is here.'

Here, being behind him, standing in the doorway.

'Is there an issue, Chief Inspector?'

'You bet your sorry fucking arse there is. Why is it that I'm only finding out about this death when I get to the office, and not the minute it came in?'

'Because, as Nadia told you two seconds ago, we thought you were on personal leave this morning and wouldn't want disturbing. Sean and I have had everything under control here, sir. There's been nothing for you to worry about.'

Nick stormed halfway across the room and held his finger in front of Victoria's face, balancing on the edge of saying something he might later regret. Tomek had seen that face before; months of pent-up frustration and aggression, of heartache and suffering, ready and waiting to be unleashed on the first person who pissed him off. Meanwhile, Victoria remained frozen, her back stiff, arms folded across her chest – the epitome of steel and resolve in the face of a terrifying dictator.

'Don't you fucking tell me what I can and can't worry about, Victoria. I do all that myself, thank you very much.'

Tomek felt the sudden need to intervene, to stop Nick from crossing the line and landing himself in a shitstorm of difficult problems he didn't need.

'Tell me what's been going on and tell me right now!'

Saying nothing, Victoria raised her arm and pointed to the series of whiteboards across the longest wall. There, hanging in the middle of the middle whiteboard was an image of their victim. Above it was the name, "Jane Doe".

Except this was no Jane Doe. Tomek knew exactly who it was. Recognised her almost instantly.

'She was found at Mulberry Harbour. Suspected cause of death is drowning. Post-mortem's being done this afternoon. Witnesses saw someone fleeing the scene, so we're assuming she was murdered. No phone or identification was found on her at the crime scene. We're trying to identify her as we speak.'

'You don't need to do any of that,' Tomek said as he brushed past Victoria and stepped into the room. 'I know exactly who that is.'

'Not one of your former lovers, is she?'

'No.'

'Fancy enlightening us then?'

Tomek noted the pleading on her face. It was only subtle – a small widening of the eyes, a brief shimmer of hope in her complexion – but it was enough.

'We just came from there...' he began. 'Guess that explains why she didn't turn up for work today. Though it doesn't explain why the deputy manager didn't turn up either...'

'Tomek!' Nick yelled, followed by a sigh. 'Get on with it, please.'

'Right. Sorry, sir. Yes. Her name's Morgana. She owns the café in Hadleigh that I go to all the time. Called Morgana's. Wonderful girl and wonderful food. She seemed really nice and friendly. I can't think for the life of me why someone would do that to her.'

CHAPTER
FIVE

Tomek felt like he was being interrogated, accused of Morgana's murder himself. For the past five minutes, he'd been forced to explain everything he knew about her. Though he didn't have much to tell them, other than that he'd spoken to her a couple of times, flirted with her on occasion (before he'd started his relationship with Abigail, he was quick to add), and that he knew she was from Ukraine. That was the extent of their personal relationship.

'All I know is that she owned the place. I don't know for how long or if there was anyone else,' he explained.

'Did she have a partner, boyfriend, husband?' Victoria asked. By now, everyone in the team, all eight of them, had been called into the incident room, and it had begun to feel like he was facing the firing squad.

'As far as I could tell, no. Like I said, we flirted a couple of times, and I'm fairly sure she did it with other customers, though I will be a little offended if that's true. That being said, I probably ended up spending a couple of quid more without realising, so I don't blame her, really. Times are tough out there. And I don't know how they keep their prices so low, but...'

Images of his scrambled egg, and Nick's double heart attack special appeared in his mind, distracting him.

Nick snapped his fingers in front of Tomek's face and told him to focus. Tomek snapped back to it and apologised.

'That's all I know, sorry. But the question is, what do *you* know?' he said, directing the interrogation at Victoria. 'What happened to her?'

Standing beside her was DS Sean Campbell, a massive six-foot-four giant of a man. The two of them had been dating since before Christmas, and it had caused a minor fracture in the fabric of the team. Not only was Tomek and Sean's relationship suffering as a result, but the make-up of the team had fallen into two distinct camps. On the one side, you had Tomek and Nick, who had known each other the longest in the team, and were collectively the most senior. Then, on the other side, you had Sean and Victoria, whose embryonic relationship had created a small bubble for themselves to confer and coincide with one another, leaving the rest of the team to choose whichever outfit they preferred. Like choosing between Mum and Dad in the divorce.

It upset Tomek to witness and be a part of but Sean was a grown man who could make his own choices.

'The body was discovered at precisely 09:52 this morning,' Sean started, jumping to Victoria's defence. 'Found by a man called Andrei Pirlog.'

'Pirlo? Andrea Pirlo? The Italian football legend?' Tomek asked.

'No. He's neither a footballer nor a legend. Nor even Italian for that matter. He's Romanian. But that's how you pronounce his name, yes.'

'How did he find her?' Nick asked this time.

'Lying face up in the water at Mulberry Harbour.'

'Yes, yes, I know that. But what was he doing there? What were the circumstances surrounding her death?'

'I was getting to that, but—'

Before Sean could finish, a knock came at the door, and two figures stepped in without waiting for approval. Tomek didn't recognise them, had never seen them before. But the expression on Nick's face suggested he had, and implied that he knew precisely why they were there.

'Good morning, everyone,' the first to enter said. 'Sorry to interrupt, Chief Inspector, but I was wondering if I could have a minute of your time?'

'Yes. Of course,' Nick said, despair and defeat lacing his words, as he headed off with his head and shoulders stooped forward. Closing the door behind him, he offered Tomek a glance that said, 'Find out everything you can for me, don't let them hide anything from you.'

Tomek understood, then turned to Sean.

'You were saying?' he continued as he found himself a seat and waited for Sean and Victoria to shuffle towards the front of the room. He acted as though nothing had happened and wanted everyone else to do the same. They quickly did. Now it was Sean and Victoria's turn to feel like they were being interrogated.

'Andrei Pirlog was walking along the estuary,' Sean started, 'during low tide. He was there to take some photographs of the harbour when he found a figure cradling Morgana's head.'

'We don't know for certain it is Morgana,' Victoria interrupted.

'Tomek confirmed that it was...?'

'Not exactly. He recognises her, that's all. We're still going to need a positive confirmation from a relative who knew her a little better than someone who saw her a couple of times at a restaurant.'

'*Her* restaurant,' Tomek corrected.

Victoria ignored the comment, and retreated behind Sean to allow him to continue, hovering over his shoulder demonically like a hospital diagnosis.

'Andrei approached the male figure and the deceased, but before he could do anything, the figure ran away. A few moments later, a tour group arrived at the harbour as well.'

Tomek nodded. 'So, she was dead by the time Andrei got to her?'

'Yes.'

'And what were the tour group doing there?'

'Touring. What else would they be doing?'

Tomek waited for Sean to answer his question properly. The response came a moment later.

'It's a small business run by a man named Warren Thomas. People pay to have a tour around the harbour. He's been doing it for the past five years. Says he knows the water like the back of his hand.'

Tomek recognised the name from school and wondered whether it was the same individual or whether it was just a lucky coincidence.

'How many people were in the tour group?' he asked.

'Five. Six, including Warren,' DC Martin Brown answered. Today, his beautiful shoulder-length hair was tied in a tight knot at the back of his head. So tight, in fact, it appeared to stretch his entire face backwards in a bizarre sort of facelift. 'They left a little after nine this morning.'

'And it took them nearly an hour to get there?'

'It's a long way. And it's treacherous. The tides are temperamental, and the mud is incredibly dangerous. Many people get stranded every year.'

'Not to mention they were delayed because a few members of the tour group kept getting stuck,' DC Rachel Hamilton added. 'You forgot to mention that bit. By the time they got there, the tide was on its way in and they only had a few minutes left until they were completely stranded themselves.'

'What happened after they'd all arrived?'

'They called the police, but we weren't going to get out there in time, so the boat unit and coastguard sent some people out. They all had to be rescued from the harbour.'

Tomek nodded as he slowly absorbed the information. He imagined the seven of them, eight including Morgana, stranded in the water, perched on the edge of the concrete harbour, awaiting rescue from the RNLI like they'd just been stranded atop the Himalayas. He could only imagine how cold they all must have been.

'Where's the body now?'

'Warming up in the mortuary,' Chey answered. 'She's scheduled for this afternoon, though I don't think we'll find much on her. Apparently, she had all seven of them manhandling her and trying to get her out of the water to resuscitate her.'

'How do you know?'

'We've interviewed them all.'

'Already?' Tomek whistled through his teeth. 'You guys aren't messing about today, are you? You're like the Tories hosting parties as soon as those restrictions were set in place.'

'We try our best.'

'Any idea on time of death?' Tomek asked to the room, then waited to see who was brave enough to answer.

'Difficult to say,' Victoria responded. 'We won't know properly until the post-mortem comes back, but Warren Thomas reckons there was a window of four to five hours between low and high tide.'

'So that's the window we're dealing with?'

'Quite possibly. But there was also a low tide last night at about ten o'clock, so it's possible she was killed then.'

That would complicate matters. It would stretch a five-hour killing window to thirteen, and if she'd been murdered during the night before, the chances of finding her killer exponentially depleted. Tomek's brain was already beginning to wonder where the killer might have gone after leaving Morgana's body in the water. If it had happened in the daylight, shortly before Andrei Pirlog and the tour group arrived, as the team suspected, then they had the chance to pick up the killer on CCTV or eyewitness accounts. But if it was in the dead of night, they might as well have tried looking for a lowercase 'L' in an infinite row of 1s.

'Suspects?' Tomek asked, even though he knew the answer already.

'Probably the guy who fled the crime scene,' Rachel said with a hint of playfulness in her voice. 'That's usually a good place to start.'

Tomek prodded the side of his head, and said, 'Great minds think alike, Rach. Great minds.'

Tomek had a lot of time for Rachel Hamilton. She was hardworking, experienced, got on with the job, and she was gradually beginning to warm to him. When they'd first met, she'd been uptight – and understandably so, given that she'd transferred her whole life from London to Southend – but after a few weeks, she'd settled in with the team, and she'd begun to tolerate Tomek's sometimes insufferable sarcasm and sense of humour. Now, she'd almost completed a one-eighty and was sounding like him too.

'How about her possessions? Her phone?'

'Nothing was found on her,' Victoria answered. 'Our theory is that she either lost it in a struggle, it fell out on the way down to the harbour, or the suspect took it.'

'That's three theories,' Tomek muttered. 'But never mind. What's next?'

'Myself as SIO, and DS Campbell as deputy SIO, need to ascertain our priorities first and then we will handle the delegation of tasks through Nadia, all right? And I want you all to accept your responsibilities without question or interrogation. Understood?'

CHAPTER
SIX

As soon as Tomek left the incident room, he made a right turn, directly towards DCI Cleaves' office in the far corner of the building. On the way, he passed the two individuals who'd come to speak with the chief inspector and offered them a polite smile, despite the fact he sensed they didn't deserve it. Something about their mannerisms and the way the air had cooled upon their arrival suggested to him they weren't there for a catch-up and a friendly pat on the back.

A moment later, Tomek knocked on the door. He entered without waiting for a response, and found Nick frozen, hovering in a half-squat out of his chair, a stunned look across his face.

'Tomek, what're you...?'

'I've come to pay for breakfast this morning,' he called loudly, lest anyone in the office overheard. He shut the door gently behind him.

'Pay for breakfast? What you talking about?'

Tomek pulled out the seat opposite Nick and leant against the back of it.

'I came to talk.'

'So you're not paying me back for breakfast?'

'Fuck no. I just said that in case anyone was listening.'

'"Anyone" being a certain inspector?'

'And her significant other.'

'Well, if they ask you anything or start to kick off then you send them my way. The mood I'm in I'll gladly deal with them.'

Tomek chewed on his bottom lip. 'What's happened?'

Nick placed his hands on the back of his desk chair, mirroring Tomek. His knuckles whitened as he sank his nails deep into the material.

'I'm being suspended.'

Those three words floored Tomek. It didn't make any sense. Suspended? Why? Nick had done nothing wrong. They spent almost every working hour of every day with one another, so what could he have done that warranted such an action?

'It's because of my ties with Brendan Door. IOPC are saying that because he and I have worked closely together over the years, my integrity's come into question, and I'm being suspended while they investigate me.'

'All that just because you worked with him and sat in the same room as him a couple of times?'

Nick dropped his head. 'Yes... but that's not all. There are... how shall I put this? A few emails... from back in the day.'

Emails? That didn't sound good.

'It was completely innocuous as far as I remember,' he continued. 'But I was copied in on a few from Brendan to the mayor and Herbert Tucker.'

'Oh, Nick... What were they about?'

'Like I say, it was innocuous, mundane stuff. Work related, but I just know those bastards'll pore over it for weeks just to make me sweat.'

'Did you know this was going to happen?'

Nick didn't answer the question, which told Tomek everything he needed to know. A few months prior, the member of parliament for Southend East, Herbert Tucker, had been abducted on his way home from work in the early hours of the morning, and killed. The investigation had exposed a sex-trafficking ring, operating in the heart of Southend, run by echelons of the political elite. Brendan Door, the

Police, Fire and Crime Commissioner (PFCC) for South Essex had been implicated, and as a result, a comprehensive investigation into everyone who'd worked with Brendan had begun.

'I found the emails while we were going through everything with Tucker,' Nick said eventually. 'I didn't say anything at the time, but I just knew they'd come back to bite me in the fucking arse at some point.'

'Well, if they're as innocuous and innocent as you say they are, then you've nothing to worry about.'

Nick released his grip from the chair, leaving indentations of his fingertips in the fabric, then shuffled around his desk.

'You don't get it. These things are brutal. The IOPC don't care who you are. They don't care what your rank is, what you've done for this service. They will dig into everything, every aspect of our shit and miserable lives until they find something.'

There was genuine fear in Nick's eyes. A fear that hadn't been there a few moments ago. A fear that unnerved Tomek.

'They...' he paused, unsure how to approach his question. 'They won't find anything else, will they?'

Nick looked Tomek deep in the eyes, hesitated.

'No,' he said. 'They won't find anything.'

That was enough for Tomek.

'Mega,' he replied, a little too loudly. 'To me, it sounds like you've got nothing to worry about. You can put your feet up during this mini-retirement and spend some quality time with Maggie, Lucy and Daniela.'

Nick offered a strained, half-smile. It was clear to see that the prospect of spending the foreseeable future at home with his family wasn't as well received as Tomek had expected. For a man on the brink of divorce, some much-needed time away from his job was possibly the best thing for him, but it didn't look like Nick felt the same sentiment.

'Bloody hell though, Nick. You kept that as quiet as a nun's bedside fucking drawer,' Tomek added with a shake of the head.

'Can you blame me? I've been shitting myself ever since it all blew up. And speaking of things blowing up—'

'Don't tell me you've got something else you want to tell me? Connections to the Middle East?'

'No, dickhead. Of course I don't. I'm talking about *here*. With Orange and Campbell. You know they're going to make life difficult without me around. You'll need to watch out for it.'

'I'm a big boy, I can look after myself.'

In fact, it was a thought that had occurred to Tomek the moment Nick had explained he was being suspended. He'd known that he wouldn't have the chief inspector on his side, fighting his corner. That he was all alone for the time being. That, if he didn't want to get passed over and pushed to the sidelines of the investigation – and ruin the faint chances of promotion to inspector that he'd slowly been working towards – then he was going to have to be clever about it.

'And you thought *I* used to make life hard for you,' Nick said.

'You did.'

'Just wait for what Victoria's got in store for you. She might come across as a mouse, but she can be a lion when she needs to be.'

Tomek thanked Nick for the warning then headed towards the exit. As he placed his hand on the handle, Nick added, 'Careful, kid, it's a jungle out there.'

Tomek smirked. 'I think I'll be all right. Last I checked, lions don't live in the jungle.'

CHAPTER
SEVEN

When Tomek left Nick's office, he stepped into an empty room – an empty room, except for one.

Chey Carter.

The twenty-five-year-old who was reminding Tomek of himself more and more every day.

'How long was I in there for?' he asked, pointing to Nick's office.

Just as Chey was about to respond, Nick slowly opened the door and poked his head through.

'They're all out in the field,' Chey responded.

'Including Nadia?'

'Well, no. Not her. She's in the toilet. You know what she's like, got the bladder of a hedgehog.'

'It's called being pregnant, thank you very much.'

At that moment, Nadia shuffled past them. Her sudden appearance made Tomek jump.

'So, if they're all out on the field, why are you still here?' Tomek asked Chey.

'I think, Sarge, the question you should ask is why *you're* still here.'

'Are you taking the piss?'

'What? No! I-I-I was just saying that...' His cheeks flushed red and his eyes frantically moved between Nadia and Tomek, as if pleading with the pregnant woman to save him. 'I just meant that we're going to be working together...'

'How?'

'Well, Victoria told me that the two of us are to be tasked with finding the prime suspect,' Chey said with a gleeful smile. The young man looked positively excited at the prospect of working with Tomek, and sitting behind a computer screen for endless hours watching the same image, hoping for the minutest of movements.

'They need us to find a drop of water in the ocean then,' Tomek replied sardonically. 'Brilliant. Where have the rest of them gone?'

Chey hesitated before answering, almost as though he was withholding the information.

'Now that they've got a name for the Jane Doe, they've gone down to the café to speak with the employees and potentially find a husband or partner, if she has one. I asked them to bring me back something, a bacon and egg sandwich, but I doubt any of them will.'

Tomek ignored Chey's last comment and turned to Nick. He whispered, out of Chey's earshot. 'They only got that fucking name from me. If it wasn't for me they'd still be wondering what colour the sun is.'

'It's started,' Nick said solemnly, then placed a hand on Tomek's shoulder. 'I wasn't expecting it to be this quick, but you're gonna have to get used to it. Either suck it up and deal with it, or fight it the best you can.'

CHAPTER
EIGHT

It hadn't taken long for Tomek to become bored. A little over an hour, in fact. And even then he'd been holding off admitting it to himself for a while. They were staring at the mind-numbing computer screen, waiting for a figure that matched the description taken from the eyewitness statements to appear. They were, as he'd made the point to Chey several times, embarking on the equivalent of trying to find Wally on the Southend seafront. They were looking for a man of medium build, with short black hair, wearing a black coat, a dark pair of trousers, and a scarf, which in this weather, was almost every man in Essex. Tomek had joked that they might even see himself, as he'd worn his black puffer jacket to the office that morning.

To make things more difficult – as if searching for a faceless man amongst a sea of anonymous, faceless figures in hours and hours of CCTV footage wasn't bad enough – they had estimated between them that they had a search area comprising six miles, stretching from one side of the South Essex coastline in Shoeburyness in the east to Westcliff-on-Sea in the west.

On a map they'd printed and stuck to one of the whiteboards in the incident room, they had circled the whole of the Southend area in a black permanent marker. Mulberry Harbour was in the bottom right of the printout, and a few inches to the left of it was Southend Pier which, according to the eyewitness reports, was the direction in which their main suspect had fled. Instead of heading north towards safety, directly towards the shore, the figure had headed straight towards the longest pleasure pier in the world. A decision that didn't make sense to him. Based on that information, however, it was Tomek's intimation that the suspect had somehow climbed up the pier and immediately blended into the melting pot of society on the platform. But, as the security footage from the shops and arcades at the end of the pier had shown, nobody had vaulted the edge and attempted anything remotely close to something from a James Bond movie. That meant the suspect had returned to civilisation somewhere along the seafront – all six miles of it.

They didn't know where.

And they also didn't know when.

It could have been twenty minutes after he'd been spotted. Or two hours. And for them to examine every camera angle from the entire stretch of the southeast Essex coastline was a massive undertaking. And one that Tomek wasn't interested in. There were better ways to spend his time and resources.

He rose from his seat and raised his hands in the air, stretching his entire body in a half-yawn.

'Come on, we're going out.'

'Where?'

'Out.'

'Why?'

'Because I'm like a squirrel in a fucking pedal bin right now. I'm going crazy locked up in here. I need to get out.'

'Can you tell me where we're going?'

'Thorpe Bay Yacht Club.'

'You mean... *the beach*?'

'Yes. But don't worry. This time I won't make you go near the sand. Not unless you wind me up. Get it – wind, *wind*?'

Chey rolled his eyes, flipped Tomek the middle finger, and then grunted as he lifted himself out of his seat. A few weeks before, during a mild storm, Tomek and Chey had ventured onto Thorpe Bay beach to speak with a kayaking and windsurfing instructor in connection with the murder of Herbert Tucker. While there, Chey had offered to hold a sail for the instructor and landed flat on his back, pinned down by the sail. It had been hilarious, and something he insisted on reminding Chey of at every available opportunity, and Tomek was keen to witness something similar this time round.

They arrived at the yacht club a little over ten minutes later. The club's headquarters was fifty yards away from the shore, and as they exited the car, Tomek joked that there wasn't a gale-force strong enough to knock the constable off his feet and send him barrelling towards the sand. At least not on this continent.

Immediately in front of the clubhouse was a car park of sailing boats of all shapes and sizes. It wasn't until Tomek saw the height of them he really appreciated how big they were, and how much of the hull was submerged under the water.

'You ever done any sailing, Sarge?'

'Only in video games I think, Chey.'

'I don't like the water, so I don't think I could try it. We had a couple of people in our year group do it on the weekends, actually. A few of them had their own boats.'

'Very posh.'

'Not really. One of them drowned in the marshes round by Maldon.'

'Oh.'

'Yeah. It was really sad actually. I knew him quite well. Sat next to him in maths for a couple of years in secondary school. Then he got moved up a set.' Chey paused. 'Shame he couldn't calculate his way out of the problem that killed him.'

'And on that cheery note...' Tomek said as he approached the building. Then he whispered, 'Keep those thoughts to yourself, yeah? I don't want you depressing everyone we speak to.'

'Aye, aye, Captain,' Chey said, with a two-fingered mock salute.

They entered a plain room. The blue carpets were filthy, bleached white from years of sunlight penetrating through the sliding doors, and years' worth of salty water being trampled in. At the back of the entrance was a desk, with a woman sitting behind it. She was in the middle of reading a book when Tomek approached her.

'Good morning,' he began. 'You're not too busy, are you?'

'I'm always busy, love. But for two young fellas like you, absolutely no chance. What can I help you with, lovely?'

'We're from the police,' he said, pulling his warrant card out as a courtesy. 'We're investigating an incident that took place at Mulberry Harbour this morning.'

'What sort of incident?' The woman's face lit up, and immediately Tomek knew that he'd started speaking with the worst type of person. The least discreet of any group, the one with the biggest mouth, the gossip.

'A body was found,' Chey answered, beating Tomek to it.

'A body?'

Tomek wanted to reach round and slap the constable on the chin, but realised violence wasn't the answer and that it was unprofessional in current company.

'We're investigating the circumstances surrounding the death,' Tomek said quickly, his tone stern. 'We were hoping you might be able to answer a few questions for us?'

'I... I can try. I don't know how much help I can be. Shall I get James?'

'Who's James?'

'He's the manager here. The chairman of the club.'

'Is he here right now?'

'No.'

'Has he been here at all this morning?'

'No.'

'But you have?'

'Yes.'

'Then we won't need James. Though it would be nice to get your name...'

'Lucinda,' she mumbled, almost shyly.

'Pleasure to meet you. How long have you been here?'

'Eleven years now. Twelve next month.'

Tomek smirked. 'That's a long time. And how long have you been here *today*? Since this morning?'

She confirmed she had arrived just after seven, and that she arrived at the same time every morning, five days a week, sometimes finishing as late as ten o'clock if there were events and functions taking place in the evenings for club members or schools in the local area. As one of only three full-time employees, she handled a lot of the admin and manual tasks about the place. She liked to think of it as her second home, and there had been a few times where it had become her first home; when she'd finished so late that she'd been too tired (or sometimes too drunk, she'd reminded them sensibly) to go home, so had fashioned a small bed for herself in the office upstairs.

'What can you tell us about the harbour?' Tomek asked. 'We understand that there are sometimes tour groups that go out there. Do you have any that you run as a club?'

'Only on the water,' Lucinda replied. 'We take some schoolkids out and our members on their sailing boats or kayaks as part of an educational trip. The tide is usually in during the middle of the day or the afternoons, so it's much better to do it on the water. That way the kids can get right up close to it.'

'That's lovely,' Tomek said, trying his hardest not to sound condescending. 'And you all set sail from the slipway?'

She nodded. 'Best and only place to do it.'

'Do you know anything about these private tour groups? Do any of them ever come here and head towards the harbour from the same place?'

'A lot of them do, yes. It's the most direct and arguably the easiest way to get there. There are a lot of routes, but only those with experience and knowledge can get you there safely. You hear so many stories about people getting trapped. About people drowning just because they're so inexperienced and don't know enough about the tides. It's such a shame.'

The thought stuck in Tomek's head. That perhaps this wasn't a murder at all. That perhaps Morgana had ventured out to the harbour of her own volition – for something to do, to tick off the bucket list, to have a moment to herself – when she'd become trapped and stranded out there. Perhaps she'd tried to swim back but, weighed down by her sodden clothes and frozen stiff by the ice-cold waters, she'd succumbed and passed away.

The thought stayed in his head for all of two seconds before disappearing again.

'Did you see any tour groups going out into the water this morning?'

'I saw about five or six of them going out with Warren. He's a friend of the club and often comes down here in the mornings with new people, providing the weather's okay, that is. If it's a clear day and there's not much wind, then he'll take them. But if it's raining or there are high winds, he doesn't want to risk it. He's done that before and he promised he'd never do it again.'

Tomek made a mental note to find out what precisely she was referring to.

'That's really helpful,' he told her. 'One last thing, before we go. Did you see anything suspicious this morning at all? Anyone going down the slipway on their own, or looking a bit... suspicious?'

'Suspicious?'

'Yes. You know. Like they were doing something they shouldn't.'

'I don't know what you mean,' she said coolly.

'Which bit are you struggling with? Let me rephrase it: did you see anyone else venturing onto the beach this morning that wasn't part of a group led by Warren or anyone else who typically runs tours?'

Lucinda considered, as though having the question spelt out for her had unlocked a key part of her brain that enabled it to work properly.

'Come to think of it, someone did park their car here this morning, and I don't think they've come back to collect it yet.'

Tomek's pulse quickened. 'Do you have any CCTV footage of the car at all that we could have a look at?'

CHAPTER
NINE

The CCTV footage from the sailing club had narrowed down the timelines of their investigation dramatically. It had shown Morgana pulling into the car park, as Lucinda had explained, shortly after eight o'clock. She'd climbed out of the car, alone, and then she'd headed off towards the beach, down the slipway, and then disappeared as she became smaller than the resolution on the footage could handle. Tomek had felt eerie watching her melt into the background, creeping towards her death. She'd moved tentatively, carefully, afraid. Petrified, almost. It was in stark contrast to the pace, power and confidence he had seen her demonstrate in her café.

But, more importantly, it had proved that she had been alive in the morning and that she'd set off to the harbour a little after eight and died shortly before ten. That meant they now had a two-hour window in which to narrow the killing and find the killer.

Outside the clubhouse, Chey had conducted a quick online search of the number plate and confirmed it belonged to Morgana. Then he'd called in a specialist team to retrieve the vehicle for inspection. They had arrived shortly afterwards and taken the vehicle away on the back of an articulated lorry. As he'd watched the back of Morgana's Mercedes shrink into a small dot, Tomek was reminded of Morgana herself, disappearing off towards her death. He wondered whether she had known it would happen. He wondered what she'd gone there for. Whether she had agreed to meet someone, or whether she'd ventured all that way to take her own life, to throw herself into the chilling water and let her soul leave the earth.

Right now, as things stood, he didn't know what to think.

His uncertainty wasn't aided by the fact that Lucinda hadn't seen anyone else following Morgana. According to her, nobody had entered the water since, except for Warren Thomas and his group of tourists.

'How did you do it?'

Chey's question took Tomek by surprise and pulled him out of his reverie.

'How did I do what? Wake up with an extra dose of awesome this morning?'

Chey rolled his eyes and shook his head. 'Forget I asked. Your ego might inflate too much.'

'If it's about my ego, then I really want to know. Go on. Out with it. That's an order.'

'You're pulling rank on this one?'

'I only do it a couple of times a year, and you've just made me use up one of my finite resources so – out with it.'

Chey placed his hands in his pockets and lowered his chin into the top of his coat until his mouth was submerged beneath the fabric. Meanwhile, Tomek, thanks to his Polish heritage, didn't feel the cold as much as his British equivalents. As a child, he was used to minus-ten-degree winters in a house that only had a fire for heating and a single bed for three young boys to huddle up in for warmth.

'I wondered how...' the young man started, then the rest came out muffled beneath his coat.

'Sorry, what was that? All I heard was "how did you know it was going to rain today?"'

Chey quickly lifted his chin out of its hole like a meerkat, asked the question, then dropped it again.

'How did I know this was the right place to come?' Tomek repeated.

He turned towards the seafront. Through the rows of sailing boats and the forest of masts, he saw the two rectangular Lego bricks of Mulberry Harbour jutting out of the water. 'I'll be honest with you, Chey, because I respect you, and I because I know you won't say anything to anyone else – and if word does get out, then I'll know exactly who to blame – but this was a complete fluke. Sometimes you need a little bit of luck in life to get by. In fact, a lot of life is luck, driven predominantly by hard work. If I had to put a figure on it, I'd say your twenty per cent of work accounts for eighty per cent of your luck.'

'You just ripped off the eighty-twenty principle.'

'Did I? Everyone else does so why can't I? As I was saying, life's all about luck, hard work, and dedication.'

'Where does that fit into the hundred per cent?'

'It doesn't. It's outside, watching in.'

'Now you're just making it up!'

'And there's your second important life lesson for the morning, young Chey. Everybody's making it up as they go along. Nobody knows what they're doing in life, so don't be afraid to admit that to yourself and make mistakes. I just got lucky with this one.'

Chey shook his head, the sound of his teeth chattering audible behind the coat. 'How the fuck did we get onto the topic of philosophy and life lessons?'

'Because we're all just making it up as we go along. And besides, if anyone asks how we thought to come to this place, tell them I spent so long looking at that bastard map on the wall in the incident room that it literally called out to me.'

'Right. Can we go back now? I want a coffee.'

'Excellent. I know the best place for it.'

CHAPTER
TEN

Tomek didn't know what to expect from the first sip of the coffee that had been given to him, but it wasn't what had touched his lip. Burnt, as though as it had been treated with a blowtorch before being added to boiling water. And he was certain he could taste chemicals in his mouth, too. Or perhaps it was salt; the smell and taste of it was everywhere in Warren Thomas's house, like it had been rubbed into the walls and the furniture, and was inside every one of the diffusers that were littered about the place.

Tomek thanked the man for the drink politely, then set it down on the table on the other side of the room – as far away as possible.

Warren Thomas was a big man. Not overweight, though there was probably some inaccurate BMI scale or new diet fad that had arbitrarily determined that he fit into the "obese" category. Rather, he was broad-shouldered, muscular, and taller than Tomek by a few inches. He looked as though he had played rugby professionally in a former life. Or at the very least continued to enjoy the sport on the weekend. And he had the scars on his face to match, too. The cauliflower ears, the broken nose that had never quite healed. Tomek remembered the day that particular incident had happened. Murray Coalfield had tackled Warren to the ground in a PE lesson and their teacher, Mr Johnson, having examined the blood streaming down the young boy's face, had told Warren to continue play. His white PE shirt had never quite recovered from the incident, and neither had Warren's bone for that matter.

'It's good to see you again, Tomek.'

'You too. I dread to think how many years it's been.'

'The less said about that the better. What have you been doing with yourself all this time?'

Tomek pointed to himself and then Chey. '*This*. The last twenty years of my life pretty much. You?'

'Nothing nearly as exciting. Couple of odd jobs here and there. Played semi-pro in my mid-twenties. Had to retire because of a dodgy shoulder. Did some more odd jobs here and there, and then after all that I started my tour guide business.'

'So I heard. Business good?'

'Business is as business does.'

Tomek had no idea what that meant but figured the man was being cagey for a reason. Perhaps he didn't want to let on to Tomek that he was struggling financially. That he didn't have the perfect job with the perfect wife and the perfect life. Tomek had always hated running into people he knew from school. It always became a competition with a lot of his former peers. "Oh, you're working in the city, are you? How much are you making a year? Oh, we've just bought our second home, a five-bed, and we've got another one in the south of Spain."

"Oh, you're still living in Essex? I moved out long ago. Had to get away from it all. Much happier now though."

"You're not married? That's all right, there's still time."

Condescending pricks he wished would all fuck off.

That was another reason he stayed away from Facebook, aside from the fact he didn't know how it worked and had neither the time or inclination to learn; because he couldn't be arsed to see where people were going on their holidays while they were ten grand in debt, staring at 60% APR on all their purchases, spread over the next forty years. So long as they looked cool on social media, that was all that mattered. It didn't matter that their homes and possessions were on the verge of being repossessed. None of that was important when you had fifteen likes and twenty love hearts on one of your Facebook posts. That was all that mattered in some of his former school colleagues' lives.

'Sounds like you're doing really well for yourself,' Tomek said. 'Shame about the rugby. I always thought you had a lot of promise, could've made it big time. A lot of people wouldn't have bounced back after what happened to your shoulder, but you've picked yourself up and by the looks of things you're in a good place.'

The look of surprise on Warren's face suggested that wasn't the response he'd been expecting.

'Shame you can't make a cup of coffee for shit though.'

The three of them laughed. 'To tell you the truth, I don't drink it that much. In fact, I think the stuff's out of date, so hopefully I haven't poisoned you.'

They laughed.

'Give me a bottle of water any day of the week,' Warren continued.

'So long as it's got salt in it.'

More laughing. 'Sorry about that,' Warren responded. 'It's a part of who I am now. I think it's in my blood and just secretes out of my pores.' Warren ran his hand up and down his bulky, fair-haired forearms.

They then moved the conversation onto the topic of the morning, of how Warren had stumbled across the body.

'Tell us about what happened. It must have been very traumatising for you.'

'I'd like to say it was. But...' he trailed off, lowered his gaze to his hairy knees. 'It's not the first time I've gone through something like that. And it's not the first time I've seen a body out there either.'

Tomek trawled through the memory bank, trying to remember if he'd ever attended or heard of a crime scene at the harbour before.

'About six years ago, I was taking a couple out there one morning. They'd lived in the area for years but had never been down to the harbour and just wanted to see what it was like. They turned up late on the morning, and the wind had picked up massively while I was waiting. It was much stronger than I would have liked. I wasn't happy about taking them but in the end I relented. When we got halfway, the tide had already started to come in and we almost got stranded out there.'

'But you didn't?'

'Fortunately, we made it back, but we were wading through the water for a good quarter of a mile.'

Tomek nodded slowly, taking it all in. 'And... and you said it's not the first time you've seen a body?'

Warren lowered his gaze. 'Yes...' he said, a catch in his throat. 'It was a good friend of mine. Not from school. I met him at rugby. He went out there one morning and didn't come back. Killed himself out there.'

Tomek allowed the man a brief moment of reflection.

'I'm sorry to hear that.'

'He was going through some stuff. A *lot* of stuff actually. He'd struggled for years after he was forced to retire from the sport like me – I went one way, he went the other. He tried to keep himself busy, but he just didn't know what to do with his life. I found him on my morning run.'

'Your morning run?'

Warren nodded. 'Every morning at low tide I run down to the harbour and back. It's the perfect wake-up call, and it gets me in the mood for the day.'

'Come rain or shine?'

'All weathers, all conditions.'

'In the same shorts as you've got on now? Brave man.'

'But why?' Chey asked suddenly. 'You go down there all day every day as part of your job...'

Tomek agreed. It was like him running to the station and back on a morning jog, only to drive down there after he'd showered and shaved. It didn't make sense to him.

'I know, but I also use it as an opportunity to scout out the weather and the tide. I've learnt after what happened before that if I don't get a good feeling, I'll cancel my bookings for the day.'

Tomek turned to the bay windows that looked out onto Warren's driveway. He was staring at a thick wall of dark grey. Rain had just started to fall, and the patter of raindrops falling onto the plastic coving echoed throughout the room.

'There it is,' Warren said. 'Later than forecast.'

'What was your feeling like for today's group?' Tomek asked.

'I didn't feel comfortable taking them out this morning. The weather was threatening, and the wind was picking up. But they insisted.'

'Why?'

'Because they're on holiday from America. Massive fans of the UK, for some reason. History buffs, too, apparently. But they leave tomorrow, and they couldn't afford to miss it. So eventually I relented.'

'What made you give in, if you knew the dangers of going out in this weather?'

Warren dropped his head in shame. 'Money,' he replied. 'They offered me double. I wasn't going to turn that down. Besides, on my run the conditions weren't *that* bad. They were manageable. Just on the edge of what I'd deem tolerable.'

'Is that why it took you nearly an hour to reach the harbour?'

'Yes. They kept getting stuck in the sand and falling over. Plus, we needed to stop so they could catch their breath every two minutes. It was a nightmare. By the time we got there, we only had a few more minutes left before the tide came in. I usually spend half an hour to forty-five minutes when we're at the harbour, explaining the history behind it, giving them some interesting facts, but that didn't happen... for obvious reasons.'

Obvious reasons that Tomek was keen to broach.

'What happened after you found the body?'

'I took control,' Warren admitted with pride. 'As I said, I'd seen it before, so I knew what to do. I carry a little radio with me every time I go out there that's connected to the coastguard. I radioed to them and told them what had happened. But because the water was coming in so fast, they wouldn't have been able to deploy as fast as we'd have liked, so they told us all to climb onto the harbour and await rescue.'

'Who lifted the body?'

'We all did. I had to help everyone up. It's taller than it looks, and there's a knack to it. People jump in all the time and injure themselves because they don't realise how high it is – and the water below isn't that deep either. Some people can be so stupid.'

Tomek continued to nod slowly, absorbing the information. Out of the corner of his eye, Chey took a final sip of his drink and set the mug on the coffee table.

'And then you were rescued shortly after?'

'Yes.'

'While you were waiting, did you try to resuscitate the body?'

Anguish washed over Warren's face. 'I tried, but it was a struggle. They... the Americans... they were hysterical. I tried to focus, but they kept screaming and distracting me. When I first found her I felt for a pulse but it wasn't there.'

'And what can you tell us about the person who fled?'

Warren tilted his head to the side. 'I didn't see him that clearly. That bloke, Andrei, had a better view. All I know is that he headed towards the pier.'

'Why might he have gone that way?'

'Because it was the only way to go,' Warren replied. 'He couldn't have run past us otherwise I would have tackled him to the ground.'

'Why didn't you chase after him? You're used to running on that terrain, you do it every day, you could have caught up to him easily, couldn't you?'

Warren hesitated and began playing with his fingernails which had already been bitten to the quick. 'It didn't occur to me. My immediate response was to tend to the woman lying in the water. I didn't think to chase after him. What are you implying?'

'Nothing. Nothing at all. It's my job to ask these questions.'

'Well, your colleagues didn't ask me anything like that earlier.'

'That's because they're not me. Did they ask you whether you saw the woman this morning on your run?'

'What?' Warren folded a leg over the other.

'This morning. Your run. What time did you leave?'

'Low tide was at nine. The water was already retreating by the time I left, so I think it was about seven-ish.' Warren's face contorted as he made the calculation in his head.

'And you headed down the slipway, right?'

'Right.'

'So, did you not see the victim on the way back? We've got footage of her heading down the slipway a little after eight this morning. Would your paths not have crossed?'

Warren hesitated. 'Not necessarily,' he replied, his voice cagey. 'She could have gone a different way. She might have tried to avoid some of the deeper puddles. Judging by her clothes she wasn't well prepared for the water and the mud. But I don't mind it. I'll just run straight through. Besides, it was still slightly dark at that point. If I hadn't been looking directly at her, I doubt I would have seen her.'

Tomek nodded slowly again, giving nothing away in his expression.

'What are you doing tomorrow?' he asked.

'Nothing special. Why?'

'I'd like you to take me down to the harbour, if that's okay? I'd like to see the crime scene. Chey will come along with me as well.'

'I will?'

Tomek turned to the young constable. 'You will.' Then back to Warren: 'He's a big fan of the beach, you see. So much so I've seen him eat sand. We're trying to wean him off it, though. It's not very good for his health.'

Warren chuckled awkwardly. 'I don't think that would be a problem. I'd... I'd have to double-check when low tide is. And we'd need to leave well in advance. But, yes, I can take you down to the harbour. Just have to hope there's not a second body down there.'

CHAPTER
ELEVEN

'Absolutely not.'

Tomek bristled with anger but swallowed it down. He didn't want to cause a scene, not yet, but he was more than happy for his resentment to show on his face, for Victoria to see that he was not the least bit pleased by her decision.

'Why not?' he asked.

'Because it's an irresponsible and inefficient use of resources and time.'

Tomek tapped the underside of his chin. 'Explain that one to me,' he started. 'This is a crime scene, yes?'

'Yes.'

'And what do we do at crime scenes?'

She could see where he was going with this, but her stubbornness kept her from answering the question immediately.

'We gather as much information and evidence as we possibly can.'

'Bingo. And what is Mulberry Harbour?'

'A crime scene,' she replied, her voice heavily laden with defeat.

'Ten points!' he said sarcastically. 'Someone died there, Victoria. More pertinently, someone was possibly murdered there. Which makes it a crime scene. The only difference between this one and the rest of them is that it's over a mile out at sea and a pain in the arse to get to. Why are we treating it differently?'

Victoria considered her answer carefully. She turned to her computer screen, as though hoping she might find the answer in there. Unfortunately, she did. Without saying anything, she grabbed the monitor with both hands and spun the device towards him. She was on the home page for the BBC Weather website. At the top of the page was a map of the UK covered in two blotches of yellow and orange. Orange in the north, yellow in the south.

'There's a storm coming, Tomek,' Victoria said with a slight West Country accent. 'And we'd all best be ready when she does.'

Tomek looked at her blankly. 'Did you just quote *Harry Potter* to me?'

'Yes. And I'm Dumbledore, you're Snape. I'm the boss and you'll do as you're told.'

'Isn't there a scene where Snape kills Dumbledore?'

'Regardless,' she started with a shake of the head. 'Strong winds of up to eighty miles per hour are expected to batter the country tomorrow, with rain forecast to fall from the early hours of the morning until the following day, with some areas reaching thirty centimetres. A severe flood warning has been issued by the Met Office in several parts of the country.'

'All right, Carol Kirkwood. So you're saying it's a matter of safety and precaution?'

Victoria replied with a short nod of the head.

'We'll be fine. We never get hit as hard as they predict. It's all a load of scaremongering. But if you're really worried about us, then we can all go the day after,' Tomek replied, smiling facetiously. 'I'd like to take Chey with me as well. He's keen on his history, particularly the Second World War, and he once told me he's a water baby. Plus, I think it would be good to get him away from his screen for a bit and out of the office. Let him run loose for a short while.'

'Like a dog, you mean?'

Tomek raised his hands in mock surrender. 'Hey, you're the one who said it.'

As he lifted himself out of his chair, abruptly calling a halt to the meeting, Victoria snapped her fingers at him and pointed for him to return. Tomek didn't appreciate that. He'd only ever been treated like that by Nick, a man who could get away with it because of their close relationship. But not Victoria. He didn't like the idea of her thinking she could do that to him on a regular basis.

'How did the rest of your investigations go this morning?' she asked slowly. 'Find anything?'

Tomek knew exactly what she was trying to achieve with a question like that. She was testing him, calling him out. Shining a light as bright as the sun on him to see whether he'd melt under the pressure.

Well, he had news for her.

'We'd have been there hours if I hadn't suggested visiting the sailing club. Now we know what time Morgana got to the beach and where she entered the water. We've also got her car, which is being forensically examined. All we have to do now is find out who else joined her and from what point along the coast, and then we should have our killer. You'll be pleased to know Chey's already on the job as we speak.'

Victoria pursed her lips and reached for her cup of tea. It had been sitting there, almost full, since the start of their meeting some twenty minutes ago, and still steam continued to float from the top of the cup. She liked her hot drinks extra, extra hot, and he'd caught her several times re-boiling the kettle twice to ensure it had reached its maximum temperature... again. He was yet to come up with a new nickname for her.

'You don't think your old school friend might be implicated in any way?'

Tomek shook his head. Almost too quick. 'No,' he said. 'The timelines don't work out. Plus, I don't know why he'd want to do it. I don't think there would be any connection between the two of them.'

'I'll get Martin to investigate. See what he can dig up.'

Tomek raised a hand in the air. 'That reminds me: what did *you* guys uncover?'

For a long moment, Victoria stared at him blankly, as though she hadn't heard the question. Then, for an even longer moment, she stayed quiet, choosing not to answer him.

'I need to process the findings once the team have written everything up,' she said, then quickly dismissed him from her office. 'And while I remember, when the time comes I want you to attend the post-mortem with Lorna.'

'Seriously? Do I have *cunt*stable in my job title?'

Victoria pursed her lips again, upset by his tone. 'Everyone else is busy.'

'Then make them un-busy.'

'Sadly, I can't.'

Rather, it was more a question of *won't*. And the worst part was she wasn't even trying to hide the fact.

———

Tomek left Victoria's office seething. He hated being pushed to the side. And if she insisted on keeping him out of the light, then he was going to have to find fun and creative ways to ensure he stayed within it.

After exiting her office, Tomek headed towards Rachel Hamilton's desk. She was one of the few, aside from Chey, Nadia and only very recently Oscar, he felt he could trust.

'Victoria's told me to come and have a chat with you,' he lied. 'Says you know the most about what's going on.'

'She flatters me,' Rachel replied.

'But you do know something, right?'

'I know a lot of things. Water's wet. Bears shit in the woods. All that jazz.'

'Think you took that line from me, didn't you?'

She said nothing.

'Next time get your own jokes. Now, tell me, who did you speak with at Morgana's?'

To assist her memory, Rachel reached for her notebook and flipped to the last page. 'We spoke with all the staff who work there,' she began. 'Seven in total, not including Morgana, and not including her deputy manager, Vlad, who runs the place when she's not there. Though he wasn't there either when we arrived, he arrived about twenty minutes later.'

'Where was he?'

'He told us he'd overslept.'

'And not that he'd just come back from killing Morgana?' Tomek asked, his mind making the more obvious leap.

'Not sure he'd admit that so freely. Oscar's looking into it now.'

Tomek waited for her to continue. Once she'd had a sip of her drink, she told him that all of Morgana's employees had said the same thing about her. That she was one of the most hardworking and generous individuals they'd ever met. They had all worked with her for several years, with most having enjoyed her relaxed and comforting managerial style ever since she first started the company. She made the café a fun place to come, and they were all impressed by how hard she worked that it inspired them to want to follow suit. Equally, they were all devastated to hear the news of her death, and when questioned whether they wanted to close the café, they'd decided to keep it open. It was what she would have wanted, they'd said.

'Very admirable,' Tomek replied. 'Did anyone take a witness statement from the deputy manager?'

'Yes,' Rachel answered. 'Turns out Morgana's got a husband. Anton Usyk. Also Ukrainian. Anna's trying to find him now. Apparently, he owns another similar restaurant in Southend.'

'Another café?'

She nodded.

'Bet that created some unhealthy competition.'

'We'll find out. Anna's going to get him in for an identification before the post-mortem can begin. Then we'll speak with him.'

'What else did Morgana's employees have to say about her character? Anyone notice anything strange, someone coming in more than usual? Someone threatening her in any way?'

Rachel consulted her notes. 'Nothing like that. The most interesting thing they said was that she was a massive flirt. Sorry to say it, but apparently she was always flirting her way around the blokes that came in, getting them to keep coming back to see her. In fact, while we were there, I shit you not, there were at least five different blokes pining after Morgana. Swear to god. I think they were more devastated about the news than her colleagues.'

'Wonder if her husband knew about that?'

Rachel shrugged. 'She had to do what she had to do to get ahead. And from what I saw, it didn't take a lot of doing. She clearly had a type: tall, short black hair, beard. And there was a fuck load of them in there, all sitting there, grinning to themselves, waiting for her to come and take their order. Come to think of it, they all looked like you.'

'Thanks?'

Tomek wasn't sure if that was a compliment or an insult.

'Then again, all you Essex blokes look the same nowadays. Nothing to differentiate between you.'

'Good thing you're gay then, isn't it? Wouldn't want you to get myself and Martin mixed up...'

'Martin's the exception. Only because he's got better hair than me.'

'What if I grew mine to his length?'

'I'd still be gay, you'd still be in a relationship, and it would look shit. Unless of course, Abigail is into that type of thing, then maybe the second portion of my statement would have to change.'

'But not the first?'

'Sadly not. They haven't invented a switch yet that instantly turns off my lesbianism. Though there are probably some people out there who are frantically trying to come up with one.'

CHAPTER
TWELVE

Less than an hour later, Tomek found himself in the Southend
Hospital mortuary with Lorna Dean, the Home Office
pathologist, preparing himself for the post-mortem. Before any of the
disembowelling, measuring, and photographing had begun, Morgana's
husband had been invited down to confirm her identity. Anton Usyk
was a thick, heavyset man of medium height, with deep pores on his
hooked nose, and thick, black eyebrows. His hair was typically Eastern
European – shaved almost to the point of being bald, save for a small
patch of black hair on the top of his head – and was covered in a thick
layer of gel. He was dressed in designer clothes – Gucci top, Versace belt,
Giorgio Armani trousers – and he smelt so strongly of men's perfume
that Tomek smelt him before he either saw or heard him.

The identification process had been conducted by Tomek with the
help of a police constable and DC Anna Kaczmarek, the family liaison
officer. Morgana's body had been placed beneath a white sheet, and
Anton had spent a fraction of a second looking at her before confirming
her identity. He had said nothing, given nothing away in his expression.
A language barrier perhaps, Tomek presumed. But as soon as he and
Anna had spoken Polish to him, Anton became more lucid, freer with
his speech. The two languages weren't too dissimilar from one another,

and Tomek found it always came in handy whenever he wanted to eavesdrop on a conversation with a neighbouring country to his native Poland.

'My colleague will be your main point of contact,' Tomek had said, gesturing towards Anna. 'She will help you with anything you need and she will keep you up to speed as to the progress of the investigation.'

'I understand,' he replied slowly in Ukrainian.

'In the meantime, we are going to need to ask you some questions down at the station. About your wife, her movements, whether you knew anything about her whereabouts this morning. We will of course find a translator to make it as comfortable for you as possible.'

Anton's face contorted in confusion. 'Why is that necessary?' he asked, this time in English.

'It's routine,' Tomek answered, blunter than he'd intended. 'Your wife has died, Mr Usyk. We believe she may have been murdered. You may not realise it now, as you're still in a lot of shock, but you might know who did this. Perhaps your wife has been followed for the past few weeks. Perhaps she had some enemies you did not know about.'

And there was always the third option: that he knew exactly what had happened to her. That perhaps he had been the one to kill her. In what manner, precisely, Tomek was about to find out. But, nine times out of ten, murder victims were killed by their relatives or someone they knew. And for Anton Usyk, that wasn't a pretty statistic.

Tomek wanted nothing more than to grill the man there and then. Find out everything he knew. Question his responses. Pick holes in all he had to say. But now wasn't the time. Nor was it the place.

By the end of the identification process, Tomek felt proud of himself for having spoken almost perfect Polish during their interaction. Sure, there were a couple of mistakes here and there, but who was counting? For someone who hadn't spoken the language fluently since he was fifteen, some twenty-five years ago (though he tried to keep *that* number out of his head), he was impressed.

A few moments later, he entered the mortuary room, a depressing and demoralising place, with an unusual grin on his face.

'Someone's got something to smile about,' Lorna said as he approached. 'Poor woman here doesn't, not anymore...'

'She will when we find her killer.'

And with that, they began. In the intervening hours following her death, Morgana's body had entered livor mortis, whereby the blood in her body had succumbed to the effects of gravity and had pooled along her back, hamstrings and calves, leaving behind purple blotches. The effect it had on her skin reminded Tomek of a painting he'd drawn in primary school. He'd been told to paint a beach scene, but had got excited and added a hue of red to the sea, which had then turned into a purple ocean, looking like it was something out of a Wes Anderson movie.

First, Lorna started by examining Morgana's head. She caressed the woman's face delicately, placing her gloved fingers on her nose and her chin, moving it from side to side, jotting down her findings as she went. Then she turned her attention to Morgana's neck. A mottled chain of blue and purple had formed at the front of her neck, wrapped around her larynx.

'Bingo,' Lorna said.

'Found something?'

The pathologist pointed at the bruises. 'These would indicate that she was strangled, possibly held under the water, forcefully.'

'That's our cause of death?'

'Nothing gets past you,' she said with a half-wink.

Tomek replied with a forced smile, then turned his attention back to the post-mortem. As Lorna continued the process, they had a brief catch-up. Discussing their respective daughters. How Carla, Lorna's daughter, had been getting on at school. Then onto how Kasia had been doing at hers. Both girls were struggling. GCSEs, exams, mock exams, boyfriends, friends, teachers, school, social media, socialising, anxiety, puberty – their whole worlds, and not to mention the hormones, were expanding, and they were struggling to keep up. Both Tomek and Lorna were looking forward to the February half-term break, though the only downside was that it took place over Valentine's Day.

'Carla's just got out of a serious relationship,' Lorna explained as she peeled back one side of Morgana's ribs.

'Oh yeah?'

'Johnny, his name was. Nice enough boy. Harmless, really. But they were together four months.'

'And that's considered serious?'

'At that age it is.'

To be fair, it was more serious than any relationship Tomek had ever had. He couldn't remember the last time he'd had one that had lasted longer than four weeks, let alone four months.

'She's pretty cut up about it,' Lorna continued, folding the other rib cage over. 'Crying nonstop. She's stopped eating. Won't go out to meet her friends. It's really affected her in a bad way.'

'And she's sixteen you say?'

Lorna nodded.

'I look forward to experiencing all this soon then.'

'You have to be careful with girls. We get our hopes up too much. Overthink things. Plus, we all know what men are like, and despite ourselves we still fall for you every time. Especially at that age. I made a few mistakes back then.'

'Didn't we all? That's the point of growing up.'

Tomek thought of Kasia. Of Billy "The Cow Fighter" Turpin, a fourteen-year-old boy in her school who had once thought he could fight a cow – and win. Their relationship hadn't lasted. In fact, it had barely even started. But he was sure that there would be other boys on the horizon. Other boys that she was talking to and getting to know on a deeper, less superficial level. Other boys that wouldn't be good enough for her. Other boys that he wouldn't approve of. He knew what they were like – he'd been one at one point – and if he wouldn't have trusted himself, then he certainly wasn't going to trust anyone else.

'All you have to do is to be there for them when they go through this sort of thing,' Lorna continued. 'Give them a shoulder to cry on and pretend you know what you're talking about when you offer them advice. Sometimes, at that age, they actually believe you when you say it'll all be okay.'

Tomek pondered on that for a moment longer, but it was a moment of reflection that was cut short by his phone vibrating against his leg. He dug into his pocket, and stepping away from the body, removed the device.

'Hello?'

'Dad?'

'Yes, Kasia. I'm at work. What's the matter? Is it urgent?'

'There's a letter for you.'

'Okay... That can wait until I get home. Thanks for—'

'It looks like it's come from a prison.'

That forced Tomek to stop.

'Which one?'

A pause as she scanned the letter.

'HMP Wakefield.'

CHAPTER
THIRTEEN

Tomek raced home straight after the post-mortem had finished. He didn't have time to condense Lorna's findings and his day's activities and share them with Victoria. His daily report would have to wait until morning. Right now, he needed to go home. The letter concerned him. But what worried him even more was Kasia. She had a tendency to open any letters or parcels with his name on and always sent him a photo of it before he got home, thinking it would help him somehow. Usually, it was just bills or statements, fairly innocuous, boring, mundane, *adult* stuff. But something about this letter had stopped her from opening it. Something had told her it was more important than the rest, one that she should leave unopened. And so, he'd urgently told her to leave it on the table, to wash her hands and to stay well back.

There was no knowing what was in it. If it had come from HMP Wakefield, home to some of the country's most notorious and violent prisoners, it could have been laced with spice, drugs, or poison of another kind. The contents could be graphic and obscene. Porn, a photo of a corpse, a piece of fabric or DNA from a crime scene or someone's cell. Nothing a thirteen-year-old girl should be seeing.

Tomek wanted to open it on his own.

Alone.

Pinching the letter in his fingers, holding it at arm's length, he shuffled carefully across to his bedroom, out of fear that any sudden movement might cause the thin envelope to explode. Carefully, he closed the door behind him and perched himself on the edge of his bed.

There it was, right in front of him. His name and address, written in scrawled, barely legible handwriting. In the top right was a stamp of HMP Wakefield, with the prison's return address beneath it. Tomek's heart began to beat faster and faster the longer he stared at it, his fingers turning clammy with sweat.

It could have only come from one person.

Nathan Burrows.

How did he know his address? How had he been able to send a letter to him? Usually, the process dictated that Tomek would have needed to agree to receive it first before anything was sent out. But that hadn't happened. The usual rules had gone out of the window. Which begged the question: *how*?

Holding his breath, Tomek turned over the envelope and ripped the edge. Then he wedged his finger underneath and began tearing the paper apart. As his finger reached the other corner, he exhaled deeply, his fingers sweating. Pinching his thumb and forefinger together like he was trying to remove a splinter from his skin, he removed the letter and held it by his fingernails. Before reading it, he gave it a sniff. Under usual circumstances, envelopes leaving any prison in the UK would have been checked for drugs (likewise, on their way in), but this wasn't a usual circumstance. Procedure hadn't been followed somewhere along the line, so he wasn't willing to take any chances.

To his great relief, he couldn't smell anything untoward. Then Tomek turned the sheet over.

At the top of the page was Tomek's address, scribbled in childlike handwriting in pencil. Beneath that was the letter:

Dear Tomek,

I am sorry we had to cut our meating short the other weak. And I am sorry for taking so long to get back to you as well. It took some time to convince the guards to give me a pensal and paper. I do hope you can foregive me.

I just wanted to let you know i enjoyed our chat. It was good to see you again. How have you been since? How has Kasia been keeping at skool? I do hope she is getting on fine with all of her classes.

If it's okay with you, and I really hope it is, I would like to keep writing to you, to open up a dialogg. I would be greatfall if you could reply. The guards and people here are giving me righting lessons. They're teaching me to spell slowly, but sometimes i don't listen and do the rest in my sell. I have problems with lissening.

It's a shame you didn't believe me about your brother. Perhaps one day we can become frends and i can tell you about what happened to him. Would you like that? I think about him a lot. I didn't tell you that either, did i? I often think about the way he died on that night. Sometimes when i'm lieing in bed i see him on the floor, covered in his blood.

Speaking of going to bed, i hope you sleep well on the night that you read this. I really hope your nightmares stop. They must have callsed you so much pane and discomfort over the years. Did you ever see the

film about the lambs? I hope yours go to sleep soon,
Tomek.

Do you think we can be friends? Please right back.
If not for yourself, do it for Michal. He would want
you too make frends and practiss foregiveness.

I look forward to hearing from you (I was told to
right that bit. Apparently it sounds proffeshonal).

Nathan Burrows, HMP Wakefield

P.S - your girlfrend is very pritty by the way. You
have good taste in women.

Tomek didn't know whether to tear it up, burn it, or scream.

In the end, he did none of those. Instead, for the first time in a long time, he cried, sobbed, and wept into his hands, unable to control the sudden flood of emotions drowning him. In his outpouring, he dropped the letter to the floor, tears streaming down his cheeks and into his palms.

But the crying stopped as Tomek's sorrow soon turned to rage.

The bastard was tormenting him, teasing him. Worse, he knew where Tomek lived. And Kasia – he knew about Kasia. And Abigail. He knew about his entire life. How? Did he have criminal contacts watching him? Friends? Relatives? How did Nathan have access to all of his information, including the nightmares? It was impossible for him to have access to his diary, or even his meeting notes with his therapist. It was even more impossible for him to have gathered the information from someone within the team. He trusted them all to his grave – even Sean and Victoria. They all knew about what had happened to his brother and how much it had affected him. There was no way they would have leaked information about his life to Nathan Burrows, was there? Tomek didn't want to go down that avenue.

Then he considered an alternative.

The second killer.

Charlie.

The anonymous, impossible to touch figure that had helped kill his brother. What if he was still out there, stalking Tomek, watching from afar? Watching Kasia, Abigail? Monitoring their movements?

He pushed himself off the bed and moved to the window. As he pulled back the curtains, his eyes surveyed the cars along the street. By now, he had learnt which ones belonged to his neighbours and which ones didn't. The ones before him were all owned by people on his street. There was nothing concerning out there. Then he tried to think whether he'd seen anyone recently, whether he'd passed someone on the way home. A particular figure he'd paid little attention to, unassumingly standing there on the pavement. Or whether there had been the same car that always followed him home.

He drew blanks on both accounts. Nothing. His mind was empty.

After a few more moments of staring into the darkness, he pulled his gaze away from the street and looked skyward. The wind had picked up, blowing the trees on the street from side to side. Leaves raced across the sky, incipient rainfall looming in the distance amongst the darkness. An ominous feeling had settled on the road, and he could feel it on his skin. He couldn't say with any certainty whether someone had been following him, or monitoring his house. But one thing he knew for sure, was that if the storm Victoria had told him about was coming, then they wouldn't be standing there tonight. For the next few hours at least, his home was safe from the threat he didn't even know was real.

CHAPTER
FOURTEEN

Plumes of water vapour exploded from his mouth in a steady, rhythmic manner. He breathed in through the nose, out through the mouth. Slow, controlled, measured, no matter how hard his cardiovascular system screamed at him to speed it up.

His legs and arms moved in the same way, steady, rhythmic. His feet pounding on the ground, the sound inaudible over the harsh wind whistling past his ears, ripping his eardrums apart. The wind was so strong that for the first few hundred yards of their run, it had felt like he wasn't moving at all, that he had come up against an immovable object, as though something was pulling on his shirt and stopping him from moving forward. Fortunately, he had Warren Thomas by his side, and the tall giant of a man was very much moving in the right direction. Though Tomek took offence at the ease with which the man moved. Gentle, graceful, almost as though he was gliding through the wind and rain, and that he could glide through any weather. It looked effortless for him, and judging by the speed at which the clouds of water vapour burst from his mouth, it was.

Earlier that morning, Tomek had messaged Warren to confirm whether they could venture down to the harbour, but the response had been no. Thanks to Storm Alisha, the tide had swelled and was too rough and dangerous. The coastguard and RNLI had been warning civilians all night not to enter the water under any circumstances, and Warren didn't think a trip down to Mulberry Harbour was worth the risk.

Tomek had reluctantly agreed.

Instead, he'd suggested a run. His first in months. The two of them, along the seafront, beyond the sailing club, further along the coast to Shoebury East Beach. Despite not having conducted any proper physical exercise since Kasia had come into his life, he was surprised at how well his body was coping. He hadn't been forced to stop. He wasn't struggling to breathe or maintain the pace. He was doing well.

And he needed it. His body needed it. His mind needed it. A release, an avenue of escape. A chance to let off steam and release the tension in his bones. Throughout the night, thoughts of Nathan Burrows had plagued him. Thoughts of the man sitting in his prison cell, penning the letter with a wry smile on his face, possibly touching himself as he wrote it. Of him writing Tomek's address with glee, of sealing the envelope and handing it in to one of the guards in the prison, unable to contain his excitement.

As he ran, Tomek envisaged the man standing there, ten yards ahead. He chased after him. Pushing, pounding, his limbs pumping. Trying to close the gap. Closer. Closer. But he was just out of reach, a fingertip away.

Along the seafront, evidence of the storm that had ripped its way through the county overnight was visible. Water had bested the sea wall defences and flooded the promenades, spilling onto the pavements and surrounding roads, leaving large expanses of water sometimes as deep as his ankles. Elsewhere, Tomek had seen further evidence: trees overturned on the side of the road, held in place by a single, powerful root; wheelie bins that had made an escape attempt and only got as far as the middle of the street, having knocked into a handful of cars along the way. On the car radio, reports had come in that power lines had gone down in the more rural areas, and the area's power network team had been working overnight to combat power cuts, though it was likely those affected would be without power until the wind had subsided. Alisha had come, caused her destruction, and gone again.

At the end of the route, they came to a stop by the East Beach booms, two kilometres of sea defences constructed from concrete poles approximately two metres tall, buried into the sand bed, held together by angled steel. First used as a defence mechanism in the Second World War to defend against submarines, mines and other surface vessels, the poles that remained had been repurposed and were largely created during the Cold War against the perceived threat of the Soviet Union. Now, they served as the boundary for the Ministry of Defence-owned land that was used primarily for military operations and weapons testing. Access to the beach beyond was strictly prohibited, and so it was the perfect place to turn back on themselves and head towards Warren's house.

They arrived forty minutes – and another mile and a half – later. By the time they came to Warren's front door, Tomek was knackered, bent double, dry heaving, his body threatening to purge its contents.

'You pushed it too hard,' Warren said.

Tomek ignored him as he focused on trying not to vomit on his old school friend's driveway. The battle was short-lived. And unsuccessful.

The contents of his stomach – what little was left, anyway – came hurtling onto the brick, splashing onto Tomek's shoes and legs.

'I'm so sorry,' Tomek said, wiping his mouth with the sleeve of his wet T-shirt. 'I'll clean it up.'

'No point. The rain'll take it away soon.' Warren chucked his key inside the lock and rotated. As Tomek made his way to the car, Warren called him back. 'Where the fuck do you think you're going?'

'To work...'

'Not like that you're not.'

'It's all right. We have showers there. I was going to freshen up in the office.'

'Not after you've just chundered all over my driveway,' Warren said, and pushed open the door. When Tomek didn't move towards it, he hurried across, grabbed him by the clean sleeve and chucked him into the house. 'You need to get warm, and you need some warmth inside you too. And sugar. Let me put the kettle on.'

Tomek hoped it wasn't another one of Warren's disgusting cups of coffee, but he was too polite to say anything. Instead, he muttered something, but wasn't too sure what. He thought it was, 'thanks', but it could have been anything.

'Let me get you a towel,' Warren said in the kitchen. Before Tomek could protest, his friend left the room, shot upstairs, then returned a moment later with a towel in hand. Egyptian cotton, dark blue. 'Wipe yourself down with that. I know the house is a bit of a mess, but I'd rather you didn't soak the sofa.'

Tomek took the towel from him gratefully and began wiping the rain from his forearms, neck, and face. Then he ran the towel over his head, picking up most of the moisture. Once the drink was made – mercifully, a tea – Warren led Tomek into the living room. It was at the back of the house and looked out onto the garden. Outside, overturned by the wind, was a two-person kayak that took up the entire length of the garden.

'Can we go out to the harbour in that?' Tomek asked.

'Not unless you want to drown.'

'I meant another time.'

'When the weather's better, I don't see why not. You ever been in one?'

Tomek nodded, confirming that he had. But chose not to explain when, or why. That was a conversation for another day.

'Let me see what the weather's like this afternoon,' Warren said. 'Forecast says the wind's due to die right down. Just depends if it's at the same time as high tide. I'll let you know.'

Placing his towel down on the sofa, Tomek perched himself on the edge and wrapped his hands around the mug. It was only a minor source of heat, but already he could feel himself getting warmer. He lifted the small cup to his mouth and took a sip. The liquid scalded the tip of his tongue and burnt his throat, but it filled him with a nourishment that spread throughout his body.

Warren removed a chair from the dining table and pulled it closer to Tomek.

'It's not much,' he said, pointing to the furniture, 'but it's enough.'

'Better than the conditions some people live in. How long have you been here?'

'I've been renting for about five years now. It does the job. But I don't need much. Give me a bed, a toilet, and a place to make some food and I'll be fine.'

Like a prison cell, Tomek thought.

Evidence of Warren's simple lifestyle was everywhere in the living room. There were no home effects, no photos, no ornaments like the ones Kasia and Abigail had told him to purchase to 'liven the place up a bit'. There was a television, yes, but it was from the late 2000s and looked as though it hadn't been used in years. Similarly, the furniture smelt, and felt, as though it had come from a car boot sale, the last possessions of someone who'd died alone. There were no books on the shelf, no DVD cases, no CDs. Not even a record player.

'What do you do all day?' Tomek asked.

Warren chuckled. 'I like to read. My collection is upstairs. You should see it. I get a lot of them from the charity shop. They're cheap and I can give them back when I'm finished with them.'

Tomek nodded politely. He had no particular interest in books but appreciated them, nonetheless. He took another sip of his tea and moved the conversation along, this time to the topic of school. It was the only thing they had in common right now. That and their mutual love of rugby. But for now, going to school together was something they'd both experienced, something they both had fond memories of. Sometimes with each other, sometimes without. They spent the next half an hour sharing stories from the classroom, discussing old colleagues and wondering what they were up to nowadays, though neither of them knew anything about anyone; they had both abstained from having social media accounts and were content to keep it that way.

'To be honest, I couldn't give a shit what people are up to nowadays,' Tomek said. 'They're all probably miserable, anyway. Doing a job they hate just so they can post it online and give the impression everything's perfect.'

'I worry about the next generation. They've grown up with it. They think they're living in a picture-perfect world, but it's not all sunshine and rainbows. Something needs to change.'

Tomek grunted as he finished the last of his drink. 'Tell me about it. Kasia spends so much time on it. She follows all these models, likes all their photos. It sets an unrealistic representation of what life should be like, and I have absolutely no fucking idea what to do about it.'

'How old is she?'

'Thirteen.'

'I didn't realise you were a dad.'

'Neither did I until about four months ago.'

Confusion crawled across Warren's face. Tomek then explained that Kasia had turned up on his doorstep one afternoon while he'd been tending to his bonsai trees.

'I love bonsai trees!' Warren interjected. 'I've got some in the shed and have a few on my bedroom window.'

'No. Way.'

'Yes. Way.'

Tomek was astounded. Usually, whenever he mentioned that he was interested in growing tiny trees in plant pots, he was met with awkward and confused stares, but now he had found someone else with the same interest. They shared a bond. Tomek had no hesitation in asking to see Warren's collection, and the man showed them to him with the same vigour and excitement that he'd shown to Abigail when he'd introduced her to his own collection. There were four on the windowsill, all different species and different sizes, with a further ten outside, sheltering in the shed at the end of the garden while waiting for the storm to pass.

'How long have you had them for?' Tomek asked.

'Since school. Some of them have got damaged over the years and I've had to replace them, but I've been collecting them since we were kids.'

Tomek shook his head as he stared into Warren's eyes. 'Where have you been all my life? I thought I was the only one.'

Warren placed a hand on Tomek's shoulder. 'You and me both, mate. You and me both.'

CHAPTER
FIFTEEN

Tomek's hair was still wet from the shower in the office when he was pulled into Victoria's office.

'Good morning, Tomek,' she said. 'Or should I say afternoon?'

Tomek looked at his watch. It was only 10:12 am. 'Wishing the time away already?'

'Some of us have been here since seven o'clock.'

'That's your prerogative. I was with Warren Thomas.'

'Why?'

'Gathering information,' he lied. 'I was hoping he could take me out to the harbour, but the weather let us down.'

Victoria smirked smugly. 'Told you it would.'

'You say that, but all is not lost, however, as he's promised to take me out this afternoon.'

'Sounds like a gentleman. Where is he taking you? Candlelight dinner by the beach? Or something a little more exciting – mini golf along the seafront?'

'Speaking from experience?' Tomek replied. 'Or are you still waiting on Sean to do either of those things with you?'

Victoria opened her mouth to reply but quickly bit her tongue.

'Very funny,' she said, 'very droll. While we're on the topic of being funny, where was your daily report for yesterday? Why wasn't it in my inbox this morning?'

Tomek took his time to respond. 'What's funny about that?'

'Your excuse, I imagine. I've heard you come up with absolute crackers in the past.'

'Jacob's or Ritz?'

Victoria gestured with her hands, pointing at him repeatedly. 'This is exactly what I'm talking about. You've always got something to say. Always got a quick remark to get yourself out of trouble, but—'

'I'm not trying to get myself out of trouble at all, ma'am. I'm as deeply concerned about this as you are. And we must get to the bottom of it.'

'Of course you fucking are. The day you care about this type of thing as much as me is the day I fucking die.'

Tomek fought to suppress the smile on his face. He didn't wish anyone dead. In fact, he did, but the list was so small that he could write it on a fingernail. For Victoria's benefit, she wasn't on it.

'This is the very reason you'll never make it as an inspector.'

The words felt like a slap to the face and a kick to the groin. At the same time.

'What're you talking about?' Tomek asked, then added internally: *You spiteful bitch.* 'What do you know? Is there a position or promotion coming up?'

Without responding, Victoria turned her attention away from him, suddenly playing shy. 'I didn't mean anything by it. Forget I said anything.'

'But you *did* mean something by it. And I want to know what.'

'And I want to know why you didn't file the report last night. This honesty thing works two ways, Tomek.'

He paused. They had reached a stalemate. He had no intention of telling her the real reason he'd headed straight home from the post-mortem and not completed her fucking report. But no excuse came to him. No apparition manifested itself in front of him like a genie from a bottle. And, he decided, by the time he eventually came up with something, the moment would have gone and she would have seen right through it.

Stalemate.

'When can I expect it?'

'Seriously?'

'Yes, seriously. You still have to submit it. You're not getting out of it that easily. Christ, you're like a child sometimes. Like asking you to do your fucking homework.'

Tomek said nothing. Instead, he offered Victoria an obnoxious and over-the-top smile.

'Without Nick here to defend you, I'm going to need to see everything that you're doing.'

'I've already told you what I've got planned for this afternoon. You're more than welcome to join us if you'd like.'

'No. What I would like is for you to do several things.' She held up her hand and started counting on her fingers. 'One, I'd like you to get that report to me as soon as you possibly can. Two, I'd like you to reach out to all the key witnesses and see how they're getting on, find out if they've remembered anything else. And third, I'd like you to get out of my office.'

Tomek waited patiently, tapping his thumb against his knee. He waited until Victoria felt compelled to say something.

'What are you still doing here?'

'I need you to tell me which one you'd like me to do first.'

Fuck off. That was the fourth addition to the list of things she wanted him to do.

Fuck off.

Get out of my office.

Send me the report.

And then visit the key witnesses.

In that order.

Unfortunately for her, Chey had completely ruined her plan for him before it had even begun.

'Sarge, there's an issue with one of the key witnesses,' he said.

'Who?'

'Kirsty Redgrave. She's reported that someone was standing outside her Airbnb last night.'

Tomek spun on the spot, then pointed to the door on the other side of the room. 'Quick Robin, to the Batmobile!'

Chey just looked at him perplexed. 'Is this some sort of joke? Are we going to be on TV?'

'What? No, idiot. I'm saying, grab your coat and keys, and we'll go down there together...'

'Together?' Chey shifted his weight from one foot to the other. 'But I thought I would stay here and finish what I was doing?'

Tomek shook his head. 'Just had a quick word with the boss and she's just told me that you and I need to speak with all of these guys, anyway. Quite handy how that's worked out in our favour, eh?'

Handy indeed.

Chey seemed to buy it. He said: 'Well, Batman, what are we waiting for?'

CHAPTER
SIXTEEN

Kirsty Redgrave was in her fifties yet looked as though she tried her hardest to make herself look anything but. Her hair was straightened, her face lightly touched up with make-up, and there was clear definition in her shoulder and bicep muscles that suggested she worked out more than she ate. She and the rest of her American family were staying in a five-bedroom house in South Benfleet. They had found the property on Airbnb and were staying there while the owners had disappeared off to their second home in the south of Spain for an extended Christmas break. It was still lost on Tomek why anyone, let alone a group of Americans who had some of the most stunning scenery in the world on their doorstep, chose a place like Essex to come on their travels. He could think of many places further north and even to the south that were better than here. The only thing South Essex had going for it was a couple of historical attractions, a pothole every few feet, and a shopping centre that attracted people from all over the country (largely because there was nothing else to do and it was an okayish way to spend an afternoon). Perhaps it was because Tomek had grown up there and seen the place change so much over the years, that his view of the area had become jaded, tinted a dull shade of grey. Even so, it still didn't make sense to him.

'Southend is steeped in history,' Kirsty said, her New York twang thick as she entered the living room.

'Technically, everywhere's steeped in history,' Tomek replied sardonically. 'The planet's been around for billions of years.'

Kirsty turned to Chey and rolled her eyes. 'Is he always like that?'

'Sadly,' the young constable answered.

'Well, there's a lot to see and do. You just have to know where to look.'

'Are you a teacher or do you just have a keen interest?'

'I'm a professor,' Kirsty replied. 'History at New York University. NYU!'

The sudden outburst took Tomek by surprise. For someone who had, according to Chey, been so panicked on the phone that it sounded like she'd locked herself out of the house with no trousers on, she was surprisingly perky.

'I've been teaching for years,' she continued. 'Entering my fifteenth now, and I love it, wouldn't change it for anything.' She turned to look out of the window. 'To think that someone, somewhere, centuries ago, came up with the idea to implement roads, irrigation systems, and currencies – where would we be without it?'

'Living in our own filth,' Tomek said. 'And don't forget the savage killing for entertainment. Though I'm surprised that hasn't stood the test of time.'

Kirsty didn't see the funny side of his comment.

'What's so special about Essex?' Chey asked, his voice laden with intrigue.

'So much,' Kirsty replied. 'Did you know that Palaeolithic stone tools were found here, meaning that humans have lived in the area ever since the first Ice Age?'

Tomek replied that he didn't.

'And that evidence from the Neolithic period suggested that man had been living in Chelmsford around six thousand years ago. And that, more recently, the Battle of Benfleet took place by the train station in AD

894. The Danes versus the Saxons. Killer! And who could forget Boudicca?'

'Absolutely,' Tomek said, though he had absolutely no idea who she was referring to. Keen to move the conversation along, he checked his watch and asked, 'I thought you were due to fly out today?'

Kirsty rolled her eyes again. 'We were, but then this bloody storm happened. Our flight got cancelled and now we can't get another one until the weekend. Fortunately, our hosts are stuck out in Spain as well, so they didn't have a problem with it.'

Either that, or they're in no rush to get home.

'At least you've got a few more nights here,' Chey said. 'Should give you some time to tick some extra things from your list.'

Kirsty's face illuminated at the thought of experiencing more historical ruins, visiting more archaeological sites, but then she quickly remembered that she and her family had crossed everything off the list.

'Where is everyone else, out of interest?' Tomek asked.

'They've gone shopping.'

'Oh, yeah?'

'Down to a place called Lakeside.'

The smirk launched itself onto Tomek's face involuntarily.

'Now *there's* a place steeped in history,' he said, with a cheeky grin.

Kirsty ignored the comment and continued. 'To be honest, I wanted them to get out of the house. I didn't think it was safe here.'

'Ah, yes. The reason we're here. Please, explain what happened to you and what you saw.'

Kirsty composed herself before she began, inhaling deeply, letting the tension in her body depress. As she started, the joy and wonder of their previous discussion left her face and was replaced with angst, as though she was re-living the experience as she told it.

'It happened last night. During the storm. The wind was blowing a gale, and I've never seen so much rain. I went to the window to shut the bedroom curtains, looked outside, and that's when I saw a figure standing there. At first I didn't think much of it, but then when I looked again he was still standing there. I told my husband, he came to look, but by the time he made his way up the stairs, he was gone.'

'Right,' Tomek said, looking at Chey, giving him the eye to make a note in his book. 'And can you remember what he looked like?'

'That wasn't the only time I saw him!' Kirsty continued. 'He appeared about half an hour later.'

'Oh yeah?'

'This time in the garden. He had hopped the fence and was just standing there, watching the house.'

Tomek tried to suspend disbelief for a moment and imagine what she'd seen. Darkness, save for the dim orange hue of the streetlights below. Cars, parked on the side of the road. Horizontal rain, distorting her view. Leaves and twigs flashing from one side of the window to the other. And a lone faceless figure, silhouetted against the blackness, standing perfectly still, staring up at her.

'Are you sure it was a man?'

'Yes,' she hissed.

'How can you be sure?'

'I know what a man looks like. I've seen them before.'

'Nobody's doubting that,' Tomek replied, sensing that she was becoming more irate as his questions continued. 'How clearly did you see the man's face?'

'I... I...' she hesitated, closed her eyes. 'I didn't get a good look at him. He was so far away, I...'

'Can you describe what he was wearing?'

Kirsty closed her eyes again. 'A black coat. A long black coat. With his hood up. It had white drawstrings, I remember that much, because they were flapping about in the wind.'

'What about on his face? A scarf? His coat zipped all the way to his chin? Any distinguishable features? Perhaps the light reflected off a pair of glasses?'

Eyes still closed, Kirsty shook her head. 'I don't think he was wearing glasses. But I could see his eyes. Like cats' eyes, glowing in the darkness.'

For a moment, Tomek wondered whether it was actually a cat that she'd seen. But his limited experience and knowledge of the animal reminded him it was unlikely one would be prowling the streets of South Benfleet in the middle of a storm, not when a warm bed and food were waiting at home for it.

'What about his shoes?' Chey asked. 'Was he wearing trainers, shoes? What colour were they?'

Kirsty squeezed her eyes shut harder, forming lines in the side of her head. 'Trainers,' she replied. 'Dark, I think. To match his coat.'

Chey made a note in his book. 'And what about his build, his size? How would you describe him?'

'He was big.' She puffed her shoulders out as she said it. 'His frame seemed to fill out the coat. He looked well built, solid, like a rugby player. And his legs were chunky as well. He looked like a bouncer or someone standing on the door. Is that what you call them here?'

Tomek confirmed that it was. Then she opened her eyes and blinked a few times to let the light back in. He reached into his pocket and produced his phone, then accessed his notes app. The night before, he had made a note of the description the American tour group had given of the man who'd fled the crime scene – their main suspect.

'Black coat,' he started. 'Black hair... medium to large build. Would you say the description of the man you saw last night matches that of the man you found at the crime scene?'

Kirsty's cheeks flushed red with worry. 'I didn't until you said it. But... I don't know. There was something different about this person. Menace, evil. Something slightly unhinged. The guy at the harbour yesterday, he... I don't know. He looked worried.'

'Worried?'

'Panicked. Like he knew that everyone would suspect him of having done something to that poor girl so he just ran away. After all, if you can't find him, you can't do anything to him.' Kirsty rubbed the side of her cheek. 'What if it's the killer? What if he's coming back to make sure that we don't say anything? Or maybe he's come to kill us too!'

Tomek raised a hand to calm her, but it had little impact.

'You have to help us. You have to protect us. What if he comes back again tonight? We need someone to stand guard. A police officer, someone. We need protection.'

'We're not the FBI, Kirsty,' Tomek said bluntly. 'We don't have unlimited resources where we can send people to babysit. But we will have a look into it and do everything we can.'

Tomek lifted himself out of the sofa and handed her a business card. 'On there is my phone number. You see anything suspicious, you let me know. I'm only a short drive away, so I can be here within a few minutes, but first, you must call the police and they can send someone out.'

Kirsty was in a state of delirium when they stood up to leave, and it was a few moments after they'd exited the living room that she realised they were going. Closing the door behind her, she chased after them and called them back. 'Please make sure nothing happens to us.'

If that were possible, he thought, then nobody would be the victim of a crime ever again.

Once they were outside, Tomek and Chey hurried towards the car. The wind had returned with a vengeance and ripped past Tomek. Meanwhile, Chey, the smaller and slighter of the two, struggled to fight the elements.

'What do you make of all that then?' he asked as he shut the door behind him, silencing the wind.

'It doesn't make sense to me that our suspect would flee the scene and then come back,' Tomek said. 'They're tourists. It's incredibly unlikely that they would know him or have any connection with him that he feels the need to come and terrify them.'

'But the killer didn't know they're tourists. He might have thought that they lived here and that he could run the risk of bumping into them in the future.'

'So you think he's going to kill them as well?' Tomek asked.

Chey shrugged.

Helpful, thought Tomek.

'One thing that doesn't make sense to me, though,' he said, staring into the dashboard, deep in thought. 'Is how he found their address...'

'What do you mean?'

Tomek pointed to the house. 'Think about it,' he said. 'These people have been in the country for a week, two. They've booked the place via a private company on an app. There's no record of them living here other than between the owner and Kirsty. How in the fuck would the suspect know where they lived?'

CHAPTER
SEVENTEEN

That thought had stuck with Tomek.

How, if the figure standing outside the Airbnb was the same person who'd fled the scene, did he know where to find them? In Tomek's mind, it was one of two possibilities: either the killer was a member of the police service and knew where to locate the information, or, and this one he thought more likely, after fleeing the crime scene, the suspect had hovered outside the police station, knowing that the witnesses would be brought in for questioning. Then he'd simply followed them back to their place of sanctuary on an island full of strangers.

If it was possible for the suspect to do that, for him to follow the Redgraves home, then it was possible they weren't the only targets.

That he had done it to the rest of them.

Warren...

Andrei...

Shortly after leaving Kirsty Redgrave, Chey had called Nadia and asked for Andrei Pirlog's address. According to Google Maps, he lived a little over twenty minutes away, in the heart of Southend-on-Sea. A small one-bedroom flat that was situated along the busy London Road. Tomek used it every morning in and out of work, and he knew how busy it could get. Like now. The constant roll of tyres, the gentle purr of engines sitting in idle, the frequent sound of a car horn as some bastard had inevitably cut someone up. It had taken them three minutes of waiting alone for someone to let them cross two lanes of traffic.

The flat was the second in a row of five. They all sat above various local independent businesses. A fish and chip shop, a newsagent's, a bakery, a tattoo parlour, and a Chinese takeaway. Andrei had the misfortune of living above the Chinese restaurant with its thick, cloying smell of vegetable oil and MSG hanging in the air. It felt as though it stuck to the back of Tomek's throat as he climbed out of the car.

'Imagine Chinese food on tap,' Chey said.

'What're you talking about? Your parents have an Indian restaurant. You have access to Indian food all the time, or as you say it, *on tap.*'

Chey shut the car door. 'Yeah, but this is different.'

'In what way?'

'Because it's *Chinese*. There's nothing better than a Chinese.'

'Don't say that in front of them. I don't want to have to deal with another murder investigation.'

The young constable chuckled awkwardly. 'Doubt you'd be allowed to do anything on that either, if this one is anything to go by.'

Tomek ignored the comment at first, started towards Andrei's flat, stopped at some steps, then turned to the man. 'What's that supposed to mean?'

Lowering his tone, Chey replied, 'I see what's going on, you know. Everyone does. Between you and Sean. Sean and Victoria. It's so obvious. But I'm on your side, by the way. Though I am enjoying the time we've been spending together.'

Like they were a couple.

'How long have you known?'

'Since we started doing all the work without Victoria telling Nick. I figured that was the start of things to come.'

Tomek was impressed. He admitted Victoria hadn't been very subtle about it, yes. But it was political, and it had taken far longer for Tomek to notice such issues when he'd been Chey's age and at that stage of his career (if he ever noticed them at all). Instead, he'd been too bothered about flirting with his colleagues, doing the bare minimum, and getting himself into trouble.

'Very astute,' Tomek replied. 'And you say everyone else has noticed it too?'

Chey nodded, his eyes widening.

Tomek suddenly felt like a coup could be coming.

'I'm impressed.'

'Does that mean we're best friends now?' Chey asked.

For the past few months, the constable had been trying insufferably to buddy up with Tomek, to become closer friends with him outside of work – and in. But Tomek had always put it off. There was a huge age gap between them. Almost sixteen years. And Tomek had made that mistake in the past, albeit with a member of the opposite sex, and he wasn't prepared to go there again. Since Sean had almost vacated his life, Tomek had joked that a position as one of his best friends had become available which had given the young man hope. Chey had been fighting for pole position ever since.

'Sorry, champ,' he said. 'But the vacancy's almost been filled. Unless you can tell me the difference between a cherry blossom and a Chinese elm bonsai tree?'

Chey reached into his pocket.

'No cheating!'

Defeat danced across his face. 'Then how else am I going to find out the answer?'

'A true best friend wouldn't let that sort of thing get in the way. Be creative. Ask around.'

Chey clapped his palms together and bowed. 'Understood, sensei.'

'You have until the end of the day.'

With that, they headed up the small flight of stairs towards Andrei Pirlog's flat. Chey was first to arrive, and he waited patiently for Tomek to follow. Just as he was about to knock on the door, something caught his eye. A gap, no larger than a few millimetres, but enough for the brain to recognise it as unusual.

The door was ajar.

Were they too late? Had the mysterious figure got to Andrei already?

He gave Chey a slight nod. The constable understood what he meant and, tensing every muscle in his body, Tomek pushed the door open.

The flat was cold, silent. As though it had been uninhabited for weeks, months, and all that had been left behind were memories and the souls of those who'd passed along the way. The hairs on Tomek's neck stood to attention as he stepped through the hallway.

Left foot.

Right foot.

Left.

Until he came to a stop. On his right-hand side was a small bathroom. Through the gap in the door, Tomek saw what he'd prepared himself for. There, lying in the bathtub, submerged under water, fully clothed, his body limp, was the man Tomek had, until now, only seen in photos. Eyes closed, mouth ajar, dead. Andrei Pirlog.

CHAPTER
EIGHTEEN

Tomek rushed towards the bathtub, crashed into the side, reached for the back of Andrei's head, and pulled his nose and mouth out of the water.

'Andrei!' he yelled in the man's face. 'Andrei! Wake up! Can you hear me?'

But the man couldn't hear him. And from the dead weight of his body in Tomek's arms, he would never hear anything again. Frantically, Tomek placed a finger on the man's neck, waiting for a pulse. Nothing.

But Tomek didn't want to take that as an answer. Wedging his toes against the edge of the bathtub, and with the help of Chey when he finally realised what Tomek was trying to do, Tomek pulled Andrei from the tub and dragged him to the floor. Water flooded the linoleum, soaking Tomek's socks and legs. He placed the man flat on his back, then began chest compressions. Pounding the man's chest with the palm of his hands, feeling his rib cage crush beneath his weight, moving Andrei's body around like a rag doll, his limbs shuddering with each compression. Staring into the man's soulless, lifeless eyes.

Eventually, after two minutes of tirelessly trying to revive him, Chey intervened and pushed him away from the body.

'He's gone,' Chey told him gently, throwing his arm across Tomek's chest. The barrier was enough for Tomek to come round and realise it was time to stop. The man was gone, had been for a long time. There was nothing more he could do.

'We need to call SOCO,' Tomek said as he pushed Chey aside, switching into work mode. 'Shut the front door. Don't let anyone or anything else into this building. And don't touch anything.'

Chey nodded his understanding, then disappeared. A moment later he called back from the hallway. 'What do you want me to shut the door with, Sarge? I don't want to contaminate it.'

'Your clothes. Do it at the top as well – someplace nobody else might have touched it.'

'Aye, aye, Captain.'

As he heard the door shut, Tomek took a step back and surveyed his surroundings, took his first proper look at the man in front of him. Andrei Pirlog was a handsome man, with a head of long, thick black hair that was enough to give Martin a run for his money. His eyes were deep set, and he had a full set of clean, well-tended teeth. He looked like someone who spent a good amount of time looking after himself, and as though he had some Italian or Mediterranean heritage in his blood; more than the Romanian name and nationality suggested.

The shower-bath occupied the length of one wall. In the corner beside his head was an opened packet of paracetamol, scrunched against the wall. Tomek counted five tabs missing. No doubt finding a home inside Andrei's intestines.

Before Tomek could examine the rest of the room, Chey returned.

'SOCO are on their way,' he said. 'ETA ten minutes.'

Tomek hadn't heard the constable call it in, but thanked him, nonetheless.

'Boy...' Chey said.

'What?'

'Nothing.'

'No. Tell me.'

Chey pointed to the sink.

'What about it?'

'He was going through some *shit*.'

Tomek looked at him unimpressed, wishing he would hurry. The longer they spent there, the longer they contaminated the crime scene.

'How do you work that one out?'

'Because you can tell a lot about a person by the state of their toothbrush.'

Tomek look at him dumbfounded.

'How?'

'Well, it looks like he's been scrubbing seven shades of shit out of his teeth and gums for a while. He must have been going through *it*.'

'*It* being suicide?'

Chey shrugged. 'I guess.'

Sighing deeply, Tomek shook his head and rubbed his face, releasing some of the tension in his muscles. Then he cautiously lifted one leg over the cadaver and stepped out of the bathroom, making his way towards the living room.

'Where are you going?' Chey asked. 'We shouldn't be—'

'We need to secure the area,' he said. 'Make sure there are no threats present.'

'Threats? But it looks like he's killed him—'

Tomek raised a hand, shutting Chey off. He didn't want to hear it. The alarm bells were sounding in his head, telling him that this was more than a suicide. That someone had entered the flat, gone there for what they needed to do, then left again. Whether it had been intentional to leave the door open, Tomek didn't know. But he would find out.

Leaving the corpse behind, Tomek jumped into the room opposite. Andrei's bedroom. Rather, what was left of it. All that remained in the room was a plain mattress, a bedside table with only a lamp to call a companion, and a wardrobe tucked into the corner. That was it. Nothing else. No decorations, no picture frames, not even a piece of linen to cover the mattress. The room looked as though it had been empty for a while.

As did the rest of the flat.

The living room had all the essentials – a sofa, a dining table – but nothing more, nothing less. As for the kitchen, it came equipped with all the typical white goods, but when Tomek checked inside the fridge and a handful of the cupboards, he found nothing. It was the world's shittest advert for a home. To all intents and purposes, it appeared as though Andrei hadn't lived there for a single night, however there was evidence of his residency: leftover food and rubbish in the bin, a handful of clothes in the washing machine, waiting to be cleaned.

The whole flat was bizarre, confusing to him. And he didn't know quite what to make of it.

Before he was able to think on it further, he felt a hand on his shoulder. He flinched and spun on the spot. Chey was standing behind him, looking sheepish, as though he'd just broken something in the garage and was coming to tell his dad.

'SOCO are here. It's time for us to go.'

CHAPTER
NINETEEN

They didn't make it very far.

Tomek knocked and waited, tapping his foot impatiently on the concrete. Behind the door, he heard pop music blasting through a set of speakers. He was surprised to learn that he didn't recognise it; since Kasia had come into his life, he'd become *au fait* with all things pop culture – or at least pretended he had – and he wasn't afraid to admit that he knew who the latest boyfriend of her favourite pop star was at any given moment, or when their new album was coming out. If the team decided to conduct a pub quiz one evening at the Last Post, their local pub round the corner from the station, he would nominate himself for the pop quiz round. There was no celebrity scandal he didn't know about, no recent release that he hadn't come across. Kasia had given him the gift of knowledge for things that had absolutely no impact on his daily life. Still, it was nice to have hobbies.

Eventually, after he'd knocked three times, the door finally opened. Standing opposite them was a woman in her early thirties wearing a dressing gown. A white towel had been wrapped around her head, and a layer of make-up applied to her face.

'Hi,' Tomek said with a forced smile.

'I don't want nuffin',' she snapped.

'That's good. Because we're not selling anything.'

'Oh. Wha' you 'ere for then?'

'Your neighbour.'

'Who?'

'Mr Pirlog. At number—' Tomek leant back to check the signage outside Andrei's front door. 'At number sixteen.'

'I dunno who tha' is.'

'You don't know anything about him?'

The woman chewed on her bottom lip and shook her head. 'Nah. Ain't never 'eard 'is name or seen 'im round 'ere before.'

'If you've never heard of him, then how do you know you've never seen him before?' Chey asked.

Tomek wished he hadn't. They were fighting a losing battle talking to this woman, and he was ready to move on to the next neighbour. Though he was fairly certain what the outcome of that one would be as well.

'Listen,' she said, this time flashing a retainer in her mouth. 'I lived 'ere for just over a year, yeah? And I ain't ever seen no one come or go from there. I'm sorry, but I ain't gonna be much 'elp to you, whatever it is you need 'elp with.'

'He's dead,' Tomek said bluntly.

'Fuck,' she replied, in kind.

'Indeed. Don't suppose you saw or heard anything strange in the past twenty-four hours or so?'

She shook her head. 'Is that 'ow long 'e's been dead for? Thought I could smell something funny. Oh wait, no, that was just the bins outside. Never mind.' She looked into the grey clouds above and began tapping her chin, as if deep in thought, though the blank expression on her face was fooling no one. 'To be honest with ya, lads, I've got my music on all day and night. I don't 'ear much other than what I'm listening to.'

'I bet you're a delight,' Tomek said under his breath.

Before leaving the woman to get back to her bleeding eardrums, Tomek handed her a business card and told her to get in touch if anything came to mind. Then he and Chey moved further along the row of flats. Their optimism that someone had known or met Andrei rapidly reduced the further along they made it. By the end of the row, they had nothing. Nobody had met Andrei, nobody had even seen him in passing. Nobody had heard of him. But as it turned out, they hadn't heard of one another either, even though they lived centimetres away from each other at all times. No one along that row of rented accommodation had taken the time to speak with their neighbours or introduce themselves; instead, they locked themselves away, confined to their own four walls.

Defeated and dejected, Tomek had passed the neighbours on to a constable, who had been more than happy to take witness statements. 'Easiest part of my day, this,' she'd said after overhearing Tomek's portion of the conversation with them. He felt inclined to agree.

While he left the neighbours in the capable hands of the constable, he and Chey headed back to the incident room. There was nothing left for them to do there: Andrei's body had been removed for a post-mortem; SOCO were in the middle of examining the evidence; and the crime scene manager was keen to get it over with as soon as possible.

'Dunno about you, mate,' Tomek said as he switched the car engine on. 'But I don't think you're going to have any time to find out the difference between a cherry blossom and a Chinese elm today. I'd rather you focus your time on finding out who killed Andrei. The bonsais and best friend thing can wait.'

CHAPTER
TWENTY

News of Andrei's death travelled fast. By the time he and Chey had returned to the incident room, word that the investigation's most important key witness was now dead had arrived before them. And Tomek had spent the best part of a few seconds trying to explain it to the team before he was called into Victoria's office. She shut the door firmly behind him, letting him know that they were going to have a problem of some description.

'I still don't have that report,' she said as she rounded the other side of her desk, keeping the table as breathing space between them.

'I've been busy.'

'So I understand. Whose idea was it to take Chey away from his duties?'

Tomek furrowed his brow. 'I believe it was Kirsty Redgrave's when she said that someone's been standing outside her accommodation.'

'Kirsty Redgrave? One of the key witnesses?' This was clearly news to Victoria, and Tomek enjoyed this moment of having one up on her. 'I thought they were due to fly back to the States?'

Tomek pointed to the window behind her. 'There was some wind and rain that delayed them slightly. Not sure if you saw or heard about it.'

At that point, Victoria channelled her inner Nick and sighed heavily.

'When do they leave?' she asked.

'Tomorrow. I think we should bring them in, or possibly protect them somehow.'

Victoria took a moment to process what he'd said. 'Why?'

'Because they think they saw someone standing outside their house during the storm – on the street and then later in the garden. Now they're worried they might come back. And after what's happened to Andrei, I'm inclined to agree.'

'And you're sure someone was there?'

'How could *I* be sure?' Tomek said, pointing to himself. '*I* wasn't there. The only way that would be possible is if I had a time travel device, or at the very least had access to one. But sadly, I don't, so I can only take her word for it. And according to her, someone matching the description of our main suspect was seen standing outside the house. We need to make sure he doesn't come back again and do to them what he's done to Andrei.'

'And what would that be?' Victoria asked. She was trying to hide the confusion and dismay in her voice, but Tomek saw right through it. She had absolutely no idea what was going on, and she needed him to explain it to her like she was a child.

'I thought it was obvious?'

'You think Andrei was killed?' She spoke with surprise, as though she couldn't believe the words had come out of her mouth.

'I have reason to believe that, yes.'

'The reports coming in say that it's a suicide.'

'Right. Reports can be wrong. That's why I haven't given you mine from yesterday.'

'Is that an admission of ineptitude, Sergeant?'

Not yet, it wasn't.

When Tomek didn't respond, Victoria asked, 'Why did you try to save him?'

'Pardon?'

'Andrei. Why did you choose to save him? Estimates coming in are that he's been dead for almost twenty-four hours.'

Tomek shook his head in disbelief. 'Are you seriously asking me that?'

'Yes.'

Tomek sighed. 'Because the front door was open. After hearing what had happened to Kirsty Redgrave and her family, I was a little on edge, and when I saw the door, I thought something might have just happened to him. Forgive me for trying to save someone's life.'

'Don't do that,' she hissed. 'Don't make me out to be the bad guy here.'

'Difficult not to when you're questioning my decision to resuscitate someone.'

'You might have contaminated the crime scene. You know better than that.'

'I also know that trying to save a life is better than preserving any sort of evidence – evidence which, from the sounds of it, you don't seem to think exists.'

Victoria turned away from him again, staring into the wall.

'We will have to wait and see what the post-mortem and forensics reports suggest, but until then, I want all of our focus on trying to find Morgana's killer. We know for a fact that someone killed her. We don't know with any degree of certainty that Andrei Pirlog was murdered, even though the scaremongering from the Americans indicates that he might have been. And I'm not ready to go chasing after people who don't exist.'

Tomek propelled himself from the chair, left her office dumbfounded, and stormed towards the kitchen, where he grabbed himself a bottle of water and a caramel Rocky biscuit bar (one of his all-time favourites) from the fridge. As he rested against the kitchen counter, he necked the water. As soon as he was finished, he began unwrapping the chocolate biscuit. He was hungry and in need of some sugar. His levels were low, and they were about to get even lower as he felt his adrenaline surge through his body. Then Sean walked into the kitchen and Tomek grabbed another biscuit in preparation. Sean didn't acknowledge him. He simply came in, headed straight for the cabinet, and removed a mug. It wasn't until Tomek slammed the door shut that Sean noticed him.

'Oh, you all right, mate?' he asked, straining whatever pleasantness he had in his voice to unprecedented levels.

'All right,' Tomek replied.

'How's Kasia?'

'Yeah, she's fine.'

'And Abigail?'

'Also fine.'

'Cool.'

'Nice one.'

Sean opened his mouth to speak but Tomek beat him to it. 'Speaking of girlfriends, you couldn't have a word with yours, could you?'

'About what?'

'Andrei. His "suicide". She seems to think matey's topped himself off in the bath.'

'I'm sure she has her reasons.'

'Even when they're wrong?'

Sean grunted.

'Something happened to him and she knows it. She's just too fucking stupid to do anything—'

Raising a finger at him, Sean replied, 'Don't talk about her like that.'

Tomek held his hands up in mock surrender. 'Not saying anything that isn't true, mate.'

Sean covered the gap between them in an instant, the momentum of his overwhelming body mass and six-foot-four frame almost knocking him into Tomek. But he held it and stood firm. They stared at each other for a long moment. Tomek observed the man's features, watching the pupils of his eyes ricochet left and right. Feeling the warmth of Sean's breath on his skin. Seeing the acne scars on his cheeks that he'd always been self-conscious about.

Before either of them could say anything, the door opened. DC Oscar Perez entered the room, frozen in the doorway.

'Sorry, gents,' he said, coy. 'Interrupting something, am I?

'No,' Tomek answered. 'Sean just told me he needed a hug. But I'm not much of a hugger. Would you mind?'

Oscar's face was illuminated beneath the LED lights. He clapped his hands together and pounced towards Sean. 'It would be my pleasure. We all need a cradle now and then. A little bro hug to make sure everything's all right.'

A second later, Oscar was ready to wrap his arms around Sean, who suddenly looked as though he was holding in an urgent and uncomfortable trip to the bathroom.

As Tomek made to leave, Oscar snapped his fingers and grabbed him by the shoulder. Pulling him back, he said, 'Uh uh uh. Where do you think you're going?'

'To my desk.'

'Nope. Not that fast. In you get, come on.'

Tomek seemingly had no choice in the matter. Oscar grabbed him by the sleeve and pulled him in. The next thing he knew, he had his arms wrapped around two men, both on the opposite ends of the height spectrum, touching their flab, feeling their muscles. Tomek wanted to get out of there as soon as possible, but each time he pulled away he felt Oscar reining him back in. This was very much on Oscar's terms and they weren't allowed to finish until he said they could.

Their time together was cut short by Nadia walking into the room, one hand resting on her baby bump. 'You know, if you're expecting to make a child that way, you're doing it all wrong.'

At that point, Tomek had had enough and pulled himself away. While Nadia busied herself with the microwave, Tomek took a step back and scowled at Oscar.

'That wasn't too hard now was it, Tomek?'

'No. But I'm a hundred per cent sure I felt something *hard* from one of you against my leg.'

CHAPTER
TWENTY-ONE

Later that evening, Tomek and Abigail were lying in bed, half-naked beneath the duvet. It was two degrees outside, but Tomek was hot, and so had one leg cocked outside the bedding. He lay with his arm behind his head, staring at the ceiling. The day's events had taken it out of him and he needed to vent, to decompress. Thoughts of Morgana, Andrei, the bathtub, and to a certain extent Sean and Victoria, plagued his mind. But tonight, there was something else concerning him.

Kasia. The teenager that continued to confuse and infuriate him, and the one that would no doubt confuse and infuriate him for many more years to come – if not for the rest of his life. She'd been quiet for the last few days, distant, distracted by something. When he'd asked about school, she'd replied with monosyllabic answers. When he'd asked about her friends and favourite classes, her expression had remained placid. Something was troubling her. And he didn't know what. Probably the social pressures of being a teenager: school, growing up, boyfriends, looks, attention. It was a fucking minefield, and he had absolutely no idea what do about any of it.

In the short space of time they'd been father and daughter, they had already battled underage drinking, vaping, and boyfriends; the trifecta of her trying to impress her peers. Not to mention the incident where she'd nearly died of anaphylactic shock which was still having a visible effect on her. But he liked to think he knew his daughter well enough to know that this was about something else, something unrelated to that particular night. She'd been resilient in overcoming that, determined, and her mental health had improved as a result of the therapy sessions they attended together. But this was a different issue altogether, he sensed. One that hadn't been discussed in a small broom cupboard with a trained professional.

He needed help. He hoped he could find it beside him. Abigail was usually a good sounding board, and he trusted her with the information he gave her. Right now, she was sitting beside him, on her laptop, typing up yet another article.

'Can I ask you something?'

'What's pi to ten digits?'

'What?'

'Nothing. Just something I was thinking about earlier.'

'Right,' Tomek stared into the blank space on the bed. 'No. It's something slightly more important than pi.'

'I'm not ready for marriage yet.'

Tomek turned to her, eyes wide. 'Is that something else that you were thinking about earlier?' He was unable to hide the concern in his voice.

She patted him on the belly patronisingly. 'Don't worry your little cottons. You're a long way from that. You've got to earn your stripes first. But you've got potential...'

'I might not want to if you keep patting me like I'm your fucking chihuahua.'

This wasn't the direction Tomek had expected the conversation to head in. In fact, it wasn't the direction he expected *any* of their conversations to head in. At least not for a few months yet. They had only been going out for a few weeks, under the official title of boyfriend-girlfriend for a little over one of those weeks, and she was already proposing the question of marriage? If she ever wanted a reason to scare him off – or any forty-year-old man who had been used to his own company for thirty years – then she was going the right way about it.

'Go on,' she said, sensing that he was distressed by the topic of conversation. 'What did you want to ask me?'

'It's about Kasia. Has she seemed... *down* to you recently?'

Abigail tied her hair in a bun, lowered her laptop onto the bedside table, then lay down beside him. 'Down how?'

'I dunno. Quieter than usual. I think something's going on, but she won't tell me.'

'Could it be school?'

'Maybe.'

'Boys?'

'We've been over that ground already. I think she might have steered clear after what happened last time.'

'What happened?' Abigail asked, suddenly intrigued.

'Nothing major. Though if I were to ask you whether you thought you could fight a fully grown cow, what would you say?'

'I'd say that you were fucking stupid for asking that question in the first place.'

'Exactly. And that's all you need to know about Billy "The Cow Fighter" Turpin.'

Abigail seemed to understand what he meant because she gave him a nod and then stroked his shoulder.

'Could it be the incident?' she asked, turning the topic back to Kasia.

'I don't think so. She's usually pretty open with me about *that*. Besides, the nightmares have calmed down since she started going to Isabel.'

'And yours?'

'Yeah, they're fine.'

'What about her classes? Maybe she's struggling in some of them and it's getting her down. What're her favourite lessons?'

'Food tech and history.'

'Right. Well, you can't really fail food tech, unless you use salt instead of sugar for something. Aside from that it's very difficult to go wrong. As for history, it's already happened, all you have to do is recount the facts, so I don't think it could be that.' Abigail hummed as she pondered. 'Is she possibly being bullied?'

'I hope not. Again, last time that happened, I made sure it didn't anymore.'

Tomek was reminded of the time he'd driven down to Canvey Island, his least favourite place to visit, and had explained to a young girl's family that circulating an image of himself naked in bed and bullying Kasia as a result was considered revenge porn, and that if she continued, he would return with an arrest warrant. That had seemed to work, as since then, neither Tomek nor Kasia had heard from her.

Unless she was being bullied about something else.

'Could it be "girl" things?' he asked Abigail, using his fingers as air quotes.

'You don't have to say it like that,' she told him. 'We are real people. We're not figments of your imagination.'

He slapped her on the arm playfully. 'You know what I mean. Could it be period things? Or…?'

'Possibly. The life of a teenage girl is filled with a cornucopia of hormones that fuck with your head. There's so much going on up there even at the quietest of times, stuff like that doesn't help. It could be "*girl*" problems'—she said, using her fingers as quotation marks to mock him—'but if you want, I can have a word with her to see if she's prepared to tell me anything. It might be good for us to have a little one-to-one, anyway. We've not really had a chance like that since we started dating. I'd like to get to know her.'

Tomek suddenly felt very protective of his daughter. 'I think that's a nice idea, but let me discuss it with her first. If she doesn't tell me, then you can go in and do what you need to.'

A slight smirk flashed across Abigail's face. Brief, discreet. 'I'd like that,' she said, then picked up her laptop again.

'Do you ever stop?' he asked.

'I could ask you the same question. We're both workaholics. It's what makes us work as a couple.'

In many respects, she was right. They were always too busy to see one another, but during whatever little time they could share, they made the most of each other's company. If work became a priority for one, the other understood completely and gave them the space and time they needed because they knew what it was like. It was a balancing act, but they were making it work. However, a part of him had quietly begun to admit that it wasn't healthy. For either of them. And he wondered how much longer the honeymoon period would last.

'What's the latest on the harbour killing?' Abigail asked.

'You're not calling it that, are you?'

'No. It would be a good title for a book, though. A little on the nose for my liking, however. How's it going?'

It was then that Tomek vented the other part of his brain that had been keeping him awake. Andrei Pirlog. His suicide. His *murder*. The Redgraves. The man outside the house. The suspect who'd fled the crime scene. He told her about it all, heedless of the conflict of interest that should have prohibited him. Unsurprisingly, Abigail listened with intent, retrieving her laptop with one hand while her full focus was on him. By the end of it, the smile had returned to her face.

'I can put something out if you'd like?'

Tomek took a moment to consider the proposition. An article, detailing the incident, and putting the main suspect's description into the public domain, would be a massive help. Though his concern was that the description was too vague, too broad. Expecting the people of Essex to find a man with short black hair and a black beard was like asking a baker to find a loaf of bread in a supermarket – they would find one everywhere they looked. Nonetheless, it could still serve a purpose, and possibly help them solve the case. Therefore, in his mind, the upsides outweighed the negatives, and so he gave her the green light to write something.

'But first, sleep,' he told her, before kissing her goodnight and rolling over to the other side of the bed.

CHAPTER
TWENTY-TWO

The following morning, Tomek awoke to the sound of his phone vibrating violently beside his head. Eyes half open, he reached for the device and stared at the screen, the harsh light almost blinding him. Victoria was calling, and according to the four missed calls from her already she'd been calling for some time. Tomek let this one go through to voicemail, then looked at his notifications.

Four missed calls. Six text messages. All within the last half an hour.

Tomek, call me.

I need you to answer. It's urgent.

Tomek?

??

???

??????

A knot began to form in his stomach. Instinctively, he rolled over and found Abigail perched in the bed, laptop on her lap, fingers typing.

The sensation in his stomach tightened.

'Do you by any chance know why Victoria's been trying to call me?'

'It might have something to do with this.'

Abigail spun the device round. On the screen at the top of the page was the *Southend Echo*'s logo, with a stunning image of Mulberry

Harbour taken by local photographer Dawid Glawdzin beneath it. The title of the article read: *Police release suspect details from Southend harbour killing.*

'Yep,' he said. 'That'll do it.'

'You sound annoyed.'

'I mean, I wasn't expecting you to have done it *this* quickly. Did you sleep at all?'

'I got a couple of hours. Don't worry, it didn't take me all night to write.'

Evidently not, as the time of publication on the website was stamped at 03:57. He also noticed that she'd been smart enough to send the article to someone else in the team to publish, so they could take all the credit – and flack. That meant Victoria had no leg to stand on when the accusations would undoubtedly come, saying that he'd leaked the information to the press. If it had been published under Abigail's name, the biggest mistake she could have made, it would be a different story.

Tomek rolled himself out of bed, his body feeling fatigued. His legs and core were knackered from the run yesterday. Christ, he was out of shape. He needed to get back into it. Seriously, this time. Actually doing it. Not just thinking about it, and procrastinating by thinking that an inadequate and tight-fitting pair of shoes was the issue. No, he needed to put them on, leave the house, and put rubber to tarmac.

One foot in front of the other.

That in mind, Tomek made his way to the shower, cleaned himself, and got ready for the day. It was a Saturday, the weekend. And yet he had to work. To spend time away from his family. It wasn't fair, but it was part of the job. And with a murder investigation as confusing and as open as this one, he couldn't afford to spend time off.

Except for this morning. He could be late into work this morning, he decided. To delay the inevitable shitstorm that would come his way. Victoria had tried calling him twice more while he was in the shower, and he didn't expect the missed calls would stop soon. Instead, she would have to wait.

Right now, he had a daughter that needed his attention and guidance.

A little after eight am, Tomek knocked on Kasia's door. Nothing. Not even the sound of movement in bed. Suddenly he began to fear the worst. That she'd escaped, run away, just as she'd done in the past, and so he knocked again but entered without waiting for an answer. He gripped the door handle hard, preparing himself to scream her name. When he saw her curled up in a ball, wrapped beneath the duvet, sound asleep, he let out a big, deep sigh.

'Wakey, wakey,' he yelled, a little over the top.

Kasia stirred, glowered at him, then rolled over to the other side of the bed.

'I've got a surprise for you this morning, Kash,' he said.

'I don't want it.'

'You don't know what it is yet.'

'Meh,' came the unequivocal grunt of a teenager begging for more sleep.

'Rise and shine,' he said, as he moved towards the window and pulled open the blinds. 'We're going out for breakfast.'

CHAPTER
TWENTY-THREE

Tomek had never seen Morgana's so empty. It was as though word of her death had spread and all of a sudden going there had become taboo. It was bizarre, eerie almost. Tomek had been there at various points in the day – early Saturday mornings, Sunday afternoons, even seven o'clock on a Tuesday evening – and yet each time was as busy as the last. Now, there were two other groups with them, and the atmosphere had dropped to match. Tomek couldn't help but think the place was unable to function properly without Morgana at the helm, leading from the front, bringing in the revenue with her flirtatious smile, her bubbly personality.

Their waitress this morning was called Helena. Ukrainian, like Morgana. Just as pretty, just as innocent-looking. Except, when it came to her personality and her ability to interact with customers, she was at the opposite end of the spectrum. Nerves plagued her speech as she addressed them both and asked for their drinks order. On two occasions she had asked Kasia to repeat her order of orange juice, and as she turned towards the open kitchen at the back, she bumped into a nearby table and chairs.

'I hope this place doesn't go under,' he said, his eyes falling on the row of flowers and teddy bears that had been left outside the front of the café.

'Yeah...' Kasia replied, despondent. She pulled out her phone and began scrolling.

'Do you know what you want to eat?'

'Egg.'

'Good start. Anything to go along with it?'

'Toast.'

'And how do you want it?'

'How do you mean?'

Bloody hell this was painful.

'Scrambled? Poached? Fried? Churned into butter and then thrown all over the walls?'

'Oh. Right. Erm... Scrambled. Please.'

Not once did she look up at him. Not once did she bat an eyelid or raise an eyebrow at his final egg option. She was distracted beyond comprehension, and despite trying his best to play it down and lift her spirits, it wasn't working.

'What's going on, Kash?' he asked. Before she could respond, Helena returned with their drinks in hand. As she set them on the table, Tomek strained a smile at her, thanked her, then placed both their orders. Scrambled eggs for Kasia, double heart attack special for him. Once Helena had taken the order and retreated out of earshot, Tomek asked Kasia the question again.

'Nothing's going on,' she answered softly, her head still buried deep in her phone.

'Is it school? Your classes going okay?'

'Classes are fine. School's fine.'

'What about food tech? Mrs Shaw hasn't been taking home more of your delicious food again, has she?'

'Not when I used salt instead of sugar...'

It took a moment for the comment to register. Salt, sugar. And then he remembered. The night before. His conversation with Abigail.

'You heard that?'

'Yep.'

Tomek thought she'd been asleep, but she'd heard everything. He tried to recall what else he'd said. What else he might have offended her about. More worryingly, however, if she heard that conversation while they'd been talking openly and fairly loudly, then that possibly meant she'd heard other things coming from their room. Adult things. Sounds that thick walls were built for.

'Is that how you talk about me when I'm not there?' she asked venomously. 'Do you say those sorts of things about me to people at work?'

Oh, fuck.

'Absolutely not. Not at all. I thought you were asleep last night. And I wasn't saying you were *bad* at food tech or anything like that. I think you're doing really well at school and I'm really proud of you. I was just saying that...'

Tomek hesitated as he tried to recall his phrasing. But he drew a blank.

'You don't know how I'm doing at school,' she snapped. 'You don't know because you never ask.'

'Hey, come on now. That's not—'

His plate of food landing in front of him cut him off. He thanked Helena, then glowered at her to leave them alone without delay. Fortunately, she was distracted by another group of customers who had just entered, and scurried away like a dog meeting new people.

'That's not fair,' Tomek continued once she was out of earshot. 'I always ask you how your day was at school. You always say it was fine.'

'Yeah, and you just leave it at that. You could at least ask some follow-up questions. Maybe ask what classes I had, what happened at lunchtime...'

Tomek nodded, realisation suddenly slapping him across the face so hard it felt like he'd just been entered into the World Championships.

'Okay. Understood. Noted. Agreed. Taken in.' He inhaled deeply, held it, then let the air out of his lungs slowly. 'I'm sorry. I should show more of an interest. That's on me. But this is all still very new to me, being a dad.'

'You can't keep using that excuse forever, *Dad*.'

Tomek didn't appreciate the way she'd said his name. There was a lot of vehemence and animosity behind it.

'Like I say. I'm sorry. Work's been busy. And things with Abigail have—'

Tomek stopped himself as soon as he noticed the change in Kasia's expression. She had rolled her eyes, shaken her head, and begun playing with her food. Within a few subtle movements, she made her opinions on Abigail very clear. Pretty sophisticated for a thirteen-year-old, he had to admit.

'Is *that* what this is about?' he asked, as his mind read between the lines. 'Is that why you've been upset the past few days? You feel like I've neglected you because I've been spending more time with Abi?'

Kasia said nothing.

'Because if it is, you need to say. You need to tell me these things. I'm not a mind reader. And despite my best efforts trying to convince the guys down in IT to create one, they still haven't come up with a way for me to read your thoughts – or anyone else's, for that matter. So, I'm having to do a lot of the legwork on my own. And I'll be honest with you, Kash, my brain isn't built for that. I wish it was. And I bet you do too.'

She grunted, meaning yes.

'So maybe it'll have to work both ways. If something's upset you or got you down, you need to tell me. You need to be honest and open with me and I will do the same with you. Agreed?'

Slowly, she picked up her knife and fork and looked him in the eye. 'Agreed,' she said, then began cutting up her breakfast.

A thin smile flashed across Tomek's face. 'Out of interest, how were your classes yesterday? What happened at lunchtime?'

Kasia set down her knife and fork. From the look on her face, she was appreciative that he had finally asked those particular questions, even if they were eighteen hours overdue. 'Classes were fine. In maths we were learning about cosine, sine, and tangents.'

'I remember doing that,' he said as he chewed on some bacon. 'I remember thinking to myself at the time that I would never need to know that in the future.'

'That's what Hayden said.'

'Well, you can tell him he's wrong. I used it the other day.'

'*Really?*'

Tomek sniggered. 'Absolutely not,' he said. 'No one in the history of the English education system has used that equation. It will not benefit you in any way.'

'I don't think you're supposed to be telling me stuff like that. Miss Hendry wouldn't be too pleased if she heard you were telling me not to worry about it.'

Tomek set his knife and fork down and wagged his finger in her face. 'No, you misunderstand me. I'm not saying don't learn it. You *must* learn it. You need to in order to pass the GCSE. All I'm saying is, don't get too excited about using it later on in life. If Miss Hendry questions whether you know the difference between cosine, sine and tangent, I want you to be able to tell her that you do, but that you also know you will never have to use it in your life. Let me know what her reaction is.'

Chuckling, Kasia replied that she would. Now the anguish had gone from her face and been replaced with a smile Tomek hadn't seen in weeks. She was a happy teenager again.

Or as happy as a teenager could be.

'What about lunchtimes?' Tomek asked. 'Do you all just sit around on your phones, not talking to each other?'

'A lot of people do. I just like to watch them. I think it's fascinating.'

'Interesting. Maybe you'd make a good detective.'

'I don't want to get into the family business thanks,' she said quickly. Far too quickly for Tomek's liking.

'There's still time for you to change your mind,' he replied, hopeful. 'What do you want to do instead?'

'Have my own coffee shop,' she said even quicker.

He was impressed. His daughter being an entrepreneur. He could brag about it to his colleagues and show off how proud he was of her.

Of course, that was a pre-requisite, a given, a non-negotiable of being her dad. But still... an entrepreneur.

And think of the cake!

'I wouldn't mind taste-testing all the new sweets and treats you decide to create. I know what I'm talking about.'

Kasia suddenly turned shy, turned her attention to her food once again. He decided to move the conversation back to its original path before he took it on a tangent.

'Who do you hang around with at lunch?' he asked. 'How's Sophia getting on?'

'Yeah, she's good,' Kasia replied, hesitation in her voice. 'I spend a lot of my lunchtimes with Yasmin now.'

'Right. But you're still friends with Sophia?'

'Yes. Of course we are. Nothing's happened between us, if that's what you're worried about.'

He was, but he didn't want to say anything. Instead, he wanted to let the situation play out naturally and be there to pick up the pieces if necessary.

Let her make her own mistakes, Tomek, he told himself.

For the next five minutes, they tucked into their food in silence. Kasia was still eating by the time Tomek finished. Except by now she had stopped eating it and was beginning to play with it, moving it about her plate. Tomek observed her for a moment. But she was oblivious to it, to the silence, to his hard stare.

'Hey,' he said, taking her by surprise. 'You all right? You sure nothing else is wrong?'

'I'm sure,' she said, too quickly again. The reticence in her voice belied her choice of words.

'Kash. What did we just talk about? Tell me.'

For a long moment, his daughter fought internally, summoning the courage to say what was on her mind. Eventually, she did. 'It's something

I've been meaning to ask for a while, but I was a bit embarrassed. It's silly really, but—'

'Nothing you say is silly, and you have nothing to be embarrassed about with me,' he said, reaching out for her hand.

'It's just that... at school, everyone's got one, and I think they look really cool, but they're really expensive, and I know we just had Christmas and everything, and I didn't want to ask for one, but—'

'Everyone has one what?'

'A mug.'

'Sorry, what?'

'A mug. A special mug. It's like a giant flask.'

Don't say what you're really thinking.

'Right.'

'It keeps things cool for a really long time and it also, like, keeps drinks really hot for an even longer time.'

'So it's a thermos?'

Don't do it.

'Yes. Well, no. Not really. This one went viral because it got caught in a house fire and it was the only thing that survived, with the drink still in it – and it was *still* warm!'

'The fire might've had something to do with that...'

Tomek took a moment to process what she was saying. She was asking him to buy her a mug, presumably because everyone else had one (including anyone who was anyone), and if she didn't have one, then that would be seen as a social faux pas and she would become some sort of social pariah.

Over a fucking mug.

'How much is it?'

'A hundred quid,' she said.

Okay, now you can say it.

'Fuck a duck,' he replied. 'Does this mug also cure cancer? Because for that sort of money, it should do. If not, I think maybe you should make *that* the family business.'

Kasia didn't see the funny side of it. She lowered her head and began playing with her food again. Sensing that he'd lost her, Tomek tapped her on the hand and said that he would have a look into the mug, see what he could do.

'You sure that's everything on your mind?' he asked for a final time.

She nodded, but from the dull glint in her eyes, he knew it wasn't. There was something else, something more important than a fireproof mug. But that was okay. She had opened the door to him. It may not have been what he wanted to hear, but she had confessed a problem to him, and left things a little open for more. And for now, he was happy with that.

With any luck, the rest would come soon.

CHAPTER
TWENTY-FOUR

Before Tomek entered the incident room, he decided he'd already had enough. He wasn't in the mood for another argument with Victoria, Sean, or anyone else.

Sadly, they didn't feel the same way.

It was a little after ten when he stepped through the door and Victoria was in the middle of leading a meeting. Surprisingly, she'd stopped calling and messaging him after he and Kasia had left for Morgana's, almost as if she'd known that he'd needed the time alone with his daughter. Either that, or she was just saving all the pent-up frustration for his arrival.

Which turned out to be the case. As he slipped into the room, he pulled out a chair at the back, hoping nobody would notice. But his plan was foiled by the screeching sound of the seat on the floor.

'Here he is,' Victoria said, halting. 'Fucking finally.'

'Ma'am.'

'Care to mention why you haven't answered any of my calls or replied to any of my messages?'

Tomek cast his gaze around the room. All eyes were on him, some scrutinous, while others (Chey and Rachel in particular) were smiling, eager to see events unfold in front of them.

'We're doing this here?' he asked.

'Yes.'

'All right then. I was out for breakfast with my daughter.'

'And you think that's an acceptable use of time during the middle of a murder investigation?'

'We were at Morgana's, ma'am. I was doing research.'

Thin, almost to the point that it didn't exist, but it was research, nonetheless.

True to her nature, Victoria asked him for a report of his findings.

'The fill-in waitress, Helena, looked tired. As did the rest of the place. It was empty. There were only three groups of customers in total. Nobody wants to go now they know what's happened. To me that was odd. I would have thought, if the number of flowers and cards outside the window was anything to go by, that people would show their support by coming in and keeping the business afloat.'

Victoria nodded slowly as she folded her arms across her chest.

'The service was slow out back,' Tomek continued. 'Our food took longer to arrive, which worries me about how long the business can survive.'

'How does that help us find the murder suspect?'

Tomek considered for a moment, hoping the answer would appear in his mind. But it didn't. He had nothing.

Until DC Martin Brown chimed in. 'Was the deputy manager not there?'

'I don't think so. Remind me what he looks like.'

As though he was secretly working for *Blue Peter*, Chey pulled up a photo of the deputy manager, Vlad Boyko, one that he'd prepared earlier on his laptop. Tomek observed the photo of the man and closed his eyes, trying to picture him in the restaurant.

'Come to think of it,' Tomek said, 'I don't remember seeing him at all.'

'Interesting,' Victoria replied. Then turned to Nadia. 'Add it to the action list please. We need to monitor him. He could be a flight risk.'

As soon as Nadia started making a note on her pad, Tomek dropped his shoulders and stooped lower in his chair, hoping to hide away from the inspector's gaze.

It didn't work.

'You came in at the right time, Tomek,' she said excitedly, as though the thought had just occurred to her. 'We were in the middle of discussing the leak.'

'Leak? Oh, that's not good. There's a pharmacy down the road. I think they do incontinence pads.'

A slight, almost inaudible chuckle bounced through the room, but it was silenced with a piercing stare from Victoria.

'You know what leak I'm referring to. The one in the *Southend Echo*. The one that released all the information we have on our main suspect. The one that announced Andrei Pirlog's death to the public. You wouldn't happen to know anything about that, would you?'

Tomek dipped his head. 'I would, yes.'

Victoria's eyes widened with delight. 'You do?'

'Yes. I now know everything you've just told me.'

The surprise at his sudden "admission" quickly bled away from her expression.

'That's not what I meant. And you know it.'

Tomek did know it. Of course he did. He wasn't stupid. But he wasn't about to admit to anything unless Victoria had evidence that could back him into a corner.

'I don't know anything about an article,' he said.

'Nothing to do with your journalist girlfriend?'

Tomek shook his head and spoke flatly. 'Nope. And I don't appreciate the allegation. Unless you have evidence to suggest otherwise, I'd prefer it if you didn't insinuate that I've been muddying the waters between personal and professional.'

Silence drifted into the office. Out of the corner of his eye, Tomek saw his colleagues' heads bounce between them like they were watching a soap opera drama.

'Fine,' she said. 'I was just curious. But if I end up finding evidence to support my theory, I swear to fucking god, I will make your life a misery for the next few weeks.'

'I look forward to it,' he responded, grinning.

CHAPTER
TWENTY-FIVE

In the hours succeeding the meeting, Tomek had been confined to his desk. He'd finally started typing the report Victoria had been chasing him for. It was a long and laborious task, condensing the progress they'd made into manageable, bite-sized chunks of digestible information. First, he'd started with his takeaways from the post-mortem. It had, in no uncertain terms, proved that Morgana had drowned. The bruises around her neck indicated that she'd been held under the water. However, there was little to no fingerprint or DNA evidence on her that wasn't from the Redgraves, Andrei Pirlog or Warren Thomas. In their attempts to lift her body onto the harbour, they had contaminated any evidence that would have pointed them towards the killer.

Aside from the bruises around her neck and the water in her lungs, there was nothing else untoward about Morgana's body. She had been in good health. She wasn't a drinker or a smoker, nor did she indulge herself in the delights of her restaurant's food. Despite that, her clothing and footwear had been sent off for external examination. However, there was a backlog and it would be another week or two before they received the results. Fortunately, all this made for a brief report, and he'd finished it within half an hour.

As he closed the document on his computer, he surveyed the office.

It was sparse. Just him, Chey and Nadia who'd been told to continue their work in the office. Meanwhile, everyone else was out in the field, collecting more witness statements, and speaking with Morgana's employees, and her customers. Whereas Chey still had the unenviable task of trying to find CCTV footage of the suspect – that, and answering the calls that had come in from the public following Abigail's online article. Since the article had gone live, the team had received hundreds of calls through the switchboard, each purporting to have information pertaining to the identity of Morgana's killer. As was often the case, a large number of them had been timewasters. There had, however, been one call to the switchboard that had been of interest. A woman from Southend had seen a man emerging from the water on the morning of Morgana's death, fully clothed and covered in sand, vaguely matching the suspect's description. As Tomek and Chey had suspected, the figure had melted into civilisation a few hundred yards from Southend Pier. Sean, the lucky bastard, had been sent to speak with her.

That suited Tomek. He thought the team were wasting their time speaking to more key witnesses. His focus was on Andrei Pirlog. In his mind, the man had still been murdered, even though Victoria disagreed and had already concluded his death was a suicide. They were still waiting for the post-mortem and DNA results, but something about the man's death disconcerted him. Why would he have killed himself? Had the sight of a dead body been too strong for him? Or had he been silenced, killed for what – and who – he'd seen on that morning?

Tomek pushed himself away from his desk and headed towards the kitchen. As he entered, his phone chimed. It was a text message from Nick.

You at the office? I see your car. I'm outside.

An arctic blast of wind battered him in the face the instant he opened the door to the car park. Remnants of Storm Alisha remained, as leaves were strewn from one side to the other.

Tomek spotted Nick a moment later, sitting in his car, his face barely visible behind the reflection of the dull sky in the windscreen. He made his way towards the vehicle and climbed in. The heating was on full blast, like stepping into a sauna.

'Don't think you've got it on hot enough,' Tomek said, immediately wishing he hadn't brought his coat with him.

'You feel the cold a lot more when you get to my age.'

'That and the weak bladder.'

'All right. That'll do. Bastard.' Nick pointed to the building. 'How's life without me?'

'Depends who you ask. Some might say it's better and they're having the time of their life. Others would happen to say it's the worst it's ever been.'

'Which camp do you sit in?'

'The latter.'

'That bad?'

Then Tomek explained to Nick all that had taken place since his suspension. The CCTV footage, the incident outside the Redgraves', Andrei's death, and the newspaper leak.

'Can I assume that you were all over that little piss party?' Nick asked.

'Like a fat kid on a cupcake.'

'And she knows that?'

'Well, she suspects it. She doesn't *know* anything.'

Nick sighed, long, deep. 'Don't get too close to the fire, mate. You can get yourself into a lot more trouble when I'm not there to defend you.'

That was the problem. Tomek didn't want Nick to defend him. Not anymore. He was old enough to look after himself and deal with the consequences of his actions – until they went too far, of course, then he might need a helping hand. But by that point, he liked to think he would know where the line was.

'How's early retirement?' Tomek asked.

'Boring as fuck. I mean, don't get me wrong, I love that I get to spend all day with Lucy, Maggie and Nella, but there's only so much looking after that Lucy needs. All she does is sit there and watch TV. We just have to make sure we're on hand when she needs us. The rest of the time it's just Maggie and me in the house while Daniela's at school.'

'How's that all going?' Tomek asked.

'Shit. Worse, maybe. Definitely no better than before.'

'It's only been a couple of days.'

'Exactly. That's what worries me. If I'm this bored, if I'm dreading going home already after less than half a week, what does that say about our marriage? What does that mean for our future?'

Tomek didn't have an answer to that question. 'Give it some time. Have you spoken to Isabel about it?'

Nick shook his head and sighed again, this time deeper. 'She's fully booked. Still got her backlog to work through. That's why I've come to see you. Take my mind off it. Vent to an old pal.'

Shit.

'Not sure how much help I can be. Got stuff going on of my own: Kasia's keeping something from me, and I can't seem to figure out what it is.'

'Have you tried asking her?'

'Yes. Obviously. Have *you* tried talking to *your* wife?'

Nick stared into the middle distance. His voice was blank, almost empty. 'Not much. I go out for a lot of walks to clear my head, process my thoughts. Although during the storm I couldn't do that so was forced to sit inside. We had a good day then.'

'Because you were forced and had nowhere else to go?'

Nick nodded. It wasn't looking good. Chatting through their personal issues was all well and good, therapeutic maybe, but Tomek wanted a change in topic.

'What are your thoughts on Andrei's death?' Tomek asked.

If Nick was offended by the sudden change in conversation, he didn't show it. Instead, he looked almost relieved. They were blokes, after all. Two men incapable of expressing themselves and confronting their emotions.

'It seems mighty convenient for him to kill himself the day after he's the key witness in a murder,' Nick said. 'And he was nice enough to leave the door open for you as well.'

'Have you ever known a suicide do that?'

Nick searched his memory. 'I've dealt with a couple that were similar in that respect. People who didn't have anyone in their life. Hoping they'd be found at some point. Making it easier for whoever did. But it's not common. Especially when it's a key witness, like I said. And even more uncommon when other key witnesses have reported a figure standing outside their window.'

'Precisely my thinking, but Victoria seems to think it's too early to determine a route into his death. She wants to wait until we get DNA and the PM done.'

'You could always beat her to it. Get ahead of the curve. My theory would be that he was silenced. That whoever killed Morgana had come back for him. The question you have to ask yourself is *how*, and *why*, and whether there's anything else that links the two of them.'

Tomek closed his eyes as he considered what Nick had said. But before he could focus on them for too long, a figure caught his attention, strolling across the car park, wearing a dark coat, with black hair, a thin black beard, and a scarf wrapped around his neck. Plumes of vapour expelled rapidly from his mouth, even though he wasn't running. Either he was seriously unfit, or he was nervous about something; his heart rate had increased for a reason.

'Excuse me,' Tomek said as he grabbed the door handle.

'Where're you going?'

Tomek pointed to the man. 'Someone who looks an awful lot like our main suspect has just entered the police station.'

CHAPTER
TWENTY-SIX

The man's name was Mariusz Stanciu. Thirty-four years old, Romanian, with short black hair and a thin black beard. Shortly after spotting him from the passenger seat of Nick's car, Tomek had raced across the car park and accosted the man, offering him help, assuming he was lost.

The man had replied, 'I've come to turn myself in.'

That had set the heartbeat racing. The potential suspect doing his job for him. Now, twenty minutes later, they were in a small room together. Nondescript, empty, save for a table and two chairs pressed against the wall. In the top corners on Tomek's left side were two cameras, watching and recording their every move. Mariusz had opted for a voluntary interview, without professional support, and Tomek was more than happy to oblige.

'Thank you for coming today,' he started. 'Though I must remind you that while this is a voluntary interview I do have the right to arrest you. You are also entitled to legal advice throughout this process, though you have already refused that. Is that something you wish to continue without?'

Mariusz offered him a blank look. His eyes were glazed over, as though he were deep in thought about something back in Romania.

'I do not wish to have any legal support present,' he responded, his accent thick.

The sentence sounded polished, almost rehearsed, as though he was dragging it from memory rather than speaking naturally and in the present.

'Very well. Then I'd like for you to begin,' Tomek said. 'Why have you come here today, Mariusz?'

'I saw... I saw...' He paused to steady himself. Looked down at his fingers, and started entwining them with one another. 'I saw on the television. The news. About the woman who died on the harbour. I saw... I saw the description of who you were looking for.'

'So why have you come in? Because you were actually there, or because you match the description of someone who was there?'

'Because I was there and I match the description.'

'And you've only come in now because you've realised the police are looking for you?'

'I... I...' Mariusz looked down at his hands again and continued playing with them. 'Forgive me, my English...'

'That's fine,' Tomek said calmly. 'Take as much time as you need.'

He wasn't willing to blow this one so quickly.

'I was there,' Mariusz said slowly, almost robotically. 'But I had nothing to do with her death.'

Tomek nodded and eased back in his seat. Now it was time to let Mariusz do all the talking. For him to shut up and listen. To find holes in his story, things he could exploit and explore further down the line.

'Tell me everything,' he said, then grabbed his imaginary popcorn and placed it beside his pen and paper.

Before beginning, Mariusz cleared his throat. 'You see, yes, I was at the harbour on that morning. Yes, I found the body of the woman – what was her name, Morgana? Yes, that's right. But I did not have anything to do with killing her. I only found her. When the other people came to the harbour, I panicked, dropped her to the ground and then ran away. I do not know what came over me. I did not want them to think that I had something to do with killing her. I panicked.'

Mariusz came to a natural stop and looked at Tomek expectantly, waiting for him to respond, but when nothing came, the man felt compelled to continue.

'I went the wrong way. I did not see where I was going. And then the tide came in. It was really fast. Faster than I expected, and then I came near the pier. You know, Southend Pier. After that I ran towards the shore, covered in sand, mud and water. Then I headed back home where I washed myself and cleaned my clothes. I did not know what to do, so I stayed inside for the rest of the day.'

Another natural stop. Another expectant look. This time, Tomek decided to indulge him. So far, everything he'd heard checked out. But it had sounded rehearsed. Some of the details that Mariusz had mentioned, like the pier, like the washing of the sand and mud from his clothes, sounded manufactured. As though he'd either been told to say them or had rehearsed them repeatedly. Tomek wanted to take the conversation down an avenue that Mariusz wasn't expecting.

'What do you do for a living, Mariusz?'

'A living? How do you mean?'

'What do you for work? What's your job?'

'Oh. I see. I... I am a lorry driver. I work for a haulier company.'

Tomek smirked at the man's mispronunciation of haulier. It came out as "hoo-liar". Had he not lived in the country for thirty-five years, Tomek believed he would have made the same mistake.

'Can I get the name of the company,' he said, more as a statement than a question.

'Of course. It's...' A brief pause as he shuffled in his seat, unsure of himself. 'It's called DWG Logistics.'

'How long have you been working there?'

'Three months. I am still in, how you say, probation?'

'Probation, yes. What have you been doing in the days since you found the body?'

'Working. I have had to drive up and down the country. Delivering orders to my customers.'

'Because you're still on probation?'

'Yes. My job is very important to me. I need to keep it for as long as I can, you understand. I have something important planned.'

Like the murder of someone else?

Tomek saw the carrot of that statement dangling in front of him and bit. 'What?'

'I am going to propose to my girlfriend.'

Tomek glanced down at the man's right hand. In Romania, as was the case in Poland and other European countries, the wedding ring was worn on the right hand, rather than the left.

'If I'm not mistaken, it looks like you're already married?'

Mariusz looked at his fingers, covered them, and began massaging them. 'This is not a wedding band. This was given to me by my grandfather before he passed. I wear it here to remember him.'

Tomek appreciated the sentiment. He'd never really known his grandparents. His paternal grandmother had passed away before he was born while his maternal grandfather had died a few months after his birth. His brothers, Michał and Dawid, had spent more time with their Polish grandmother before eventually leaving her in Poland when they emigrated to the UK. He'd only seen her a handful of times since, on holidays, anniversaries, and funerals. As for his remaining British grandfather, he had moved to Scotland for love. It had come out that, while his nan was dying, his grandad had been sleeping with another woman and was waiting for her to pass before moving up to Scotland with his new lover. Naturally, it had caused a lot of arguments within the family, and Tomek had neither seen nor heard of him since. He doubted the man was still alive.

'Where is your girlfriend now?' Tomek asked.

'She... she is... back home in Romania. She had to go back for some family... some family issues.'

'Right. And does she know what's happened?'

Mariusz shook his head innocently. 'I did not want to worry her,' he explained. 'Are you not going to ask me why I was at the harbour?'

Mariusz's question took Tomek by surprise.

'I had planned on it,' he replied. 'Are you going to tell me?'

'Of course. I want to help the investigation as much as possible. It is important to me. You need to catch the killer!'

Tomek kept his expression blank as he waited for the man's psychological anxiety to take over.

'I visited the harbour because I am going to propose there, as I have said. I wanted to, how you say, *scout* the place out. I wanted to do a test run and see what it is like for me and my girlfriend to go down there when I propose. I needed to see if it was muddy or wet, and what the tide is like. I was not expecting to find a dead body there.'

'Certainly not,' Tomek replied flatly. 'Can you remember what time you arrived at the crime scene?'

Mariusz looked down at the table as if hoping to find the answer there. Then he said, 'Nine thirty am. Just after. I think I made it back to the beach after eleven.'

'Over an hour later? That's a long time to get back...'

The little lightbulbs inside Tomek's head were starting to blink.

'I had to run and avoid the puddles. Plus, I went the wrong way. I already told you this.'

'You're right. You did. My apologies. Did you, on your initial journey to the harbour that morning, see anyone acting strange or anything out of the ordinary? Did you see anyone fleeing the scene of the crime? Did you see the murder take place?'

Mariusz shook his head. Slowly. 'I'm sorry,' he said, 'but I did not see anything. It was just me. I wish I could be more help.'

'You really want to help the investigation in any way possible, don't you?'

Mariusz tilted forward in his seat, straightening his back slightly. 'Of course I do. It is important to me. Whatever you need.'

Tomek had heard enough.

'In that case, Mariusz Stanciu, I am arresting you on suspicion of the murder of Morgana Usyk. You do not have to say anything, but it may harm your defence if you do not mention when questioned something which you later rely on in court. Anything you do say may be given in evidence.'

CHAPTER
TWENTY-SEVEN

Tomek had been left with no choice but to arrest Mariusz and place him in a holding cell. He'd confessed to being at the scene of the crime and being the only one in the area at the time of Morgana's death. For the next twenty-four hours, at the very least, Tomek and the team had the luxury of being able to investigate his connection with Morgana's death without the risk of him escaping or destroying any evidence. The only problem that remained now, however, was confirming his whereabouts, his job, and his movements following her death. It was a race against time, but fortunately, Tomek thought they had the team to do it.

Shortly after being arrested, Mariusz had been taken down to the booking-in desk – or as Tomek liked to call it, the arrest desk – where he'd handed over his possessions, been given a tracksuit to change into, and his fingerprints and DNA samples taken. Tomek had also ensured that he retained a copy of the man's mugshot. Annoyingly, Mariusz looked remarkably handsome in it. There was none of that washed-out look, none of that withered and worn-out expression on the man's face. Instead, he looked youthful and vibrant, as though he knew he had nothing to worry about.

Tomek ran the photograph through his fingers as he waited for the front door to open. Beside him was Rachel, who had today opted to let her hair hang loose. A moment later, the door opened, and they were greeted by the large man. He was so big his body barely fitted through it. This morning, he was dressed in a pair of short rugby shorts that were tighter than a duck's arse and bulged in all the wrong places. On his top half, he wore an old, torn, and battered rugby shirt that looked as though it hadn't fitted him in twenty years.

'Tomek...' Warren said sheepishly. 'And...?'

'DC Rachel Hamilton,' she replied.

'You don't sound like you're from around here.'

'That's because I'm not. Though I wear that particular badge with pride. I'm a North London girl.'

'What brings you down here? It certainly wasn't Tomek's leadership skills, I know that much. I've seen him on a rugby pitch at school. He didn't know his arse from his elbow.'

Warren placed his hand on the top of the doorframe and rested against the side, displaying his large triceps and latissimus dorsi muscles, the muscles on the back that made it look like he had wings. The obvious flirtation and attempt to spread his feathers like a peacock were commendable, but futile. Unless Rachel had had a sudden and pretty drastic change of heart in the past few weeks, she was still gay and very much playing on the same side of the field as both of them. But Tomek didn't want to tell him that. He was enjoying watching the car head towards the impassable tree.

'Actually, it was,' Rachel said. 'I'd heard such wonderful things about him, and then I was bitterly disappointed when I finally met him in person.'

'They say you should never meet your heroes,' Tomek interjected.

Rachel rolled her eyes, then turned to Warren, asking if they could come in. The man stepped aside to let them through. As Tomek sidled past him, squeezing himself past like a fox trying to fit though a badger's hole, Warren said, 'Why don't you leave the banter to me, mate?'

'You thought that was my attempt at flirting?'

'Wasn't it?'

'Of course. Sorry, yes. Terrible, you're right. In fact, I think I will leave it up to you. And if you need any tips, she's really into jokes about absolutely slating ABBA.'

'ABBA?'

Her favourite band.

Tomek nodded, suppressing the smirk from leaping onto his face. 'Hates them. Can't stand them. Thinks that virtual show they've got going on at the moment is the biggest waste of money known to man.'

Warren's face lit up like an alcoholic being gifted a drink. 'Great, thanks! I hate ABBA too!'

A moment later, Tomek and Warren joined Rachel in the living room. She'd already made herself at home by finding a space on the sofa opposite the television. Warren offered a drink, but both refused.

'Sounds serious,' he said as he shuffled towards the centre of the room.

'This morning, we arrested someone on suspicion of murdering the woman from the harbour,' Rachel said, blunt and straight to the point.

'Arrested someone already? Who?'

'That's why we're here,' Tomek said, reaching into his pocket.

As soon as Tomek made the movement, Warren stepped backwards, holding his hand out in front of him as though he were fending off a rugby tackle from an opponent. His eyes were wild with fear.

'Me? Is this some sort of sick way of saying you've come to arrest me?'

Tomek and Rachel glanced at one another. Then burst into laughter.

'I think it might take more than two of us to do that,' she said.

'Though if you make a run for it, I might be the only one who can catch you,' Tomek added.

That seemed to allay Warren's fears. He lowered his hands and dropped his shoulders a few inches.

'We wanted to see if you can confirm the identity of the person we've arrested, whether it fits the description of the person you saw that morning?'

'Have you been to see the Americans?'

'We've just come from there.'

'And?'

'I'm not going to tell you. I want you to have a look at this photo first and tell me whether it matches the description you gave.'

Tomek reached into his pocket and produced the mugshot of Mariusz Stanciu. He passed it across to Warren, who took it warily from Tomek and observed the face from afar, his eyes squinting. Then he realised that he was fooling nobody and hurried into the kitchen to get a pair of reading glasses. When he returned he examined the photograph. It took him all of three seconds to come to a conclusion.

'I can't say for certain,' he said. 'I didn't see the bloke's face all that well. The only person that got the best shot of him was the guy who was there before us. You should show it to him.'

'We'd love to,' Tomek responded as he took the mugshot back from Warren. 'But he's dead.'

'Dead?'

'Sadly.'

'How?'

'Suicide. Supposedly. But we're investigating it.'

Warren's gaze turned towards the bay windows. 'If he was murdered... does that mean he might have been killed because he saw the man's face?'

'If that's the case, then you and the rest of the tour group don't have anything to worry about,' Rachel answered.

'They didn't see him clearly enough either then?'

Rachel shook her head.

'It seems the only person who can undeniably confirm whether this is the guy who fled the crime scene is dead.'

'I'm sorry,' Warren replied.

'What are you apologising for?' Tomek asked.

Pointing to the document in Tomek's hand, he said, '*That*. I wish I could confirm whether that was him. But I just didn't see his face. All I saw was his coat. I was too busy helping Kirsty's husband at the back of the group. The fat bastard kept getting stuck in the mud.'

'It's no problem,' Rachel replied coolly. 'You've been a great help in this investigation so far anyway.'

'Of course.' Warren snapped his fingers, as though something had just occurred to him. 'Hey, have you considered that this might be an ABBA-obsessed assassin? Because, if so, he's having the time of his life.'

Silence. Rachel's face dropped. Tomek could barely contain the laughter.

'What?' Rachel asked.

'What?'

'What?' Tomek said, chiming in.

Suddenly, the giant rugby player shrank to half his size and looked like a child who'd just been embarrassed on the playground. 'ABBA... "Dancing Queen"... No?'

'No. Not really.'

Rachel shot him a scornful look, then turned to Tomek, glowering at him. It was at that point Tomek lost control and burst into a fit of laughter, bent double, holding onto the side of the sofa for support.

'I'm sorry. I told him to. I thought you might like an ABBA joke that didn't come from me for a change...'

'You set me up?' Warren babbled. 'You set me up? Arsehole.'

'Yes, I echo that sentiment,' Rachel said, shuffling towards Warren's side so that the two of them ganged up on him. 'Probably the biggest arsehole I know. If not the world's biggest.'

Regaining composure, Tomek smiled smugly at them, then mock bowed. Rachel quickly called an end to the visit. Tomek was more than happy to stay and hear some more of Warren's quality ABBA jokes, but according to Rachel, there was no time. Their window of finding evidence against Mariusz Stanciu was closing fast.

'You still need to take me out to the crime scene,' Tomek told Warren as they headed to the front door.

'Not after that little set-up, I don't.'

'Great. Shall we say tomorrow, same time as our run?'

'You want to go running again?'

'If that's all right with you? My body was feeling it the day after, but once I get back into the swing of it, I'm sure I'll be all right.'

Warren's face beamed at the prospect of having a running partner. Long term.

'Come on, Mo Farah,' Rachel said, tapping Tomek on the shoulder, 'we need to get back to the office. There's a murder investigation to run, remember?'

CHAPTER
TWENTY-EIGHT

Tomek pulled the chair out from beneath the table and sat. Beside him was Chey, who, in the space of a few hours, looked as though he'd turned into a father of five, all of whom were under the age of ten. His eyes had sunk, he'd lost some colour in his cheeks, and there was no cheeky-chappie smile that Tomek was used to. He looked broken, beaten.

'Long day?' Tomek asked.

'Like you would not fucking believe.'

'You look like you could do with some Adderall.'

'What's that?'

'I dunno,' Tomek answered. 'It's one of those things Americans say when they see someone who looks tired.'

'If it's American, I don't want it. I've seen the Netflix documentaries.'

Tomek was about to ask him to elaborate, but Victoria had just entered the room, so he caught himself. As she made her way past him, Tomek felt the atmosphere drop.

'Right, everyone,' she began, 'I want to keep this short and sweet. I want updates from all of you, and I want to confirm whether we can formally charge Mariusz Stanciu with the murder of Morgana Usyk.'

She slapped a folder of documents on the desk unnecessarily hard, then turned to the whiteboard at the head of the room. Standing beside her was her loyal dog, Sean, with the training collar still attached to his neck, and dry-wipe marker in hand.

'Chey,' Rachel started. 'Would you like to kick us off?'

All eyes turned to Chey.

'Don't think I have a choice,' he muttered under his breath. He rustled some papers to mask it, but it was still audible. If Victoria heard it, she didn't let on. 'Where do you want me to begin?'

'With the headline facts.'

'All right. Fine. So, I've done all I can in terms of looking through the CCTV footage of the pier and surrounding seafront. Now that we know where and when Mariusz says he returned to dry land, that's helped narrow down the field, but I still can't find any images of him along the seafront. There's nothing that points to that section of water at that time of day. So, he could have come out of the water at that particular time, but I can't see any of it.'

'Or he was lying,' Tomek remarked.

His comment was ignored.

'Martin? What do you have?'

Now it was DC Martin Brown's turn to speak. He, in complete contrast to Chey, looked fresh, as though it was his first day on the job and he'd only been there for ten minutes. Which, compared to the rest of the team, he had; along with Victoria, he'd joined from Colchester a few months ago. He was still embedding himself in the team, but it was still clear to see the close ties with the inspector remained.

Before speaking, he brushed a stray strand of hair behind his ear. 'I've spoken with his employer, DWG Logistics, and they've confirmed that Mariusz works for them. They've sent across his right to work, a copy of his passport – everything. They've even confirmed that he was working the past few days, and have sent across the delivery notes for his journeys up and down the country.'

'Chey...' Victoria started. 'Can you check those on ANPR and CCTV, please?'

'Could someone else not do it?' he responded, in his politest voice. 'It's just that I'm swamped with the other footage you need me to find.'

'But you've already ascertained you can't find him. Now I'm asking you to find him on a separate occasion.'

The constable lowered his head, nodding absent-mindedly and scribbling a note down in his book.

'Tomek...' Victoria continued, turning to him with a hint of disdain in her voice.

'Yes, ma'am?'

'What did the key witnesses have to say about Mariusz?'

'They don't know him from Adam,' he replied. 'Or, in this case, Andrei.'

'What?' Sean asked abruptly, taking Tomek and everyone else in the room by surprise.

'They couldn't definitively say that it's the same man. The only person who got the best look at him was Andrei Pirlog.'

'And now he's dead...' Victoria said softly, as though talking to herself.

'Still think it's a suicide, ma'am?' Tomek asked, but his question was met with silence. 'Oh, and before we move on, I told the Redgraves that you've authorised another week's stay in their Airbnb.'

'Why the fuck would you do that?'

'Well, I thought we might need them for the investigation, and they were due to fly back to America tomorrow. I didn't think we could afford to lose them.'

'So, you told them they could stay for another week?'

'All expenses paid. Food, accommodation, security. They're very grateful.'

Victoria's eyes narrowed as she clenched her jaw. 'I don't fucking believe you. What do you expect me to do?'

'I expect you to be true to your word, ma'am.'

'I never agreed to this.'

'Do you want to be the one to let them down, or would you rather I pass on the message?'

'I don't have a fucking choice but to approve the cost now, do I?'

Victoria needed a moment to control her anger before she continued the rest of the meeting. Her face had swollen red with fury. She turned to DC Anna Kaczmarek, the family liaison officer.

'Can you please deal with this? Give them a budget. I don't want them living like they're on death row.'

Anna confirmed that she would. Then Victoria addressed DC Oscar Perez. The Captain as he was affectionately known in the office, owing to his constant correction of anything anyone ever said, had stayed quiet throughout the conversation. Unlike him. He always found something to say. He was a good detective, and Tomek had a lot of time for him. He knew what he was talking about. He was thorough, level-headed, and efficient. Everything the team could have asked for.

'I've trawled through Mariusz's social media, and it appears that he only recently came to the country. As far as I can make out, he arrived here a little over three months ago. He doesn't post a great deal, but there's enough for me to gain an insight into his life. Nothing more, sadly. Nothing to indicate that he was there on the morning of the murder.'

'Anything to suggest a connection with Morgana?'

'Not yet. But I'm still searching.'

'Great. What about his girlfriend?' Victoria asked. 'What do we know about her?'

'She's more prolific on social media. Posts a lot of content. Rather, she did. Until they came to the country she was posting almost every day. Now, not so much.'

'Can you speak with her? Find out if she knows anything about her boyfriend's whereabouts.'

Martin nodded. 'I'll try to make contact with her.'

Victoria clapped her hands. 'Excellent. Great work, team. Really, great work. You're all doing a fantastic job. I'm proud of you all. But there's still lots to be getting on with. Lots to do in the next nineteen hours. A lot of hard work, with heads down and dedication is expected from you all. And I want to be able to charge Mariusz Stanciu for Morgana's murder by the end of the countdown.'

Tomek thought Victoria's rallying speech was more Boris Johnson than Winston Churchill. Conceited, dull, and uninspiring. Perhaps it was just the way she was. Or perhaps it was his rapidly growing disdain towards her.

As he slipped out of the doorway, one of the last to leave, he felt a hand on his back.

Sean.

'Would you...' he paused. 'Would you mind if we had a chat?'

'Okay...' Tomek replied, hovering in the threshold. 'Sounds ominous.'

Sean gestured for Tomek to move aside, then closed the door behind him like he was in a spy movie.

'You're not dying, are you?' Tomek asked.

'No. Well, we all are. Just at different rates.'

'Brilliant.'

'But no, I'm not dying. Not anytime soon at least. I just...' Sean placed his hands in his pockets and looked to the floor. Tomek felt like he was about to be asked to the prom. 'Some things have been happening at home.'

'Oh?'

'Yeah. Nothing major. I missed... I missed a few rent payments and now the landlord's kicking me out. Plus, he's also looking to sell the place as well, which doesn't help.'

'Paying the rent on time probably would,' Tomek remarked. Such was their relationship – rather, what had once been their friendship – that they could speak so candidly to one another, without the need for pandering, coddling. Everything they said to one another was unserious – even the serious bits. The way it should be. 'What's happened?'

'I just got caught in some finance problems,' Sean replied.

'You didn't buy a vending machine, did you?'

Tomek was referring to their mutual friend, the landlord of a pub they used to frequent, who had fallen victim to a potentially lucrative business venture involving a vending machine inside the pub, stock that supposedly replaced itself (and sold in the first place), and a passive income that never stopped. Since Tomek had last spoken to him, only the first point had come through – at an expensive initial cost.

A smirk flashed across Sean's face. The first Tomek had seen in a long time.

'No,' he replied, 'I'm not that stupid.'

'I'll be the judge of that, depending how you lost your money.'

'I just lost it. Too much spending. Too much going out. Too many unnecessary purchases.'

'Like what?'

Tomek didn't realise he was interrogating his friend, but Sean was doing nothing to stop him.

'I bought a computer I don't use. Some new headphones. A new watch. A new car.'

A new car? Now Tomek really felt out of the loop. That was the sort of thing they would have shared with one another. Even though Tomek had very little interest in motor transport, he would still have asked to go on a joy ride with him. Within the boundaries of the law, of course.

'What'd you get?'

'Tesla. Brand new.'

'How long have you had that?'

'About six weeks. Early Christmas present.'

'Finance?'

Sean dropped his head lower. 'All of it was.'

'So, you missed a payment.'

'There was a problem with my bank. They fucked up.'

They always did in situations like this. Always the bank's fault. Or someone else's. But never the victim's, never the one whose name was on the finance agreements.

'Now you're being kicked out of your house?'

'That, and the landlord's selling.'

How could he forget?

'What compelled you to buy all that shit?' Tomek asked.

'I don't know! I thought I wanted it.'

'You wanted it all in the space of a few weeks?'

The human brain, and the way it had been conditioned towards the latest thing, the hottest thing, the shiniest thing, continued to baffle him. Growing up, he and his brothers never had the money to purchase whatever they wanted. Instead, they were always forced to window shop, to hope, to want, that one day things might change. And even when that had begun to change for them as a family, when his parents had set up their respective businesses back in the UK, they still kept money tight, they still kept it from them. Essentials only. They didn't know what turmoil was on the horizon, and so they were cautious with it. They were smart, conservative, and it helped him appreciate what it was like to have nothing.

Interestingly, the same had also applied to Sean. As a child, Sean had known what it was like to have nothing as well, especially when his father had passed, and so he'd been forced to become entrepreneurial at school, by selling sweets and snacks at a significant markup. He'd then used the profits towards the essentials. Food. Water. Heating. Rent. Like Tomek's parents, Sean had been sensible. But now something had switched. The dopamine receptors in his brain had become frazzled. And Tomek thought he knew why.

Victoria. Either he was doing it to impress her or she was the driving force behind it.

'Does she know?'

Sean shook his head. 'And I'd like to keep it that way. It's embarrassing.'

'Embarrassing for who? You or her?'

Sean opened his mouth but could not answer the question.

'Have you spoken to HR?' Tomek asked. 'They probably need to know, so there aren't any nasty surprises later down the line. We don't want to find you dead in a ditch because you couldn't repay a loan shark.'

'No, no. Just the debt collectors instead.'

'Brilliant.'

A moment of silence rolled through them. Sean massaged his face as he struggled to find the words. The sound of his skin brushing past his stubble was deafening in the almost silent room. Thirty seconds passed before he finally said what he needed to.

'I was wondering if I could stay at yours for a couple of nights, maybe weeks? I would only need a sofa—'

'Good, because that'd be all you're getting.'

'And I can pay for my own food and everything. I wouldn't take up too much space.'

Tomek eyed him from head to toe. 'You've seen the size of you, right? You'll be lucky if half of you fits on the sofa. Leave it with me. I'll have to double-check with Kasia, see if she's happy with it.'

'Of course.'

'And Abigail.'

'Abigail?' There was hurt in his voice, as though he felt second best. 'What do you need to ask her for?'

'She stays over quite a lot. She might find it awkward.'

'You've only known her two seconds.'

Tomek took a step back, raised a hand to Sean. 'Do you want the sofa or not?'

CHAPTER
TWENTY-NINE

The smell of bacon and vegetable oil was the same, familiar, yet simultaneously different, alien. Like climbing into the same make and model of bed, only to find out it wasn't your own.

Like Goldilocks breaking and entering the Three Bears' house, something just wasn't right about Iliana's Café. The atmosphere was off. There were fewer customers, and the spaces between tables were too narrow, meaning you were almost on top of one another, overhearing everything that was said around you. To top it all off, the coffee tasted grim.

While Victoria and the team placed all their focus on trying to find evidence to accuse Mariusz Stanciu of killing Morgana Usyk, Tomek had different ideas. For starters, he didn't think the man had had anything to do with her murder (he'd only arrested him to begin the custody clock and ensure that he didn't become a flight risk). There were holes in Mariusz's story, not to mention the fact Chey couldn't confirm his whereabouts and that none of the key witnesses could positively identify him. Even if Andrei were still alive, Tomek was almost certain that the key witness wouldn't have recognised him.

Instead, Tomek suspected there was something else at play. That someone had put Mariusz up to the task. His responses and monologue sounded too polished, too rehearsed. And the minor hole in his story where he'd said that he had dropped Morgana back to the ground, when the witness statements had said he'd dropped her in the water. Not to mentioned, his eagerness to please and assist their investigation suggested to Tomek that it was something someone had told him to say. Why, and who, he didn't know. But he intended to find out.

And so, he'd come to Iliana's Café along the Southend seafront, amid a small promenade of shops looking out onto the water, a few miles away from its sister, Morgana's, in Hadleigh. The restaurant was owned by her husband, Anton Usyk, a man whom Tomek had been keen to meet for a second time. Very little progress had been made into him, and as far as Tomek was aware, it needed to be. The first place they typically looked in an investigation like this was the victim's closest relative, particularly the husband. And so far, Victoria had let him slip.

Tomek was keen to get to know the man. And he often found that a familiar setting yielded the greatest results.

'Good... afternoon,' said the waitress. 'Can I... get you... something?'

Her manner was all off. Discordant, flappy. There was no confidence in her expression, nor her smile. At least Helena, the waitress in Morgana's, had looked happy to be there. This one, the name tag on her breast read Gina, was miserable. Though when she repeated the question, Tomek decided to cut her some slack. She was Polish, and her English was less than sufficient. So, to put her at ease, he spoke in their native tongue.

'*Dzień dobry*,' he said. Good afternoon.

'You speak Polish?'

'I *am* Polish, so I'd hope so.'

That elicited a laugh. Though it didn't last long. As soon as the sound had blurted from her mouth, she snapped her head towards the back of the restaurant.

Iliana's had almost exactly the same layout as Morgana's, with the booths on the sides of the room, the cash register in the far right, and the open kitchen in the back with the chefs visible over a metal countertop.

Curious, Tomek rotated in his seat, hoping to get a glimpse of what she was looking at, but she distracted him.

'Which part of Poland are you from?' she asked.

'Katowice. You?'

Another look to the kitchen. 'Gdańsk.'

'Nice. I've never been. How long have you lived here for?'

'Three months.'

'Nice. How you finding it?'

Gina hesitated, turned to the kitchen, then shrugged her shoulders. 'Is okay...' This time she spoke in English.

'What made you leave home?' he asked.

But before she could answer, a figure came up to her, placing a hand on her shoulder.

'Is everything all right over here?' the man asked bluntly. Then, as soon as Anton Usyk recognised Tomek, he said, 'Ah, Detective. It is good to see you again.'

He spoke plainly, devoid of emotion. His face was empty, blank. Difficult to read. Tomek hated talking to people from his part of the world. They never gave anything away. Never let the other person know what they were thinking or feeling. It was like they were all Russian spies facing trial.

'Good to see you too,' Tomek said.

'I hope you are here under better circumstances than last time?'

'I'm not here to tell you another loved one is dead, if that's what you mean.'

'That's better news than none at all.' Anton turned to the waitress, then back to Tomek. 'How rude of me. You were in the middle of ordering. Apologies. What can we get you?'

'Flat white is fine.'

'Perfect. Anything to eat?'

Tomek refused the offer. Anton turned to Gina and whispered to her in Ukrainian. Then she scurried away to the back of the café, where she immediately began busying herself with her tasks. Without saying anything, Anton helped himself to the chair opposite, his pectoral muscles flexing beneath the tight-fitting Hugo Boss designer T-shirt. 'I hope you don't mind the company?'

'Not unless you swallow really loudly?'

Anton chuckled. 'Only when I'm talking with someone I don't want to.'

A moment later, their drinks arrived. Gina set them down on the table tentatively, cautiously, almost spilling Tomek's flat white onto the surface. Keeping his eye contact firmly focused on Tomek, Anton Usyk held the cup to his mouth and drank. The sound was inaudible.

'I told you,' he said. 'I did not lie about it, did I?'

'No,' Tomek replied but wondered whether there was anything he *had* lied about.

'How is the investigation coming along?' Anton asked. 'I have not heard anything.'

'Slow. But we're making good progress.'

'Have you made any arrests yet?'

'Not yet,' he lied. 'We're still working on it. The area in which the killer fled the scene is so big, it's proving more difficult than we anticipated. So far we've got an idea that the killer may have emerged on the seafront by the pier. We're currently looking into CCTV and any eyewitness accounts around that time and area. Our team think they may have caught a screenshot of him on one of the cameras. The plan is to potentially release the information to the public soon.'

Anton's face was blank, empty. Still giving nothing away. Tomek had tried to goad him into letting something slip, but the man had a poker face like a professional.

'I trust you and your team are doing everything possible. If there is anything I can do to help, then please, you must let me know.'

An alarm bell started to ring in Tomek's head.

'You might be able to help, in fact,' he said, as he reached into his pocket to produce his notebook. 'I was wondering if you could tell me what you were doing the morning of your wife's murder.'

For the first time, Anton's head flinched. Subtle, almost invisible to the naked and untrained eye. But not Tomek's.

'I have already given a witness statement. I have told you already where I was.'

'The passage of time sometimes allows us to reflect differently on situations and view them in a new light,' Tomek explained, being purposely philosophical and obtuse. 'Besides, you told my *colleagues*. You didn't tell *me*.'

'I see...' Anton sipped his drink. 'What is it you wish to know?'

'Everything. But first, let us begin with yourself, your story, your wife's story.'

'Could you be more specific?'

'How long have you been in the UK for?'

'Thirteen years,' he replied without hesitation. When faced with that question for himself, Tomek always had to think back and calculate his age before giving an answer. Whereas, for Anton, the answer had come at the snap of a finger. Either he knew the information off the top of his head. Or it was a lie. 'Morgana and I came over when we were in our mid-twenties. Southend has been our home ever since.'

'And the two of you have set up some very successful businesses, by the looks of it?'

Anton gave a slight dip of the head. 'We have worked hard to get to where we are.'

'I'm sure you have.' Tomek drank some of his flat white, licking his lip free from foam. 'Tell me,' he continued, 'why do you have two restaurants?'

'Because, as you say, we are successful.'

'Do the two businesses operate individually from one another, or do you see yourselves as part of a chain?'

'Separately. Morgana manages Morgana's. I manage Iliana's. They are two separate businesses.'

'Did that ever cause any friction between the two of you, any arguments, competition, disagreements? If one of you was doing so much better than the other, I can certainly see how it might. If I'm honest, I've only ever been to Morgana's. I didn't know this place existed until the other day. And I feel it's the same way with a lot of people.'

'I am sorry you never made the discovery sooner.'

'I'm not. Morgana's was much better.'

Another head tilt. A moment for Anton to consider his response. 'That is your opinion.'

And several thousand others, if the Google and Tripadvisor reviews were anything to go by.

'Have you come here to insult me, Detective? I do not like to be insulted. Especially from a man of your profession.' Suddenly, Anton's stare narrowed, his brow furrowed. Now he was giving away a lot in his expression. One emotion in particular: rage.

'I've come to do no such thing,' Tomek answered. 'I am just curious, did the two of you never fight about the competitive nature of your business?'

'No. We are a team.'

'So, the state of the businesses never came between the two of you?'

'No.'

'How about Morgana's flirtatious side? I am told she was very friendly with a lot of her customers.'

'That is why her restaurant was much more successful. She knew how to be friendly to her customers. Me, I like to be funnier.'

Because you've been such a barrel of laughs so far.

'Sex sells, as they say,' Anton added.

That it did. And Tomek was ashamed to say that he'd fallen for it a little bit. The nice eyes, the smile. Hook, line, and sinker. If it hadn't been the place where he'd met Abigail on a semi-professional basis, they would have been his only reasons for returning.

'The two of you must be very busy,' he said, moving the conversation along.

'Yes. I start at seven am, and leave after eight or nine o'clock on some evenings. For Morgana, it was very much the same. Sometimes we stayed even longer. There are a lot of things to manage.'

'I imagine you spent very little time together.'

'This is the sacrifice you must make if you want a successful business.'

'I can imagine. The two of you coming home late, tired from the day. It must have put a real strain on your marriage. Getting frustrated with one another. The little things getting on your nerves. But neither of you says anything because you're tired and stressed. Then those little things begin to grate on you more and more. And still, you don't say anything because you know how it is. Until one day that little thing turns into a big thing. And something snaps.'

'No, Detective. You are wrong. We know what it is like to have nothing at all except each other. We know what it is to be at the bottom. And now we are at the top, that's never changed between us. We are humble, simple. Nothing has come between us. Nothing you say is true.'

Tomek didn't believe it. There was still a germ of doubt in his mind about Anton's movements and behaviour. He was a muscular, well-built guy, who clearly worked out. The rounded shoulders, the bulging biceps. Tomek glanced down at Anton's hands. He hadn't noticed it, but they swallowed the mug with ease. Strong and powerful, yet there was a delicate touch to them. It would have been very easy for him to strangle his wife to death with those.

'You still haven't answered my question,' Tomek said, finishing the last of his drink. 'What were you doing on the morning of your wife's death?'

The side of Anton's mouth rose. 'That is not the question you originally asked me. You asked *where* I was on the morning of her death. But I will answer both for you at the same time. I was here, working, in the office. As I said, I start at seven, and I do not leave the office until late. There is important admin I must take care of.'

'Every morning?'

'Every morning.'

'Without exception?'

'Without exception.'

'So who left the house first thing on that morning?'

'I did.'

'And you don't know where your wife went?'

'No.'

'And you don't know why she was there?'

'No. I do not know why she was there.'

Tomek turned to face Gina, then began admiring the scenery, surveying the customers. By now, the number had grown to five.

'One more thing,' he said, 'before I forget.'

'Yes.'

'Where does the name Iliana come from?'

'It is the name of our daughter. She died during Morgana's pregnancy ten years ago. She is the reason we started this restaurant. Iliana's was first, then Morgana's.'

Tomek offered his condolences. Anton dropped his head. He could see pain on the man's face, an emotion for the first time. And a little shame too. Perhaps it was because the restaurant in her name wasn't as successful. That he'd let her memory down somehow.

Then the thought of Morgana losing the baby during her pregnancy caught up with him. How horrible it must have been. How traumatising. Three months ago, these thoughts wouldn't have entered his mind; now that Kasia was in his life, things had changed.

With that, Tomek pulled out his wallet and placed a tenner on the table. Anton picked it up and handed it back. On the house, he said. A special favour, for all his hard work. Tomek thanked the man, then left the café.

The team were expecting him back shortly after, but there was somewhere else he wanted to visit first.

Someone he knew for certain wasn't at work when they were supposed to be on the morning of Morgana's death.

CHAPTER
THIRTY

Vlad Boyko lived in a one-bedroom ground-floor flat near Leigh Cemetery. Tomek knew very little about the man who lived there. Sean's report on him, which was readily available on the PNC, had been vague, and the quick search he'd asked Nadia to do had returned little information.

Tomek knocked on the door and waited. Overhead from the flat above came the sound of heavy music and deep bass.

A moment later, the door opened, and standing there, dressed in a plain white T-shirt that was several sizes too small and a pair of grey jogging bottoms, was Vlad.

Tomek had taken a punt on Vlad being at home. Though what the deputy manager of a café that was missing its owner and manager was doing at home, Tomek didn't know.

He wanted to find out.

'DS Tomek Bowen,' he said, flashing his warrant card in front of the man's face. 'Might I come in?'

'Something wrong?'

'Not yet. Just got a few more questions for you about the morning of Morgana's death. It's a bit cold outside, and I'd hate for you to lose all the heat. Could I come in?'

Reluctantly, Vlad stepped aside. He had no power in this situation, not unless he wanted to make himself look suspicious by refusing entry.

As Tomek stepped inside, the noise of the music above grew. The ceiling and walls vibrated sharply, and he felt his skin crawling in time with the beat.

'Considerate neighbours you've got there.'

'Yeah.'

'How long does it usually last?'

'All day. All night sometimes.'

'You should complain,' Tomek said.

'I'm used to it.'

Tomek didn't doubt that, but it was still an inconvenience. Fortunately, he'd been blessed with a wonderful neighbour in the form of a seventy-something-year-old pensioner who kept noise to a minimum and put up with a lot from himself and Kasia, including his lead feet stomping across the floorboards in the early hours of the morning when he couldn't sleep.

Vlad then took Tomek into the kitchen area, where he offered a drink of tea or water. Tomek refused both.

'If I have any more caffeine, I'll be sprinting up and down the seafront all night.'

'Right,' Vlad said, half-interested as he busied himself with the kettle for a drink of his own.

'Have you ever done it? Run along the seafront, that is?'

'No.'

'You should. It's fantastic. Exhilarating. Do you like running?'

'No. Can't I say I do.'

'I noticed you had a nice pair of Hoka running shoes by the door, though. Forgive me...'

'They're just for comfort. A lot of the reviews I read online said they're like walking on clouds.'

'I've been eyeing a pair up for a while but can't justify the cost. They're really expensive.'

Vlad shrugged, implying that while the cost might have been high for

Tomek, it certainly wasn't for him. Shortly after, the kettle finished its boil and the deputy manager made his cup of tea.

'How have you been coping with the news the past couple of days?' Tomek asked.

'It's been a shock. Tough.'

'How come you're not at the restaurant?'

'It's my day off.'

'And how's everyone at the restaurant doing? Are they suffering as well?'

'Of course they are. We all loved Morgana. We can't believe she's gone.'

To Tomek's right was a small, circular, wooden dining table. He pointed to it and asked if it was safe to sit. Vlad confirmed it was.

'How long have you known Morgana?' Tomek asked.

'Since we were seven.'

Interesting.

'And how long have you worked with her?'

'Several years. She gave me the job when I first moved across. She helped me out when I needed it most. I would never have done anything to hurt her.'

'Nobody's saying you did,' Tomek replied.

Answers like that were always more alarming than most. Telling, in fact. There was always a hidden meaning behind them.

'You say you were friends since childhood,' he continued. 'Have the two of you always been close?'

'Yes.'

'No arguments or disagreements between the two of you?'

Vlad shook his head and folded his arms across his chest.

'I imagine the two of you trusted each other, right? I mean, you've known each other since you were seven. I bet she probably told you things that you promised not to share with anyone else, and you probably shared some things with her that you didn't want anybody else to find out.'

Tomek had a pickaxe in his hand and was digging away at the stone wall of Vlad's expression. There was a diamond beneath his tough exterior, Tomek could tell, and he was going to get to it.

'We trusted each other, yes.'

'Did she ever tell you about any disagreements that she'd been having with Anton? Any times he might have hit her, or when the violence had escalated?'

Vlad smirked, letting out a small snigger. 'You think you are so clever,' he said. 'But you have it all wrong. Anton never hit her, he never hit anyone.'

'Perhaps she didn't trust you as much as you think she did.'

A mixture of concern and confusion flashed across Vlad's face. 'What are you talking about? I know Morgana better than most people. She is like a sister to me.'

'Not a lover?' Tomek asked, continuing to hammer away, trying to find the right angle to crack the stone open.

'Excuse me? What are you saying?'

'Did your feelings ever progress from friendship to something more? Are you sure you never saw her as more than a friend?'

Tomek was reminded of his childhood relationship with Saskia Albright. She'd been the only person to come up to him in the playground on his first day at school in England. After that, they had become best friends. Though their relationship had grown distant over the years, Saskia was now back in his life and Tomek was keen to keep her there. While their friendship had been strong, Tomek had always wondered whether there was anything more there, anything that they could both explore but had always been worried about jeopardising their relationship. It was a difficult and fine line to walk. One he wasn't sure if he wanted to know the outcome of.

'I... I don't know what you mean,' Vlad said. Except the intonation in his voice and shaky expression told a different story.

'You never at any stage wanted to ask her to be your girlfriend or to go on a date with her?'

'No...'

'You never tried it and she shot you down?'

'No...'

'I bet that hurt, didn't it? Imagine that, seeing her every day, knowing that she was with another man, possibly another man you don't approve of. I bet you think she can do much better than him, don't you? Do you wish it was you she was married to?'

'I don't understand what you are talking about...'

'What happened before her death?' Tomek asked. 'Did you ask her to leave her husband? Did you promise she would be happier with you, that the two of you could live life in the restaurant together? But then she said no—'

'You are wrong,' Vlad snapped.

'And you didn't like that, did you? So, you wanted to make sure that, if you couldn't have her, then nobody could.'

'Enough!' Vlad's voice boomed throughout the ground-floor flat, drowning out the sound of the music above. He slammed his fist on his leg, his body tense, his chest rising and falling deeply.

Tomek smiled inwardly. He had just found the diamond he'd been looking for.

'Why were you late to work on the morning of Morgana's murder, Vlad?'

'Because I overslept,' the man hissed through gritted teeth. 'I have told you this already.'

'Not to me, you haven't. Can you remember when exactly you woke up?'

'It was after eleven.'

'That's some lie in. What time do you usually wake up for work?'

'Six.'

'What time are you supposed to start?'

'Eight.'

'Has it ever happened to you before?'

'No.'

'But you didn't get to the restaurant until lunchtime.'

'What took you so long?'

'It takes me a while to get ready.'

Two hours. That was some time.

'What were you doing the night before?'

'Why?'

'I just want to know why, for someone who's never late, you suddenly turned up to work three hours later than you were supposed to.'

'I was tired,' he replied. 'Working at the restaurant is full-on. It takes it out of me. By the end of the day, I am tired. All I do is go to work, come home, and sleep. I don't eat. I don't shower. But I still do it. Do you know why? Because I love it.'

And because you love Morgana.

'I had nothing to do with her murder, and I don't know anything about it. So you can stop asking me all these questions.'

Tomek took that as his cue to leave; with the diamond he'd excavated nestled delicately in his pocket. He shook Vlad's hand, then told him that he could show himself out. Rather suspiciously (and Tomek couldn't blame him for this), Vlad ignored the offer and followed Tomek to the door. As he wandered through the corridor, music still reverberating through the walls, something caught his eye. A patch of mud on the floor by a small cupboard, and the small, yet distinguishable marks of footprints.

'What's that?' Tomek asked.

'Mud,' came the blank response. Like Anton Usyk, Vlad gave nothing away in his expression.

Without asking permission, Tomek opened the cupboard. Inside was a selection of coats – from thin to thick, waterproof to fashionable – and a small collection of shoes. The most notable of which was a pair of red trainers with plastic spikes sticking out of the toes.

'The fuck are these?'

'Christian Louboutin. They're designer.'

'You trying to make contact with aliens with these?'

'No.'

'Mind if I take 'em?'

'What for?'

'Evidence. Run some tests on 'em.'

Vlad hesitated. 'Guess I don't have a choice, do I?'

'Of course you do. You could say no, and allow me to leave suspicious as to why you didn't want to give them up. Or you could hand them in and have nothing to worry about.'

Either way, it wasn't a good look for Vlad.

Eventually, after a few grunts and disparaging looks, Vlad relented and allowed Tomek to take the shoes with him. Fortunately, he had a large evidence bag in the back of his car for just such occasions.

As Tomek pulled away, he wore a smile on his face. Success. Not only had he come away with a diamond in the form of Vlad's undying love for Morgana, but he'd also left with a physical, tangible one as well. And they were currently sitting beside him in the passenger seat, strapped in with the seatbelt.

CHAPTER
THIRTY-ONE

The final destination on Tomek's list for the day was Red Birch Farm, in South Woodham Ferrers. The farm was a little over twenty minutes away, but it was rush hour, and so the journey was made frustratingly longer. By the time Tomek arrived, it was starting to get dark.

Red Birch Farm was owned and run by Stanley Hutchinson. Earlier that morning, Tomek had looked through the suspect list and found his name right at the bottom. He, with a lot of help from the animals on his farm, supplied Morgana and Anton with the meat and produce for their business. Usually, it was imported from overseas at a cheaper rate, but somehow, Stanley and the cattle were able to charge it to Morgana and Anton at a ridiculously low price. Tomek didn't know what their profit margins were, but if the couple could charge five pounds for a full English breakfast, someone was getting ripped off somewhere, and it didn't feel like the customer.

Tomek thought it was worth speaking with the man who had close business relations with the husband-and-wife partnership. His view of their relationship would be more subjective. There may have been things – underhand comments, decisions the other knew nothing about – that he'd picked up on and kept to himself. He might possess valuable insight that might have been overlooked by Victoria and the team.

Tomek swung the car into the farm's entrance. An enormous banner reading "Red Birch Farm and Petting Zoo" dominated a small row of hedges to the left. As Tomek entered a large expanse of gravel that had been used as a car park, he drove through a pothole. His body bounced and ricocheted from side to side, and he winced at the thought of the damage done to the underside of his car. It sounded expensive, but it was no different to the copious potholes up and down the county. (He'd driven through over a dozen on the way there alone.)

The first thing Tomek noticed when he stepped out of the car was the smell. Manure, mixed in with the smell of freshly cut grass. A unique, yet oddly quite enjoyable, blend. The farm comprised four large hangar-sized structures, and a few smaller brick buildings situated a small distance from one another. Tractors and other heavy-duty machinery littered the forecourt. Beyond were vast expanses of green, dotted with animals the size of ants. In the distance, the perimeter of the land was lined by thick rows of trees.

As Tomek shut the car door, a man wearing wellies and a thin fleece walked across the forecourt from one building to the next.

'You all right there, mate?' he called to Tomek in a thick Essex accent. 'Petting zoo's closed for the day now, fella.'

'Good thing I'm not here for that,' he replied, as a gust of wind pummelled him from the side. 'I'm looking for the owner.'

The man prodded the breast pocket of his fleece. 'You're looking at him. There some sort of problem?'

Stanley Hutchinson looked completely different to what Tomek had been expecting. In his mind, he'd envisaged an overweight, pompous man, with a gut larger than his wallet and a blood pressure that suggested he never did any of the heavy lifting. The man in front of him, however, was the complete opposite: tall, skinny yet muscular in his upper body, and much younger. Tomek placed him in his early thirties and the man's grip took Tomek by surprise too. That was what hurling dozens of bales of hay all day did to you, no doubt.

'No, there's no problem,' he replied. 'I'm from Essex Police.'

'This about Morgana?'

Tomek nodded slightly.

'You'd better come inside.'

Stanley was referring to his office, a state-of-the-art, modern interface complete with a standing desk, iMac computer, and sleek furnishings throughout. Nestled in the corner of the room, with accompanying coffee machine, was a small seating area, equipped with two black leather sofas and a small coffee table.

'This is where we have our morning meetings,' Stanley said. 'Nothing like a bit of caffeine to wake me up in the early hours of the morning.'

'Or to keep you going throughout the night.'

'Precisely. Summer's our busiest time with all the harvesting, so that's why we've got the petting zoo as an extra revenue stream that's open all year round. Kids love coming down here in the mud and seeing all the animals. The parents, not so much.'

Tomek was reminded of the time he'd been to Marsh Farm on a school trip during primary school. His recollection was vague, but the smell was vivid and was what had stuck in his mind after all these years.

On the wall to Tomek's left was a small row of awards and shields addressed to Stanley and the farm. Tomek shuffled closer for a better look. They were from various charities across the country, congratulating and thanking Stanley for his patronage and fundraising schemes.

'What's all this then?' Tomek asked.

'Just my way of giving back to the people,' he said.

'Business must be good.'

'It's all right. We've struggled since Brexit, but they don't want you to hear about that.'

Stanley offered him a cup of coffee, but Tomek refused. He'd had enough for one day.

'I understand one of my colleagues has been to see you since Morgana's death earlier this week?'

'Yes. Nice woman. Rachel, I believe her name was. It's terrible what happened to her. We're all still a little bit shell-shocked, but we've not had time to grieve or process it as things don't stop around here. I wish they did, but you must know what it's like. Constant, constant, constant. Like a hamster in a training wheel.'

'Or a chicken laying eggs,' Tomek added, to an appreciative smirk from Stanley. 'Did you know Morgana very well?'

Stanley shrugged. 'I'd say so. We've been her and Anton's supplier for over ten years, ever since they started the business. Anton handles all the logistics, while Morgana's in charge of the financials.'

'Really? So she's the boss of the business?'

Stanley nodded. 'The stereotype's flipped on its head with that one. She's a real businesswoman, a proper entrepreneur. She knows how to haggle, negotiate and get what she wants. That's probably why a lotta the boys round here liked her so much. She's always coming down to see how her meat's being prepared, how the eggs are coming along, how things are going.'

'Is that how she got away with paying so little for her produce?' Tomek asked. 'Because she fluttered her eyelashes at you?'

Stanley didn't appreciate the underhand comment. 'Like I said, we do a lot of business with her,' he said, a hint of disdain in his voice. 'She was one of my first customers when I took over the business from my dad after he passed, and since then I've never seen a reason to charge her more than I need to. We ship about two tonnes of produce to them every year, most of it our finest pieces of meat. Don't get me wrong, we still make a profit from her business with us, but the margins are razor thin.'

'How do you afford to run this place then?'

'We have other customers. We do a lot of wholesale to the grocers and other restaurant chains, that's where we make the bulk of our money, but we just offer our best pricing to our best customers. That's the way it's always worked.'

'Do you see that changing going forward?' Tomek asked.

'That all depends on what Anton decides to do with the business. He might close down Morgana's, he might keep it open. I think there were even discussions of opening a third.'

'Who would run that one?'

Stanley hesitated, shrugged, non-committal. 'I tried to stay out of those conversations. It was nothing to do with me, and whenever I heard things getting overheated between them, I took myself away.'

Interesting, Tomek thought. Something that Anton had neglected to mention. Perhaps that had been the disagreement that had set them over the edge. Perhaps it was the disagreement that had led to Anton killing her. Tomek made a note.

'And what about your personal relationship with Morgana?' he asked.

'What do you mean?'

'I understand she was quite flirty. You've just said yourself that all the boys around here loved her. Did you ever try anything on with her?'

Stanley's offence turned to rage. 'Absolutely not! Why would I jeopardise our business together over something stupid?'

'Because some things are bigger than business.'

He shook his head violently, almost to the point it made Tomek feel sick just looking at him. 'Never. I would never do anything immoral and conceited like that.'

'I take it there's no Mrs Hutchinson then?'

He shook his head. 'Used to be. She decided she couldn't stand the smell of shit anymore. That and the long hours. She accused me of being more married to the farm than her, though it helped pay for her Range Rover and jewellery, didn't it? She wasn't too happy to hear any of that. Anyway, it's been and gone – *she's* been and gone – and I've moved on.'

Tomek nodded, then moved the conversation along.

'Did my colleague ask you about your whereabouts the other day?'

'Yes. And I told her that I was here. Early. Probably before you were awake.' Stanley's tone had dropped suddenly, helped, no doubt, by Tomek's accusation that the man had also fallen in love with Morgana.

'Anyone corroborate that?'

'How about the fifteen people I have working for me?' Stanley pointed towards the door. Then, almost as if rehearsed, a figure walked past the floor-to-ceiling glass window. 'And don't forget the twenty-five cows, the hundred and fifty sheep, the thirty-seven chickens, and the nine pigs – sorry, *eight*, we've just had to take one of them to slaughter.'

'Can I have a look?' Tomek asked.

'Around the farm? Is that because you want to see the animals or because you want to interrogate them about my whereabouts?'

'Both.'

Tomek was warming to Stanley. The man possessed a sense of humour, and it was nice dealing with someone who didn't look as though they'd just been told the price of their milk was going up by an extra twenty per cent. Perhaps it was because he was an Essex boy through and through – from the way he spoke to the way he dressed, even to his hair which had been combed backwards – that Tomek felt a certain affinity with him.

The walk to the animals was brief. The first ones they came across were the pigs. Eight of them in total, all in varying states of filth, all almost as large as Tomek's car. As he came up to the edge of their pen, they hurtled towards him, grunting and snorting like fiends. There, Stanley explained that they behaved that way because they were probably hungry as they'd last eaten a few days before. He was trying to keep them as lean as possible, as it was good for the meat when they eventually went to slaughter, Stanley'd added.

Next, were the chickens, which Tomek didn't have much time for. He didn't know why, but they'd always scared him. His body tensed and the hairs on his arms tingled every time he saw one. Perhaps it was the way they walked or the way their heads bobbled back and forth with each step, but there was just something about them that unnerved him. He was keen to get out of there as soon as possible, though not before Stanley had asked him to imagine what being pecked to death would feel like. And, with that horrifying image in his head, they ventured towards the cows. Tonight, they had been brought inside and were all in a line, hooked up to milking machines. The sound of heavy machinery was deafening and took Tomek by surprise. When they left, the sound still ringing in Tomek's ears, they went straight across a small field to a series of pens. The real petting zoo, Stanley had called it. There, they found a small flock of sheep, lambs, donkeys, llamas, goats, rabbits and a porcupine, which threw Tomek off a bit. Throughout the tour, Tomek listened politely, but his brain was busy surveying and scanning the faces of those working on the farm, matching them against the description of their main suspect. While Stanley may not have had anything to do with Morgana's murder, if his colleagues really could corroborate his whereabouts, there was nothing to say that someone else on the farm hadn't. And so far he'd seen none.

'Thanks for showing me around and answering my questions,' he said to Stanley just before he left. 'I might have to bring my daughter down when the zoo's back open.'

'Oh, is she a little one?'

'She's thirteen. So not that little. But I didn't mean for her to come and see them,' he replied. 'I meant as a job. Something for her to do. Can't help but think that shovelling some shit might entertain and excite her as much as it does the kids. I know it would certainly make me happy to get her off her phone. She could do with a distraction.'

CHAPTER
THIRTY-TWO

The smile had disappeared from Tomek's face by the time he made it home. On the twenty-minute drive back, Tomek had received a phone call from his mum, the first in a long time, inviting him, Abigail and Kasia over for dinner the following evening. Tomek had stalled and delayed as much as possible until his mum had hounded him for an answer. By the end of the call, he had agreed to let her know that evening.

It wasn't that he didn't want to see his parents; it was just that the past few times hadn't ended well. Not to mention their relationship had been disjointed for almost thirty years. Since his brother's death, his parents (in particular, his mum) had excluded him from the family, but in recent times they'd all begun to make amends. Tomek had introduced Kasia to them, which had come as a shock. He couldn't blame them for that. "Hey, Mum, here's a teenage daughter I knew nothing about until a few weeks ago." That was the sort of news that needed some groundwork and an unhealthy dose of alcohol.

Before that, Tomek had taken a former partner to a meal once, to honour the anniversary of his brother's death. It had ended with a massive argument and Tomek storming out during the main meal.

And it was *that* which concerned Tomek. Taking Abigail. His new girlfriend. Introducing her to the family.

It was a big step in their relationship. It signified long-term commitment, that he was in this for the long haul. Tomek could only remember two other girlfriends that he'd introduced to the family. One had turned out to be the mother of his child, the other a serial killer. It wasn't a decision he took lightly. And on the drive home, he'd boarded the flight to Second Thought Suburbia, where he'd overthought every detail of his and Abigail's relationship. Did he love her, or was it too soon? Did he see a future with her, or was it just a bit of fun for now? Did he want to be with her long term? She was a few years younger than him, and even though they hadn't discussed it, he knew that she wanted children. Would Kasia be enough, or did she want more? Was he ready to welcome another Tomek Bowen spawn into the world? He was forty years old, at a comfortable spot in his career. Did he have it in him?

He didn't know. And he wasn't ready to confront those sorts of questions just yet. So, like he always did, he pushed the questions – and answers – to the back of his mind, where he would deal with them later.

Whenever that may be.

Fortunately, when he got home, he was distracted by Kasia. His daughter had changed into her casual clothes and was in the middle of watching the television, sprawled across the sofa, face engrossed in her phone, as he stepped through the front door.

'How was school?'

'Fine.'

'Sure?'

'Yeah.'

'Would you tell me if it wasn't?'

'Yeah.'

Liar. It had taken a great amount of effort for him to pry the information out of her in the café the other day, and even then she hadn't been truthful with him.

'You'll never guess where I went today,' he said.

'Okay.'

'Want to know where?'

'Yeah.'

'Then guess.'

She groaned and rolled her eyes, face still melting into her mobile phone. 'I don't know. Can't you just tell me?'

'No. You need to guess.'

'I don't know. Work?'

'Yes. I did go to work, you're right. But that's not what I'm talking about. I went to a petting zoo today. Up near Nana and Grandad's.'

'Why?'

'For work. It's open to the public. I thought you might like to go?'

'To the petting zoo? I'm not five, Dad.'

Tomek smirked. 'I didn't mean for you to go and have fun there. I meant for you to work – milk the cows, feed the chickens, clean out the pigs' pens.'

'Eww, no!' She sat bolt upright, swinging her legs off the side of the sofa in disgust. 'Why would I want to do that? That sounds horrible.'

The suggestion landed just as he'd expected.

'Besides,' she continued, 'I'm thirteen. I can't work yet. It's against the law.'

'I am the law.'

Kasia rolled her eyes again. 'You're so annoying sometimes,' she said, then quickly lost interest and turned her attention back to her phone.

'How about we go to your nan and grandad's tomorrow for a meal instead?' he asked as he made his way to the dining room table.

'All of us?'

'I haven't asked Abigail yet. I wanted to see if you were up for going, and if you're happy for her to be there.'

Kasia lowered her phone to her chest. 'Why wouldn't I want her there?'

'Just asking.'

He'd taken the coward's way out. Putting the decision on her. This way he didn't have to face the awkward conversation afterwards; Abigail wouldn't be able to argue or pick a fight with Kasia for not wanting her to join. She would be the bad person.

'I don't have a problem with her coming,' Kasia replied. It had been decided for him. 'And I don't have any plans with any of my friends, so we can go.'

But Tomek had stopped listening. His attention was focused on the pile of letters on the dining room table that had been hastily placed there, sprawled across the surface. His eyes scanned for his name in the handwritten lettering, for the HMP Wakefield stamp at the top of the document.

But there was nothing.

Not today.

'Dad?' Kasia's voice pulled him away from his thoughts.

'Yes' he answered half-heartedly.

'Did you hear me?'

'Yes, mate,' he said, staring at the letters still, in case his mind had overlooked it somehow.

'What did I say?'

'That... that you don't have any friends.'

'What? No! I said that I'm not doing anything with my friends, so we can go. I can't believe you said I didn't have any friends.'

Fuck.

Now he had no other choice but to invite Abigail along. He just hoped that she would be too busy.

CHAPTER
THIRTY-THREE

I t was pitch dark when Tomek joined Warren at the launch ramp a little before six am. The man had come well equipped for the journey: a cagoule that came down to below his knees, a thick pair of shorts with a thermal layer underneath, and a head torch that blinded Tomek as he swung it into Tomek's eyes.

Tomek, by comparison, was massively under-prepared and underdressed. His only saving grace, however, was the head torch he'd found in the cupboard under the sink. Aside from that, he was in his best trainers, a thin hoodie, and a pair of running shorts – minus the thermal layer. An oversight, in his haste and tired state.

'I hope you're not expecting those shoes to be functional by the time we get back,' Warren remarked.

'If not, I'm charging your tour company for a new pair.'

Warren chuckled, then gestured for them to start. As Tomek breached from behind the seawall, setting foot on the sand, he was hit in the face by a gust of wind. The last few gusts from the storm had been blasting his window all last night and had robbed him of sleep. That, and the excitement of finally making it out to the harbour.

At the foot of the ramp, Tomek paused and surveyed his surroundings. Blackness everywhere. No matter which direction he looked. The clouds overhead were thick with cover, there was no sign of the sun on the horizon, and the only light that he could see in the distance were the small pinpricks of streetlights coming from Kent on the other side of the estuary.

There was, however, one particular light that caught Tomek's eye. Red, flashing rhythmically in the distance.

'That where we're headed?'

'You bet.'

'Good thing we've got the head torches.'

'Trust me,' Warren replied. 'You wouldn't want to be without them.'

He was right about that. The first few hundred metres were shaky and unnerving. Tomek constantly looked down at his feet as he trundled through the rivulets and grooves in the sand, lest he trip and twist his ankle. The further they left the safety of the shore behind, the darker it became, and Tomek was grateful to have a friend with him, someone who knew what they were doing. Warren, meanwhile, looked relaxed, a natural. He jogged at his usual pace, head held high, lighting the path a few metres in front of him at all times. His feet pounded the sand methodically. He'd settled into the rhythm of the run with ease, whereas Tomek was trying to fight it every step of the way.

It took him another few hundred metres to get into the groove of it, and by the midway point, he eventually found his rhythm. From that point onwards, he was able to keep pace with Warren, and they ran shoulder to shoulder, splashing each other's legs with the last of the tide. They jogged in silence, focusing on their destination and the rhythm of their breathing.

A little over thirty minutes later, they arrived. The deep trenches on the beach had forced them to snake their way around them, adding another mile to their journey. When the silhouette of the harbour finally came into view against the backdrop of black, Tomek's knees felt like jelly. Trundling through the soft sand and mud had been harder on his muscles than he'd been expecting. He needed to sit down. But there was no time. Before leaving, Warren had impressed upon him the importance of being as quick and efficient as possible. By his estimates, they had a little over thirty minutes before they needed to head back and avoid the oncoming presence of the tide. Typically, he gave his customers less than that. But, thanks to Tomek's justification for being there, he had been afforded more.

Panting heavily, Tomek bent double and rested his hands on his knees. 'I'm so glad you were with me for that,' he said. 'I would've had no clue where I was going.'

'I'm starting to have second thoughts about charging you,' Warren replied as he came over, grabbed Tomek's hand, and pulled him upright. 'You need to stand up and open your chest if you want to catch your breath.' Then he slapped Tomek's chubbier than normal stomach. 'And breathe through your gut. You'll fill more of your lungs up.'

Tomek did as he was told, and within a few minutes, he felt normal again. Forty-year-old men weren't supposed to do that sort of exercise, especially considering they hadn't done so in months. (And the run they'd been on the day before had done little to prepare him.)

Placing his hands on his hips, Tomek surveyed the harbour. It was larger than he was expecting, but at this level of light, it was almost impossible to search through the site. And there was only so much the head torch could do.

While they waited for the sun to creep over the horizon, Tomek imagined the events that had led to Morgana's death. Warren had pointed to the spot in which they had found her body, and Tomek had envisaged her standing there, waiting in the cold, cowering against the wind and rain. Then a figure had appeared. The two of them began talking, quietly, amicably at first. Then something changed. Things became heated. Someone threw a punch, missed. Then Morgana was pushed to the sand. A struggle ensued. She fought off her attacker, but it was no use. He overpowered her, was stronger than her, and used all his weight to push her down. To drown her. Tomek imagined Morgana's struggle: face submerged below the waterline, bubbles escaping her mouth as she screamed for her killer to stop, her hands flailing at the attacker's face – *missing*, as well, as there was no DNA evidence found underneath her fingernails.

Whoever had killed her had done so quickly and efficiently, leaving no trace at all.

Twenty minutes later, the sun eventually made an appearance, breathing life into the surroundings. Now Tomek could clearly see the harbour and all its intricacies. The only problem was, they only had ten minutes left to search it.

Tomek didn't know what he was expecting to find, if anything at all. There was the very real and worrying possibility that he was too late. That anything that had been inadvertently left by the killer had already fallen victim to the storm and the raging tide, including Morgana's phone.

Tomek waded through the small moat of water until it came to his kneecaps. Then he reached overhead, his fingers searching for a groove or rivet, something for him to secure his grip on the concrete. When he found it, he wedged his foot onto the wall and heaved himself onto the top of the harbour. He couldn't imagine the strength required to lift someone else onto there, let alone a dead body. Andrei and the Redgraves, and even Morgana herself, were lucky to have had Warren there with them.

As soon as Tomek climbed over the top, he was met with an overwhelming sense of disappointment. The inside of the harbour was divided into giant hollow squares, three by four like a new version of Sudoku. He looked down. Water gently lapped against the insides of the structure.

But there was nothing. Nothing floating in there, nothing wedged into any of the nooks and holes that had formed over the decades.

All hope of finding something had completely disappeared.

'And you say this is where you lifted her body?' Tomek called to Warren down below.

'Right where you're standing.'

'And then what?'

'The kids were screaming, making it difficult to focus. We tried to revive her but Andrei had already done that. I then called the coastguard as I had my walkie talkie with me, and we waited. Down the bottom at first, but then as the tide came in, we moved further to the top. After about ten minutes of waiting, Andrei and I went up to that pylon and started waving our arms about for them to see us.'

Tomek turned towards the pylon. Its bright red light continued to flash every few seconds. As he started towards it, his phone vibrated in his shorts pocket.

It was Rachel.

He answered.

'Morning, Sarge,' she said. 'Hope I didn't wake you up.'

'Not at all.'

A gust of wind blew through the phone. 'Bloody hell, where are you?'

'At the foot of Mulberry Harbour. Freezing my legs and arse off.' It was then that he realised he hadn't felt the lower half of his body since they'd arrived. 'What's the matter? What's so important you had to call me during my meditation period?'

'Some of us have been working through the night to get evidence together against Mariusz,' Rachel explained, with a hint of sarcasm. 'While you've been meditating, Lorna's just reported that she's found DNA evidence underneath Andrei Pirlog's fingernails.'

'Whose?'

'Andrei Pirlog,' she said. 'The guy you found in the bathtub.'

'No, not him. I know who he is. I meant, whose DNA?'

A soft chuckle. 'I know what you meant. I was joking. I think you need to go back to meditating, your head's all muffled still.'

Tomek sighed. The sensation in his legs worsened as the wind continued to batter him. 'Just tell me,' he screamed into the handset.

'The DNA under Andrei Pirlog's fingernails belongs to Mariusz.'

CHAPTER
THIRTY-FOUR

The smirk on Tomek's face as he wandered through the incident room was one of vindication. And from the look on Victoria's, she wanted nothing more in that moment than to wipe it off for him.

His first words to her did nothing to stop that desire.

'What were you saying about Andrei's death being a suicide? I got the impression you were confident enough to stake your house on it.'

'What were *you* saying about Mariusz having nothing to do with Morgana's murder?' Victoria said in retaliation.

'We still don't know that for certain.'

'The causes of death are the same.'

Tomek shrugged. 'Doesn't prove anything. The DNA proves my theory was right. Yours is still just a theory.'

'Enough.'

'I'm just saying.'

'Well, don't. No one wants to hear what you have to say.'

Tomek had heard that so many times in his life he was starting to think it might be true. But when he'd just been proven right like that, how could he stop?

'Where's Mariusz now?' Tomek asked, suddenly aware that there were other people in the room.

Martin Brown answered by pointing to the flat screen television on the adjacent wall. Tomek had been so preoccupied with goading Victoria, that he hadn't even noticed the man on the screen, sitting in an interview room, with a solicitor present. Opposite him were Sean and Oscar.

'Twenty minutes in,' Martin added. 'Just in time. He's about to find out about the DNA.'

Captivated, Tomek pulled a seat from the table, his attention engrossed by the screen.

'Do you recognise this man?' Sean asked Mariusz, then slid a photo of Andrei across the table. 'This man was killed in his flat in Southend a few days ago. Do you recognise him?'

'No... no comment,' Mariusz replied, cagey.

Already, Tomek picked up on the hesitation in his voice. The man on the screen was entirely different to the one he'd sat across from only twenty-four hours before. His shoulders were stooped, his back arched in the shape of a hunchback, and his head hung low. He was playing with his fingers, and he bounced his knee vigorously. Tomek hadn't noticed any of that. Before, he had been the model of composure. But now, he was fraught with fear. Tomek suspected it wasn't entirely due to the image in front of him. Tomek suspected there was something else to blame.

'His name is Andrei Pirlog,' Oscar continued. 'Do you recognise that name?'

'No... no comment.'

Mariusz was unable to take his eyes off the photo in front of him. He stared at it intently, as though it were speaking to him.

'We have reason to believe you know him,' said Oscar. 'In fact, we have reason to believe you know where he lives as well. Are you sure you've never met this man before?'

'I... I don't know what to say. I... I...' Mariusz turned to his solicitor. The man sitting beside him raised his hand slightly, then lowered it. In turn, Mariusz's heavy breathing steadied, and he said, 'No comment.'

'Interesting.' It was now Sean's chance to take the helm. 'This morning, we found your DNA underneath Andrei's fingernails. We also found some of your DNA in his bathroom and around his throat. The evidence suggests you were there when he was killed. Maybe you were the person that killed him.'

'No... I...' Another turn to his solicitor. 'Please, help me.'

The man offered nothing in response.

'You should be helping us, Mariusz,' Sean continued. 'Now's your time to tell us what happened. You killed him, didn't you, Mariusz?' Sean's voice commanded authority and attention in the small confines of the interview room. 'You killed him and then made it look like a suicide.'

'No. Please. I didn't. My girlfriend, she... I...'

'Were you working with your girlfriend?'

'No! Never. No.'

'Did she have anything to do with Andrei's murder? Was she your accomplice?'

Mariusz shook his head frantically. 'No. You must understand, she had nothing to do with this. She is innocent. As am I. I don't know what to do.'

'The evidence indicates otherwise,' Oscar interrupted. 'The DNA evidence is incontrovertible. You cannot hide behind it.'

'What will... What will happen to me?' Mariusz asked.

Suddenly, his rapid breathing slowed, and his leg stopped bouncing.

'We're going to charge you with the murder of Andrei Pirlog,' Oscar answered. 'Shortly after this, you will be sent to prison where you will stay on remand. Is there anything else you'd like to say?'

'Help me. Please. I do not know what to do. My girlfriend.' Mariusz's voice was blank, emotionless, almost robotic. It unnerved Tomek, raising the hairs on the back of his neck. Then Mariusz added: 'I did not do it. I did not kill Morgana. You have to believe me.'

―――

Sadly for Mariusz, nobody in the team believed him. Instead, they were all gunning for him, all eager to find the evidence they needed to prove he'd been the one to drown Morgana. After all, as Victoria had already pointed out, if he could do it to a fully grown man in his bathtub, then he would have no trouble doing it to a woman in the middle of the open beach, surrounded by nothing but water.

Everyone in the team believed Mariusz was responsible for Morgana's murder.

Everyone except Tomek.

He didn't know why, but there was something that didn't sit right with him. That Mariusz had gone to the middle of the estuary in a bid to find the perfect location for his proposal, found Morgana, killed her, fled the scene, and then murdered Andrei Pirlog in the same fashion. The evidence against him for Andrei's murder was irrefutable. Tomek couldn't deny that. The evidence had put him in the bathroom at the time of Andrei's death. And as for the motivation behind his murder, it was conceivable that Mariusz had followed him and killed him for being in the wrong place at the wrong time. That all made sense to Tomek. But what didn't make sense to him was the connection between Mariusz and Morgana. And as far as their initial investigations had confirmed, there wasn't one.

Tomek sensed he would have a hard time selling that to the team. To Victoria in particular.

He had tried, shortly after the interview had concluded, but she'd shot him down, reminding him of the evidence against Mariusz: several eyewitness accounts, one of whom was now dead; a figure matching his description outside the Redgraves' Airbnb property; and a cover story that had more holes in it than a colander. In short, it wasn't looking good for the HGV driver.

But Tomek was still convinced there was something else going on. And if the team weren't willing to find out what it was, then he would have to do it alone.

But first, he had a call to make.

All this talk of prisons and arrests had reminded him of one thing. Of one person.

Nathan Burrows.

The letter.

Things had been so busy with the investigation that it had completely skipped his mind to call the prison. After leaving the incident room, Tomek snuck away to a small room that was typically used for one-to-one meetings and private conversations. Or, if you were Rachel or Martin, some quiet time to get your head down and focus on important tasks.

Tomek eased the door shut and pulled out his phone. As he sat at the table, he dialled the line for HMP Wakefield. He was expecting the call to be quick, but prison bureaucracy and budget cuts had put paid to that. The first hurdle was the robotic automated system that offered him eight separate options. Then, after navigating the first set of choices, he was given five more to choose from. Eventually, after progressing through the automated labyrinth, he was able to speak to a human.

'Is this someone from the postage team within the prison?' he asked, doubtful.

'No, you've come through to the wrong team, love,' replied the woman in a strong Yorkshire accent.

Fuck's sake. How hard could it be?

'Can you pass me through to them?'

'Sorry, love.'

Then the line went dead. Tomek clenched the phone in his fist and gritted his teeth.

He tried again. On the second time, he got through to the main switchboard.

On the third time, he made it.

'Fucking finally,' he said to the person on the end of the line.

'Sorry, pal,' the voice said. 'They make these things difficult on purpose, I swear. I don't even reckon one of them lot from NASA could come through to us on the first time if they tried.'

Tomek immediately calmed, his frustration dwindling as he listened to the man's dulcet tones put him at ease.

'How can I help?'

For once, it was nice to speak to someone over the phone who didn't sound like they hated their job. It made a pleasant change to some of the conglomerates and banks that he'd spoken to in the past.

'My name's DS Tomek Bowen, from Essex Police. I visited the other week, an inmate called Nathan Burrows.'

'Ah, Mr Burrows... We all know him around here.'

That did little to allay Tomek's fears.

'Well, earlier this week, I received a letter, delivered to my home address, from Nathan.'

'I understand.'

'What I want to know is how he found out my address. This man killed my brother thirty years ago. I do not want him having easy access to my address. He also knows about my daughter and partner, which is something I've certainly never told him. That information is not supposed to be common knowledge.'

The man on the other end of the line paused a moment.

'When did you say you visited?'

Tomek told him.

'And what time?'

'Three o'clock.'

Another pause. Another moment of waiting.

'I've just checked the visitor system log, and I can see your details are on here.'

'Including my address?'

The man confirmed his home address was on there. 'But this is a secure system. There's no way he would have been able to access it.'

'What about one of your team?' Tomek asked, realising how bad the question sounded after he'd asked it.

'What do you mean? Are you suggesting that one of our prison guards leaked your address to him?'

It was a keen possibility. One that he wasn't willing to disregard on account of a current prison worker trying to convince him otherwise.

'I know you might think we're all bent, but we're not,' the man said, suddenly getting defensive.

'Hey,' he replied, 'I know what it's like. I'm a cop. We get that sort of stick all the time. Comes with the territory. But what I meant was maybe someone in the service gave it to him inadvertently, without realising. Maybe they looked away from the computer one time and Nathan saw it. Or...'

Or someone on the take noted it down and passed it under the door. He could only imagine what sort of remuneration the guard would have received. Drugs, money? It wouldn't take much.

'Unfortunately, our systems do not let me see who, if anyone, has accessed your information. I will have to investigate this further.'

'You personally?'

'Well, no. I mean, someone will have to investigate this. I can ask around in the meantime.'

Tomek was dubious. The chances of anyone admitting to leaking his private and confidential information to a convicted murderer were as thin as the envelope the letter had come in. And he didn't think the person responsible was ready to make any sudden changes to their career prospects and come forward. It was a lost cause.

'Anything you can do to help would be greatly appreciated,' Tomek said, massaging his forehead.

'Great. Is there anything else I can help you with?'

CHAPTER
THIRTY-FIVE

The rest of the afternoon disappeared in a flash. Tomek had spent that time digesting Mariusz's interview, watching it over again and again. After his third time round, he was still convinced there was something untoward. The only problem was, he didn't know what. The atmosphere in the office was one of jubilation and triumph. They'd caught their man, and many were going to the pub to celebrate at the end of the day. Fortunately for Tomek, he had an excuse.

A forty-minute drive to his parents' house for a dinner that he wasn't too keen on.

Tomek had opted to drive. Partly because he knew the way, and partly because Abigail didn't like driving in the dark. On the journey, the three of them had caught up on their day. Kasia's, as always, had been fine, and nothing else. Abigail's, similarly, had been relatively quiet. There had been no breaking news to report, no exciting stories to share with the community. Her face had beamed after Tomek had told her the news about Mariusz. Though he'd asked her to keep the information to herself for now. Or at least wait until it was shared with the paper officially.

'Why are you making me wait?' Abigail asked as he swerved the car round a narrow country lane.

'I'm not convinced it's our guy,' he answered.

'That spidey-sense of yours tingling?'

'Eww!' came the response from Kasia in the back. Her face was illuminated a pale blue glow from her phone. 'That's disgusting. Don't say stuff like that while I'm here. *Please*.'

Tomek scowled at her in the rear-view mirror. 'You know that's not what she meant, Kash.'

'No, I don't. I know what you two are like. It's disgusting.'

'It's natural,' Abigail interrupted. 'You're a little too young to get involved with that sort of thing, but it's important you know about it, and you know how natural it is.'

Tomek couldn't believe he was hearing this. The last thing he wanted right now was to hear his daughter and girlfriend have the sex chat right before he was about to meet his parents. But he was too dumbstruck to say anything.

'I know how it all works,' Kasia replied venomously. 'You don't have to teach me anything.'

'So, you know about orgasms and ejaculation?'

'What?'

'Abi!' Tomek yelled, then turned to her. She looked back at him, confused, as though she'd just crossed the starting line of a race and didn't know what she was supposed to do next.

'What's the matter?' Abigail asked.

'She's *thirteen*.'

'And? I knew about those sorts of things when I was that age. It's important to know your body and to be comfortable enough to explore it. I've got a good book that you can—'

Tomek slammed his hand on the steering wheel. 'Right, that's enough. No more talking. Nothing out of the two of you until we get there.'

Mercifully, the rest of the journey only lasted ten minutes. Tomek was still in shock as he stepped out of the car. As the three of them made their way to the front door, a security light switched on, and Tomek saw pain and anxiety on Kasia's face, and a sense of pride on Abigail's. Meanwhile, his was one of shock and horror.

'Tomek, Kasia!' his mum, Izabela, screamed as she opened the door. '*Cześć*!' She bent down to embrace her granddaughter, then reached for a hug with Tomek. As she pulled away, she eyed him suspiciously. 'You all right? You're very pale.'

'A bit mortified, but I'll be fine.' Then he remembered his girlfriend standing awkwardly beside him. 'Mum, this is Abigail. Abigail, this is Mum.'

'Pleasure to meet you,' Abigail said, as she reached out to shake Izabela's hand.

'The pleasure is all mine.' Izabela swatted away Abigail's hand and instead wrapped her arms around her. 'We're huggers in this family,' she said. 'I must say, you're very pretty. I bet you have loads of men throwing themselves over you. What's wrong with you? What made you choose my son?'

The comment elicited a small laugh from the girls, but Tomek was the only one not joining in.

'Well, I—'

'Don't actually answer the question!' he said to Abigail, then grabbed his mum by the shoulders, turned her round, and ushered her in. As soon as he stepped inside, he hurried off in search of his father, Perry. The man would be able to save him from being ganged up on by the three most important women in his life.

Tomek found him in the kitchen, finishing pouring the last of a bottle of wine into four separate glasses. 'Hope you like white,' Perry said.

'I'm happy with whatever,' Tomek replied.

'Not you. Your date.' Perry looked round Tomek's side and held out a glass for Abigail, who was following closely behind. Once they'd introduced themselves, without launching any more verbal assaults at Tomek, Perry handed out a glass to the adults. Then he turned his attention to Kasia. 'And for the designated driver this evening, a bottle of Fentimans cola.'

'You remembered?' Kasia's face illuminated.

'Of course I did.'

'Wow, thanks! Dad never lets me have this.'

'Because it costs a fortune,' Tomek replied. 'Maybe if you took that job I got for you at the zoo you'd be able to buy as much Fentimans as you like.'

'A job? At a *zoo*?' The anguish in Izabela's voice was palpable as she massaged her perfectly manicured nails into her hair.

'It's not a real job,' Kasia replied in a huff. 'It was just Dad's idea of a joke.'

'He's good at those,' Perry replied with a slap on Tomek's back. 'I think I started work when I was about your age, actually, Kasia. In a workshop with one of my dad's colleagues' sons.'

'You sure it wasn't a chimney? They still sent kids up there when you were that age, didn't they?'

Perry winked, slapped Tomek on the arm playfully. 'See, there's your dad's sense of humour again. Not sure where he gets it from. Because mine's far superior to his, don't you think, Kash?'

'Yeah,' Kasia replied as she sipped on her drink. 'Dad's is more embarrassing than funny.'

'I keep telling her it's my job. It was always yours for me.'

'But you always took it so seriously,' Izabela said as she placed her hand on his forearm. 'You were so sensitive to it. Do you remember that one time you cried when Dad told you that your eyes would go square if you kept staring at the TV and that eventually they'd fall out of your head?'

'I was seven!' Tomek shook his head and turned to Abigail, who wore a massive grin on her face. It was clear to see she was enjoying herself. That she didn't feel awkward at all. And that it had all come at his expense. 'My parents, ladies and gentlemen,' he added, 'terrorising a seven-year-old.'

'You weren't special. Your brothers got the same treatment.'

And that was just it. He wasn't special. Not in his parents' eyes. Not compared to his brothers. He'd never been made to feel like he was the favourite, growing up. As the youngest, that was what he'd anticipated. It was what all the sitcoms and TV series made you believe. But it hadn't been his reality. And that feeling had only compounded following Michał's death.

Fortunately, someone else had come up with another conversation topic – possibly Abigail, possibly his mother – but he wasn't paying attention. His mind had wandered off to thoughts of Michał and Nathan Burrows. To the letter. To the conversation they'd had a few weeks before.

Discussing Michał's death never ended well between the three of them. It was a sore topic, for obvious reasons, but it was made worse by the fact Tomek had never been able to give his parents, in particular his mum, closure over what had happened to him. The possibility of a second killer being out there somewhere, avoiding capture after all these years, and nobody except Tomek being able to identify him, had created a gulf between them. Tomek didn't believe a word of what Nathan had said. He knew what he saw, and he saw a second figure hovering over his brother's dead body. But did his mum need to know that? Could he mend things and bridge the gap between them by finally admitting that it had all been part of his fragile and distorted imagination after all this time? Would she believe him? Would it finally grant her the closure she needed after over thirty years of hurt?

Tomek wasn't so sure. But there was only one way to find out.

For their evening meal, Izabela had made the family favourite: *pierogi*. A simple meal consisting of dumplings filled with meat, served in an unhealthy dose of gravy.

'For Abigail I made something else, in case you don't like them,' Izabela said with a warm smile.

'I'm open to anything,' Abigail said as she forked one past her lips.

The noise that came from her mouth belied the expression on her face. As did her words. 'Delicious,' she said.

Everyone in the room sensed she was lying, but like her, they were all too polite to say anything.

For a brief moment, they ate in silence. It didn't take long for the conversation to get round to work. Tomek had hoped they'd get to know Abigail a little better, but he'd had more luck on the lottery.

'Got any big cases at the moment?' his dad asked.

'Just a couple.'

'Any we can help with?'

'Abigail's done all I need anyone else to do.'

'Oh yeah?'

Tomek nudged her to explain. It was safer that way. She could only relay the information she'd picked up from Tomek or Anna. That way, nothing important that she didn't know yet could get out.

Abigail finished her mouthful, painfully, and said: 'You know that woman who was found in the estuary the other day?'

'No?'

'Well, she was killed about a mile away. Drowned. I put out the suspect's description.'

'*And*?' Perry asked, eyes transfixed on Tomek.

'We arrested someone in connection with the death this morning,' Tomek replied blankly.

'Why do I sense a "but"?'

'Because I don't think he did it. I think we've got the wrong guy or that someone else was involved somehow.'

Perry chuckled. 'Story of your life that, eh, kid?'

Tomek chewed on his bottom lip. He'd expected the comment from his mum, but not his dad. Perhaps that was why Perry had said it, because he knew Tomek wouldn't retaliate.

'Speaking of which,' Tomek started, clearing his throat. 'The other week I went to see Nathan.'

'Nathan?' Perry repeated. 'Who's Nathan?'

'You didn't...' Izabela said, her voice unusually deep.

'I did, Mum.'

'Who's Nathan?' asked Perry, but no one answered.

The conversation between Tomek and his mum continued.

'Why would you do that? How could you?'

'I needed to know.'

'Not like that. He doesn't deserve that.'

'Is someone going to tell me who Nathan is?' Perry asked.

The sound of a fork slamming on the table distracted them all. 'The person who killed Michał!'

All eyes turned to Kasia. Both her knife and fork were on the table, leaving smudges of gravy across the perfectly white and recently ironed tablecloth.

'Thank you, Kasieńka.' Perry turned to Tomek, his face sullen. '*The* Nathan? Really? Why did you go there?'

'Like I said, I needed to know. I needed answers.'

'And did you get them?'

Tomek lowered his gaze, then raised it to Kasia, then Abigail, before eventually making his way back to his parents.

'I did.'

'Are you going to tell us, or are you going to talk in riddles?'

Tomek inhaled deeply, slowly. 'There was no one,' he said. 'There was no other killer. He told me I'd got it all wrong. All these years it had been in my head.'

CHAPTER
THIRTY-SIX

Tomek awoke with a start.

Not because he was having a nightmare. Not because he was conjuring images of Nathan Burrows and the second killer in his mind. But because his phone started to ring beside his head. It sounded like a gun going off, vibrating on the IKEA furniture.

Eyes half open, he reached for the device. Saw Sean's name at the top of the screen. Groaned. It was just before six o'clock. His alarm was due to go off in twenty minutes' time. But something told him he wouldn't be able to go back to sleep after the call.

'Yes?' he said.

'Morning, Champ,' came the annoyingly cheerful response. 'Didn't wake you, did I?'

'Do planes fly in the sky?'

'What? Oh. I get it. Good one. Clever.'

'Not my best. But then again, what can you expect when I've just woken up?'

As he said it, Abigail stirred beside him. She was usually a light sleeper and had woken up during several of his alarms since they'd started dating, but the three glasses of wine and several plates of food had put paid to that. He slipped out of the bed and scurried into the living room.

'Am I going to like what I'm about to hear?' he asked.

'Probably not. Mariusz Stanciu's dead. Murdered. Killed in his prison cell last night.'

CHAPTER
THIRTY-SEVEN

According to the prison guards' report, Mariusz had been pronounced dead at 22:39, approximately ten minutes after he'd been placed in his cell for the night. The cause of death had been attributed to stabbing. Thirty-eight times. His killer had broken out of his cell, overpowered the guards, and slipped into Mariusz's cell. Mariusz had been alone, breaking into his new prison life without anyone to console him, when the killer had charged in. By the time the guards had reacted and found a separate key, some three minutes later, Mariusz had bled out and died on the floor. Meanwhile, his killer was standing at the back of the cell, face pressed against the wall, arms above his head like he was being arrested for the first time. He was surrendering, admitting defeat. But that didn't stop the guards from pummelling him into the wall, seven armed bodies crushing him into the concrete. Nor did it stop them from hammering him repeatedly with their truncheons and throwing him to the ground like he was a piece of meat.

The man's name was Denis Danyluk, and he was currently serving a life sentence for murder.

Tomek and Sean had been sent to interview him. The decision had come from Victoria. As the team's largest and most physically imposing figures, they were the perfect candidates for the job. It also helped that they were joint second-in-command behind her.

They were both ushered into a small, blank room that reminded Tomek of the interview rooms at the station. In the middle was a small table, barely large enough for one, let alone three. Slouching in his chair, facing them, was a thick, heavyset bald man, with shoulders almost as broad as the table itself. He wore a deeply unimpressed expression on his face. Above his left eye was a two-inch long laceration that looked as though it had cut through to the bone. His eyes were the colour of the ceiling, and his nose was broken in at least two places. Denis wasn't overweight, but he wasn't exactly sporting five per cent body fat either. Despite living in a prison twenty-four seven, he looked as though he ate well – very well indeed.

As they approached, Denis rose out of the chair and extended his hand. Tomek was taken aback by the sheer size of him. Like staring at John Coffey from *The Green Mile* in the face. Now he understood why the two of them were the best people for the job. He put on a brave face.

'My name is Denis,' he said, in a thick Eastern European accent. 'It is good to meet you. I have been waiting.'

Neither Tomek nor Sean opted to shake his hand. Instead, they pulled their chairs out and sat. In the top corners of the room, single red lights flashed as the video cameras recorded their every move. It was a thin consolation knowing that protection was only a few seconds away, though, given the size of him, Tomek felt confident the man could dispatch them both by the time reinforcements arrived – and stand with his face against the wall and his hands above his head with a few seconds to spare.

'We need you to tell us everything that happened in the build-up to Mariusz's death,' Sean said.

Denis shrugged. 'It is simple. I broke into his cell. Then I killed him.'

'How did you get into his cell?'

'The guard came in. I stole his key.'

'How?'

'I took it from the guard.'

'And?'

'I pretended to have stomach issues.'

'Then what?'

'I stole the key, went into Mariusz's cell, then I killed him.'

'How?'

Without saying anything, Denis pushed himself away from the table and stood. Tomek immediately tensed, readying himself for an altercation. But it didn't come. Instead, Denis proceeded to act out how he'd killed Mariusz.

'I rushed in,' he started, 'grabbed him by the shirt, then pushed him against the wall. Then I stabbed him. Thirty-eight times. I counted. One for each year of Morgana's life. He was dead by the time he hit the floor. Then I dropped the knife and stood by the wall. Like this.' Denis pressed his body against one side of the wall and placed his hands above his head.

'Shortly after that, the guards came. Is that right?'

'That is right,' Denis replied, speaking into the wall.

'You can come back now,' Tomek said.

A deep chuckle. 'Forgive me. I am used to being in this position.'

Tomek didn't doubt it. Nor did he doubt the man's version of events. It matched what he'd read in the report. That he'd stormed in and killed him without a moment's hesitation. That it had been pre-meditated. That Denis had known Mariusz was coming into the prison, that he knew which cell he would be in.

The questions on Tomek's mind were how, and why?

'Why did you kill him?' he asked once Denis had returned to his seat.

'Revenge.'

'Revenge for what?'

'Because he killed Morgana.'

'Why should that impact you?'

'Because she is my sister.'

CHAPTER
THIRTY-EIGHT

The news had floored Tomek, and he'd needed time to process the information, but it wasn't time he could afford to spare. Fortunately, Sean had come to his rescue and conducted the rest of the interview until Tomek had regained enough composure to join him. He couldn't believe it. Rather, didn't.

It was the first Tomek and the team had heard of Morgana having any family outside of her husband, let alone a brother who was in prison. He hadn't come up in any of their investigations, witness statements or research. He hadn't existed. But now he did. Perhaps that was the way Morgana had wanted it. Perhaps she'd been so disgusted and disappointed with her brother's actions that she'd completely shut him off, locked him up inside her mind and thrown away the key, and told everyone else to do the same. It wouldn't be the worst thing she could have done.

Sean had questioned the validity of his claims. But, to combat that, Denis had agreed to take a DNA sample, and by the time Tomek and Sean left, they had it bagged and ready to be sent off for testing. Only time would tell whether Denis was telling the truth.

Regardless, the man had still killed Mariusz, slaughtered him to the ground, and for that, he was looking at an even longer sentence. Added to his current sentence, it was looking like Denis would never get out of prison. Already inside for the murder of a twenty-five-year-old male in a random killing incident, it was obvious Denis was going to die inside the four walls of his cell. And there was nothing he could do to change that fact. No amount of DNA tests, no number of confessions.

As he entered the incident room, forty minutes later, Tomek's mind was swimming with ideas, thoughts. He needed to process them all, and before doing anything else, he headed straight towards his desk and began jotting them down on a notepad. When he finished, the notes were barely legible:

Morgana's
> **Iliana's**
> **Denis and Mariusz link - what connects them?**
> **Denis - organising it all from prison?**
> **Mariusz and Andrei - connection?**
> **Maybe no links at all?**
> **Random?**
> **Andrei, Andrei's address - Mariusz**
> **Connection?**

For a long moment, Tomek stared at the list. Until the words became meaningless, nothing but scribbles and lines on a page. In his head, it all made sense, but there was something missing. Something in the back of his mind that he couldn't reach, couldn't grab and chuck onto the page.

He stared at the list a moment longer.

Indecision crept in, and he suddenly had no idea where to start.

Fortunately, the decision was made for him.

'Sarge,' came the call from a hesitant Chey.

'Yes, Mr Pepper?'

'Call me doctor.'

'No. I'm not going to do that.'

Chey shrugged, then said, 'You're missing out on some top-quality banter there.'

'I'll take my chances. What do you need me for?'

Chey pulled out the chair beside Tomek and plopped himself onto it. As he folded one leg over the other, he said, 'I was doing some looking...'

'Be careful where you do that and who you do it to, mate. Don't want to have you arrested as a peeping Tom.'

'Funny. But that's not what I meant. What I meant was, I was doing some *thinking*—'

'Some might argue that's even more dangerous.'

The earlier excitement on Chey's face gradually dwindled the more Tomek drained it from him.

'Sorry,' he said, punching the constable on the arm playfully. 'I'm just messing, getting the creative juices flowing, that's all. You have my full attention.'

Chey looked uncertain. 'Well, while you were out, the team has been looking into Denis, finding out everything they can. But I wanted to stick with Mariusz for a little bit longer.'

'Right.'

'I've been looking through CCTV footage along the seafront again, trying to find any sign of him around the time of Morgana's murder. I even looked at footage from the morning to see if I could find him going out to kill Morgana.'

'And?'

'Still nothing.'

'Have we found a connection between Mariusz and Morgana yet?' Tomek asked. His mind was trying to wipe out the thoughts and ideas and start anew with Chey's information.

'No, but the team are still looking.'

'Okay. Is there anything else, or is that all you've come to tell me?'

Chey shook his head. 'Of course not. I found something that I think you might find interesting.'

Tomek rubbed his hands together. 'Go on.'

'Well, I was thinking back to something you said about the figure outside the Redgraves' Airbnb. How could the figure, assuming it was the killer, have found out that information? It's only available on our systems, or he knew the Redgraves well enough to know where they were staying. The only person who fits that bill is Warren Thomas.'

Tomek bridled in his seat uncomfortably.

'But then he doesn't fit in with the profile and the description they all gave about the attacker. I mean, I've *seen* Warren, and you'd *know* the difference between him and Mariusz. So then that got me thinking. The other possibility is that he somehow got access to the Redgraves' address via our systems.'

'Or he followed them home after they gave their witness statements at the station?' Tomek said.

Chey snapped his fingers into a gun. 'I was hoping you'd say that. In fact, I knew you would. Can read you like a book, Sarge. In fact, you were the one who gave me the—'

'You were saying?' Tomek interrupted.

'Yes. Right. Sorry. I was hoping you'd say that because I looked into Mariusz's involvement with Andrei. Again, as far as we can make out, there's no direct relation or connection between the two of them.'

'Which implies that Mariusz killed Andrei because he was in the wrong place at the wrong time.'

'Correct, yes. That's the implication, at least. And the only way he could have found out where Andrei lived is either by accessing the information on our systems, or by...'

'Or by following Andrei home after his witness statement.'

Another finger gun. 'Exactly! So, thanks to your wise and professional inspiration, I looked at the CCTV footage of the station around the time he came in for his statement and at the time he left. I also looked at CCTV from around his flat above the Chinese takeaway shortly after, matching any cars that had left the station and had driven past the nearest camera.'

'And?' Tomek felt himself inching forward slightly.

'And nothing.'

'What do you mean, nothing?'

'There's no sign of Mariusz outside the station at all. I also couldn't find any matching vehicle descriptions or registrations from both here and Andrei's flat, which means that he wasn't followed home by car either.'

'So how did Mariusz know where Andrei lived?' Tomek asked, though he became lost in deep thought again.

'Isn't it obvious?'

It was. But Tomek needed to consider the implications.

'It's the second possibility,' Chey continued. 'Mariusz managed to access the information from our systems. Or someone did it for him.'

Tomek slowly turned to him, eyes widening with despair.

'Do you... do you know who?'

Chey was unable to shake the excitement from his face. 'I was waiting until you came back, Sarge,' he said. 'Victoria gave me another task to focus on while you were out.'

Figured.

Tomek glanced towards Chey's desk. 'Have you got it open now?'

Chey nodded. Tomek climbed out of his chair before Chey and rushed over to his desk. He tapped on his wrist repeatedly, as if to hurry the young man up.

The constable sensed the urgency and skipped the last few steps. In his seat, he logged in to his computer and loaded the screen. At the top was a small search bar. Chey entered Andrei Pirlog's name and hit enter.

A moment later, a small log popped on the screen. Tomek's eyes quickly scanned the information, looking first at the dates and then the name of the account that had accessed his file.

And then he saw it.

CHAPTER
THIRTY-NINE

M ercifully, Tomek didn't recognise the name on the screen. He didn't want to begin to imagine how the conversation would have gone if it had been someone on the team. That someone he knew intimately had leaked Andrei's private information to a killer.

The name that had appeared on the screen belonged to a Mr Gavin Barker.

A quick search of Gavin's name in the police internal database had concluded that he worked for the Safer Policing team, in the same office as the Police, Fire and Crime Commissioner, Brendan Door. After seeing the PFCC's name, Tomek's mind had started to spin. A few weeks before, Brendan, along with some of the city's elite and most respected individuals, including the local MP, the mayor, a prominent businessman and head of Abigail's newspaper, the *Southend Echo*, had been charged with trafficking women from Eastern Europe so they could be their decadent and debauched playthings in their exclusive members' only club in the heart of Southend, and he was currently on remand while the investigation progressed.

Tomek and Chey were sitting patiently in a small reception area. They were perched on a pair of uncomfortable seats made from a coarse material that reminded Tomek of his grandparents' sofa back in Poland. Behind the desk was a woman who looked like the type to lose control of herself in the event of a fire safety test, someone who would be the first to scream and sprint out of the window if the situation demanded it – slightly neurotic and tightly wound. As soon as she realised who Tomek and Chey were, and what they were there for, she was straight on the phone, dialling through to Gavin, eager to contact him, apologising profusely as they waited.

Five seconds for him to answer.

Five minutes for him to appear.

Gavin was a small, unassuming man, with a large mouth and short spiky hairstyle that required far too much hair gel, and hadn't been fashionable since the early noughties. Despite his size, he had one hell of a grip on him.

'I trust this'll be quick?' he asked as he lowered his hands to his sides.

'Probably not,' responded Tomek. 'You might want to think about cancelling any appointments or meetings you've got lined up.'

Without saying anything, Gavin spun on the spot and shot off through a set of double doors. His office was a short walk away, but the man was well ahead of them, and by the time they caught up, Gavin was already sitting behind his desk, waiting for them like a headteacher expecting a pair of truant children.

'If this is about the investigation into Brendan, I've already answered every question there is to answer on it.'

'We just have a few more, if you'll indulge us.'

'Indulge you? What's that supposed to mean?'

'We just have a few more questions that require some answers.'

'I already told you, I've discussed everything there is to discuss on Brendan.'

'Who said anything about Brendan?'

'You did...?' He seemed uncertain of himself now.

'No, we didn't. If that's what the receptionist told you, then I'm sorry, but you've been misinformed.'

'If it's not about him, then what is it about?'

'We think you know.'

Tomek perched himself on the edge of the chair, placed one hand on the table, then gestured to Chey. The constable reached into his pocket and produced a piece of paper.

'Have you heard about the body that was found by Mulberry Harbour the other day?'

Gavin's eyes bounced between Tomek and Chey. 'I think I saw something about it.' His voice was shaky, nervous, as though he knew where this was headed.

'Well,' Tomek said, 'shortly after all of that happened, one of the key witnesses was killed. Don't say anything though, we're keeping this part pretty hush-hush. It's such a shame, because he was a really nice guy. Like the woman, he was taken from us too soon. Can you believe the bastard that did it, he came forward out of nowhere?'

'Out of nowhere,' echoed Chey.

'Well, not exactly out of nowhere. He had a little helping hand from the *Southend Echo*. After they released his description to the public, he felt compelled to come forward, you see? But that's not the only helping hand our killer had, is it, Chey?'

'No, Sarge.'

'No, sirree,' Tomek continued, with a shake of the head. 'You see, Gavin, someone gave our killer the eyewitness's location. Can you believe that?' Tomek leaned closer. Gavin felt obliged to do the same. The lines in his eyes had creased and his brow had furrowed. Tomek thought he also saw a droplet of sweat forming at the edge of his thinning hairline.

'And... the crazy thing is...' Tomek continued. The apprehension on Gavin's face grew. 'It came from somewhere in *this* office.'

The relief on Gavin's face was so sudden and forceful, Tomek almost felt it on his cheek.

Tomek lowered his voice. 'And we think *you* might be able to help us work out who...'

Gavin's eyes widened. 'You think... you think someone from this office leaked someone's address to a... to a killer?'

'Oh, yeah.'

'And you think I can help you find out who might've done it?'

'Yes, but we're going to need you to be super quiet about all this. We can't have word getting out. There are some dangerous people in this world. It's a jungle out there, and who knows what they're capable of.'

'Right. Yes. I see. That's... that's interesting. Very interesting.' Gavin suddenly became deep in thought, tapping his chin, turning his head away from Tomek. 'Have you... have you any idea who it might be?'

'Tim from accounts.'

'Tim from accounts? Really? I... I never thought he had it in him.'

'That's because he's not real,' Tomek said abruptly. 'There is no Tim from accounts. We made him up. But you didn't make up Andrei Pirlog's address, did you? You found that right where you needed to, and you gave it directly to his killer, didn't you?'

Gavin's face contorted into a knot of protestation. 'What're you talking about? How dare you accuse—'

Tomek shut him up with the piece of paper he'd been waiting to unleash.

'That's your name right there, isn't it? And that's the IP address for this very computer – don't worry, we had IT check before we came over. We also checked your calendar, and the CCTV in the building, and they all say that you were right here, sitting at this very desk when you viewed Andrei's profile on the system.'

Gavin opened and closed his mouth to speak, but nothing came out.

'I can't believe you were going to let an innocent, albeit fictional, man go down for something he didn't do. Poor Tim from accounts. Have you no shame, Gavin?'

'You can't do this to me,' the man replied. 'You have no proof.'

'I've just shown it to you. Are you delusional?'

'No, I—'

'Who asked you to leak the address?'

'No one, I—'

'Who asked you?'

'I don't know. I just received a text message.'

'Saying what?'

'It just asked for the address. That was it.'

'Do you still have the message?'

'No. I deleted it as soon as I'd sent the information.'

'Why? Why you?'

'I don't know. I... I wish I could tell you.'

'You're lying.'

'No! I promise you, I'm not!'

'Then I suggest you tell us everything we need to know.'

Out of the corner of his eye, he saw Chey remove a small audio recording device from his pocket and place it on the table. Gavin studied it suspiciously, and as he spoke, his eyes flitted to it frequently.

'Listen, I...' he started, babbling incoherently, unable to get his words out. He inhaled sharply, composed himself. 'I know how it looks. Really, I do. But I didn't do anything wrong. I didn't. The other day I was in Leigh, walking along the Broadway with my wife and two daughters, just minding my own business, when I got this text. It was from an unknown number, with a photograph of my family walking along the street. It must have been taken about five minutes before. They were standing outside the Co-op, waiting for me while I'd popped into the gift shop over the road. I looked around to see if anyone was still there, but I had no idea who I was looking for. And it was busy, too, so I had no chance of finding them.'

'What did the message say?' Tomek asked.

'Something along the lines of, "We know everything about you, we know everything about your family. Reply with the address of a Mr Andrei Pirlog" – I don't know if I'm pronouncing that correctly—'

'I don't think he'll mind,' Tomek interrupted. 'He's dead because of you.'

Gavin flinched at the remark but continued regardless. '"Give us the address for a Mr Andrei Pirlog otherwise we will kill your family." Naturally I wasn't going to sit around and do nothing about it.'

'So you got someone killed instead.'

'I didn't kill anyone!' Gavin slapped his palm on the table. The only person to flinch was Gavin himself.

'No, you're right,' Tomek said, lowering his tone slightly. 'He was just drowned in his own bathtub while you practically stood by and watched.'

Gavin chewed on his bottom lip. A thin layer of tears began to settle at the bottom of his eyes as realisation sank in.

'Was that the only thing you were asked to do?'

They'd lost him. Gavin was staring blankly into the middle space of the desk, lost in his deep, spiralling thoughts.

'Gavin, I'm going to need you to answer.'

Eventually, after what felt like a long time, he lifted his head. 'They told me to go to the prison as well.'

'When?'

'Yesterday. I had to go before a new inmate arrived.'

'Who did you speak with?' Chey asked.

'A man named Denis. I... I was told to find out when someone was coming in, someone called Mari-*oosh*, or whatever his name was. They... they wanted me to pass on the message.'

'What message?'

'Do I have to spell it out?'

'It's the least you owe these people,' Tomek replied bluntly.

Gavin cleared his throat. 'They wanted Denis to kill Mari-*oosh*. He was due to go into prison that evening, and they wanted Denis to kill him.'

'And you went along with it?' Chey asked.

Gavin slowly turned to the constable. 'Do you have a family, mate? No, of course you don't. Look at you, you're about twelve. What do you know? You can't pass judgement unless you know what it's like to have your loved ones threatened. I did what I had to do in order to protect my family.'

'Even if that meant killing two people?'

Gavin's expression suddenly dropped. 'I did what I had to do in order to protect my family.'

This time there was no remorse in his voice, as though he'd suddenly come to terms with his decision and the subsequent penalty that would follow.

Tomek was infuriated with the man. If he had only come to the police first, they could have protected Gavin and his family, and potentially saved two lives. But the man had taken matters into his own hands, and now he would pay the ultimate price for it.

CHAPTER
FORTY

The atmosphere inside the incident room was sullen, morose. Hopes and expectations had fallen, and there were a lot of confused faces staring blankly into the table and onto the walls. Optimism, despite having a successful charge for the murder of Andrei Pirlog, was ebbing as fast as the retreating tide.

'I'm saddened and shocked to hear the news of Mariusz's murder,' Victoria said slowly, calmly, with a sense of measure in her voice. She stood with her head up and her back straight. This time, there was no loyal hound by her side; instead, Sean was sitting amongst the rest of them at the table. 'But thanks to Tomek's and Chey's diligence, we've managed to find a reason as to why he's dead. Gentlemen, would you care to explain?'

And so they did. But not before Tomek had pointed out the glaring error in Victoria's original statement: that the thirty-eight puncture wounds in Mariusz's body had been the *actual* reason he was dead, not their thoroughness at doing their job. Regardless, Tomek had allowed Chey to explain Gavin's active involvement in the man's death to the team. It was a chance for the constable to develop and grow more confident in his role. When he'd finished, Victoria opened the room up to questions, which Chey had been able to answer concisely and without hesitation.

'I'd like to use this time to go through what we know, what we don't know, and what we want to know. I think we all need to wrap our heads around what the fuck's been going on these past couple of days so we can all make sense of it and finally put it to bed.'

A soft murmur rumbled through the team.

With the troops rallied, Victoria set off into battle and turned to the boards behind her. Over the course of the past few days, the team had placed documents, information, facts, images, crime scene photographs, and evidence on the wall to build a complete mind map of the investigation. In the top left was a small photograph of Mulberry Harbour, with some brief facts about the monument. Beside it was an image of Morgana, taken from her social media; the thirty-eight-year-old was smiling ebulliently into the camera. 'At 9:52 am, we received the emergency call from Warren Thomas at Mulberry Harbour to say that they'd found Morgana's body. Present at the time were Andrei Pirlog, now deceased, Warren Thomas himself, Kirsty Redgrave, and her family of four.' Their names were written beneath the image of Morgana, and Victoria pointed to each one as she spoke. 'A suspect, of medium build, with short black hair and a thin black beard, wearing a black coat and scarf, was seen holding Morgana's body. He later fled the scene, heading west, towards Southend Pier, where he later resurfaced somewhere around here.'

With her pen, Victoria drew an arrow on a map of Southend from the harbour to the pier, then another line pointing upwards. She stopped when she hit land.

'At that time in the morning, the tide was coming in fast, leaving our key witnesses stranded. As a result, they were forced to lift the body, and themselves, onto the harbour, where they awaited rescue. Once they'd been brought ashore, they were taken to the station for statements. The only person to get the best view of our suspect was Andrei Pirlog.' Victoria prodded the man's name with the pen. 'Shortly after, Andrei was found dead in his bathroom. Originally believed to be suicide, DNA evidence later found under Andrei's fingernails confirms that Mariusz Stanciu, a haulier for DWG Logistics, was present. We now know that Mariusz killed Andrei, the evidence is irrefutable, and we also know that he was the one to flee Morgana's crime scene.'

'No, we don't,' Tomek interrupted.

Victoria shot him the look of someone who had just been stopped from coming first at the finish line of a marathon. Fury crawled along the creases of her face.

'Yes, we do.'

Tomek shook his head. 'All we have is his word for it. He came forward out of nowhere because he matched the description in the newspapers.'

'Which you leaked.'

'That's got nothing to do with it.'

'So you admit it?' Victoria pressed.

'No. Now will you let me finish? Thank you. As I was saying, Mariusz came forward because he matched the description in the newspaper. When he spoke to me, he told me he had nothing to do with Morgana's death, that he found the body like that, and that he fled the scene because he knew how it would look. When I showed his photo to the Redgraves and Warren Thomas, they couldn't definitively say it was him. The only person who could was Andrei.'

'Who he killed.'

'Yes, but that doesn't mean to say he was the one who killed Morgana, or that he was even there.'

'It all but does,' weighed in Martin. 'He was there at the harbour, he was spotted, he fled, and then he killed the person who got the best sighting of him. It doesn't look good.'

'I know how it looks,' Tomek replied with a heavy sigh. 'But you weren't sitting opposite him in that interview room. You didn't hear him. You didn't hear how calm and... robotic he sounded.' Another sigh, this time deeper, longer. 'I believe what I believe, and I don't believe he killed Morgana.'

'What about his girlfriend?' Martin asked, continuing to weigh in.

'What about her?' Tomek asked.

'In his statement, he said that he was there to find a perfect spot to propose to his girlfriend. Where is she? Does she exist?'

'Yes,' came the blunt response from Oscar. He lifted himself out of his chair and pointed to a photograph on the other side of the wall. It contained a sprightly-looking woman, smiling behind a thick scarf that was wrapped around her neck and chin. In the background was a set of steps and a building. 'She exists,' he continued, 'but I've been unable to contact her because she's back in Romania.'

'Which supports what Mariusz said about her,' Tomek added. 'He said that she'd gone back home to see her family.'

'None of that's relevant,' Sean interrupted. 'What is relevant is why Mariusz, a man who appears out of the blue – literally, in this case – would kill Andrei if he had nothing to do with Morgana's murder. Why would he kill an innocent man if he was innocent himself?'

Tomek didn't have an immediate answer, so instead asked a question of his own. 'Has anyone found a link between Mariusz and Morgana yet?'

All eyes turned to one of the boards. In the centre were two images, Mariusz and Morgana, with a line stretching between them and a large question mark underlined several times beneath.

'No, in short,' Rachel answered.

Tomek shrugged, offered a smug look to the rest of the team. 'Point proven.'

'Moving on,' Victoria started. 'We can come back to Mariusz and Morgana. But while we're on the topic of Mariusz, he's just been killed in prison by Morgana's brother, Denis Danyluk. Who's got the latest on him?'

'We're still looking into him,' Rachel answered. 'We've not had enough time to piece much together.'

'Nothing at all?'

'Well, he comes from Ukraine, the same as Morgana. He was imprisoned for the murder of a twenty-five-year-old man. Stabbing him to death. There was a concern that it had been tribal, drug, gang, or even turf related, but there was no evidence to support it. One day, Denis got into a disagreement, lost the plot, then stabbed a man to death. We won't know if he's related to Morgana until the DNA results come back.'

'There's no mention of her on any of his records? Never had her down as a next of kin? Vice versa?'

Rachel shook her head. Then Victoria moved to a clean section of the whiteboard and began scribbling a brief to-do list. The first task on the list was to speak with Morgana's husband and associates to find out the validity of Denis Danyluk's claim. Those closest to her would know whether she had a brother or not. Particularly her husband, Anton.

Then the conversation briefly moved on to Gavin Barker's involvement with Mariusz's prison murder, and how he'd informed the prisoner of Mariusz's imminent arrival.

'Someone told Gavin to leak Andrei's address,' Tomek explained. 'Then, once Mariusz had been charged, they told Gavin to forewarn his arrival to Denis Danyluk. Someone, whoever's behind those messages, clearly wanted Andrei and Mariusz dead. Now do you understand why I don't think Mariusz killed Morgana? Someone else did it, they sent Mariusz to confess, and they've been covering up after themselves ever since.'

Nobody responded. All eyes avoided one another, until Martin was brave enough to speak up again. He brushed a piece of hair out of his eyes and stroked it behind his ear. 'Perhaps they're unrelated. Perhaps Mariusz's murder is a separate event. There's still a lot we don't know about Mariusz. Perhaps he had enemies.'

Tomek scoffed. 'Please. He's only been in the country three months. Keep thinking that if you want, but I think our focus should be on finding out who sent those text messages. And I plan on doing it while digital forensics are trying to do the same.'

'So you can beat them to it?' Victoria asked, a hint of indignation in her voice.

'No, so that we can be ready with an arrest warrant when the time comes.'

CHAPTER
FORTY-ONE

'T eflon Tommy!'

The cry had come from behind him as he'd stepped out of the incident room, and it took a while for him to realise he was being addressed.

He hadn't heard that nickname in a while. Teflon Tommy. So named because shit didn't stick. And there had been a period, a time during the early stages of his career, when he'd upset a few people, ruffled a few feathers, broken the rules a few times, and yet nothing had been able to stick. Thanks, in no small part, to Nick. The chief inspector had always been there to defend him, and the nickname had been born between the two of them. The ironic thing was that, at first, the name had stuck, but over time, and as he'd matured and developed into a more competent and rule-following detective (those terms were loosely used to describe him), it had stayed true to form and slipped out of use.

'T-Bone!'

Another call, another nickname. This time referring to his love of T-bone steak. Tomek had been the one to appoint himself the moniker, but not everyone had adhered to it.

Confused, Tomek turned round to the owner of the voice. He'd been half expecting to see a former colleague, one who'd sidled up to him at every available opportunity, clung to his hip and laughed at every one of his jokes. He'd known a few leeches like that in his time, sucking the blood out of his sense of humour. Instead, it was Sean. Holding the door open with his hand, fingers spread across the surface like a blood splat.

'All right, mate?'

Tomek answered slowly. 'Yeah... What's with all the nicknames? You flirting with me, or are you after something?'

'Bit of both. Whichever one works.'

'This about the room?'

Sean suddenly turned shy, lowered his voice. 'Yeah. I was just wondering if you'd had a chance to speak with the girls yet, get their approval?'

Tomek scratched his cheek. 'Sorry, mate. Not yet. It's completely slipped my mind – a bit like my name, eh!' But Sean didn't see the funny side of it. His eyes lowered, and he nodded slowly. 'Listen, let me speak to them tonight. I'll get an answer to you tomorrow, how's that?'

'Yeah. Great, thanks.'

'When do you need to move out by?'

'ASAP really. I'd love to stay for as long as possible, out of spite really – I mean, the fucker's kicking me out, after all. But it's getting a bit toxic staying there, and I think it makes more sense to get out of there sooner rather than later, if you know what I mean?'

Tomek understood perfectly. He placed a hand on Sean's shoulder. 'Leave it with me, mate. We'll find you somewhere.'

Sean's face filled with warmth. 'Thanks, mate. Really appreciate it. You're a good friend. You know that, right?'

CHAPTER
FORTY-TWO

Ever since he'd first seen Gavin Barker's name appear on the screen, Tomek's mind had immediately leapt to one man having an involvement somehow. Brendan Door, the Police, Fire and Crime Commissioner for Essex. Brendan was an evil man who had shown little remorse for his actions, and it was impossible for Tomek not to think of him.

The man was currently on remand in HMP Bedford while the investigation and trial into his sex trafficking progressed. Tomek had tried to get a meeting shortly after Victoria had finished with the emergency debrief, but it had been too late. Visiting hours had passed, and there was no chance of speaking with him that night. So Tomek had been forced to delay to the following day.

He had set off to HMP Bedford before sunrise, missing his morning run with Warren. The journey had been long and tiresome, as it had felt like the whole world and his dog had decided to leave the house at precisely the same time as him, and he'd been nose to arse the entire way. The only positive he'd taken from the experience was that he'd been able to listen to a few episodes of a new podcast he'd been trying out. *The Crime Detectives*, it was called, which involved a husband-and-wife team who fancied themselves as amateur detectives, and spent the entire episode discussing real-life cold cases. Each week they went away, did some research, and came back with some more facts, gradually progressing the investigation along. Tomek admired their ingenuity and tenacity, and from the two episodes that he'd listened to, was envious of the progress they'd made. He knew first-hand how hard it was to conduct an investigation and find the killer sometimes, and he admired them greatly, nonetheless. He wasn't sure if it was a podcast he'd continue to listen to, however. Not because he didn't like how much progress they were making and it made him feel redundant, but because he'd become so involved in their discussions and hearing their voices, that he'd almost crashed on several occasions. It appeared he was incapable of handling heavy machinery and listening to a podcast at the same time. He thought they should have put that on the packaging, same as they did for medication.

After arriving at the prison and going through the various checks, Tomek had been directed to a separate meeting room, away from the general population, where he'd been waiting for Brendan to arrive. The prisoner had been required to approve the meeting before Tomek could sit in front of him, and to his surprise, Brendan had agreed. Eventually, after ten minutes of waiting, the man entered the room, and Tomek got an immediate sense of what prison had done to him. In such a short space of time, his face had become haggard, his jowls sagging from the sudden and drastic weight loss. He walked slowly, his back hunched, shoulders stooped, head low. Here was a man who, on the few occasions Tomek had met him, stood proudly, cockily, with the power of anonymity and status behind him. Now he looked broken and withered. The air of arrogance beaten and stolen from him. Police officers, even the corrupt ones, were still among the most detested inmates in prison, behind rapists and paedophiles. But despite this, there was still a thin veil of power behind him, as though it hadn't been beaten out of him completely.

Brendan pulled the chair from beneath the table and sat.

'I've been up all night thinking about today,' he said in his usual deep, gruff voice.

'Likewise,' Tomek replied.

'Though for very different reasons, I'm sure. They wouldn't let me know what this is about, so my imagination's been going wild.'

Tomek considered that statement for a moment.

'Hopefully I won't disappoint.'

Just as he was about to explain the reason for his visit, Brendan interrupted him.

'How's my mate?'

'Which one?'

'Nick. My mate, Nick. How's he keeping?'

'Suspended, thanks to you.'

'Really?'

Tomek dipped his head slightly. 'Suspended, pending full investigation into any connection with you and what you and your mates were up to.'

A hint of a smirk flashed across Brendan's face. Some of the power returned. 'Ah, yes. There was that one time I invited him to become a member of the Southend Seven.'

That was news to Tomek.

'Good thing he said no,' he replied, trying to hide the surprise in his voice.

The smirk grew into a knowing grin. 'Is that what he told you?'

Tomek's eyes narrowed. 'What's that supposed to mean?'

'Nothing,' Brendan replied. 'I'm sure your saintly chief inspector has got nothing to worry about. I'm sure he'll be back by teatime.'

That unnerved Tomek slightly. That the possibility of one of his closest friends in the service could have agreed to becoming a member of a club that was directly involved in sex trafficking. Moreover, that Nick had lied to him. He had sworn blind that there was nothing else Tomek needed to know, just that he'd been included in a few and had had absolutely no involvement in the club whatsoever.

Now Tomek wasn't so sure.

'Anyway,' Brendan said, 'now that little parasite is swimming around your head, would you like to explain why you're here?'

Tomek cleared his throat. 'Does the name Morgana Usyk mean anything to you?'

'You mean the woman that died on the harbour the other day? Is that why you're here?'

Tomek said nothing.

'What's that got to do with me? I've been in here the whole time. Scout's honour.' Brendan held three fingers in the air.

'So, you've never heard that name before?'

'Only on the news.'

'What about Mariusz Stanciu?'

Brendan searched his memory for an entire second. 'No. Sorry.'

'Not a problem. This one might jog your memory,' Tomek continued. 'What can you tell me about Gavin Barker?'

'Who?'

'Gavin Barker, from your office... the head of the Safer Policing team.'

'Oh, you mean Gammy Gavin! Why? What's he done? Not had something to do with those people you mentioned, has he?'

Tomek pursed his lips. This wasn't going how he'd expected. Last night, he'd put together a plan – brief, simple – to get the information he needed. But it wasn't working. The man knew nothing. Perhaps Tomek had wanted so much for Brendan to be involved he'd almost convinced himself that he was, but there was something about the man's reaction that suggested he'd had no involvement with Morgana, Mariusz, or any of it.

'What can you tell me about Gavin?' Tomek asked, trying not to let his disappointment show.

'What would you like to know?'

'His personality. What's he like in the office?'

'A pushover. A coward. Next, come on, I can see on your face that you've got something you really want to ask me, but something's stopping you. Come on, Tomek, what is it? It's unlike you to shy away from saying what's really on your mind.'

Tomek didn't think the man knew him well enough to make that sort of judgement, but on the balance of things, it was pretty accurate.

'What about a man named Andrei Pirlog?' Tomek asked, his voice faltering slightly.

'Never heard of him.'

Almost as quick as the last one.

'You sure?'

Brendan folded his arms across his chest. 'Absolutely. Never heard of him. And that's the sort of name you'd remember, isn't it? Like the midfielder. Now, if you're not going to say what you've come here to say, then we might as well call it a day. Prison can be a busy place sometimes, and I've got plenty of things to be getting on with.'

'Like planning someone's murder?'

Tomek had originally intended to keep the comment in his head, but it had escaped his lips without hesitation, as though it had a mind of its own.

Excitement registered on Brendan's face, and he tilted forward in his seat.

'There it is. Bingo. You think I had something to do with a murder? Let me guess, you think that I, for whatever reason, had this Morgana woman killed, and that it had something to do with Gavin and those two other fellas you named? Oh, Tomek. You've not really thought this through, have you? I don't know any of those people. I've never heard of them in my life. And you know I don't, don't you? You haven't got any evidence to suggest I do, and you know it. You came in here thinking I would roll over and tell you anything you wanted to hear. But it didn't work out the way you wanted. Funny how life works that way. Any cards that you did have are now out on the table, face up, and you've lost. It's the shittest hand I've seen. You're supposed to be smart, a detective sergeant, no less. I expected better from you.'

And he expected better from himself. He'd completely fucked that entire interview. He'd crumbled. While it was still possible that Brendan was lying, that he knew about Morgana, Andrei, or Mariusz, and that he had known about the messages to Gavin, Tomek knew when he was beat.

He exited the interview room with a lump in his throat and a heavy weight on his chest. As soon as he jumped into the car, his Bluetooth automatically connected to his phone and began playing the podcast. He reached for the device and switched it off. The last thing he wanted to be reminded of was that a husband-and-wife partnership, with no prior experience, no training, no nothing, was doing a better job than him at the one he'd been doing for nearly twenty years.

Before pulling out of the car park, Tomek changed the address on his satnav. He had a detour to make.

CHAPTER
FORTY-THREE

Nick lived on the outskirts of Rochford, a small town that was a short drive away from CID headquarters. On the drive down, Tomek had passed at least half a dozen pelotons. Approximately twenty individuals cycling in the middle of the day, in the middle of the week. What were they doing for the rest of the week? Did they not have jobs? Or perhaps they were all so well paid they could afford to take four hours a day off to cycle around the countryside.

Tomek had never been big on cycling. Running, football, rugby, yes. Physical contact sports, whether it be with his feet against tarmac or a shoulder into the abdomen. Plus, he didn't think he had the body for it. He was over six feet, legs as thick as tree trunks, and judging from the average size of those he passed, he was the same width as three of them. He was top-heavy and would topple over at the first sign of a strong wind.

The cyclists, however, weren't the worst part of the journey. Coming directly from HMP Bedford had taken longer than he'd expected, this time thanks to an accident on the M25. He'd thought about postponing the visit and saving it for the day after, but he didn't want to wait, to let his thoughts and suspicions fester in his mind.

Better to do it this way.

Tomek pulled off the road and onto Nick's driveway. There, sitting in the middle of the gravelled driveway, was Nick's boyish Range Rover and Maggie's quiet, understated Citroën Berlingo. Since their daughter's accident, they had been forced to modify the family car to fit Lucy and her wheelchair into it. The same sort of modifications hadn't been made to the Range, he noticed.

The front garden was filled with stone statues and ornaments. A few metres from the front door was a small pond. A marble statue of a young boy with wings, water gushing from his mouth, stood proudly in the middle. The sound of the water cascading into the pond soothed him, and as he waited for the door to open, he closed his eyes and focused on his breathing.

In. Out. In. Out.

Processing the conversation in his head.

'Tomek?' came an excitable voice, pulling him out of his thoughts. 'What are you doing here? This is a pleasant surprise!'

Tomek opened his eyes to see Maggie, Nick's wife, standing in front of him. She seemed smaller than he remembered, older, more frail. In a short space of time, the bags beneath her eyes had grown, and they were now sagging on her face. Her eyes were bloodshot, and her cheeks had lost their colour. Caring for their now-disabled daughter had been unkind to her, and Tomek felt a pang of sympathy swell in his stomach.

He reached out his arms and embraced her.

'I thought I'd drop by to say hello,' he lied. 'It's been a while.'

'No Kasia?'

Tomek shook his head, then looked behind him in case she'd miraculously appeared without his realising. 'I've come from work,' he said. 'But I can always bring her over another time.'

'Oh, that would be wonderful. We'd like that. We could all have a lovely dinner together. Sunday roast. It's our family favourite.'

Tomek grinned. 'Sounds perfect. Tell me a time and date and I'll make sure we're available.'

'Oh, you bet!'

The excitement in Maggie's voice was overwhelming. Like it was the first time she was meeting him after having heard so much about him. Like it was the first time she'd seen or met someone other than her husband and daughters in over ten years. She eagerly pulled him into the house, told him in no uncertain terms that he could keep his shoes on if he wished, that it was no bother to her or anyone, that she could clean it up after, and then took him into the kitchen. The space was exactly as he remembered it. Stone tiled flooring, wooden dining table and chairs, island in the centre of the kitchen, cast-iron Aga on the side. Rustic, old-fashioned, like something out of an episode of *Escape to the Country*.

Maggie hurried to a cupboard and reached for a glass.

'Water? Wine? Whisky? Whatever you want, we've got it.'

'The lesser known who, where, what, why, when,' he joked. 'Water's fine. Don't want to go home driving under the influence. Think of the example that would set!'

Maggie cackled. 'Ha! Of course. How silly of me.'

When she handed him the glass, she massaged his arm innocuously. Possibly the first piece of human contact that she'd in a while.

'How have you been keeping?' she asked.

'Oh, you know, busy with work. Busy with Kasia.'

'She keeping you on your toes?'

'You can say that again. Who knew teenagers could be so confusing?'

'Try having two of them.'

'How are they getting on?' Tomek asked. 'Daniela getting on all right at school?'

'Oh, she's flying. Top in all her classes. She's loving it. We're so proud of her.'

Part of the way she said it made it seem like they weren't proud of Lucy, the one who was currently sitting in one of the rooms of the house somewhere, staring at the television, causing the massive rift in Nick and Maggie's marriage.

'I'm pleased to hear it,' Tomek said. 'Have you heard from Robbie recently?'

At the mention of her son's name, the excitement on Maggie's cheeks washed away. After several years of disagreements and bickering,

Robbie had left for the navy when he turned sixteen. He'd deserted the family, and kept contact to a minimum. The departure had been tough on them as a unit, and Tomek had been there to help pick up the pieces with Nick, consoling him in his office, offering what few words of wisdom he could draw upon. Incidentally, Tomek's experience of feeling like an outsider in his own family had helped Nick look at things from Robbie's angle, from the angle he potentially hadn't considered, and make some inroads to improving their relationship.

Maggie lowered her head, placed a hand on the kitchen surface for support. 'No,' she replied, weakly. 'We've not heard from him in a while. Though we do know that he's safe and being well looked after.'

'I heard on the news the other day that they might be bringing back national service if shit ever hits the fan. Fortunately, by the time it happens I'll be just outside the age bracket.'

Tomek didn't know why he'd said that. To fill the void, mask the silence, perhaps.

'Yes, you should consider yourself lucky.'

A brief pause.

'And...' he started. 'And how are *you* keeping? Looking after yourself?'

Maggie opened her mouth, but was cut off by the kitchen door opening. Standing there, frozen in the doorframe, was Nick.

'Tomek... What are you doing here?' He looked as though he'd just been caught with his trousers down.

'Tomek's just popped by to say hello.'

'Hello?' Nick repeated. 'Nobody pops by to say hello anymore. This isn't the eighties. And Tomek *especially* doesn't pop over just to say hello. He wants something. What do you want, Bowen?'

Nick released his grip on the handle and moved into the room.

'Don't talk to our guest like that,' Maggie said, jumping to Tomek's defence. 'You see, this is why we don't have people over.'

'No, we don't have people over because we don't invite people over.'

'And whose fault is that?' she said. 'You're the one who's out all the time. You're the one who knows more people than I do.'

Maggie folded her arms across her chest and sighed heavily. Must have been in the family.

Tomek's head bounced between them as they began their argument. He hadn't intended to cause a disagreement, but now he understood what Nick had been complaining about. The bickering, the tiniest things blown out of proportion, the sour taste it had left in everyone's mouths. There was a lot they weren't saying to each other, and some of it was coming out in front of him.

'We're not doing this here,' Nick said, quickly shutting the argument down. 'Not now.' He turned to Tomek. 'You're here to see me, I presume?'

'Well, I—'

'You don't have to lie anymore, kid.'

Tomek slowly turned to Maggie, who wore a look of defeat on her face. 'Could I see Lucy before we go up?'

'You want to *see* her?' Nick asked.

'Yeah, if that's all right?'

'Why do you say it like it's a bad thing, Nick?' Maggie asked, the disdain in her voice palpable.

Nick instantly shot her a look that said, 'don't start'. Then said: 'I just wasn't expecting you to come all this way to want to see her as well.'

Tomek shrugged. 'It's no problem at all. I'm sure she could do with the company, and Kasia's always asking about her.'

A half-lie. Kasia had mentioned Lucy's name twice since the incident, but they didn't need to know that.

A smile Tomek hadn't seen in a while stretched across his friend's face. 'In that case, come on round.'

Tomek followed Nick through the corridor and into their second living room at the back of the house, where Lucy was sitting on the other side of the door. Through the walls, Tomek could hear the sound of the television playing loudly. Something filled with canned laughter.

As Tomek stepped up to the door, Nick placed a hand on his chest.

'I must warn you, she's not the same as she used to be,' he said.

'I know,' Tomek replied. 'You've told me. Several times. But I'm not afraid. She's not contagious. Besides, I've seen worse. Much worse, remember?'

Nick grunted, then opened the door. It took a few moments for Lucy to register their arrival, and when she did, she turned her head slowly. Calculations played on her face as she tried to remember who Tomek was. With a little help from Nick, she remembered.

'How you doing, kid?' Tomek asked as he glanced at the television screen. She was watching *Friends*.

'Aside from a massive hole in the side of my head, I'm okay,' Lucy replied in good spirits. 'Though Dad will probably tell you I've got the plague or something.'

Tomek chuckled. 'He's just worried because he's getting old. He thinks next time he gets the flu that might be it for him.'

This time it was Lucy's turn to laugh. Her voice drowned out the sound of the TV and carried through the rest of the house. Tomek wondered how long it had been since the sixteen-year-old had last laughed like that. Since she had last felt even a morsel of happiness. If Nick's stories were anything to go by, not at all since the accident.

'Have your teachers been sending you homework and revision notes?' Tomek asked.

But she didn't reply. At least, not at first. Her brain had switched off and focused back on the programme before eventually returning to him.

'Homework?'

'Yeah. Kasia got loads of homework and lesson notes when she was off for a week or two. The teachers said it was to keep her busy, but that was the last thing she wanted to do.'

'Oh... No... I don't think so.' She turned to Nick. 'Do I... Dad?'

'No, sweetheart, you don't. And even if you did, I wouldn't give it to you. Schoolwork is the last thing you should worry about.'

'Oh... Okay.'

'You should consider yourself lucky,' Tomek told her. 'I wasn't that nice to my daughter.'

'Yeah...'

And then he lost her completely. Her eyes washed over and her attention gradually returned to the television like a wind dial on a still day. Nick took that as their cue to leave and pulled Tomek out of the room. Shutting the door behind him, he said, 'Thanks for doing that. You didn't have to.'

'I wasn't doing it for you. I was doing it for her. I'd like to bring Kasia down one afternoon. It might cheer her up a bit, get her mind working in a different way. Plus, I think Kasia's probably bursting at the seams with gossip from school.'

'But they're different year groups.'

'Kids gossip regardless, Nick. You went to school, right? Or were they just introducing them to the general public when you were that age?'

'Fuck off.'

With that, Nick took him upstairs to his office. The room was dark, but not in a depressing way. There was little light in there, and what light came through the windows was absorbed by the dark wooden furniture of the bookshelves and large desk in the middle. It was more like a study taken from an Agatha Christie novel than a detective chief inspector's place of work.

Nick didn't bother sitting behind his desk.

'What's this about, Tomek? Should I be worried that you've come here unannounced?'

'That depends on what you tell me.'

'About what?'

'About Brendan.'

'What have you got to do with that?'

'I've just spoken to him. Someone from his office has been leaking information.'

'About what?'

'The harbour case. He told Andrei Pirlog's killer where Andrei was living, and now his killer's been killed, thanks to someone from the PFCC office leaking that information as well. There's a lot to catch you up on.'

'So, someone's been pulling strings and pushing the right buttons to get the necessary people killed?' Nick asked, the calculations inside his mind playing on his face.

'Can see you're not going to dust between the ears just yet,' Tomek remarked.

'And you think Brendan had something to do with it?'

'I *did*. But now I'm not so sure.'

'So how do I fit into it?'

Tomek held his breath.

'He said something that raised suspicions. About your involvement with the Southend Seven.'

Nick sighed heavily, ran his hand over his scalp. 'And you believed him?'

'I just need to know if it's true.'

'What did he say?'

'Is it true?'

'Don't you trust me?'

'Is it true, Nick?'

The chief inspector's blatant avoidance concerned him.

'I'm not going to answer the question unless I know what I'm being charged with.'

'He was vague,' Tomek replied. 'He made me doubt your version of events. He alluded to the fact that you *had* joined the club, and that you had been to a few events there...'

Another sigh, this time filled with less despair.

'And you believed him?'

'Right now, I don't know what to believe. You promised that the IOPC wouldn't find anything.'

'Then believe what I'm about to tell you.' Nick stopped running his hands over his head and stood upright. 'Yes, he's right, I went to the Southend Seven – *once!* – but I never saw anything, and I never did anything. There were no drugs and there was definitely no prostitution going on while I was there. It was a quiet evening, I guess you could say. After that I never went back.'

'What made you stay away?'

Nick lowered his head. 'It was too... too far removed from life – *my* life – from society. All those people there hate themselves, they hate their lives, their marriages, their kids. They live in their own little bubbles where they're the only people that matter. They're all there just tossing off each other's egos, and I didn't want to be a part of it. It's not who I am, it's not what I stand for. So, I politely declined. And now it feels like Brendan's dragging my name through the mud, that little fucknugget cunt.'

'Don't be afraid to say what you really think about him, sir,' Tomek replied with a weak smile on his face.

The two laughed, but it was tinged with a slight hint of awkwardness. Tomek believed the chief inspector, his *friend*, of course he did, but Brendan's seed of doubt was still firmly planted in his mind, and he didn't know what it would take to suppress it.

CHAPTER
FORTY-FOUR

Tomek pushed the seed of doubt to the back of his mind as he drove past Southend airport towards the city centre. The wind had picked up, and a light rainfall was knocking on the metal roof. He switched off the sound of the gentle, dull, thudding windscreen wipers that cut across his vision. His mind was totally focused on the next task.

Anton Usyk.

Morgana's, supposedly, loving husband.

Rachel had called him while he was at Nick's house, asking to meet her at the Usyk family home at four o'clock. But owing to Maggie's caring nature, she had insisted he stayed for another glass of water and some more chat. As a result, he'd pushed Rachel back to five o'clock. By the time he finally arrived, she was waiting for him in her Ford Fiesta, parked up at an awkward angle on the kerb.

Tomek slotted his car a few cars behind her and approached slowly. Her face was illuminated in the wing mirror a soft shade of blue. Distracted by her phone. Oblivious to his movements. Then he opened her car door suddenly and took a step back. The scream that erupted from her mouth travelled up and down the street, and rattled around his eardrums for a few seconds.

'Fuck me!' she yelled, unbuckling herself and launching out of the car. 'You could've given me a heart attack, for fuck's sake, you silly chino-wearing dickhead!'

Tomek chuckled, then looked down at his trousers. 'Hey, what's wrong with my chinos?'

'Nothing, I just wouldn't have picked that colour for you,' she said calmly. Then she remembered she was supposed to be angry with him and slapped him on the chest. 'The fuck did you do *that* for?'

'Funny.'

'You won't be laughing when I get you back ten times harder.'

'That sounds like a threat. Did your mum never teach you to treat your elders with respect?'

'Not when they're arseholes.'

When Rachel settled down, a minute or two later, they made their way to Anton and Morgana's house. Immediately after her death, a team of uniformed constables and forensics officers had been sent round to gather samples and DNA evidence, so Anton was no stranger to having police officers inside his home. However, when he opened the door, he looked concerned to see them standing there.

'What is this about?' he asked. 'Let me guess, you have a few more questions?'

'They're important,' Rachel answered. 'We'd appreciate it if you could let us in,' she added politely, though from her intonation he had no choice.

The inside of the Usyks' house was in stark contrast to Nick's. There was no identity, no sense that anyone had lived there for the last thirteen years. The walls were blank, the kitchen tiles plain, the furniture lifted straight from an IKEA catalogue. For a couple that were clearly successful, with both Morgana's and Iliana's turning a profit (according to the research Nadia had done at Companies House), Anton and Morgana's house was modest, understated, flying well below the radar. There was nothing extravagant about it, nothing showy, nothing over the top. They were living well within their means, and it showed. Perhaps it was because they were hardly home that they hadn't given it any character, or perhaps it was just a reflection of their personalities. Instead it was clear to see Anton spent all their profits on designer clothes. Though Tomek was pleased that the house didn't match the garish diamanté mirrors and pink furniture of their respective restaurants.

Anton ushered them into the kitchen. The room was complete with a small dining table and chairs, and was separate from the rest of the house. A small window looked out onto the side of the property next to them.

'I would offer you a hot drink, but I've seen enough of it for one day,' Anton said, already hinting that he was going to be less than cooperative.

'I suspect you probably feel the same way about food when you get home as well?' Tomek mocked as he pulled out a chair from the dining table and placed one leg over the other.

'I imagine you can't stand *people* at the end of your day,' Anton said, his voice sullen.

'This should be an interesting conversation then.'

Sensing the tension in the air, Rachel cleared her throat and stepped between them. In situations like this, she was the more professional representative, and in this instance, Tomek was more than happy to let her take over. 'Mr Usyk, the other day, a man was killed in prison. He was arrested and charged in connection with your wife's murder.'

'Good.'

'Excuse me?'

'It is good.'

Tomek's intuition started to tingle. As did Rachel's, because her face tightened.

'What do you mean, "good"?'

'He received what he deserved.'

'You say that as though you know something about what happened to him?'

Anton, straight-faced, his piercing black eyes staring into Rachel, shook his head. 'Does the penguin think it is bad when the killer whale eats a seal?'

Tomek sniggered at the cryptic Eric Cantona-like quote, then asked, 'Which one are you? The penguin, the killer whale, or the seal?'

It was obvious to everyone in the room that Mariusz had been the seal, which left only two options for Anton: the killer whale, or the penguin. And right now, Tomek's intuition was telling him that Anton Usyk was the black and white orca, the four-tonne predator. But that left the obvious question: who was the third member? Who was the penguin?

'*I* am the penguin,' Anton replied. 'The man who was killed is the seal, and the man who killed him is the killer whale.'

Rachel and Tomek shared a disconcerted look.

'The man who killed the victim – the man you are calling the killer whale in this bizarre, confusing analogy – was someone we believe you know. Someone we believe you know very well.'

'Who?' Anton's voice remained flat, static.

'A man named Denis Danyluk.'

'We do not speak his name in this house.'

'You know him?'

'Yes.'

'Who is he?'

'Morgana's brother.'

'Why are you not allowed to mention him?' Tomek asked, leaning forward in his seat.

'Because Morgana banned it. He betrayed her and her family name when he killed that man.'

'But what about now? Has he not redeemed himself now that you know he killed the man arrested in connection with your wife's murder?'

Anton didn't answer.

'Surely he must have found retribution in your eyes? He got justice for the man who killed Morgana.'

Anton's face didn't move. Like the last time they'd met, he gave nothing away in his expression.

'What he did to that man was unacceptable—'

'Which one? The guy he killed years ago or the one he killed just the other day.'

'Both.'

'So, killing on the whole is bad in your eyes?'

Anton shifted his weight from one foot to the other. Rachel took a step back to clear the floor between them. 'Do you not agree? Killing of any kind is not permitted.'

'Why is that?'

'Because it is against God,' Anton replied.

Tomek smirked. 'I see. So where does God fit into your little food chain hierarchy?'

Anton flexed his muscles. It was only a small, minute movement, but Tomek saw the man tense up. 'He doesn't,' Anton replied.

'Interesting.' Tomek leant back in the chair.

'When was the last time you spoke to Denis?' Rachel interrupted, keen to move the conversation along from whatever was going on between Tomek and Anton.

'Not since before he was sentenced.'

'And when was that exactly?'

'I... I do not remember the exact date.'

'What about the month?'

'I... I do not remember. It has been so long.'

'Could you give us the year, at least?'

Anton's face contorted, deep in thought. 'Eight years ago, I think. Like I said, we do not talk about him. We did not discuss him since he went to prison. It upset Morgana too much. She always cried whenever he came up in conversation.'

'I see. I can understand that. It must have been very tough on her and her family.'

'It was. She cried for months afterwards.'

Rachel moved towards the other side of the kitchen and leant against the counter. She straightened the front of her jacket and folded her arms. 'Why didn't you mention she had a brother to us sooner?'

'What do you mean?' Anton asked, obviously stalling.

'If you knew she had a brother in prison, why didn't you say something when we first spoke to you about her murder?'

'What difference would it have made? He had nothing to do with her death. There was no need to mention him. As far as we are concerned, he does not exist. That is why I did not say anything to you.'

Rachel nodded, cleared her throat. She had no response. Neither did Tomek. There was nothing more they could discuss. Tomek thanked the man for his time, apologised for disturbing him, then left. As he exited the kitchen, he asked if he could use the bathroom.

'No,' Anton replied. 'The toilet does not flush at the moment. I have been trying to fix it this afternoon.'

'What have you been using in the meantime?'

'The restaurant.'

'That's a hell of a journey just for a piss. Bet you wish you really were a penguin, don't you? That way you can just go whenever you want.'

The sides of Anton's lips moved in a forced grin as he held the door open for him.

'Good to see you, Detectives,' he said. 'Take care of yourselves.'

As they stepped out of the house, Tomek turned to Rachel and whispered, 'Something tells me he doesn't mean that in the slightest.'

CHAPTER
FORTY-FIVE

S omething was missing. Something Tomek couldn't quite put his finger on.

The atmosphere. The smell. The sight. The location.

Iliana's was completely different to Morgana's in every way, except when you boiled it down to the fundamentals, they were exactly the same. They both served the same food. They were both styled in a similar fashion. And they both occupied great positions in their respective areas – if nothing else, Iliana's had the higher footfall along the seafront. It didn't make sense to Tomek why then Morgana's was financially the more successful restaurant. He didn't think it was down to just her meeting and greeting customers with a warm smile. There must have been something missing.

Though he had an idea, a justification for the significant turnover differences.

The possibility that Morgana and her husband were selling drugs through their restaurants had briefly entered his mind after the connection between Gavin Barker and Brendan Door had been made. It was no secret that drugs, in particular cocaine, had been prevalent at the parties inside the Southend Seven Gentlemen's Club. It had been well-documented in the newspapers following the investigation, and Tomek had seen it first-hand on a photograph hanging from one of the walls in the building. But the drugs had found their way in there somehow, which meant they had needed a supplier. The theory had been that Richard Stafford, wanted and investigated by the drug squad for years, had supplied them, however, nothing had come from it.

Tomek had started to think that there might have been a link there somehow. A tenuous one, but a link, nonetheless.

Perhaps Morgana and her husband had been propositioned by Richard Stafford. Perhaps they agreed to sell the drugs through the restaurant, launder the money, and then give a portion of the product to the gentlemen's club. In return they would be protected by the police through Brendan Door. Perhaps there had been a disagreement following Brendan's arrest. Perhaps the Usyks had feared that their names would come out in the wash. Perhaps Brendan and Richard Stafford had ordered Morgana to be killed, that Mariusz had been a hired hand, and that he'd leant on Gavin to cover up the loose end in the aftermath. Perhaps Morgana's killing had been a message to Anton: continue selling the drugs, continue following our orders and sending the money our way, otherwise we will kill you.

Tomek thought it was a bit of a stretch, but he'd experienced far stranger situations. And at least it would go some way to explaining why Anton was such a miserable bastard, aside from the obvious fact that it was because his wife was dead.

Tomek nursed those thoughts, juggled with them, as the waitress approached his table. It was the same girl as before. Gina. Wearing the same outfit that she'd been wearing the last time Tomek had seen her, except this time it was slightly tighter, cropped in the middle, and she was wearing considerably more make-up, in an effort, he supposed, to bring more punters in.

'You're back,' she said.

'I enjoyed myself so much last time, I couldn't wait to come again.'

She saw through the lie, but still offered him a muted, stilted giggle. As she handed him the menu, she cast a quick glance back to the kitchen.

'Is the boss working this morning?' Tomek asked.

'Yes. He is out the back.'

'Did he manage to get his toilet fixed?'

Confusion swept across her. 'The toilet? There is one down there on your left.'

'No, I meant Anton's toilet has—' Tomek looked up at her, smiling. 'You know what? Never mind.' He set the menu down. He already knew his order. 'How long have you been working for Anton?'

Gina glanced back again. Tomek felt inclined to do the same, but he kept his gaze focused on her.

'A few weeks now,' she replied, her voice as low as a whisper.

'You enjoy it?'

'It is okay, I guess.'

'What were you doing before working here?'

'I was in another coffee shop.'

'Morgana's?'

At the mention of her name, Gina's eyes widened slightly, and her pupils dilated.

'It's okay,' he said. 'You can say her name.'

'Yes. Of course. I know. It's just...'

Tomek took a moment before replying. She was swaying from one foot to the other, scratching at her thigh with fingernails that had been chewed down until there was almost nothing left.

'Would you prefer to talk in Polish?' he asked in the language.

Hesitation. 'Please,' she replied in kind.

'Did you know her? Morgana?'

'I only met her once, maybe twice. She...' Another look towards the back. 'She came in one day, angry, but—'

And then she stopped, withdrew into herself, and continued scribbling on the piece of paper in her fingers.

A moment later, Anton arrived, placing a hand on her shoulder. She began to shake, the paper and pen bouncing from side to side as she was suddenly gripped by nerves.

'So that's a cup of coffee and eggs on toast?' she said.

Tomek was bemused for a moment, then he realised what she was doing.

'Yes, please, that would be great.'

She left. Anton watched her go, then once she was out of sight, sat opposite him.

'Morning, Anton,' Tomek said as he poured himself a glass of tap water from the jug that had been provided. 'You all right, mate? How's the plumbing? Get it all fixed?'

'Not quite,' Anton replied dryly. 'I am expecting someone to come over this afternoon.'

'Great. Well, like I said last night, it's a good thing you've got this place, otherwise, you'd have been shitting outside like a wild fox, or in your case, a wild penguin. Or was it a killer whale?'

Anton said nothing, continuing to stare at him. He sat with his fingers knitted together, hands resting calmly on the surface. Today he'd opted for a Prada top and a matching pair of trousers.

'Why are you here, Detective?'

Tomek shimmied his body to the side, so that his legs stuck out of the booth, then placed one leg over the other.

'I'm here to sample some more of your fine food, of course. After seeing the latest accounts at Companies House, I thought this place could do with the business.'

'Thank you,' he said, 'but we do not want your business here.'

'Now it makes sense why this place hasn't been doing so well. I don't know anything about the hospitality industry, but I wouldn't recommend insulting all your customers. Think of the Tripadvisor reviews!'

The unassuming, unyielding face said nothing.

Before Tomek could antagonise him any further, Gina returned, two cups and saucers in hand. She delicately set the cup in front of Tomek, smiling down at him as she did so.

'Thanks.'

'*Nie ma za co.*'

'Yes, thank you. You can go now,' Anton instructed her with a dismissive flick of the hand.

Without saying anything, the woman left and hurried away, back to the kitchen. As soon as she was out of earshot, Tomek grabbed a sachet of sugar from the small container on the table, flapped it between his fingers, then decanted it into his drink. As he stirred the contents, he felt Anton's unrelenting stare burning into him. The man hadn't moved in the last five minutes, and the only indication that he wasn't dead was the steady rise and fall of his chest.

'I always look forward to our chats, Anton,' Tomek said. 'Speaking of which, I'm glad you dropped by, actually. You... you wouldn't happen to know the name Brendan Door, would you?'

Anton's face gave nothing away.

'No? You wouldn't happen to know anything about the rumours going around, would you?'

Tomek could see it in the man's face that he wanted to nibble on the comment. All Tomek had to do was give him enough time to convince himself it was the right thing to do.

'What... what rumours?'

Hook. Line. Sinker.

'Some people are saying you guys are pushing drugs through the restaurants – both of them. You wouldn't be doing that, would you, Anton?'

'Of course not. You can check if you like. We have nothing to hide.'

Tomek was thinking he might do just that, when Anton thanked him for his custom, said that he wasn't welcome back, then stood up to leave.

'So soon?' Tomek asked. 'I was hoping to find out more about you.'

But then the food arrived, and the desire to antagonise and interrogate Anton quickly disappeared. For the next ten minutes, he took his time with the food, delicately cutting his toast into little squares, chewing slowly, pausing after every mouthful, staring out at the seafront below. Taking in the sights. It was the first time he'd noticed the water on the horizon, shimmering beneath the weak sunlight as the ripples continued their random and mindless path towards London. In the distance, Tomek thought he saw the small blotch of Mulberry Harbour. Then his mind turned to the morning of Morgana's death. Had she driven past Iliana's on the way to the slipway? Had she stared at the harbour as she'd driven along the seafront? Had she known she was heading towards her death?

Tomek's thoughts were disturbed by a customer entering the café. He quickly returned his attention to his food. After he finished the last few mouthfuls, he pushed the plate to one side and drank the last of his drink. Far too sweet for his liking, but tolerable. As he slid it in front of him, he noticed a small, white piece of paper tinged with a hint of brown, wedged underneath. Looking around him, making sure that Anton was out of sight, he pinched his fingers together and carefully removed it.

It was a note. Handwritten.

From Gina.

In Polish.

Outside. Tonight. 10 pm. There is something you must know.

CHAPTER
FORTY-SIX

As soon as Tomek stepped through the entrance, he was stopped by a soft, gentle voice calling out to him.

'Good evening, Tomek.'

His neighbour. Edith. The retired woman who lived beneath them.

'Heya,' he said. 'Is everything okay? Is it time for me to take another water meter reading already?'

'No. Nothing like that.' She shut her door behind her. She was dressed in a thick coat, and a dark green woolly hat. They lived in a converted house, and the only space they shared was the small hallway that separated their two flats. It was cramped, and a chilly breeze crept in through a gap in a brick wall. 'I'm off out for dinner with an old friend actually,' she continued.

'That's nice.'

The countdown in his mind until ten o'clock was ticking.

Ticking.

Ticking.

He forced himself not to check his watch.

'Yes, it should be nice. She's an old work friend. It's been a few years since we last saw each other. Too long, in fact. Much too long. This is something we should have done months ago, if not years. But... you know how it is. Life gets in the way. We all get so busy with our own lives that we forget to include other people in them sometimes.'

'Yeah,' Tomek said, his mind drifting gently towards Sean and Warren.

'And then by the end of it all, you spend your last few years alone, trying to make up the ground you lost.'

Tomek placed a hand on her shoulder. 'You're not alone,' he told her. 'You've always got Kasia and me. Any time you feel lonely, you can always knock and see what she's up to.'

'Oh, you're too kind, bless you, but I imagine she's got so many friends at her age that they're all keeping her busy from one day to the next.'

Tomek wasn't sure about "so many". One or two, yes, but what harm would one more do? Perhaps it might do Kasia some good to speak with someone outside of her age range. Perhaps she could confide in Edith. Perhaps the pensioner could be the quiet, calm, experienced ear she needed. The mother figure that Kasia didn't have.

'Nonsense,' he said. 'I'll send her down at the weekend. I'll give her one of our board games you two can play, and if I'm free, I'll come and join you too, if that's all right?'

Edith's face warmed. 'I'd like that. Thank you.'

As soon as she was gone, Tomek thrust his key into the lock and sprinted up the stairs two at a time. He burst through the door at the top of the steps and found Kasia sitting on the sofa again, scrolling, staring into her phone.

'There you are,' he said. 'Just the person I'm looking for.'

'Hey.'

'Did I get any post?'

Without responding, her attention entirely focused on her screen, she pointed to the table. A large brown box had been discarded on the surface at a jaunty angle.

'Aren't you going to open it?'

'Why would I?' she asked. 'It's addressed to you.'

'Yes. But it's *for* you.'

Intrigued, Kasia rolled her legs off the side of the sofa and, like a wary animal approaching another predator's kill, she tentatively reached for it and began opening it. She hacked at the tape and the corners with her fingernails before eventually conceding defeat and asking for a pair of scissors. Tomek handed them to her, and she cut her way through with ease.

When she finally opened it, her face illuminated. Inside, beneath the cardboard and paper packaging, was the salmon pink of the bottle she'd asked for the other day. A Winston cup. Nearly a foot tall and a couple of inches wide, it was large enough to knock someone out.

'Fuck a duck,' he said. 'Look at the size of it. At least you get your money's worth.'

'And when there's a fire, this thing will still be standing – now *that's* value for money.'

Tomek took it from her to inspect for himself. 'Well, let's hope there won't be any of those any time soon. At least not around here.'

The cup was heavy, like a cinder block, and had a matte finish to it. He unscrewed the cap (after a couple of unsuccessful attempts) and peered inside. The contents of the container were made of steel and at the bottom, he saw his reflection, enlarged in all the wrong places thanks to the concave design. Tomek gripped the handle tightly and began swinging it around, lashing it in a downward motion. 'Come to think of it, you can always use this thing for self-defence.'

As Tomek raised it above his head to throw the final blow at his imaginary opponent, Kasia intervened and took it from him. 'Well, let's hope nothing like *that* happens, either.'

'Yes,' he said. 'You're right.'

A few moments passed, and he watched Kasia interact with the cup. By now the excitement had gone and it had just become another inanimate object. Though he didn't think there was much to get excited about when it came to a cup – it was hardly an iPhone – he would have thought she'd be a little bit happier.

'What's the matter?' he asked. 'Is it not the right one?'

'No. Yes! Yes, it is. I love it. Thank you.'

She shuffled towards him and gave him a hug.

'Then why do you look like you're not happy?'

'I am. Honestly. Thank you, but you didn't have to. I feel guilty now, bad that I even asked for one. You were right, it's stupid.'

'Not if it makes you happy. Remember that.'

The life lesson was lost on Kasia, as she offered him a forced smile, said thanks again, then returned to her space on the sofa.

Tomek checked his watch. 8:30 pm. He still had a little under two hours until the meet, but he was nervous, anxious to get there on time, to make sure he didn't miss it. He didn't know what Gina had to tell him, but if it was something she didn't feel confident or comfortable telling him in person – under the all-hearing ears of Anton – then it must have been important.

Tomek spent the next hour on edge, constantly checking his watch, and looking at his phone for the time. He was caught in that infuriating waiting stage. Like at the airport, waiting for the plane. Or a doctor's appointment. When you can't do anything except wait, and nothing you try as a distraction works. In the end, he kept himself occupied with looking after Kasia. Feeding her, watching the television with her, pretending to take an interest in her mind-numbing programmes.

He tried to switch off, but to no avail.

When the time finally came for him to leave, it occurred to him he hadn't told her about his day; he'd been so focused on the meet that it had completely slipped his notice.

'I went to see Lucy today.'

'Lucy who?'

Tomek looked at her blankly. He hoped the disappointment on his face was obvious. 'Your friend, Lucy. Lucy Cleaves.'

'Oh, right. Sorry, I thought you meant someone else.'

'Hmmm. Anyway, I've said we'll go over there one time as a family to see her.'

'Why?'

Tomek couldn't believe what he was hearing. 'Because she's your friend, and she needs your support. She's been lonely since her incident.'

'But I was going to meet up with someone else this weekend.'

'Who?'

'Yasmin.'

'Yasmin, who was there on the same night on the beach?'

'Yeah.'

'Not anymore. You're coming, and that's that. No more talk on the matter. If you were in her position, you'd appreciate the company. Don't be so selfish.'

Kasia lowered her phone to her chest. 'Will Abigail be coming?'

Tomek hesitated before answering. 'I haven't invited her. But I wasn't going to if you must know.'

He placed his hand on the door. One last check of the time.

'Before I leave,' he said, 'do you remember Sean, my colleague?'

'The big guy?'

'Yeah.'

'Yeah, I remember him.'

'Well, he's being chucked out of his house and needs a place to stay. He's asked if he can sleep on the couch for a couple of nights until he gets himself somewhere to stay more permanently, but I said I'd ask you first.'

'And what do you feel about the situation?'

'I don't like the idea of it, but I'll only agree to it if you're comfortable having him there.'

'So *now* you consult me. When it comes to your friends. But when it comes to seeing my friends and my plans, you've already decided them for me.'

'I don't do that.' Tomek inhaled deeply. 'It's not the same, and you know it.'

It wasn't the same, was it?

CHAPTER
FORTY-SEVEN

A light rainfall had started almost the moment he stepped out of the car. After five minutes of waiting, it had become heavier, and heavier, until eventually he'd been forced to retreat to the safety and cover of his driver's seat, where he would have to watch and wait for Gina from the comfort of his leather upholstery.

But she wasn't there.

After ten minutes, there was still no sign of her.

Then ten minutes turned into twenty.

Twenty into thirty.

By minute thirty-one, the rain had become horizontal and was lashing at the car from all angles. The windscreen wipers, despite giving it their best, were fighting a losing battle. And Tomek quickly felt the same way.

What infuriated him most was that he didn't have a contact number for her, no way to reach out and speak with her discreetly.

All that waiting. For nothing.

He tried not to think that something bad had happened to her. Rather, he hoped that she'd got cold feet, or had second thoughts. Or maybe even just got distracted by something at home. A family emergency, a family event she'd double-booked on the calendar. But from the way Anton had been around her, the way he'd spoken to her, touched her, the way he'd been surreptitiously intimidating... and those quick, nervous glances back to the kitchen – Tomek hadn't liked those.

The sensation that Anton could appear at any moment crept into the car, and his imagination got the better of him; as he glanced in the rear-view mirror, he thought he saw the man sitting in the back seat, his impervious stare chasing him down.

'Christ on a fucking bike!' he yelled, his heart rate spiking.

It was just a reflection of light bouncing awkwardly off a seatbelt. But as he turned round to catch his breath, something else caught his eye. A figure. Slight, small, the same build as Gina, wearing a light coat with a hood pulled over her head. It looked as though it was ill-equipped to deal with the rain.

Uncertain it was her, Tomek gently opened the door and made his way towards the figure.

'Hello...' he said cautiously.

At the sound of his voice, the woman spun round. The low light from the streetlamp not too far from the café's entrance revealed her to be someone else, a stranger.

She let out a little squeak. 'You what?' she hissed, her Essex accent thick. 'Who're you?'

'Nobody. Never mind.' Tomek turned to leave. 'Sorry I disturbed you. Have a good—'

'Help! Somebody help me!'

Her voice carried on the wind. As soon as Tomek heard it, he panicked, forgot that he was a police officer, and hurried to his car. By the time he made it, she was already gone; had sprinted into the darkness of the seafront a few hundred yards away. Tomek decided he didn't want to stay any longer, that it wasn't worth the fight, and so headed home.

Tomorrow, he told himself as he tore through the streets of Southend, on edge. Tomorrow. He would come back tomorrow and speak with her then.

CHAPTER
FORTY-EIGHT

Tomek was sitting in the same parking space. It was a little before eight o'clock, and there was no sign of life outside Iliana's. The pavements, however, were busy with commuters rushing towards the train station, cutting through the various alleyways and shortcuts, but still no sign of Gina.

No sign of anyone he recognised, in fact.

Shortly after eight, a woman Tomek didn't know approached the restaurant. She walked with the confidence of someone who knew what she was doing, rather than a customer tentatively tiptoeing towards the restaurant to see if it was open for the day.

When Tomek saw her keys, he hopped out of the car and skipped over.

'Sorry, we are not open yet,' she said without looking at him. 'Please wait.'

Tomek opened his mouth, but nothing came out. Something had washed over him, switched his mind off, and he couldn't think what to say. In the end, he settled on, 'Of course. I'm happy to wait.'

Then he spent the next ten minutes standing outside like an angry customer wanting to return something they'd bought the day before, except when he entered, he didn't storm up to the cash desk and throw the item down as though it was the assistant's fault the item didn't fit. Instead, Tomek headed straight to his booth on the side of the room. This time, he faced the other way, and was now watching the kitchen. He scanned the faces. He didn't recognise any of them. It was a completely new roster of workers: all men, all wearing the same white apron. Tomek was certain he hadn't seen any of them before.

That thought reminded him.

As he sat there, waiting for a member of staff to come up to him, he pulled out his phone and loaded Iliana's website. At the top of the page was a white banner, with the Tripadvisor logo on it. Tomek clicked on the banner and was taken to Iliana's page on the review site.

Just beneath the café's logo was their star rating: 2.4/5.

Less than attractive to prospective customers or tourists looking for a nice place to visit. Morgana's, by contrast, was sitting proudly with a healthy 4.3/5. Not perfect by any means, but far better than Iliana's. Anton was running the café into the ground, and when he read some of the customer reviews, obviously starting with the lowest, he found out why. A litany of messages saying that the customer service was crap, that the staff were rude, and that they never saw the same employee twice. Some of his favourite responses were: "Probably get better service in a Russian prison", "Think I'd rather shit in a cup and eat it than come back here – it'll probably taste nicer", "There's someone new there every five minutes, they must have a higher turnover than a prostitute's bedroom". And his personal favourite: "Wouldn't even bring my worst enemy here. This place is worse than hell." Tomek thought it might have been a bit too much, but people were entitled to their opinion, and he wasn't about to start arguing with them online. That was when the craziness started.

Fortunately, he was pulled away from the scathing reviews by the woman he'd met out the front. Her face was flat, and she had an attitude to match. They'd only been open five minutes and already she looked like she'd had enough.

'What do you want?' she asked. Eastern European, though she spoke with an American accent.

'Where's the woman that was here yesterday?' he asked.

'What woman?'

'Gina.'

'I... I don't know. This is my first day.'

'Okay,' he said, confused. 'I don't want a drink or anything. I'm all right for now. I'll wait.'

'You want to wait?'

'Yes.'

'You're going to just sit there?'

'Yes.'

'You don't want a drink or anything?'

'Not for now, thanks.'

'Okay...'

With that, she turned away from him and started towards the kitchen. For a long while he was the only person in there, and since he hadn't ordered anything, there wasn't a lot for the kitchen staff to do, so they huddled together, discussing amongst themselves, constantly looking at him. Tomek tried not to get paranoid about it and take it personally – that they were taking the piss out of his hair, or mocking him for the way his beard didn't quite meet up on his cheek – instead he tried to listen, to observe. Over the years he had developed the art of listening without listening, and liked to think he could pick things up from afar (though Abigail would say otherwise). From what he could decipher, they were speaking Romanian. But while the languages were very similar, he was unable to decipher any meaning.

It wasn't until a second customer came in that he hailed the waitress down again.

'Where's Anton?' he asked her.

'Anton?'

'The bloke who hired you.'

'Yes...' She suddenly turned tense, afraid. 'I know Anton. I... I do not know where Anton is. Nobody has seen him since yesterday.'

'Who?'

'Pardon?'

Tomek realised he was going to have to speak in full sentences if he wanted a response out of her.

'Who from the kitchen staff that is working today hasn't seen him since yesterday?'

The cogs slowly turned in her head as she struggled to process the question. *Fuck this*, he thought. He didn't have time to wait. Not when there was still no sign of Gina. He shuffled out of the booth, peeling his arse and legs from the faux leather, and stormed towards the kitchen. He banged his fist to grab the chefs' attention, then once he had it, said, 'Does anyone know where Anton is?'

Five bemused and perplexed faces stared back at him, as though he were speaking a foreign language. It wasn't lost on him that many of them probably didn't understand him.

'Anton. Your boss,' he reiterated. 'Does anyone know where he is?'

Still nothing. Then one of them stepped forward. He looked tired, beaten, with a pair of broken glasses hanging loosely on the end of his hooked nose.

'Anton's not working today,' the man said in almost perfect English.

'Do you know where he is?' Tomek asked.

'No. He did not say.'

'And *you* spoke to him, did you?'

'Yes.'

'When?'

'This morning. On his mobile. He called to say.'

'Right.' Tomek turned away to process the information. Neither Anton nor Gina had turned up. It was a little after nine am and there was still no sign of her, and Tomek was starting to think she wouldn't show. Had Anton found out about their secret meeting? Had he done something horrible to her?

Tomek started to think the worst. Before he could act on it, his phone vibrated in his pocket. He thrust his hand in there and retrieved the device. In his haste, he answered the call without looking at the caller ID.

'DS Bowen,' he said.

'Tomek? It's Rachel.'

Tomek moved away from the kitchen and returned to his seat. By now, the waitress had moved on to another customer.

'Ah, Miss Hamilton. If you're asking on behalf of a certain inspector why I haven't come into the office yet, then you can tell her I'm doing some important work.'

'What? Shut up. It's nothing to do with that. It's about Mariusz's phone.'

Tomek began digging the knife into the napkin, tearing through the fabric. 'I'm listening,' he said.

'Digital forensics has just finished going through it. I've got their report right in front of me.'

'And?'

'And they found a photo on Mariusz's phone that he'd sent to a withheld number on the morning of Andrei's death.'

Tomek already knew what was coming.

'The photo was of Andrei Pirlog, dead in his bathroom. There was no wording, no context behind the picture. It was almost as if it was—'

'Proof,' Tomek finished for her. 'Evidence that Andrei was dead.' He swung his legs out of the booth and began shimmying his body out again. 'I'm on my way now. I'll be there in five.'

He hurried out of the restaurant and sprinted towards his car. As he shut the door behind him, his phone began vibrating again. Again, in his haste, he answered without checking.

'Don't tell me you've found another photo,' he said.

'Erm...' came the confused response. Tomek glanced down at his phone, saw the caller ID, and swore under his breath. 'Is that Detective Bowen? It's Kirsty Redgrave. Where are you? Can we meet? We have something you might want to hear...'

CHAPTER
FORTY-NINE

Tomek had chosen Morgana's.

By the time he arrived twenty minutes later, the Redgraves were already waiting for him. Kirsty leapt out of her seat and shook his hand as soon as she spotted him.

'Thank you so much for coming,' she said, gratitude lacing her every syllable.

'It's no problem at all,' Tomek replied. 'Sorry I'm late. The bastard traffic was a nightmare.'

'Oh, yes. We're aware. Lots of traffic lights here. But that's something we Americans do really well. You should have seen us when we got to our first roundabout.'

Tomek smirked politely, though he was eager to get this over with as fast as possible. The news of the photograph had played on his mind on the drive over.

Kirsty introduced him to her family.

'This is Jimmy, my husband. Patricia, my daughter. Annabel, my mother-in-law, and Nelson, my son.'

Tomek immediately thought of the bully from *The Simpsons* – ha-ha! – and he had to admit the resemblance was almost uncanny. His hair was slicked back in a quiff, parted either side of his forehead, his shoulders were a combination of fat and the early signs of muscle, and his pudgy nose was too on the money.

Tomek seated himself opposite the young man, wedging himself between Kirsty and her husband. Annabel, the mother-in-law, wrapped an arm around Nelson.

'Would you like a drink of anything?' Kirsty asked Tomek.

He was about to say no when he realised they would only put it through on the expenses before flying back to America anyway, and so if he could have one on Victoria, then he would be a fool to say no.

'I could murder one, thanks.'

After he'd ordered, he asked, 'How have you been enjoying your extra-long stay? I trust everything's been sorted with the accommodation and the car rental?'

'Yes,' she said as she placed a hand on his shoulder. 'Everything's been magnificent. Everyone's been so helpful. And Anna – oh my god, we *love* Anna.'

'Yeah, she's a good egg.'

'Not only that, but she's so kind and compassionate. We could do with someone like her at the university.'

'Well, she's ours,' Tomek said, 'and you're not allowed her.'

The Redgrave family chuckled, whispering to one another as though he was on the outside of an in-joke that only Anna would get. A part of him wondered whether they were members of a cult, and this was a part of their initiation process to try to get him to join. First, they'd got Anna, now they were on to him.

He pushed the thought to the back of his mind.

'What about the figure you saw?' he asked, moving the conversation along. 'Any more sightings since?'

Kirsty placed a hand on his. 'Thankfully, nothing. We've not seen or heard a peep from any other neighbours, or noises from the garden, or even anything standing on the other side of the road. Something seemed to have scared them away.'

Yeah, a bloke called Denis Danyluk might have had something to do with that, Tomek thought.

'I'm glad to hear it. But if that isn't what you called me down for, then what is?'

Kirsty didn't answer. Instead, she pointed to her son.

At first, the young lad couldn't meet Tomek's gaze. He looked down at his fingers and played with them. Then, after Nelson looked to his mum for support, and she gave it to him with a gentle nod, he summoned enough courage to speak.

'Well, the other day – I mean last night…'

Ha-ha! Tomek heard that iconic sound in his head as soon as the teenager spoke.

Nelson hesitated. He'd hit a stumbling block and didn't know how to continue.

'It's all right, Nels. You can tell him. You're not in trouble,' said Kirsty, coming to his rescue.

That seemed to comfort the boy. 'Well, it was last night. We were walking along the seafront. We'd just been out for a meal on the high street and I wanted to have a look at the arcades. First, we did the one by the Kursaal then we made our way down. Then, as we came out of one of the places along the strip, something caught my eye.'

Strip, like Southend-on-Sea was the grimier, poorer equivalent of Vegas.

'It was a man, dressed in black,' Nelson continued.

'Right.'

'The same clothes as the man who fled the crime scene on the beach.'

'Right.'

'It reminded me of him.'

'Who?'

'The person who ran away!'

'Okay… Do you think it was him?'

'I don't know.'

'Right.'

Tomek didn't know where this was going. All they'd seen was a man who looked like the figure who'd fled the scene – Mariusz, who was dead.

'Tell him the rest,' Kirsty insisted, reaching across the table for her son's arm. 'There's something he's not telling you,' she said to Tomek.

Nelson turned shy again, lowering his head. 'I... I didn't think it was important at the time, you see, and it was because nobody else noticed them that I thought maybe I'd imagined them on the beach.'

'Noticed what, Nelson?'

'Last night, the man from the seafront was wearing the same shoes. That's what made me remember...'

'What shoes?'

'He was wearing a pair of red Christian Louboutins.'

Tomek looked at the kid blankly.

'Designer shoes,' Patricia, Kirsty's daughter, said as she thrust her phone in his face. On the screen was an image of a pair of red hi top trainers with studs that looked like they'd come from a BDSM sex toy on the toecaps.

Tomek recognised them instantly.

CHAPTER
FIFTY

S he had never expected this. It wasn't what her life was supposed to be like. It wasn't what she had planned. She'd hoped for a more fulfilling, more fruitful existence, for both her and her family back in Romania. But things had changed so quickly, so dizzyingly quickly, that she'd had barely any time to comprehend and process it.

She was in a small room. She knew that much. It was pitch dark, that much was decipherable as well. But she had no idea how long she'd been there for. Time had become distant, out of reach, but she knew she'd been there long enough to know the box. It's nooks and crannies. It's smooth, solid surfaces. So much so that it had almost become a friend.

At first there had been screaming, crying. Pounding her fists and kicking her feet against the concrete walls. Until the pain had become too unbearable for her to continue.

She didn't know what she'd done to deserve this, what sort of series of unfortunate events had led her here. Nor did she know how she was going to get out of it.

It seemed a certainty she was going to die. No water, no food. Soon there would be no air.

She would either starve, dehydrate, or suffocate. Whichever came first.

Though she didn't like to think about it. Instead, she occupied her thoughts with home, her husband, her mum and dad. How they had cared for her growing up, how she was grateful for everything they'd done, the sacrifices they'd made. They were all probably wondering where she was, like the last time something like this had happened. When she'd been younger. A toddler. She'd been playing at the beach with her sister on holiday. The two of them had gone off in search of a toilet. After ignoring their dad telling them several times to use the sea as their bathroom – "Dad! That's disgusting!" – they eventually set off, hand in hand, the sand moving beneath their toes. They had found a suitable cubicle a few hundred yards inland a short while after, but it was dirty, sweaty, covered in piss and with used toilet paper on the floor. The handle was rusty and required a great deal of effort to get it open, and graffiti covered the walls like the inside of an insane asylum. All in a foreign language. None of it made sense. But perhaps that had been a good thing; she'd seen some of the stuff that vandals and kids wrote on the walls nowadays and it disgusted her.

The cubicle was barely large enough for one of them, let alone two, and as the youngest, her selfish older sister had sent her in first. She'd been so desperate for the wee that she'd been able to ignore the mess, and had even forgotten to place toilet paper on the rim so fewer germs would come into contact with her skin. After she was finished, the filth of the place dawned on her and she tried to escape as quickly as possible. In her haste, however, she'd snapped the handle from the door, locking herself in. She'd banged on the door repeatedly, screaming until her lungs burst and she ran out of air. Her sister had screamed too, their cries separated by only a thin piece of metal.

Then her sister had told her she would find help, that she promised to return. A few seconds later, she was gone, leaving her alone in the putrid cubicle.

The first ten minutes had been filled with optimism, and hope that her sister would find support and return promptly. But as time gradually passed, the feeling dwindled, and the panic began to sink in. What if they weren't coming back? What if her sister had forgotten about her, or was playing some elaborate trick on her? What if something had happened to her sister?

Screaming. Punching the door.

Just as she was now.

Though by now the hope had all but gone.

After what had felt like two hours in the cubicle but had only been thirty minutes, her sister returned with support. And a few minutes later, she was saved. She had never hugged her family so tightly.

But now there was no one to hug. No one to save her. No one to rescue her from the darkness.

She searched for the corner of the room, her fingers running along the smooth surface. When she found it, she slid down to the floor, scrunching into a ball, and tucking her knees into her chest. Then she began to sob, thick tears streaming down her face. They didn't last long. Her body was so dehydrated that she had nothing left, nothing more to give. Instead, she lowered her head to her knees and forced her eyes shut. Her delirious and dehydrated imagination began creating wild scenarios and images in her head – cowboys, mountains, fish that she'd only ever seen on a television screen, her favourite shop she was allowed to visit.

And then she heard a sound.

At first, she thought it was the cash register opening in her mind. But then she heard it again and realised it wasn't that at all. It was *something*.

Something in the real world.

Something nearby, outside the confines of the small box.

A moment later, she heard the sound of metal clanking against metal.

Then the light came flooding in. Blinding her.

It was a long time before she could open them again. When she did, she saw a figure standing in front of her, a solid black demon against a backdrop of pure white.

'Get up,' it said. 'Come with me.'

CHAPTER
FIFTY-ONE

Tomek had found the man he was looking for in Morgana's café, sitting in the back room, pretending to be busy. With the help of two uniformed constables, Tomek had arrested him on suspicion of the murder of Morgana Usyk.

The man was now sitting opposite him in interview room one. Beside him was his solicitor, and next to Tomek was Rachel. They had reminded him of his rights and were now ready to proceed.

Tomek cleared his throat before beginning.

'Vlad, there are just a few more things we'd like to know regarding your whereabouts on the morning of Morgana's death.'

The man said nothing.

'In an original statement to us, you said that you had overslept and were still in bed. Do you remember saying that?'

'No comment.'

'You later went on to say that you'd woken up just after eleven. That right?'

'No comment.'

'You still stand by that?'

'No comment.'

'Can you remember what time you got into the café that morning?'

Vlad's expression remained blank. 'No comment.'

'Let me help you out then.' Tomek pulled open a small folder and placed a sheet on top of it. 'Our team got there at 12:45 and you were still nowhere to be seen. According to our team's reports, you didn't turn up until just after one. Do you see where I'm going with this?'

'No comment.'

Tomek let out a small sigh.

'Is there anyone who can corroborate your whereabouts for that morning?' Rachel asked. 'Because right now, all we have is your word for it. And with the way things are looking, that puts you firmly in the frame for murder.'

Vlad's eyes narrowed as he turned his head slowly to Rachel. 'No. Comment.'

'Very well,' she replied.

Tomek opened the folder again and produced two new sheets. On them were four still images taken from various CCTV angles across Southend seafront. After the Redgraves' discovery about the shoes, Chey had taken another look at the CCTV footage from across the seafront, this time looking for a pair of red Christian Louboutins, and had found who they believed to be their main suspect, emerging from the water by the pier. The figure's face, however, was still distorted and covered by the hood and scarf. But it was clear to see who they believed it to be.

In the photos in front of Vlad, Tomek had taken the decision to crop out the shoes.

For now.

'Do you recognise the man in these photos?' Rachel asked as she slid them across to him.

Vlad completely ignored them.

'No comment.'

'This is the person who we suspect of killing your boss, your closest friend. Do you recognise this person?'

Rachel prodded it with her fingers repeatedly, eliciting a quick glance from the man. A flicker of the eyes.

'No comment,' he said, then did a double take as he eased himself back in his seat. A small hint of recognition flashed in his eyes.

Another sheet. Another photograph. This time it was the image Mariusz had taken of Andrei in the bathtub.

'What about this image? Do you recognise the person in this one?'

Now Vlad was unable to tear his gaze from it. He picked up the sheet and studied the photo of the dead man.

'No comment.'

Tomek sighed again. They were in for a long afternoon.

'Have you ever seen this photo before?' Tomek repeated.

'No comment.'

'Do you know anyone who has?'

Vlad's eyes flickered to the wall.

'No comment.'

'Where were you last Thursday?' he asked, the day of Andrei's death. 'Walk us through what you were doing.'

'No comment.'

Dead end. He was giving nothing away. They were going to have to try harder than that. Tomek reached into the folder again and produced his ace card: the same images of the man on the seafront, except with a subtle difference. The red shoes, enhanced and saturated to make them even more obvious on the page.

'What about the man in *these* photographs?' Tomek asked. 'Recognise anything about him now?'

Tomek slid the paper containing the seafront images across to Vlad. Finally, the man cracked and glanced at the pictures. He picked them up, holding them directly in front of his face so neither Tomek nor Rachel could see his reaction. Then, a few moments later, he set the paper down and whispered into his solicitor's ear.

'My client would like to request a break, if that's at all possible? He needs the bathroom, and we have some things we need to discuss before we take this any further.'

———

Tomek gave them fifteen minutes. While they waited, he and Rachel headed back to the incident room. The space was muted, silent as they returned, all attention focused on them for an update.

'We're having a little siesta,' Tomek declared. 'Recess is over in fifteen.'

As Tomek returned to his desk, a voice called to him.

'Sarge!'

It came from Chey's desk. The young constable climbed out of his seat and hobbled over.

'What's the matter with you?' he asked.

'Tripped up outside. Complete accident.'

'No... because doing it on purpose would be weird. Unless you were looking to sue us, in which case, all the more power to you.'

'Thanks for the idea,' Chey said. 'You got a min?'

'For my friend? Of course.'

Chey smirked, then dragged Tomek to his desk.

'You're having a break at the right time,' he said. 'I didn't want to interrupt, but the composition analysis has come through on the shoes retrieved at Vlad's place.'

'And?'

'There's a match between Vlad's shoes and the mud and sand samples found on Morgana's clothing.'

'Meaning?'

'That those shoes were present at the crime scene on the mudflats.'

'Meaning that Vlad was the one Andrei had spotted cradling Morgana's head.'

'Meaning that Vlad might know what happened to her,' Chey added.

'Or may have done it himself.'

Tomek suddenly swelled with euphoria. The shoes. Those bastard, garish, horrible shoes. He'd been right to suspect them. He couldn't help but feel a little pride wash over him.

At the end of the fifteen minutes, Tomek and Rachel headed out of the incident room. Before Tomek could reach the lift, Sean accosted him.

'Can it wait, mate?' he asked. 'We're about to go back down.'

'Yeah. It's only a quick one – the room.'

'What about it?'

'Don't need it anymore anyway,' he said. 'I'm gonna be moving in with Victoria.'

'That's good. Saves us having an awkward conversation.'

'Oh?'

'Yeah. Kasia wasn't too keen on the idea of having a strange man living in our house,' he lied. Kasia didn't have a problem with it. After he'd pressed her for a yes or no answer, she'd said that it was fine so long as she was able to shower in the mornings first. But Sean didn't need to know that.

Tomek was last to enter the interview room.

'Apologies,' he said as he hurried back into his chair. 'Trust I haven't missed anything.'

'Not yet,' Rachel responded. 'We were waiting for you. I understand Vlad has something he'd like to share?'

'Yes,' the solicitor replied as she turned to Vlad.

Tomek braced himself. Was he going to confess? Or was he going to try to wriggle himself out of the situation somehow?

Tomek was almost on the edge of his seat.

Leaning forward, Vlad placed his elbows on the table, and said, 'I know what you're going to say. The shoes. The ones you sent for testing the other day. I know that they're going to come back with a match. I know that you're going to find the same mud and sand that was on Morgana's body.'

Tomek took a moment to compose himself. 'How do you know that, Vlad?'

'Well, there's only one possible way, isn't there? Because it looks like I killed her.'

'Sounds about right,' Tomek replied, trying his hardest to keep his cards close to his chest.

'But I want to make something perfectly clear. On the record.'

Tomek said nothing. Waited for the man to continue.

'Go on...' responded Rachel.

'I had nothing to do with her murder. On the morning she died, I overslept, like I told you I had. But I didn't kill her.'

'Elaborate, please.'

'I don't know anything about what happened on the beach that morning. That's a fact. But I do know what happened to those shoes.'

Tomek was struggling to keep up. 'I'm going to need you to spell it out for me.'

Vlad sighed. 'The shoes. They're not mine. I was given them, told to look after them.'

'By who?'

Vlad paused, and stared Tomek and Rachel down for a few moments before responding.

'They belong to Anton Usyk. And I can prove it.'

CHAPTER
FIFTY-TWO

According to Vlad's "proof", Anton had dropped the shoes off one morning and he'd documented it all on his security doorbell camera. Following the interview, Tomek and Chey remotely accessed the video footage from Vlad's phone, searching for the evidence. They'd found it an hour later: Anton standing by the front door, wearing a thick black coat with a scarf wrapped tightly around his neck, holding the red shoes in his hands, passing them to Vlad. He then entered the house, bringing the shoes with him, and left twenty minutes later, hurrying towards his car.

The video all but confirmed Anton had been at the crime scene, that he'd been the one Andrei had spotted, that he'd fled the harbour. As a result, it put him in the frame for his wife's murder. The only problem now was trying to find him. According to reports, he still hadn't turned up for work that morning, and nobody had seen him since last night.

'So that's it then,' Anna said, after Tomek had called a meeting and got Chey to explain the video footage to the team. 'Anton killed Morgana. He's the one who did it?'

'Possibly, yes,' Tomek said. He raised his hands in surrender to allay the furious stares. 'But we're not done yet. There's still a lot that doesn't make sense.'

'Like what?' Victoria hissed, as though it was his fault the investigation was so complex.

'Like the fact that Morgana drove to the harbour – *alone*. She'd gone there to meet someone, or possibly just for a walk – we don't know. But when she got down there, she bumped into her husband, and then he proceeded to kill her. He's then caught red-handed, flees the scene, gives his sandy shoes to the deputy manager of one of his restaurants for "safe keeping", and then proceeds to send Mariusz in as a fall guy to take the blame for it. What I want to know is, what's the connection between the two of them? What's the connection with Gavin as well? Was it Anton telling him to leak the information, or was Vlad involved somehow?'

'You think Anton has been orchestrating this thing the entire time?' Victoria asked. She couldn't have sounded more unintelligent if she'd tried, like asking a Gen-Z for the first prime numbers and them thinking it had something to do with the customer service contact details for the streaming service.

'That's my hypothesis,' Tomek answered. 'Anton killed his wife, fled the scene, and passed the evidence to Vlad. He then realised the net would soon close in on him, as he's the husband and the obvious choice, and so he got Mariusz to kill Andrei in his flat, then hand himself in to confess to being at the harbour. He probably didn't bank on us finding out the truth about the fake suicide so soon.'

'So, the photos on Mariusz's phone were sent to Anton?'

'That would be my guess,' Tomek replied with a dip of the head.

'And the messages to Gavin, our whistle-blower?' Victoria began moving about the whiteboards, prodding everyone's name and face with her marker as she spoke. 'You think Anton applied the pressure to Gavin to get him to leak the information to Denis Danyluk in prison?'

'As I see it.'

'But if Denis is Morgana's brother, why didn't he go straight to Denis for the murder of Mariusz in prison?'

Tomek pondered on that a moment. 'Maybe he knew that would be the obvious route we'd go down. He got Gavin involved to cover his tracks and throw us off the scent. He's clever. He's not done any of this himself. In all instances, except for the murder of his wife, he's got someone else to do it for him: Mariusz to kill Andrei; Denis to kill Mariusz; and I imagine if we send Vlad and Gavin to prison, he's going to get them killed as well somehow.'

The sombre thought brought a moment's reflection to the team.

'I'll make sure Gavin's placed in vulnerable protection, same with Vlad if we find enough evidence to prosecute.'

'Enough evidence?' Tomek repeated. 'We've got evidence of him helping cover up a murder. He's lied to the police about what happened that day. He knew way more than he was telling us, and I think he knows a lot more that he's yet to tell us. There's nothing "if" about it. We've got twenty-four hours to find more concrete evidence against him, and I say we use every last second of it.'

Tomek propelled himself out of his chair, shuffled past his colleagues around the oversized table, and took the whiteboard marker from Victoria. Grabbing the eraser, he rubbed out some unnecessary scribbles and created a massive circle in the middle of the space. Within it, he wrote Anton's name, then added five separate strands to the spider's web with a name in each.

Mariusz Stanciu.

Gavin Barker.

Vlad Boyko.

Brendan Door.

Denis Danyluk.

As he snapped the cap back on the pen, he prodded the names in clockwise order.

'We need to find connections between Anton and all of these men. How do they fit together, what made Anton choose them? Barring the obvious ones – Vlad, the deputy manager, and Denis, his supposed brother-in-law – we need to ask ourselves what connects them.'

Tomek paused and surveyed the room. He was looking down at a bunch of applied, eager and ready faces. He couldn't recall the last time he'd seen that. In that brief moment, in that short interlude, it felt like the investigation was his, and he was managing the team from now on.

Sadly, the reality would be slightly different.

Just as Tomek was about to return to his seat, Chey tentatively raised his hand. 'I can go one step further and answer some of them.'

Tomek took a step backwards, maintaining his perceived position of authority.

'By all means, Mr Pepper, the floor is yours.'

Chey cleared his throat. 'Firstly, Denis Danyluk was lying when he said he was related to Morgana.'

'Come again?'

'I've checked her social media accounts and requested documents from back home in Ukraine, and there's no mention of Denis Danyluk in any of them. They don't even share the same name. Nothing on socials. Nothing on any next of kin. Nothing on birth certificates or family trees or medical documents. Nothing to suggest they're remotely related.'

Tomek turned to the board and underlined Denis's name. 'Make that four connections we need to find,' he said, then turned back to the young constable. 'Good work, mate. Anything else?'

The man sat upright, buoyed by the positive feedback. 'Well, while we're on the topic of social media, I've been looking into possible connections between the Usyks and Gavin and Mariusz, using the restaurant's accounts as a basis. It looks like they were set up by Morgana, as she was much more prominent on the likes of Instagram and TikTok than her husband. In a couple of posts, I've seen Gavin go into Iliana's several times. He's been featured on their pages quite a lot and has even left one of the more positive Tripadvisor reviews on there.'

Tomek pointed to Oscar and told the man to make a note to question Gavin on it at some point.

'Anything else?'

'I've also briefly looked through Vlad's phone before we sent it down to digital forensics, and I don't think he's been the one sending the messages to Gavin, nor do I think he received the photos of Andrei in the bathtub.'

'So, Vlad's off the hook?' Anna mentioned.

'Not quite,' Tomek corrected. 'Like I said earlier, he's not squeaky clean in all of this, and I guarantee there are still some things he's keeping to himself. So why don't we get everything we need together, all the ducks in a row and all that, then bring it to him at the last moment.' He turned to Victoria. 'Could we look at getting a custody extension?'

Victoria pondered for a moment. 'I can look into it.'

'Great, thanks.'

Tomek could feel the tides of the investigation rapidly turning in his favour. If Victoria wasn't careful, she might get stranded by the harbour and drown.

Then a thought occurred to him. 'What about a connection between Anton Usyk and Mariusz Stanciu?' he asked Chey, but the question was open to the rest of the room.

Martin grabbed the opportunity with both hands. 'Might have something for you there, Sarge,' he said. 'Turns out that the haulage company Mariusz works for, DWG Logistics, delivers the food and supplies to the cafés.'

'Is that right?'

'Yes, Sarge.'

The cogs began to turn in Tomek's brain.

'That's our focus.' He drew a large circle between Anton and Mariusz's names on the board. 'We need to find out how closely these two know each other. Bearing in mind Mariusz has only been in the country for three months... And another thing we should look into: does anyone know where the fuck Anton is?'

CHAPTER
FIFTY-THREE

With Mariusz dead in prison, and Anton having disappeared off the face of the earth, that left only one person Tomek could speak with who knew them both.

Red Birch Farm was still open, and to his surprise, was still busy. It was nearing the end of opening hours, and there were at least ten cars sitting in the car park. After narrowly avoiding several of the potholes, Tomek parked, climbed out of the car, and made his way towards Stanley's office.

Tomek knocked on the window but there was no answer. Cupping his hands on the sides of his face, he pressed his nose to the glass. Empty. Then he spent a few moments looking around for someone, for help. When it didn't appear, he set off in search of it.

'Excuse me, mate,' Tomek called to a man carrying a broom, who had just emerged from the horses' enclosure. He wore a pair of overalls tucked into a pair of wellington boots. His hair was flame red and he had a thick ginger beard to match.

'Hello...' he said cautiously.

'Do you know where I might find Stanley?'

The man pointed without looking. 'With the pigs,' he said, then carried on with his errand.

'Bringing home the bacon, eh?' Tomek said to the man but it fell on deaf ears.

On the way to the pig pen, he passed a young family of four, dragging the two children away from the sheep. They were screaming, begging to stay, but the parents had to get back for dinner, they said.

Eventually, he arrived at the pig pen and found the man he was looking for.

'Detective...' Stanley said sternly, a hint of caution in his voice. 'You haven't come to tell me someone else has died, have you?'

Today he wore a different-coloured body warmer. His trousers and boots were khaki but had become soiled with mud. In his hands he held a green bucket with a pair of gloves.

'Millions of people have died since we last spoke,' Tomek said.

'Well, that's... I guess... I guess you're right.'

Tomek pointed to the bucket.

'What you doing?'

'Feeding time.'

Tomek turned to the pigs. Seven of them in total. One less than last time, though it didn't take a genius to figure out why. They were ugly, foul creatures. Hairy, filthy, covered in their own shit. Tomek had never liked them. But he did like to eat them. He liked to think they were the epitome of beauty always being on the inside.

'You want to have a go?' Stanley asked, holding the bucket out for Tomek. 'They're pretty full but I reckon they can handle a couple more mouthfuls.'

Tomek raised his hands and stepped back a few paces, shaking his head. 'I couldn't. No thanks. Not for me.'

'You sure?'

'Yeah. This suit... it's really nice. Designer. Needs to be dry-cleaned every couple of weeks. I wouldn't want to get it dirty. Besides, I wouldn't want to overfeed them.'

Stanley scoffed. 'They're pigs. They'll eat whatever you give them so long as they're hungry enough. They taste better that way.'

Tomek turned to face them again. One of the beasts had just come up to him, grunting and sniffling away like a zombie in a disaster movie.

'He likes something on your trousers,' Stanley said.

'Yeah. It's called money,' Tomek replied, pulling his leg away. As he did it, something caught his eye, flashing amongst the dirt. A green jewelled earring, glistening in the light. Tomek was too afraid to pick it up so pointed at it. 'Think someone lost something.'

Confused, Stanley crouched down to inspect it. He placed his hand into the pen with ease, and swatted away the pigs' curiosity with a hefty shove.

'There it is!' he exclaimed. 'There's the little bastard. One of our customers earlier lost this. We were looking all over the place for it. You should've seen us. I got mud in places I didn't even think possible.'

Tomek thought of a joke but decided to keep it to himself. Neither the time, nor place, nor company.

Stanley pocketed the earring and stood up. 'I'll give her a call later. In the meantime, how can I help?'

'Would we be able to speak in your office?'

'Somewhere more private? Absolutely.'

On the way to the office, Tomek saw the ginger man with the broom again. He nodded at him, but didn't receive one in reply.

'Don't worry about him, he's just grumpy because I told him he's working off-site for the rest of the week,' Stanley said as he held the door open for Tomek. 'Drink? Tea? Coffee?'

'Irish?'

Stanley looked shocked. 'Only if you want it!'

Tomek shook his head and ordered a cup of tea. The scalding liquid warmed his body and eased the soreness that had started in his throat that morning.

'So...' Stanley began as he flopped into the leather seat opposite. 'Do you have an update on what happened to Morgana?'

'Yes. Which is partly why I'm here.'

'Okay.'

'Two reasons, actually. First is whether you've heard from Anton recently. Has he tried to contact you at all?'

The man's eyes widened. 'Anton? Anton did this?'

'We're looking into it,' Tomek replied, deflecting the question. 'But right now we can't seem to locate him. Do you know where he might be?'

Stanley shook his head slowly, staring into the farming magazine on the coffee table, deep in thought. 'No, I haven't heard anything from him since the morning of her death.'

'And would you be willing to provide evidence to support that?'

'Of course. Here.'

Stanley reached into his breast pocket, removed his phone and passed it to Tomek – unlocked and ready to go. Tomek took it from him and began scanning through the man's latest text messages, emails, WhatsApp, even his social media accounts. It felt like an invasion of privacy, which it essentially was, but the man had consented. And there was nothing there. Nothing that immediately leapt out to Tomek. No messages with an unknown number, very few recent chats that fitted the timeframe since Morgana's death, and there were no photos in his deleted album or recently deleted folder. Tomek had looked at the photos cautiously, lest he find something more than he'd been expecting. Instead, he found close-ups of some of the farm animals. Some cute, some not so much. As he handed the phone back, he thanked the man.

'No problem. Can I ask, why are you looking for Anton? Just out of curiosity. You don't have to say if you can't.'

Tomek paused. 'Let's just say we think there are things that he's not telling us.'

'Hopefully he hasn't gone too far.'

'You haven't seen him hiding around any of the animal paddocks, have you? I'd say he probably fits in quite well with the donkeys.'

Stanley burst into a cackle of laughter. 'We've got a particular llama that never took a liking to him when he came to visit. Always used to spit at him.'

'He's probably not the only one. Some of the Tripadvisor reviews gave the impression that they would spit at him if they could.' Tomek sipped his drink, set it down.

'If I see anything, I'll contact you right away. Same goes for my team.

We want to help your investigation in any way we can.'

'That's great. We really do appreciate it. Do you have time for some more questions?'

'Of course. Anything.'

Tomek pulled out his notebook, pressing pen to paper. 'Does the name Mariusz Stanciu mean anything to you?'

'Little Mario?' Stanley's voice filled with glee. 'He's our courier. He collects our produce and delivers it to all of our suppliers. He also delivers other stuff for us as well.'

'Like what?'

'Boring bits. Hay. Seeds. Fertiliser. Anything that we need in order to run the farm.'

Tomek knew nothing about farming so couldn't comprehend the scale of what was required, but he imagined it was a lot.

'I think we started using DWG Logistics about five years ago,' Stanley continued.

'And how long has Mariusz been doing deliveries?'

Stanley blew hot air through his teeth. 'A couple of months? Maybe three? But he's already a firm favourite around here. Got a decent sense of humour on him.'

Shame, Tomek thought, that he didn't get to experience that side of Mariusz. Instead, he had dealt with a frightened and panicked little man. A frightened and panicked little man who had been instructed to kill Andrei Pirlog and then document it.

'Do you happen to know anything about his relationship with Anton?'

'Working relationship or personal?'

'Any,' Tomek said with a shrug.

'I know Mario did a lot of deliveries for me to Anton. I know he was always on the phone to him it seemed, probably discussing work things, and sometimes the football, but other than that, I couldn't actually tell you. Sorry.'

'Not to worry,' he said as he slapped his knee and made to leave. 'I wasn't expecting much.'

CHAPTER
FIFTY-FOUR

Two days had passed and there was still no sign of Anton Usyk. A warrant had been put out for his arrest, and Abigail and the team at the *Southend Echo* had released a photograph of him online. The coverage had even reached national headlines, and so hordes of journalists and reporters had flocked to the headquarters like a rock band's fan group. Each time Tomek tried getting through the crowd, it was like fighting the pigs at the farm. And so far all of it had been in vain.

They had exhausted every available opportunity. Contacts in his address books, friends on social media, even other business suppliers and customers that they'd found on the books. Two unlucky souls within the team, Chey and Anna, even had the unenviable task of ringing round to all their former employees and meeting with the ones who still lived in the country. A lot had either moved back to their home country or were uncontactable.

Meanwhile, Vlad was still in a holding cell. In Nick's absence, Victoria had sought approval to extend the clock up to thirty-six hours. By Tomek's estimations, they had a little under two hours left. The team were still gathering as much information as possible, and the feeling was that they had enough to charge him for perverting the course of justice. Several attempts had been made to break him open, and cause a crack in his façade, but he hadn't budged. He still maintained that he had no idea where Anton was.

The man's phone was off. He hadn't logged into his social media accounts, or even his email, for three days, since the night before Tomek was due to meet with the waitress, Gina, and nobody seemed to know where he was. An all-ports warning had been put out for his name and face, so if he tried to flee the country, he wouldn't be able to. Some, not Tomek, had postulated that perhaps he'd fled the country back to Ukraine on the back of a lorry. But if that was the case, there was little to nothing Tomek and the team could do except speak with the Ukrainian authorities and put them on alert for his return.

He had to be *somewhere*. He had to be hiding, lying in wait, hoping that this would all blow over. Tomek was adamant.

As for Gina, she too appeared to have vanished from the face of the earth. Tomek had spoken with as many of Iliana's employees as possible, but nobody had seen her, heard from her, nor even remembered her. It was as though she hadn't existed.

Tomek pulled into the car park and stepped out of the car. Before him was Iliana's. Through the floor-to-ceiling windows, with condensation slowly creeping up them, he saw that it was empty. There was no manager, no assistant manager. Tomek was curious how the place was functioning. There had to be a leader in there somewhere, a second-in-command who knew what they were doing but had perhaps flown under the radar, had kept themselves hidden all this time. Tomek was willing to put money on it that they would know where Anton was hiding.

He slammed the car door shut and made his way to the restaurant. The atmosphere inside was as it always had been. The sound of fat and grease sizzling away in the kitchen at the back, the music playing in the background, the coffee machine whirring as it blended coffee beans, the sound of Eastern European chatter, all speaking over one another. The only difference was the staff within. Tomek didn't recognise any of their faces from the other day. Even the waitress who approached him was different to the lady who had replaced Gina.

Where the fuck do they keep coming from? he wondered. It was as though they were growing them in a laboratory out the back.

'Good morning, sir,' she said, more jovial and enthusiastic than her predecessors. 'Table for one?'

'Please,' Tomek said, his attention focused solely on the kitchen area.

Something had flashed across his vision, distracting him. A shock of red hair, with a beard to match. Wearing an apron. As the woman directed him to his seat, he ignored her and continued towards the kitchen. There, he rounded the counter and waded through the bodies. The man he was after had his back turned to him, busy flipping two eggs at once, using a technique and a spatula Tomek had never seen before.

He tapped the man on the shoulder.

As he flinched, the man flung round and dropped one of the eggs onto the floor. Grease and yolk splashed onto Tomek's shoes and the cuffs of his trousers. It would no doubt leave a stain, but Tomek didn't care. He was more enamoured with the man in front of him. With the red hair and beard. The cheekbones and vacant stare. The man who, only forty-eight hours prior, had been holding a broom instead of a spatula. A man who had been shovelling shit instead of flipping eggs.

'You shouldn't be back here, sir,' he said, his expression vacant, lost. 'This is for staff only.'

Then the rest of the cries came. The hands, pulling him back. The antagonised faces squaring up to him. Tomek, dumbfounded and astonished, felt himself being manhandled and manipulated out of the kitchen.

For a long time, he stood there, frozen, on the other side of the kitchen counter, staring intently into the chef's face. It was a while before he eventually came to and realised what he needed to do.

Tomek reached into his pocket and pulled out his warrant card. Then he pointed at the man with the red hair.

'Can I speak with you regarding—'

The man bolted. He threw the spatula in Tomek's direction, missing him by miles, then grabbed a frying pan from the surface and chucked it after him. Tomek gave chase, charging towards the kitchen's entrance, barging through the static bodies in his way. The man was small, nimble, and much faster than Tomek who, despite the two runs he'd been on recently, was struggling to keep up.

He chased him through the back of the building, and into the small staff car park that was only large enough for two cars. The rest of the space was occupied by wheeled recycling bins. As soon as he breached into daylight, the chef grabbed one of the bins and rolled it in front of Tomek in an attempt to delay him. It had little effect as Tomek was able to skip past it – a throwback to his rugby-playing days. Then the man rounded the corner of the building and headed towards the seafront. Tomek continued to chase, legs pounding, feet stomping on the tarmac. He kept his breathing steady and rhythmical, in through the nose, out through the mouth. Wishing, praying that the man didn't make it onto the seafront. It was busy, filled with obstacles – people – that didn't always move out of the way.

The only advantage Tomek had was that he knew the seafront well, had run along it hundreds of times, and so knew how to pace himself, how to keep himself in the race. That momentum, that advantage, would be lost if the assailant headed onto the sand, however. Which was precisely what he did.

'Stop!' Tomek screamed. 'Stop right now!'

A group of male runners, dressed in bright neon clothing and skimpy shorts that showed too much for Tomek's liking, were coming towards them. Stupidly, they listened to his command and stopped running, letting the chef shuffle around them and set foot onto the beach.

Tomek cursed them as he passed, hoping that each one twisted their ankle or popped a knee.

The surface beneath his feet went from solid, sturdy tarmac to labouring, uneven and unpredictable sand. Pieces of stone and seashells flicked up behind the chef, and in the wind carried into Tomek's face. He spat and closed his eyes to prevent them from entering, but it was no use.

He was, however, more to his own surprise than anyone else's, gaining ground. Either the run with Warren down to the harbour had

had an impact, or the chef had wildly underestimated the effort required to run on sand. They were nearing the pier, moving closer to the waterline. Tomek didn't know what the man's strategy was, but it wasn't well thought through. And within a few hundred yards, his body screaming at him to stop, he caught up with the man and leapt onto his back.

The landing was soft, for the most part; in the fall, Tomek felt a knee clatter into his groin. Pain flashed in that area and quickly swelled to his stomach. He screamed in agony, but now wasn't the time. He couldn't afford to let the man go, and so, in his anguish, he straddled the man, pinning him to the ground, one hand holding his groin, the other pressing on the back of the man's head.

'I haven't done anything!' the man yelled, spitting out sand and seaweed.

'Innocent people don't run, mate.'

CHAPTER
FIFTY-FIVE

Tomek had been in the meeting room for twenty minutes, breathing steadily, trying to overcome the pain in his stomach, when Chey and Rachel entered.

'You feeling any better, Sarge?'

'No. It's come up to my chest now. I can feel it in my throat.'

Rachel scoffed. '*Men*. You love to blow things out of proportion. Man-flu—'

'That's a real thing, by the way!'

She continued: 'Any aches and pains, and you expect us to be at your beck and call every time.'

'Is that why you chose women over men?'

'Obviously. That's the only reason I'm a lesbian.'

Chey's eyes widened, and he turned to face Rachel like a cartoon character. 'You're a—?'

'Yes, Chey. I am. I like women, and I wasn't hoping it would get out this way, but I guess it has. But we're not talking about me right now, we're talking about Tomek and the little knock he's taken to his genitals. To that I say, welcome to our world. Try that for one week every month, but instead of a one-off pain, imagine you're being punched in the balls repeatedly. Again and again.' She mimicked punching a boxing bag.

'I commend you for it,' he said. 'I really do. Kasia tells me all about it. Sometimes too much. But I think you need to work on your right hook.'

'Even when you're in pain, you're still an arsehole.'

He shot her a finger gun with thumb and forefinger. 'Nothing's gonna make me change, baby. What's our Usain-Bolt-wannabe saying?'

The constables looked at one another. 'Actually, sir, it's what Vlad's saying that's the priority right now.'

'In what way?'

'Well, he knows the time on his clock is up and he thinks it's bargaining time.'

'He wants a way out?'

'Well, there's no chance of that happening,' Rachel answered. 'Rather, he wants half the cake and he wants to eat it. He reckons he's got something we might want to know.'

'If it's what I think it is, we don't have any need for him,' Tomek said, as he carefully lifted himself to his feet. His knees creaked as he stretched his legs.

'Then I think you might need to have a word with Victoria,' Chey said. 'The interview's already begun.'

Fuck's sake.

Tomek shuffled past them and wedged through the door, limping as he walked towards the major incident room. There, in the middle of the room was Victoria and the rest of the team, watching Martin conduct the interview on the television screen like they were in the cinema.

'Don't agree to anything,' he said.

Victoria turned to face him, disdain in her eyes. 'Excuse me?'

'Don't agree to anything he wants. Not yet.'

'Why should we wait? This is nearly over.'

'The bloke I arrested,' Tomek said in between pants. The walk from to the interview really took it out of him. 'I recognised him from the farm. I think something's going on over there, and I think he might be able to tell us what exactly.'

'So, what are you suggesting?'

'That we call Vlad's bluff. Tell him that we've arrested someone from the farm – it's important that you mention that specific point – and that we're just going to get everything we need from him. Vlad's already going to prison for a very long time, there's nothing he'll be able to do to stop that. Then, once we've got the information we need from this ginger matey down in the holding cell, we'll present it to Vlad and possibly get him to fill in some of the gaps if necessary.'

Victoria considered for a moment. He could see on her face that she wasn't prepared to make a deal of any kind with Vlad for information he may or may not possess. But he could also see that she didn't want Tomek to be right.

She had a difficult choice to make. Ego or the lives of innocent people.

In the end, the lives of innocent people won.

'What are you going to do if you're wrong?'

Tomek shrugged. 'Then someone's got to have the awkward conversation with Vlad where we admit we might have placed all our cards down too early.'

A few moments passed. Victoria wrestled with the decision.

Then she turned to Sean, and said, 'Get down there now. Tell Martin to wait. Let's see what Tomek can get out of his suspect first.'

CHAPTER
FIFTY-SIX

Tomek liked to think that he didn't feel pressure, that he was immune to it in some way. That, over the years, he'd learnt to deal with it and process it, manipulate it for his own benefit. After all, he'd dealt with the death of his brother on his own. He'd learnt how to grow up and deal with life's struggles and setbacks without advice or a guiding hand from his parents. And yet, as he entered the interview room, he felt a slight wobble in his knees, a slight knot tightening in his stomach.

Either it was the nerves or the sensation from being kneed in the genitalia was still hassling him.

He put it down to the latter.

In his hand, he held a small document that had been given to him by the custody officer. On it was the man's name, date of birth, and other information that had been extracted from him when he'd been signed in at the station

'So... Alfie,' Tomek began as he sat opposite the man. 'How are you doing today?'

'I ain't done nothing wrong.'

'That remains to be seen. Like I said on the beach, innocent people—'

'Yeah, they don't run. I heard you all right.'

'Great. So, we've already managed to ascertain that your listening skills are up to standard. What about your ability to understand and answer questions?'

'What?'

Tomek tilted his head. 'Off to a shaky start. Let's try that again, shall we? Can you please confirm for me your name, age and date of birth?'

'They're the same thing, idiot.'

Tomek pointed the pen at him. 'That's a tick on the logic portion, congratulations.'

'What the fuck are you even talking about, pal? Why the fuck am I here? I ain't done nothing wrong.'

Alfie was a small man, a little under five-eight, with small shoulders, but there was a heritage in his make-up that suggested he wouldn't look out of place in a boxing ring. His movements were jittery, as though he had taken a little sniff of something before his shift in the kitchen, and he repeatedly cracked his knuckles. Tomek liked to think he could outmuscle the man, but he wasn't prepared to get into a fistfight, not when the lower half of his body was still recuperating from its earlier bout in the ring.

'I was wondering if you could answer some questions,' Tomek said. 'Are you capable of that?'

'Not when I ain't done nothing wrong.'

'Excellent. I'd like to start by knowing how long you've been working at Iliana's.'

'I don't work there.'

'Then what were you doing in the kitchen? A spot of volunteer work?'

'As it happens, yes.'

Tomek was taken aback. He hadn't been expecting that response.

'Elaborate.'

'I was helping out,' he said. 'Stanley asked me to go and give them a hand. Said that they needed me to cover a shift.'

Tomek recalled Stanley's words: *Don't worry about him, he's just grumpy because I told him he's working off-site for the rest of the week.*

'Why?'

'Because they haven't got anyone in charge there. Stanley said they needed to keep the business afloat somehow. They're one of our biggest customers.'

'You're aware that one owner is dead and the other is wanted in connection with her murder?'

Alfie shrugged. 'I wasn't, but now I am.'

'And Stanley knows that too. So why is he sending you to help out?'

Alfie threw himself into the back of his chair and folded his arms across his chest. 'Fuck a man for doing some philanthropic work, helping out his community.'

Tomek was reminded of the awards and accolades in Stanley's office.

'Yes... he's good at that, isn't he?'

'I think he might try buying the place if anything happens to it.'

Interesting, Tomek thought. Very interesting.

'How many times have you been told to help out at the restaurant?'

'Which one?'

'Either.

'Only the once,' Alfie replied.

'And how long have you worked for Stanley?'

'About six years now.'

'Long time.'

Alfie shrugged. 'I like it. He's a good employer. Pays fairly. Doesn't take no extra money for himself. Plus, I like the work. I don't see what the problem is?'

Tomek chose not to answer the question. At least not right away. Either Alfie was an exceptionally good poker player and was giving nothing away, or he genuinely had no idea what was wrong. There was only one way to find out.

'Why'd you run?' Tomek asked.

'Reflex.'

'From when you were younger?'

As soon as Alfie's name had been entered into the system, a handful of former arrests had come up. Vandalism, truanting, petty theft.

Throughout his teenage years, he'd spent his time graffitiing the walls of Basildon and stealing sweets from shops when he should have been at school.

'As soon as I saw your ID, something came over me.'

'Guilt? Paranoia?'

'Instinct.'

'Shame your feet don't work as fast as your instincts,' Tomek said as he glanced down at the sheet. 'Four arrests. Now five. Lucky none of them ever decided to press charges.'

Alfie tucked his hands deeper into his armpits. The sound of knuckles clicking echoed from beneath his skin. 'It ain't a crime to help people out. You ain't got nothing to charge me with. Same as all them previous ones. Now, if that's all, I'd like to go please.'

CHAPTER
FIFTY-SEVEN

Tomek didn't have a choice but to let Alfie leave. No crime had been committed, and he couldn't hold him in a cell while they waited to gather evidence. Instead, it would have to be done the other way round. Find the evidence then bring him in. But unless Tomek could put him anywhere at the scene of Morgana's murder, he wasn't hopeful.

He returned to the major incident room with a forced, pretentious smile on his face.

'You fucked it, didn't you?' was the first thing Victoria said to him.

'Well, I wouldn't put it like that.'

'How would you put it?'

'It was a non-starter. He was just helping out at the restaurant.'

'Right. And so you've let him go?'

'Yes, ma'am. Don't want to put any more strain on our otherwise limited resources.'

Victoria placed her hands on her head, a little too theatrically for his liking. 'I don't fucking believe this. You assured me this was a win-win.'

Tomek shrugged. 'You win some, you lose some.'

'How can you be so blasé about this? We've now got to go back in there with Vlad, with our tails between our legs and our fucking shorts down. He's not going to give anything up unless he gets exactly what he wants.'

'Yes, he is,' Tomek replied.

He was met with a blank face. His point had gone straight over Victoria's head.

'How do you mean?'

'He doesn't know that we've fucked it—'

'That *you've* fucked it,' Victoria hissed as she insisted on correcting him.

'Potato, *potahto*. Right now, he's sitting in the holding cell paranoid that he's going to be spending the next several years in prison with the regret of not sharing his information with us sooner. He's going to want to do anything to tell us what he knows, to bargain with us as much as he possibly can because we're going to tell him that we already know everything. We're still the ones with the power.'

Now it began to make sense to her. Her eyes fell to the floor and she lowered her hands to her hips.

'But this will only work,' Tomek continued, 'if we give the impression that we know everything. If he sees through our façade, *then* we're fucked.'

'Oh, so only at that point we should consider ourselves up shit creek? Brilliant.'

The smile returned to Tomek's face, this time with a little more truth behind it. 'Exactly. Hence why I'm not worried.'

'That's because your arse isn't on the line.' Victoria turned to the team who were sitting around the table. 'What other lines of enquiry do we have open at the moment?'

Silence, save for the sound of rustling papers as his colleagues pretended to find an answer to the question that didn't exist.

'Nothing? Shit!' She turned back to Tomek. 'So, this is the only solid source that we have available to us.'

Tomek shrugged. 'Would appear that way, ma'am. It's your decision. That's why you're paid the big bucks.'

She shot him a look of derision.

'You're right, Tomek. It is why I'm paid the big bucks, which is why I'm giving it to someone I trust, someone I think is going to see this through to the end.' She gestured to the man closest to her. 'Sean, I'd like you to take care of this please.'

Quelle surprise.

The rotten owner and her loyal guard dog looking out for one another again.

'Perfect candidate,' Tomek said through gritted teeth, then returned to his seat as the team began coming up with a strategy for the second part of the interview with Vlad. In all honesty, Tomek was a little relieved not to hear his name. He had been expecting Victoria to choose him as some sort of chance to redeem himself for making the fuck-up in the first place, but now that responsibility had fallen to someone else, he could relax knowing that it wouldn't be on his shoulders if it all went tits up. And they said he wasn't a team player...

Thirty minutes later, the team had finalised the strategy and, armed with it, Sean left for the interview room. By the time Martin and Oscar had set up the live video feed, the interview had begun.

It was the first time Tomek had seen the man since his initial arrest. He looked beaten, withdrawn, skinnier – much skinnier, as though he'd gone on hunger strike and nobody had noticed. Beside him was his solicitor, slouching forward on the table, back as arched as the Golden Arches of the McDonald's sign. On the screen, Sean had his back to them, but Tomek knew his friend had his game face on – a stern, stolid expression that would give nothing away.

'Thanks for coming back,' Sean began.

'How'd it go? Did your other suspect tell you everything?'

'That remains to be seen,' Sean said. 'We're just hoping you can fill in some of the gaps for us.'

A brief pause entered the room, and for a few moments, nobody moved. At first, Tomek had thought the feed had frozen, but when he saw Vlad wipe the underside of his nose, he realised he was wrong. He also realised that Sean had given it away.

'Fill in the blanks?' Vlad repeated. 'You don't know shit, do you? You want *me* to fill in the blanks? That's basically asking me to give you everything I know for free.'

Fuck.

Vlad folded his arms across his chest and slouched in his seat. 'That sort of information don't come free, and it certainly doesn't come cheap either, I'm afraid. My original offer still stands.'

Double-fuck.

Sean had given it away. He'd blown it faster than a virgin losing his virginity. Sure, they'd come up with a contingency plan during their ad-hoc strategy meeting, but they hadn't expected to need it so soon.

Tomek looked around at the muted, surprised faces of his colleagues. Victoria's, however, was a masterpiece. She was sitting forward, with her elbows resting on her knees, cupping her face in her hands, squinting through the gaps between her fingers.

'I don't fucking believe it,' she said. 'Christ on a fucking bike. Can someone go down and help him?'

'I think it's beyond salvation right now,' someone in the team said.

Tomek was paying too much attention to the screen to notice who'd said it. On the feed, Sean shifted in his seat uncomfortably and began playing with the documents in his hand again.

'We can't give you immunity,' he said.

'Why not?' Vlad responded.

'Because it doesn't work that way. If a crime's been committed, you will be punished for it.'

'So, you definitely don't know anything,' Vlad said. He knotted his fingers like Mr Burns from *The Simpsons*. 'I think that means you'll want to agree to my terms.'

'We can't. How do we even know that you've got evidence and information relevant to the case?'

Vlad tilted forward in his seat. 'How about we make a deal? First, you either give me immunity or witness protection. Then I will tell you. If you do not think the evidence I give you is worth it, then the deal is off.'

'So, you'd be willing to let us decide whether we value the information enough to grant you immunity?'

Tomek screamed internally. *No! Don't say that you fucking melt!*

'Actually, you're right,' Vlad continued, 'that doesn't make sense. Ignore that. Either you take it or leave it.'

Tomek couldn't believe what he was hearing. Not only had Sean blown their cover, but he'd also managed to talk Vlad out of giving them the best deal. If Vlad had given them information that had led to an arrest, they were under no obligation – except Sean's word – to follow through with any sort of paperwork that might lead to immunity of some kind or entering him into the witness protection programme. It was their best shot of getting the information out of Vlad's head, and he'd squandered it.

Tomek had never seen a car crash happen right in front of him before. But now he had. And it was spectacular.

CHAPTER
FIFTY-EIGHT

There had been no smile on Sean's face when he'd returned to the incident room. He didn't have a backup plan like Tomek had, and he'd been unable to look his colleagues in the eye. The first thing he and Victoria did was head to her office, where Tomek imagined she was consoling him in her bosom. That left the team not knowing what to do with themselves. There was a lack of direction following Victoria's sudden escape, so Tomek took it upon himself to take charge, give some semblance of leadership and fall upwards into the role, a skill which he'd seen many before him do, so how hard could it be?

Tomek turned to the wall of whiteboards in front of him and spent a few moments scanning the information, looking at the links, the lines that connected their suspects to one another.

'Ladies and gents,' he said, 'our main goal right now is finding Anton Usyk. If we can find him, we might be able to get him to sing like a canary, or piss like an octogenarian, as Chey has so eloquently put it in the past.'

'Too right, Sarge,' came the remark from the constable.

'Before I head off in one direction, does anyone have an update on his movements? Any possible sightings?'

Martin was first to speak. He lowered his hands slowly. 'I've been fielding a lot of calls from people answering the news press releases and so far they're all reporting seeing the same man matching Anton's description. But no one's come up with anything of any significance. It's surprising the amount of people, particularly old people, who are calling in to wish us the best of luck with it all.'

'Doesn't do us much good.'

'I know, but it sort of restores your faith in humanity a little bit.'

'Hmm. It's like when celebrities post on Twitter their thoughts and prayers with the families of war or the latest gun shooting. Vacuous, empty, meaningless words.'

'It's called X now, Sarge,' Chey added.

A phone began ringing in the main office. Martin hopped out of his seat and rushed to answer it.

'Nobody calls it that,' Tomek continued. 'They always refer to it as "X, formerly Twitter". But that's beside the point. I think we have bigger things to worry about than the name of a social media company.'

Tomek looked around the room, waiting for someone else to speak. Just as he was about to open his mouth, Martin reappeared at the door.

'Sarge,' he said, panting, 'not sure if it's worth checking out, but a body's just been found on Two Tree Island. The cyclist who found it reckons it could be Anton.'

CHAPTER
FIFTY-NINE

Two Tree Island was nearly three hundred hectares of salt marshland. As a Wildlife Trust nature reserve, it was home to thousands of wildfowl and waders. The land had been reclaimed in the eighteenth century from the sea after a sea wall had been erected around the area and had been used for farming, but it was now a popular spot for walkers, cyclists, wildlife enthusiasts and birdwatchers, with several hides dotted about the area.

Tomek and Rachel arrived thirty minutes after the phone call. Access to the island was only available via one of the various footpaths, and they had spent twenty minutes trying to navigate their way through the walkways. It wasn't until they spotted a uniformed constable heading back from the crime scene that they found it.

'Do you know what,' Tomek said. 'In all my thirty-five years in this country, I don't think I've ever been here.'

Tomek looked behind him. In the distance was the South Essex coastline. Hadleigh on the left, with the castle protruding from the skyline atop the hill, then on to Leigh-on-Sea, Chalkwell, and Southend beyond. On a good day, Tomek would have been able to see the pier, but the weather had deteriorated. In the past few hours, clouds had formed overhead, threatening rain, and bringing with them a cloak of darkness.

A few hundred yards away, a white forensics tent had been erected over the body, the path had been shut off by blue and white police tape, and a small outfit of uniformed constables were tending to the scene. Just in front of the police tape was a man dressed in Lycra, holding onto his racing bike with one hand, talking with a police constable.

Beside them was another constable holding a clipboard and pen.

'Afternoon,' Tomek said as he flashed his warrant card and signed in.

'Afternoon,' the man replied.

Tomek and Rachel were already dressed in white forensics suits. He always kept a couple in the back of his car for such eventualities. Once they'd both signed in, they ducked beneath the tape and sauntered towards the crime scene. There, they found a man who introduced himself as Leon Ridpath, the crime scene manager.

'Victim is a man in his thirties,' he said as he efficiently began to describe the scene for them. 'From the looks of it, he's been bludgeoned to death with some sort of blunt instrument. Trauma to the back of the head, possibly execution style. Little bit of blood down his neck, but some of it must have been washed away in the rain.'

'How long's he been here?'

'Not my place to say. But not long. I mean... look for yourself.'

Tomek was first into the tent. He pushed the flap aside, then held it for Rachel. The figure was lying face down on the grass, his features hidden from view. He was wearing a pair of dark blue jeans, running trainers, and a light green waterproof coat. There was nothing about the man's outfit that suggested the victim was into the same designer and luxury brands as Anton, but perhaps that was the perfect disguise for a man who was on the run for killing his wife.

'Any ID found in his pockets?' Rachel asked as Tomek placed a hand on the man's shoulder.

Leon called to one of the scenes of crime officers. A moment later, a figure answered, 'Yeah. His driver's licence.'

'What's his name?' Tomek asked, as he rolled the man onto his side.

But he knew the answer before he heard it.

'It's not him,' Tomek said.

'Who is it?' Rachel asked.

'Reece Cartwright,' the SOCO answered.

The sigh from Rachel's mouth was audible over her face mask and the wind that had started to ripple the fabric of the tent.

'Fuck,' Tomek whispered.

'There a problem?' Leon asked.

'No. It's just... we thought it might have been someone we were looking for.'

It was dark by the time Tomek and Rachel had finished with the scene. They had a new victim. Someone's relative, someone's friend, someone's loved one. They couldn't have just left him there because he wasn't Anton Usyk. It would have been immoral and unethical. Someone had killed Reece Cartwright, so another murder investigation would have to be launched. But right now, that wasn't Tomek's priority. They had everything they needed to begin – a witness statement from the cyclist who'd found him, a report from the crime scene manager, and a pathologist's report coming through within the next few days. Tomek and the team would have to begin questioning the man's family, and his friends. But first Tomek wanted to see Morgana's murder through to the end. He needed the closure of resolving her death. And that sensation, that satiating desire, wouldn't end until they found Anton.

But life didn't always work like that. It wasn't always that kind.

As he'd learnt the hard way.

Thoughts of Nathan Burrows and the letter returned as he stepped out of his forensics suit and climbed into his car. It had been several days since he'd received the letter, and he'd hoped that it was a one-off. But the thought that the man now had his address had continued to weigh down on him, and he'd begun to suspect and question those who had access to that information. Someone must have leaked it to Nathan. For a brief moment, Gavin Barker's name popped into his head. That the man had been put up to the task by Brendan Door somehow – trying to get revenge for arresting him in connection with the Southend Seven – but he quickly dismissed it. It was a ridiculous thing to think.

As Tomek inserted the key into the ignition, Rachel slipped into the passenger seat. The sound of rain hitting the roof filled the cabin. She was in the middle of tying her hair in a ponytail when she said, 'We'll find him. I've got a feeling in my stomach.'

'You sure it's not just this morning's coffee?'

'Could be a bit of both.'

Tomek was about to respond when his phone rang. Chey was calling. 'Hold that thought,' he said, then answered. 'Mr Pepper... You better have something exciting for us.'

'Only if you promise to let me be your best mate.'

Tomek rolled his eyes.

'You carry on with the blackmail, you'll move further and further down the list.'

A moment's reflection.

'Fine. But you'll regret this.'

'Go on. Just tell me. *Please.*'

'Digital forensics have finally been able to locate the source of the blackmail text messages that were sent to Gavin Barker.'

'Right.'

'They came from a burner phone.'

'Right.'

'They've also got a ping on Anton Usyk's phone.'

'The fucker's alive?'

'And stupid, it would appear.'

'Where? Tell me where!'

Tomek started the car, and was already reversing out of his spot when Chey answered.

'Both have come from Red Birch Farm, Sarge.'

CHAPTER
SIXTY

Tomek had been disappointed not to find Anton on Two Tree Island. He'd got his hopes up, only for them to be brought back to the ground again. He tried not to do the same now, but it was proving an impossible task. This was a lead. A proper, concrete lead. There was no ambiguity or doubt when it came to phone records, technology and data.

Anton's phone had been switched on. For what reason, they didn't know. But they were going to find out.

The only thing that was ambiguous, was who had switched it on. Anton? Or somebody else at the farm?

Which meant there was only one other person it could have been.

Stanley Hutchinson.

Tomek was at the front of the convoy, leading the way. Trailing behind him was the entire team, driving two to a car. At the back of the pack were two liveried police vehicles, with more from other nearby stations coming. It was important that they all arrive at the same time, that they spring the attack by surprise. The other problem they faced was the sheer size of the farm. At over three hundred acres, it was estimated that they would need to situate at least a hundred officers around the perimeter of the entire piece of land to stop anyone from fleeing. A massive undertaking that required planning and time – time which they didn't have. Anton, or at least his phone, could switch off and move at any time. They had to balance efficiency with working smarter. And that task had fallen to Tomek and Victoria.

It was dark outside, had been for a little over two hours, and the roads were quiet. By now the rain had worsened, and they were each dressed in their anoraks and hiking boots – ready and prepared to chase across the fields if necessary.

Tomek swung the car off the road, entered the car park, accelerated as fast as possible to the farmer's office, and then skidded to a halt, kicking up stones and gravel behind. Before the engine had switched off, he was out and was sprinting towards the office. Blue and white lights danced off the surrounding buildings' surfaces, and the still air was punctuated by the sound of cars coming to a stop, footsteps on gravel and car doors slamming.

Tomek was first to the office.

Locked.

Cupping his face with his hands, he peered through the glass. The lights were off and nobody was inside.

'Bollocks.'

Then he set off, heading to the next building. By now, the team had begun to fan out around the estate, moving as quietly and surreptitiously as possible, approaching each building with caution, searching for signs of life.

Then the screaming started. Deep, terrified, in agony.

At first, Tomek thought it was coming from one of the team. That perhaps they had fallen over or injured themselves in a heavy piece of machinery. But as soon as he heard the pitch change to a shrill cry, he bolted towards it. The sound was coming from the pig pen, on the other side of the farm. Of all the buildings, it was the only one with lights on.

A few moments later, he charged through the heavy wooden door, heedless of what he was walking into. He felt a sharp pain shoot up and down his shoulder, but he ignored it because the pain of opening a door was nothing compared to the pain of what was happening right in front of him.

Standing outside the pig pen were Stanley Hutchinson, Alfie, and several other faces that Tomek recognised from his various recent visits to Iliana's. Inside the centre of the pen, however, was Anton. Surrounded by seven ravenous beasts. On the floor, wriggling, writhing, trying to fight his way out. He was naked, and covered in blood.

So much blood.

So much screaming.

Tomek didn't think. He just acted.

He vaulted the barrier and jumped into the enclosure. He was grateful for the hiking shoes as he waded his way through the filth. Behind him, someone called, 'Police! Stop!' But it was already too late. Stanley and his accomplices had bolted. While some officers gave chase, others stayed behind.

'Tomek!'

He looked behind him to see Sean climbing over the fence. Tomek returned his attention to the man in the middle of the enclosure. As the sound of screams continued, Tomek wrapped his arms around one of the pigs' necks and began yanking him away from Anton, but it was futile. The beast outweighed him twenty to one. Sensing his struggle, Sean joined in, and between them, they were able to push the beast back a few feet. But they were outnumbered and outmuscled. As Tomek turned his attention to another pig, he felt something sharp in his back. A bullet? A knife? Neither. The rock-solid head of the pig he'd just pushed away, tearing him down. Tomek was thrown to the ground. He fell face-first into the mud. And as he looked up, he saw Anton amongst it all. Amongst the hay, the filth, the blood, the pigs. His skin had been ripped from his body, his limbs hanging on by their last shred, by chunks of flesh and muscle. His face had been torn in half, and as Tomek reached out to grab what was left of him, one of the pigs wrapped its mouth around Anton's throat and ripped it away. Blood sprayed in Tomek's face like a Jackson Pollock painting. He screamed.

Then realisation settled on him: that if he didn't move – *now*! – he would be next. The pigs would have him for dessert.

Sinking his fingers into the filth, searching for purchase amongst the mud, he pushed himself to his knees. But there was a pig atop him, straddling him. He could feel the animal's hot, steaming breath bearing down on his neck and head, the wet snout sniffling and rustling his hair.

'Tomek!' someone called, but he couldn't hear them. The noise was drowned out by the sound of grunting, of the two tonnes of flesh and meat standing over him.

All he could think to do was place his hand over his head and lie still, to play dead. That they might get bored of him, that their stomachs might be full enough to ignore him.

It didn't work. As he lay there, he felt something on his foot, then—

His body slid across the mud, flying underneath the pig. Hands began to grapple him, hooking under his arms and lifting him to his feet. Through the mud in and around his eyes, he saw Sean in front of him. His friend had pulled him from beneath the belly of the beast and yanked him to safety.

'Sean...' he said.

'No time for that now, pal,' his friend said as he placed Tomek's arm over his shoulder and crouched down to place his arm between Tomek's legs. It was the first time he'd ever been fireman carried. In his delirious and bewildered state, he stumbled once his feet came into contact with solid ground, and he collapsed onto the concrete.

'You're safe now, mate,' Sean said, slapping him playfully on the cheeks.

'Anton...' he whispered weakly.

Sean turned round to face the pigs. 'Gone. You did your best, but we were too late.'

'And Stanley?'

'We got him!' someone called from the other side of the pen. 'Putting him in the back of the car now.'

Sean shuffled round to Tomek's side, placing a hand on his back. 'Hear that, mate? We got him. It's all done. Come on, let's get you cleaned up. You look like shit.'

CHAPTER
SIXTY-ONE

Several hours later, Tomek was cleaned, debriefed and ready to continue his job – against Victoria's wishes. She'd hounded him to get some rest, get some sleep, process what had happened to him, but he couldn't, didn't want to.

Instead, he wanted to hear what Stanley Hutchinson had to say for himself, how he fitted into all this, and what he had to do with Morgana's death.

But his interview had been disappointing. Rather unsurprisingly, the man had answered "no comment" to everything. The same had gone for his accomplices and the rest of the farm staff that had been arrested on site. They were all keeping shtum, united in their desire to withhold the truth.

In the end, after what had eventually been an unsuccessful night, Tomek had taken Victoria's advice and gone home. He arrived after midnight. Kasia had been asleep, so he'd headed straight to bed, where sleep had evaded him. Thoughts and images of what had happened played in his head, appearing in his mind, blown up, zoomed in like they were under a microscope. For the first time in years, he'd had a different nightmare. A new nightmare. One where he dreamt that he was being eaten by pork.

By morning, he was awake before it was light. Instead of getting himself out of bed, he stayed beneath the covers, staring into the ceiling, missing the comfort that Abigail offered beside him. It had been a few nights since she'd last stayed and he was beginning to miss her.

When it was time for Kasia to wake up, he rolled his legs off the side of the bed and went to her bedroom.

'Morning,' he said, waking her up. 'Time for school.'

She opened her groggy eyes, wiping the sleep away from them. 'When did you get home?'

'After midnight. How was last night?'

'Fine. Got some work done.'

'Great. Well, there's something I need to tell you when you're ready for school. I'll get the eggs on in the meantime.'

The toast and scrambled egg breakfast he'd made her had been sitting on the counter for five minutes by the time she finally arrived. As he looked at her, he noticed something different about her.

Her hair had been brushed and curled, and she'd applied more make-up than usual.

'You look nice,' he said. 'Who's that for?'

'Why does it have to be *for* anyone? Why couldn't I have just done it for myself, to make myself feel good?'

Tomek raised his hands in surrender. 'Yep. Good point. You got me there.' He set the plate in front of her. 'Eat them quick, they're about to go from cold to frozen.'

'Ha ha...' she said sardonically as she hopped onto the chair. 'Go on then, what have you got to tell me? You finally got rid of Abigail?'

Tomek closed the cupboard door. 'No, but good one. Good to see where your head's finally at. No, it's about last night. Why I was late...'

And then he told her. To the last detail, barring some of the graphic information that she didn't need to know. Like the way Anton's neck had exploded in his face. How he'd been covered in another man's blood and had spent thirty minutes in the showers at the station, scrubbing, cleaning himself of the indelible stain until his skin had turned red.

'Oh, my god, you nearly died!' she yelled after he'd finished.

'*Nearly* being the important word. If it hadn't been for Sean I possibly might have.'

'Bet you feel guilty about him not being your friend anymore...'

Tomek shot her a derisive look. 'Now isn't the time for a moral of the story, Kash. I just thought you should know. In the name of being honest and transparent with one another. Now get yourself ready. I'm going to drop you off.'

As he'd lain there awake, turning over the thoughts in his mind – chief of which was how close he'd come to death – he decided to spend more time with her, to do the little things more often, like taking her to school, making her breakfast fresh in the morning. It was only minor, but he knew they would both appreciate it in years to come.

Their time was precious, and he didn't want it to slip away.

Twenty minutes later, he waved goodbye to her at the school gates, then headed to the station. The office was bustling with activity. Faces and bodies he didn't recognise moved from one side of the room to the other. Detectives from other parts of the region had been swiftly drafted in to help, including a stranger who was sitting at his desk. Tomek spent the next few seconds looking for Sean. He found him in the kitchen, making a cup of coffee.

'Get you one?' Sean asked.

'Please. Though I'm so used to Morgana's recently, I don't think anything will compare.'

'Well, you're going to have to get used to that,' Sean said as he set about making Tomek a cup of instant coffee.

After he handed it to him, they left the kitchen and headed towards the incident room.

'What've I missed?' Tomek asked.

'Nothing. Anton's still dead. The post-mortem on his body is being done this afternoon, though it won't take many guesses how he died, given that we were all there.'

'In the thick of it. Literally.'

Sean smirked. 'Stanley's still not budging. He's still giving no comment. Same goes for his mates from the farm.'

Sean pointed to the whiteboards. Since he'd last seen them, all the information surrounding Morgana's death had been cleaned away and replaced with images of the farm and Stanley Hutchinson.

'Do we know why Anton was there?' Tomek asked.

'Our suspicion is that he was kept there by Stanley and that his phone may have been turned on by mistake. Right now, we think Stanley kept him captive for some reason – possibly in retaliation for killing Morgana, and in a bid to escape, Anton switched his phone on. We don't know. And we might never know.'

Tomek scanned the information on the boards that had been hastily thrown together overnight.

'I wonder how he fits into all of this?' he said, looking at the image of Stanley Hutchinson.

'Victoria thinks he might have been the one to kill Morgana.'

'But he doesn't match the description. He looks nothing like the person we've been looking for. And we've got proof that Anton was there, the CCTV footage, the shoes, Vlad's witness statement.' Tomek turned to Sean and saw the belief in his eyes. 'You feel the same way, don't you?'

'I'm inclined to agree with you. I don't see how he fits.'

An idea popped into Tomek's head. He slapped him on the back. 'You can be the one to tell her then, mate. Just remember to keep the personal and professional separate, all right?'

Tomek turned and headed towards the exit.

'Hey, where you going?'

Tomek placed a hand on the doorframe.

'To speak with someone who I think can finally answer all of our questions.'

CHAPTER
SIXTY-TWO

Tomek despised the level of smugness on the man's face. But he had to give it to him: if the shoe was on the other foot, he would have done exactly the same. That didn't make him like the man's behaviour any more.

Tomek had lost count on Vlad's custody clock. All he knew was that it had been a long time, and they were going to need to charge him with accessory to murder and perverting the course of justice soon. And he could add a murder charge to that rap sheet.

He placed a document face down on the table and flattened his hand against it.

'Vlad...' he began.

'I'm not talking unless I get my deal. The offer's there, on the table. I can tell you who killed Morgana.'

'I think I already know.'

'If you say so. But you won't know for sure, will you?'

Tomek hesitated, tapped the paper. 'We've been thinking about your offer. Truly, we have. It all seems very promising. But what assurances do we have that what you say is true?'

'I have evidence—'

'Because firstly I wanted to give you an update on what's been happening outside the four walls of your cell. Last night, Anton was killed. Would you like to know how he was killed?'

'I can guess.'

'He was mauled to death by pigs.'

Tomek paused to gauge the man's reaction; his pupils dilated and his lips parted.

'Is that what you guessed?' Tomek asked.

Shock and acceptance seemed to come over him. As though he'd been expecting to hear it, but it was still a surprise.

'Yes... that might have... did you see it?'

'I was right in the middle of it,' Tomek replied. 'Tried to save him, but I was too late. As a result, we've arrested Stanley Hutchinson and the rest of his staff at Red Birch Farm and Petting Zoo for his murder. And now that Anton's dead, we no longer need to continue our investigation into Morgana's murder.' Tomek made a tick sound and gesture. 'We've got Anton for Morgana's murder. We've got Stanley Hutchinson for Anton's murder. We've got Denis Danyluk for Mariusz's murder. We had Mariusz for Andrei's murder. We've got Gavin Barker for leaking private information. And, we've got yourself for perverting the course of justice, of course. It looks to me like everything is case closed.'

The smirk of Vlad's dwindled a little.

'You're wrong,' he said, flat.

'About which bit?'

'The person who killed Morgana. He's been dead for a while now.'

Tomek was stunned by the statement. Vlad had just given away his ace card without coming to any sort of agreement. Tomek placed it down to pride getting in the way, of wanting to prove Tomek wrong, and that he really did have the information they wanted.

Sometimes people just couldn't help themselves.

The ego got in the way.

That's how you do it, Sean!

Though the next question proved to be tricky. *Who* had killed Morgana? It was a toss-up, a fifty-fifty, either wrong or right, and he staked his entire backing on it as only one name came to his head.

'Mariusz?' he said. 'It really was Mariusz who killed Morgana, then he killed Andrei afterwards?'

Vlad shook his head. As he was about to respond, his solicitor leant across to whisper in his ear, to offer a sage word of advice. But Vlad shoved him away with a flick of the hand. This was his playground now, and nobody else was allowed in.

'Wrong. It was Andrei.'

Tomek felt his eyes widen with surprise. 'Andrei Pirlog, the key witness? From the harbour?'

Vlad nodded, his gaze narrowing.

Tomek was struggling to wrap his head around this.

Andrei. Morgana. Anton.

How did it all fit together?

He felt like he needed a minute. But he didn't have one. Hundreds of thoughts, images and scenarios were racing around his head. Fortunately, what he did have was a man willing to share everything with him.

'Andrei killed Morgana,' Vlad said with a sense of relief in his voice. 'She... she... how should I say this? For the past few years, she has been bringing... smuggling people into the country. From her home country and nearby countries. Romania, Poland, Latvia, Belarus. They pay her large amounts of money to be here, but then she keeps them, locks them up and forces them to work in the restaurant.'

'The restaurants?'

'No. *Restaurant*. Singular.'

'Which one?' The images had now stopped, and instead his brain had entered hyper-focused mode, where he listened to every syllable, every pronunciation coming out of Vlad's mouth.

'Iliana's. Anton used to oversee them. He was in charge of watching them while Morgana orchestrated everything from her office.'

That explained the high turnover of staff and the Tripadvisor reviews.

'What do you mean he was watching them?'

'He made sure they didn't step out of line, that they didn't talk to anyone about what was happening to them.'

Gina... from Poland. Anton must have got to her. He must have found out... A knot formed in Tomek's stomach. He tried to swallow it down, but it didn't budge.

'How do they get out?' Tomek asked, then explained to Vlad that each time he'd gone to the restaurant there seemed to be a new face. 'Where do they go?'

'Somewhere else. The farm, the—'

'Red Birch Farm?'

Vlad nodded. 'They work there, between the farm and Iliana's. It's how they keep them under close control. They get them working long hours and pay them nothing for it. Then they keep the profits for themselves. Stanley's been in on it from the beginning.'

Tomek let out a slow breath through his nostrils. He had been wrong. There had been no drug angle. Instead, it had been trafficking of a different kind.

'How does Andrei fit into this?' he asked, the questions swirling around his head like they were stuck in a blender.

'I lied when I said that nobody gets out. *He* did. The first and last time.'

'What do you mean? Tell me how it happened.'

Vlad's shoulders had dropped slightly. It was clear to see from his reaction that he'd been holding onto this information for a long time, and it was a relief to get it all out in the open.

'Andrei had come over with his wife, Tatiana. They were going to start a life together here in the UK, but it was robbed from them by Morgana and Anton. Morgana – she, she was head of it all. The snake head. She was in charge of everyone who came over. Stanley helped facilitate them coming into the country...'

Mariusz and DWG Logistics.

'But I didn't want anything to do with it. I told her from day one that it was the wrong thing to do. But I didn't want to leave the restaurant, and she couldn't let me leave because of what I knew. So, we came to an agreement. There would be nothing like that in our restaurant. It would be a legitimate business with legitimate owners.'

Semi-legitimate owners, Tomek thought.

'Everyone of our employees at Morgana's is kosher, above board. They have no idea what's going on. They were kept completely separate from it. But there was a problem. One day, Andrei was working with us. I don't know how, nor do I know why. Morgana treated him as though he was a new starter to the rest of the staff. And on his "first day", he decided to steal money from the cash register. He wanted out, he wanted his freedom. So he took it. But before he could get back to his wife, Anton got to her first. Andrei disappeared for a short while. We didn't know where he went or what he'd done with the money.'

That explained why the flat they'd found him in looked as though it had been empty for some time.

'For all they knew, Andrei could have gone to the police. But his love for his wife was so strong that he laid low for a few days. In the meantime, Morgana had told the rest of the kitchen staff that he couldn't hack it, that he couldn't handle the pressure of being in the kitchen. Until a few days later he came back into the restaurant. He and Morgana sat down at the table, deep in discussion. It looked as though he'd come to ask for his job back. That was when they agreed to meet—'

'At the harbour?'

'Yes. Andrei would return the money and Morgana would be there with his wife, Tatiana.'

'And he believed that they would hand her over, just like that?'

'He was desperate. He was in a foreign country, with little money, no place to stay, and no one to keep him company. What would you have done?'

Tomek reflected on that point for a moment. The answer was he wouldn't have had a bloody clue.

He was transfixed. He needed to hear more.

'What happened next?'

Vlad cleared his throat. 'Well, as I understand it, Andrei went there with the money, but when he got there it was just Morgana. There was no wife. No exchange.'

'So he killed her?'

Vlad nodded. Tomek tried to picture the scene in his head. The man, trafficked into a foreign country, alone, desperate, his last chance at getting his wife within reach right before him, only to find out it was gone and he would never see her again. Rage, envy, fury would have come over him. Then he got his revenge and drowned her. But then what?

'Andrei was one of our key witnesses,' Tomek said, confused. 'All the other key witnesses corroborate and say they saw Andrei *walking towards* the scene, then someone else running away.'

'Anton,' Vlad answered bluntly. 'Anton was watching the whole thing unfold. He was there as backup, you could say. It was my impression that they were going to kill Andrei that day, but he beat them to it. And after he'd killed Morgana, Andrei fled the scene. But for whatever reason, he went back. That was when he saw Anton in the water, holding his wife's head. Then the Americans arrived.'

Tomek inhaled deeply. He'd got it all wrong. *They* had got it all wrong. Anton hadn't killed his wife. Andrei had. The man who'd been there from the start. The key witness nobody had thought to second guess.

He could put the rest of the story together himself: Anton, enraged at the death of his wife, had sought retribution. He'd known that Andrei would be forced to give an address at the police station, and so he'd leant on the only person he knew who could access it, Gavin Barker, who had visited Iliana's on his various lunch breaks in the past few weeks. Then he'd convinced Mariusz to kill Andrei and make it look like a suicide. And as the only loose end, he'd then sought the help of Denis Danyluk to tie it all off.

It had been an elaborate story of revenge and betrayal, one that Tomek had never seen coming.

'How do you know all this?' he asked.

'Anton told me everything when he dropped off the shoes.'

'And that was why you needed the witness protection, the immunity...?'

Vlad nodded. 'Now I have nothing to fear.' For the first time, the smile on his face was filled with a slight sense of hope, that he could fulfil his sentence without the threat of Anton or Stanley Hutchinson looking over his shoulders.

There was one more question on Tomek's mind.

'Why did Stanley kill Anton?'

Vlad shrugged. 'You'll have to ask him.'

Tomek dropped the sheet of paper face down on Victoria's desk. She brushed a strand of hair aside and looked down at it.

'You got it?' she asked.

'Signed and dated,' he replied. 'Have a look.'

Tentatively, Victoria flipped over the paper. The hope in her eyes burnt out immediately. At the bottom of the document that agreed to enter Vlad into the witness protection programme, Tomek had scribbled the words, "VLAD THE IMPALER, ROMANIA" in block capitals.

'What's this?' she asked, scowling up at him.

'A joke. My way of saying that's how it's done.'

'What're you talking about?'

Tomek brushed his shoulder. 'Didn't need it. Got him to piss like an octogenarian.'

'A full confession?'

Tomek mock bowed. 'At your service, Your Royal Highness.'

'Arse.'

'An arse who gets results, mind. Remember that.'

Tomek made his way towards the exit, unable to wipe the smug smile off his face. Now he knew how Vlad had felt all this time.

'Wait! Wait!' she called him back. 'Aren't you going to tell me what the fuck's going on?'

Tomek placed his hand on the door handle. 'You know, since you've been sitting in Nick's seat you've become a lot more sweary.'

'Because fuckers like you keep winding me up with petty shit like this!'

You haven't seen anything yet.

Tomek opened the door.

'You can't leave until you tell me what happened...'

'Don't worry, ma'am,' he said as he stepped out of the room. 'It'll all be in my report.'

The sound of the door shutting was deafening. From the other side, he heard Victoria groan and then sigh heavily.

Turning his back on her, he headed into the incident room, where he found the majority of his colleagues replacing some of the images and information from the investigation with the victim that had been found on Two Tree Island the day before.

'Already?' Tomek said.

'The inspector's asked us to focus on this as a priority.'

No rest for the wicked.

Tomek decided to help. As he pulled down some of the sheets of paper, his mind became blank, and he began to think about Andrei, about the case, about the unanswered questions. Like where were the victims being kept? What had happened to Andrei's wife?

And then he saw it.

A printout of a selfie, taken from a restaurant back in Romania. Andrei and his wife, Tatiana smiling, all dressed up, holding her hand to the camera. Andrei had just proposed, but it wasn't the ring on the finger that caught his attention. It was the green jewelled earring hanging from her left lobe. The same one Tomek had found in the pig pen the other day.

What was it Stanley Hutchinson had said to him on his first visit?

They're pigs. They'll eat whatever you give them so long as they're hungry enough.

She too had been fed to the pigs.

Tomek couldn't believe it. The evidence had been right there, right in front of him. And he'd completely missed it. How many more had died like that? How many more people had been eaten by the pigs on the farm? What if they never made it off the farm?

And then it dawned on him. The more apt question was: how many times had he ended up inadvertently eating human flesh?

The pigs... the bacon... Morgana's... Iliana's.

We ship about two tonnes of produce to them every year, most of it our finest pieces of meat.

Was that what made the bacon taste so good? Human flesh?

Sometimes in life there were some things that just weren't worth knowing.

CHAPTER
SIXTY-THREE

Tomek relished the rain gracing his face, the wind biting into every pore of his skin, the water splashing onto his legs, numbing his thighs and toes.

He needed to process everything, absorb it, digest it. And there was no better way to do that than with a run. Alongside him, struggling to keep up with Tomek's pace, was Warren Thomas who, for a time, Tomek had considered Morgana's killer. But he was glad he'd never voiced that concern, even if he'd felt rumblings of it amongst his colleagues. What an embarrassment that would have been.

It was the day after Vlad's confession, and his first full day off in a while. The team had pressed charges against Vlad, Stanley, Alfie, and the rest of the farm's employees. They had begun the process of trying to find the victims of Morgana's and Anton's human trafficking ring, but it was proving difficult. Teams of volunteers and support staff, along with SOCOs and uniformed officers, had sealed off the farm and begun seizing all assets for evidence, while searching the hundreds of acres of land for signs of life.

Tomek wasn't hopeful.

They were twenty minutes into their run. They'd started a little further inland, running along the coast first before setting foot on the sand, and were now halfway to their destination. The harbour loomed in the mid-ground, intimidating, eerie. He wondered how many secrets it had, how much life and death it had seen over the years, what stories it had to tell.

Andrei and Morgana had given it one more to add to the list.

The remainder of the run to the harbour was surprisingly easy. Tomek had found an extra gear and raced ahead, beating Warren by a few hundred metres.

'Someone's got second wind,' Warren said as he caught up. 'Or have you got actual wind?'

Panting, Tomek was bent double, hands on knees. 'I've got something in me that I need to get out, that's for sure.'

Anger. Frustration. Grief.

Angst. Fear. Guilt.

He was feeling it all.

Falling backwards, he sat on the wet sand, and caught his breath.

'I need a minute,' he said.

'I'm not surprised.'

'No, not about that.' He turned to the harbour on his left.

'About what happened?' Warren asked.

Tomek nodded. 'I've got a lot I need to process. Just think about it... someone died right here. Someone was murdered.'

'Tragic, I know. But from what you've told me, it sounds like they deserved it.'

'That may be... but...'

Tomek trailed off. Something had caught his eye. The red flashing light at the top of the harbour. Curious, he climbed to his feet and pointed to it.

'Run me through what happened on that morning.'

'Really? We've been through this.'

'I know, I know. But a lot's happened since then and I've forgotten.'

Warren sighed, placed his hands on his hips. 'We found the body, called it in, then climbed on top of the harbour.'

Tomek moved slowly towards it, unable to take his gaze away from the pylon. 'Yes, but what *specifically*? Last time you said you and Andrei went to the highest point?'

'Thought you said you couldn't remember?'

'Warren...' Tomek shot him a derisive look. 'Please. This is important.'

The man sighed. 'Fine. You're right. That guy and I went to the top.'

'Right. And what did the guy do exactly?'

'What? What's the significance of this?'

But Tomek was off, wading through the water, climbing the structure.

'Did you see what he did when the two of you were up here?'

Curiosity eventually got the better of Warren, and he joined Tomek, climbing the structure with ease.

'I mean... I was too busy looking out for the coastguard.'

'Think, mate. I need you to think. Did you see where he went? His movements?'

Warren's face fell deep in thought.

'Don't think I've ever seen you think so hard in my life, not even when we were back in school.'

'Fuck you,' he said, then without warning started towards the pylon.

Tomek watched in hope as Warren relived his movements. The man traversed the structure with ease, his long legs striding over the large gaps in the middle like they were cracks in the pavement.

'We came up here...' he started. 'We were panicked, breathing a lot. The wind was picking up. I sensed that the tide was going to come in super-fast so we needed to do something.' He pointed to a spot in the structure. 'I almost slipped and fell here, but he caught me and held me. Then when we got to the top, we...' Warren stopped right by the pylon. Tomek made his way towards him. 'I thought I saw something over there. I thought it was a boat coming towards us, so I flagged it down...'

'And what was he doing?'

'I... He...'

Warren's eyes fell towards the foot of the tower. There was a small hole burrowed into the cement.

'He was down there…' Warren continued. 'At… at first I didn't think much of it. I… I was too busy flagging down the boat. But…'

Tomek wasted no time. He skipped past Warren, spread his legs across one of the sections in the structure, and using one of his arms for support, reached into the small hole.

The concrete was coarse and abrasive on his skin, but he paid it little heed. Within a few seconds, he found what he was looking for and pulled it out.

Something they'd been searching for all this time. Something they'd believed to be gone.

Morgana's phone. Perfectly intact.

CHAPTER
SIXTY-FOUR

Two days had passed of hoping, praying, waiting. Of tirelessly wishing that Morgana's phone would turn on. They had tried all the usual methods – putting it in a bowl of rice, wrapping it in a tea towel and placing it on the radiator – but nothing. Until, when all the other options hadn't worked, a member of the digital forensics team had been able to unscrew the device's components and dry them out individually. It had taken longer than expected, as it was an intricate piece of kit, but that had done nothing to abate the nerves. The team had waited for the office phone to ring, to eventually confirm that it was working.

Finally, the call had come that morning. The digital forensics team had managed to dry the machine, put it together again, and then plug it into their computers. From there, they'd reviewed the entirety of Morgana's phone: her app downloads, search history, message history, her photos. The latter two had been of most importance to the investigation, and they'd conducted a full post-mortem on them, looking for reference to where the victims were being kept. A message, a keyword, a set of phrases that she and Stanley and Anton might have used to denote their location.

In the end, it had come down to a photo. Two, in fact. The first was of Andrei's wife, cowering in the corner of a small, white-walled room. There was nothing in there other than a bare mattress. No windows, no comfort. Complete sensory blindness. In the photo, she had been holding her wiry hand up to protect her eyes from the light. Weak, malnourished. There was no telling how long she'd been in there. From the complete lack of evidence to suggest that she'd been fed or at least given water, Tomek suspected it had been days. Possibly since Andrei's theft that had started the entire ordeal.

The second photograph that had caught the digital forensics team's attention was a photograph of the farm. A nondescript, plain, generic piece of land that was bordered by a thick row of trees.

Tomek, alongside a small army of constables, sergeants, inspectors, civilian support staff and even the general public – including Warren Thomas and the Redgraves – was standing in front of that very spot now, looking out at it as though it was about to be mowed down. They were part of another search party. The police's initial searches on the farm had garnered no fruit; all they'd been able to find were a series of documents and bank statements, along with a small bin full of cash.

That had been two days ago. Two long days since the people they were looking for – if they were still there – had last been fed, given water, since they'd last been tended to. There was no knowing what conditions they'd been living in, but the theory was that it hadn't been pleasant, that they were living in squalor, atop one another in cramped, confined spaces, like Andrei's wife had been before she died.

Underground.

A bald man with a thick black beard stepped in front of the crowd. All the attendees had lined up in a row, side by side, two metres apart.

'Right, ladies and gentlemen,' he began, his voice rolling over the land with ease. 'Make sure to stay in a line. One step at a time. If you see anything of interest, do not touch it. If you see anything move, do not touch it. I want you to scream, "Help!", and then we will all stop and those of us at the back will inspect what you've found. It is vitally important that you do not touch anything. Does that all make sense?'

A chorus of yesses echoed around the farm.

Then they began. Small steps at first, feet rustling through the grass, eyes and heads down, scanning the earth like metal detectors. The atmosphere was quiet, tense. Over fifty people united by their desire to find the victims.

Tomek remained optimistic, but as they reached the tree line, they still hadn't found anything, and he started to feel the optimism wane. In his mind he tried to visualise what they might find – on both ends of the spectrum. The good being everyone alive and well, looking like they'd just come back from a holiday in the Arctic. And the bad, which contained the same amount of white skin, except this time it was because they were all dead, having succumbed to hunger and dehydration.

He prayed for the first scenario.

Ten minutes into the search, they had already stopped three times. All nonstarters. Pieces of rubbish, oddly coloured leaves, a flower mistaken for something important.

With each find, Tomek's optimism continued to decrease.

Until the fourth call.

He didn't know why, but there was something about this one that felt different.

The man who'd called it in was only a few feet from him. He tapped his foot on the ground. The sound was hollow, louder than it should have been. The officers at the back of the line joined his side and tested it with their feet. Anticipation and angst descended on the woodland. Then they began removing the surrounding earth. Leaves, mud and twigs flew into the air, revealing a large, metal hatch.

An underground bunker, buried deep in the heart of the woodland.

Tomek's heart leapt into his mouth. He didn't wait. As the most senior officer that was closest to it, he hurried towards the hatch and threw it open. Immediately, he was hit in the face by a wall of warm, stale, sweaty air.

'Hello!' he called into the pit of darkness. 'This is the police, can anyone hear me?'

Gentle murmurings echoed up through the chamber. Within a few seconds, the murmurs turned to screams and shouts.

Life.

Tomek pulled out his phone and switched on the torch function. Then he descended the steps as fast as possible. Once at the bottom, he turned round and headed into the darkness. The corridor was small, narrow, not built for someone his size. But at the end of it, he saw a dim light. A deep orange. And figures, emerging, getting in the way.

'Police,' he said calmly. 'It's all right. Everything's going to be okay. I'm the police. You're all safe now.'

Tomek hadn't known what to expect when he reached the bottom, but it wasn't what he saw in front of him. A large, underground space, the same size as one of the warehouses on the farm, filled with over thirty people, living and breathing in the darkness, buried twenty feet beneath the surface. Like zombies clamouring for blood, they hurried towards him, clinging to every part of his body. Some tried to hug him while others, in their desperate state, searched his pockets.

Shortly after, the senior members of the search party joined him.

'Holy shit,' someone said.

'How many people are down here?'

'I don't know exactly,' Tomek asked. 'I haven't stopped to have a chat with them just yet. I think we should be more worried about getting them out first, don't you?'

Tomek took charge of the evacuation. Using the torch on his phone, he funnelled the human trafficking victims towards the exit, consoling and reassuring them as they went past. With the help of two members from the search party, they grabbed what little food and water was left in there, and took it up with them.

Tomek was last out, and as he breached into the open, blinded by the light, a soft, steady round of applause ensued. They'd done it. They had rescued everyone involved in the horrors of Morgana's and Anton's machinations. More importantly, they were all alive.

CHAPTER
SIXTY-FIVE

S*ix weeks later*

Tomek knocked on the door and entered without waiting for approval. Inside, he found Nick and Victoria sitting opposite one another, deep in discussion.

'Sir, you're back! You cheeky fucker, kept that one to yourself, didn't you?'

Nick turned round to face him, then lumbered out of the chair and shook his hand. 'Always a pleasure to see you, Tomek.'

'Does anyone else know you're here?'

'Not yet.'

'Victoria smuggle you in through the back door, did she?'

'I don't officially return until next Monday, but I wanted to come in to get a handle on things ready for when I do.'

'Mega,' Tomek said. 'Well, we can't wait to have you back.' He placed a firm grip on the man's arm and squeezed. 'Victoria been telling you how well we've been doing since you left?'

'Yes, but between you and me I think she's gone a bit brain dead.'

Victoria's face dropped.

'I am right here, you know?'

Nick ignored her, and said, 'She's been singing your praises. Fuck knows why.'

'Couldn't possibly imagine how hard it must be for you at this difficult time,' Tomek mocked. 'Though I would love to hear what you've had to say, Victoria. Maybe I could elaborate on a few things for you?'

The inspector rolled her eyes. 'Put your ego to one side for a moment please, Bowen. But if you must know, I said that despite our obvious differences, you did really well. Without you I doubt we could have found what we were looking for.'

Tomek crossed his arms. 'I'm sorry, Inspector, I didn't quite hear you.'

'Don't make me repeat it,' she said.

'She's put in a recommendation for inspector,' Nick interrupted.

Tomek looked at her, floored. 'You did *what*?'

'You'll have to take all the relevant exams and wait for something to come available, but I think you proved yourself.'

Tomek hesitated. 'A lifetime of sitting behind the desk... I'll have to think about it.'

'Really? I thought you'd be happy. You've been badgering me for the past couple of months about this?' came Nick's response.

'I am happy. Honest. I'll just need to think it through...'

'Well, there's no obligation to do anything,' Victoria said. 'If you're happy where you are, then that works for everyone.'

The smirk on Tomek's face returned. 'I must say I am surprised though, ma'am. Does that mean you'll start to respect me as much as you do your toy boy out there?'

The sentimental moment between them didn't last very long.

'I'll fucking withdraw it if you carry on.'

Tomek replied with a cheeky-chappie grin.

'Was there a reason for your intrusion, Tomek?' Victoria asked, moving the conversation along.

'Only to tell you that the DNA analysis of the mud from the farm's come through.'

'And?'

'Four people's DNA were found in there. Anton's and Andrei's wife's, Tatiana.'

'And the third? Mariusz's girlfriend?' she asked.

Tomek dipped his head. 'Afraid so. Mariusz never worked for the haulier. Anton, Morgana and Stanley owned that company separately, and he was just another victim of their trafficking like the rest of them. I don't know why they chose him, but they used him as a fall guy to kill Andrei and take the rap for it. They even used him as the person outside the Redgraves' Airbnb. His girlfriend was the blackmail to get him to do what they wanted, and they somehow made it look like she'd gone back to Romania so Martin couldn't contact her.'

'Poor thing. Can't imagine how painful it must have been for them to die that way.'

Tomek could. He'd seen it first-hand. And had continued to do so for the past few weeks in his nightmares.

'What about the fourth?' she asked.

'A woman named Gina. She was one of the workers at Iliana's I was speaking with. She was supposed to share information with me, but she never made it. Now I know why.'

Tomek paused to compose himself.

'Was there anything else?'

'Yes. Couple more things that have answered a few more of our questions. Stanley Hutchinson, the bastard, still isn't saying anything. But fortunately for us that little ginger prick I arrested on the beach has found his voice. Funnily enough it was when he found out we were pressing charges. According to him, Stanley killed Anton because they'd had a falling out. Stanley wasn't happy with the way Anton was handling things, so he chucked him underground with the rest of them. I guess Anton must have found a way out, made a break for it, then paid the ultimate price.'

'Nothing less than he deserved,' Victoria said slowly.

A few moments later, Tomek said his goodbyes, then headed out of the room. That evening, when he got home, the thought of the inspector's exam played on his mind nonstop. It was something he'd considered for a long time, only exacerbated by Kasia's arrival in his life. It was more pay, more security, and there was less field work, less chance that he'd get himself killed by a serial killer or find himself inside a pig's stomach. But that was what he loved about the job, the rush, the thrill of it. He wasn't sure if he wanted to be confined to a desk all the time, dictating what others should do, when he wanted to lead from the front, lead by example.

It was a decision that required his input as much as Kasia's.

But before he could begin thinking about how to approach the topic with her, something on the floor caught his attention.

An envelope. The HMP Wakefield stamp in the top right corner of the document.

A second letter.

He'd hoped the first was a fluke, a one-off. But Nathan Burrows had been true to his word. He wanted to open up a dialogue with Tomek, befriend him almost.

Inhaling deeply, holding it there, listening to the sound of his heart beating like a thousand drums in his head, Tomek tore open the envelope and read the letter.

TOMEK BOWEN RETURNS IN...

Death's Angel

Every angel deserves their wings...

When flight attendant Angelica Whitaker is reported missing after a night out at one of the most popular night clubs in Southend, the case is handed to DS Tomek Bowen for the first time in his career.

As soon as the investigation begins, the finger is pointed at the man she danced with at the club, but when her body is later found in a church, posed like an angel, the same fingers begin to point towards a calculated, composed and sadistic killer.

But as the investigation progresses, and as Tomek delves deeper into the victim's life, it becomes clear that there is no shortage of suspects, and everyone's got their secrets — some more than others...

Coming soon...

ALSO BY JACK PROBYN

The DS Tomek Bowen Murder Mystery Series:

1) DEATH'S JUSTICE

Southend-on-Sea, Essex: Detective Sergeant Tomek Bowen — driven, dogged, and haunted by the death of his brother — is called to one of the most shocking crime scenes he has ever seen. A man has been ritualistically murdered and dumped in an allotment near the local airport. Early investigations indicate this was a man with a past. A past that earned him many enemies.

Download Death's Justice

2) DEATH'S GRIP

Annabelle Lake thought she recognised the Ford Fiesta waiting outside her school, and the driver in it. She was wrong. Her body is discovered some time later, dangling from a swing in a local playground on Canvey Island.

Download Death's Grip

3) DEATH'S TOUCH

When the fog clears one December morning in Essex, the body of a teenage girl is discovered lying face down in a field. But as soon as the investigation begins, Tomek discovers Lily's death may be linked to a killing spree that has lain dormant for many years — with no one ever being brought to justice for it.

Download Death's Touch

4) DEATH'S KISS

The body of a teenage girl is found face down in the middle of a field. The evidence surrounded her death is scant, until a vital clue uncovers a terrifying serial killer lying in wait...

Download Death's Kiss

5) DEATH'S TASTE

The body of a homeless man is found wedged between the beach huts of Thorpe Bay. But it isn't until the victim's identity is revealed that the town begins to sit up and wonder: who killed him, and why?

Download Death's Taste

The Jake Tanner Crime Thriller Series:

Full-length novels that combine police procedure, organised crime and police corruption.

TOE THE LINE:

A small jeweller's is raided in Guildford High Street and leaves police chasing their tails. Reports suggest that it's The Crimsons, an organised crime group the police have been hunting for years. When the shop owner is kidnapped and a spiked collar is attached to her neck, Jake learns one of his own is involved – a police officer. As Jake follows the group on a wild goose chase, he questions everything he knows about his team. Who can he trust? And is he prepared to find out?

Download Toe the Line

WALK THE LINE:

A couple with a nefarious secret are brutally murdered in their London art gallery. Their bodies cleaned. Their limbs dismembered. And the word LIAR inscribed on the woman's chest. For Jake Tanner it soon becomes apparent this is not a revenge killing. There's a serial killer loose on the streets of Stratford. And the only thing connecting the victims is their name: Jessica. Jake's pushed to his mental limits as he uncovers The Community, an online forum for singles and couples to meet. But there's just one problem: the killer's been waiting for him... and he's hungry for his next kill.

Download Walk the Line

UNDER THE LINE:

DC Jake Tanner thought he'd put the turmoil of the case that nearly killed him behind him. He was wrong. When Danny Cipriano's body is discovered buried in a concrete tomb, Jake's wounds are reopened. But one thing quickly becomes clear. The former leader of The Crimsons knew too much. And somebody wanted him silenced. For good. The only problem is, Jake knows who.

Download Under the Line

CROSS THE LINE:

For years, Henry Matheson has been untouchable, running the drug trade in east London. Until the body of his nearest competitor is discovered burnt to a lamppost in his estate. Gang war gone wrong, or a calculated murder? Only one man is brave enough to stand up to him and find out. But, as Jake Tanner soon learns, Matheson plays dirty. And in the estate there are no rules.

Download Cross the Line

OVER THE LINE:

Months have passed since Henry Matheson was arrested and sent to prison. Months have passed since Henry Matheson, one of east London's most dangerous criminals, was arrested. Since then DC Jake Tanner and the team at Stratford CID have been making sure the case is watertight. But when a sudden and disastrous fraudulent attack decimates Jake's personal finances, he is propelled into the depths of a dark and dangerous underworld, where few resurface.

Download Over the Line

PAST THE LINE:

The Cabal is dead. The Cabal's dead. Or so Jake thought. But when Rupert Haversham, lawyer to the city's underworld, is found dead in his London home, Jake begins to think otherwise. The Cabal's back, and now they're silencing people who know too much. Jake included.

Download Past the Line

The Jake Tanner SO15 Files Series:

Novella length, lightning-quick reads that can be read anywhere. Follow Jake as he *joins Counter Terrorism Command in the fight against the worst kind of evil.*

THE WOLF:

A cinema under siege. A race to save everyone inside. An impatient detective. Join Jake as he steps into the darkness.

Download *The Wolf*

DARK CHRISTMAS:

The head of a terrorist cell is found dead outside his flat in the early hours of Christmas Eve. What was he doing outside? Why was a suicide vest strapped to his body? And what does the note in his sock have to do with his death?

Download *Dark Christmas*

THE EYE:

The discovery of a bomb factory leaves Jake and the team scrambling for answers. But can they find them in time?

Download *The Eye*

IN HEAVEN AND HELL:

An ominous — and deadly — warning ignites Jake and the team into action. An attack on one of London's landmarks is coming. But where? And when? Failure could be catastrophic.

Download *In Heaven And Hell*

BLACKOUT:

What happens when all the lights in London go out, and all the power switches off? What happens when a city is brought to its knees? Jake Tanner's about to find out. And he's right in the middle of it.

Download *Blackout*

EYE FOR AN EYE:

Revenge is sweet. But not when it's against you. Not when they use your family to get to you. Family is off-limits. And Jake Tanner will do anything to protect his.

Download *Eye For An Eye*

MILE 17:

Every year, thousands of runners and supporters flock to the streets of London to celebrate the London Marathon. Except this year, there won't be anything to ride home about.

Download *Mile 17*

THE LONG WALK:

The happiest day of your life, your wedding day. But when it's a royal wedding, the stakes are much higher. Especially when someone wants to kill the bride.

Download *The Long Walk*

THE ENDGAME:

Jake Tanner hasn't been to a football match in years. But when a terrorist cell attacks his favourite football stadium, killing dozens and injuring hundreds more, Jake is both relieved and appalled — only the day before was he in the same crowds, experiencing the same atmosphere. But now he must put that behind him and focus on finding the people responsible. And fast. Because another attack's coming.

Download *The Endgame*

The Jake Tanner Terror Thriller Series:

Full-length novels, following Jake through Counter-Terrorism Command, where the stakes have never been higher.

STANDSTILL:

The summer of 2017. Jake Tanner's working for SO15, The Metropolitan Police Service's counter terrorism unit. And a duo of terrorists seize three airport-bound trains. On board are hundreds of kilos of explosives, and thousands of lives. Jake quickly finds himself caught in a cat and mouse race against time to stop the trains from detonating. But what he discovers along the way will change everything.

Download Standstill

FLOOR 68:

1,000 feet in the air, your worst nightmares come true. Charlie Paxman is going to change the world with a deadly virus. His mode of distribution: the top floor of London's tallest landmark, The Shard. But only one man can stop. Jake Tanner. Caught in the wrong place at the wrong time. Trapped inside a tower, Jake finds himself up against an army of steps and an unhinged scientist that threatens to decimate humanity. But can he stop it from happening?

Download Floor 68

JOIN THE VIP CLUB

Your FREE book is waiting for you

Available when you join the VIP Club below

Get your FREE copy of the prequel to the DS Tomek Bowen series now at jackprobynbooks.com when you join my VIP email club.

ABOUT THE AUTHOR

Jack Probyn is a British crime writer and the author of the Jake Tanner crime thriller series, set in London.

He currently lives in Surrey with his partner and cat, and is working on a new murder mystery series set in his hometown of Essex.

Don't want to sign up to yet another mailing list? Then you can keep up to date with Jack's new releases by following one of the below accounts. You'll get notified when I've got a new book coming out, without the hassle of having to join my mailing list.

Amazon Author Page "Follow":
    1. Click the link here: https://geni.us/AuthorProfile
    2. Beneath my profile picture is a button that says "Follow"
    3. Click that, and then Amazon will email you with new releases and promos.

BookBub Author Page "Follow":
    1. Similar to the Amazon one above, click the link here: https://www.bookbub.com/authors/jack-probyn
    2. Beside my profile picture is a button that says "Follow"
    3. Click that, and then BookBub will notify you when I have a new release

If you want more up to date information regarding new releases, my writing process, and everything else in between, the best place to be in the know is my Facebook Page. We've got a little community growing over there. Why not be a part of it?

Facebook: https://www.facebook.co.uk/jackprobynbooks

Printed in Great Britain
by Amazon